# NOT
# MY
# HOME

LOOK FOR THESE EXCITING WESTERN SERIES
FROM BESTSELLING AUTHORS
WILLIAM W. JOHNSTONE AND J.A. JOHNSTONE

*The Mountain Man*

*Luke Jensen: Bounty Hunter*

*Brannigan's Land*

*The Jensen Brand*

*Smoke Jensen: The Early Years*

*Preacher and MacCallister*

*Fort Misery*

*The Fighting O'Neils*

*Perley Gates*

*MacCoole and Boone*

*Guns of the Vigilantes*

*Shotgun Johnny*

*The Chuckwagon Trail*

*The Jackals*

*The Slash and Pecos Westerns*

*The Texas Moonshiners*

*Stoneface Finnegan Westerns*

*Ben Savage: Saloon Ranger*

*The Buck Trammel Westerns*

*The Death and Texas Westerns*

*The Hunter Buchanon Westerns*

*Will Tanner, Deputy US Marshal*

*Old Cowboys Never Die*

*Go West, Young Man*

Published by Kensington Publishing Corp.

# NOT MY HOME

## WILLIAM W. JOHNSTONE

### AND J.A. JOHNSTONE

**Pinnacle Books**
Kensington Publishing Corporation
www.kensingtonbooks.com

PINNACLE BOOKS are published by

Kensington Publishing Corp.
900 Third Avenue
New York, NY 10022

PUBLISHER'S NOTE: Following the death of William J. Johnstone, the Johnstone family is working with a carefully selected writer to organize and complete Mr. Johnstone's outlines and many unfinished manuscripts to create additional novels in all of his series like The Last Gunfighter Mountain Man, and Eagles, among others. This novel was inspired by Mr. Johnstone's superb storytelling.

All Kensington titles, imprints, and distributed lines are available at special quantity discounts for bulk purchases for sales promotion, premiums, fund-raising, educational, or institutional use.

Special book excerpts or customized printings can also be created to fit specific needs. For details, write or phone the office of the Kensington Sales Manager: Attn.: Sales Department. Kensington Publishing Corp., 900 Third Avenue, New York, NY 10022. Phone: 1-800-221-2647.

PINNACLE BOOKS, the Pinnacle logo, and WWJ steer head logo Reg US Pat. & TM Off.

First Pinnacle Books mass market printing: June 2024

ISBN: 13: 978-0-7860-5058-1
ISBN: 13: 978-0-7860-5059-8 (eBook)

10 9 8 7 6 5 4 3 2 1

Printed in the United States of America

# CHAPTER 1

Randall Early never understood what the phrase, *you can't go back home*, really meant until he'd come back to his childhood home of Springerville, South Carolina, four months ago with his new bride. He'd been excited to rescue her from the big-city life and worries of Chicago to the place he'd waxed poetic about ever since they'd met in basic training. To her credit, Ashley was game for it, happy to start their new lives in the place that made him happiest.

A lot had changed since he'd left to serve in the Army for five years, with another year living with Ashley in Oak Park. Sure, when they walked down Main Street there was still the Iron Works Bar and Grill with its tattered front awning, Fuller's Luncheonette with the best biscuits and gravy in all of South Carolina, and Banks Fill and Go. Randall had gotten his hair buzzed just the other day by Al Keene, who had been cutting his hair since he was old enough to sit in the chair by himself. Mrs. Wallace, still chubby and bubbly, manned the realtor office her late husband had left her.

From the outside looking in, Springerville was trapped in amber.

But outsiders were the problem.

A few of Randall's classmates and childhood friends were still kicking around, now with budding families of their own, but whenever he walked or drove around town, he saw too many faces to count that weren't familiar to him. According to his father, there had been an influx of folks from all points of the compass seeking "the slower pace of life," now that they could work remotely. Most of all, they came seeking to get more bang for their buck. Unfortunately, their money brought a rising tide in the price for goods and services, which was fine for them with their big-city paychecks, but was making life a struggle for those who had called Springerville home for generations.

The hope of Randall and Ashley was to buy a house, preferably somewhere close to his parents now that his mother was diagnosed with Parkinson's disease. The problem was, the price of the few houses left on the market were astronomical. Because of that, they'd had to move in with his parents, which made it easy for Randall to help care for his mother, spelling his dad so he could take a moment for himself from time to time. It wasn't easy for Ashley, no matter how much she told him she loved being there. It was one thing to uproot your life, and another to navigate the first year of marriage while living with your in-laws.

Which is why they needed tonight.

"You want some more?" he asked Ashley, holding the half empty bottle of chilled white wine.

"Don't mind if I do," she replied, with a smile that never failed to quicken his heart.

He reached into the cooler and got another bottle of beer for himself, because this moment was too special for cans. A lesson his father had taught him long ago.

"I haven't seen this many stars since we were deployed in Guam," Ashley said.

They sat on a blanket on the eighth green at the Spring Golf Course. Randall used to caddy here when he was a kid, hitting the links every now and then when he turned eighteen, just before he headed off to serve. Back then, like the housing, it was affordable. It had also been open to the public and getting a tee time was never a problem.

Now, the course was private, and the membership fee was beyond rational. Most of the locals had been priced out, having to travel as far as an hour or more away to play a round. Randall may not have had the expendable funds to buy a membership, but he still knew where the breaks were in the surrounding fences. The eighth green was on top of a hilly section that overlooked a pond and the rolling greens below, and the panoply of stars above. He'd always wanted to take a girl out here when he was a caddy.

At this moment, sitting close to his new bride, he was glad he'd been so woefully unsuccessful before Ashley. It made the moment even more special.

As she rested her head on his chest, he said, "I know you've been wanting to talk about having a baby and I've been telling you we should wait until we're more settled."

"I get it, Randy. We have time. Besides, your father keeps telling us to enjoy the honeymoon." She snickered and Randall joined her. It was hard to fully enjoy the honeymoon when your parents were right down the hall.

"I was wrong."

Ashley sat up and searched his eyes, looking to see if he was playing a joke. Randy smiled.

"I mean it. I can't think of anything more important and wonderful than bringing a new life into this world . . . with you."

Tears welled in his and Ashley's eyes. "Do you really mean that?"

He cupped her face in his hand. "I do. I really, really do."

"But what about waiting until we have a little more, you know, security?"

Randy kissed her long and lovingly. "My parents had me when they barely had two nickels to rub together. We'll figure it out. All three of us."

Ashley threw her arms around him, quietly sobbing into the side of his neck. When she settled down, she said, "Or the four of us."

"Four?"

"You know twins run in my family."

"Oh boy."

Ashley gently pushed him to the ground while unbuttoning his shirt. "Oh boy is right."

Their clothes were cast off with practiced abandon while frogs and crickets hidden in the darkness provided a little background music. Nothing young Randy the caddy could have dreamt up was better than this moment.

Neither of them heard the approaching footsteps.

Randy felt a sharp kick in his side. It was hard enough to roll him off his wife. With his hand clasped to his ribs, he looked up to find they were surrounded by four men, all of them wearing hoodies and black surgical masks so he couldn't make out their features. One of the men had grabbed all of their clothes and rifled through the pockets until he found Randy's wallet.

"Got it," he told his shadowed cohorts.

"What about her?" one of them asked, pointing at Ashley who was desperately trying to cover her nakedness.

Randy wanted to jump to his feet and take on the four men. What was surely a broken rib and realizing he was outnumbered and nude kept him on the ground. He shifted on the grass so he could position himself in front of his wife.

"Just take the wallet and go," Randy said. He had twenty-three dollars in cash and a lone credit card, along with his driver's license. It could all be easily replaced.

"What about hers?"

Ashley gripped Randy's arms, pressing herself against him. "I don't have a wallet, dumbass," she said. "You got what you wanted. Now go before things get worse." Ashley could be tougher than most of the men Randy had served with. She could also let her temper get the best of her.

One of the men chuckled. "Get worse? For who? Us? I don't think so."

The man had an accent Randall couldn't place. He was certainly not from around these parts, that was for sure.

Randy got to his feet, still clutching his side. "You've gotten all you're going to get. You should call that a win and go back to whatever hole you came out from."

The men creeped forward. Randy couldn't see their eyes in the gloom, but he could feel their gazes locked on his wife and sense their intention.

"Step back," Randy said.

Ashely was on her feet now, unabashed by her nudity. They both raised their fists and took a fighter's stance. "We don't want to hurt you," Ashley said.

"But we will," Randy added.

He heard the metallic click of a friction lock baton expanding. He knew the sound well. He had one of his own . . . back home.

"I don't think so," the one with the baton said.

Before Randy could react, slowed by his broken ribs, the baton cracked the side of his knee. He went down hard, lifting his arm up just in time to take the brunt of the next blow aimed at his head. Randy lashed out with his leg and connected with the thug's ankle. The hooded piece of trash landed beside him, but that didn't stop him from bludgeoning Randy with the baton.

Ashley cried out. The sound of fists on flesh cut through the still night air as she tried to fight off her attackers.

Even she was no match for three men who each must have outweighed her by fifty or more pounds. They drove her to the green. Randy reached out for her but received a sharp blast to his wrist for the effort.

"Get the hell off of her!"

"Randy!"

He rose just in time to see the baton headed for his eyes. And then he saw and felt nothing.

# CHAPTER 2

Augustus "Gus" Fuller turned on the flat top before he hit the lights. He liked getting to the luncheonette before sunrise, when everything was still and peaceful. While the flat top warmed up, he would go in back and make the biscuit mix and get started on the sausage gravy. Then he'd whip up some pancake and waffle batter.

Gus had called Springerville, South Carolina, his home all of his life. His family could be traced all the way back to when the town was incorporated back in 1827. Springerville was the very definition of a bucolic suburb, with the nearest big city being Charleston forty miles to its east. The tree-lined business district consisted of four blocks with one streetlight at their midway point. From his front window, he could see clearly from the library at the southern end to the Iron Works Bar and Grill in the north. City hall was just a block away, with its grassy oval complete with large gazebo that hosted most town events for as long as anyone could remember.

His grandfather had opened the luncheonette to great fanfare before Gus was a twinkle in his father's eye. It had become a staple of Springerville over the years, host to every hungry belly in town, four marriage proposals, one wedding, innumerable high school lunches and book club breakfasts, hotly contested bridge tournaments, as well as a meeting place for folks to talk of frivolous and serious topics, all over a cup of coffee and fresh biscuits slathered with butter.

Even after his stint in the military, serving during wartime in the Middle East, there was never a doubt in Gus's mind that he would return to the town and luncheonette he loved. Being in service to others gave him true joy, which is why he never missed a day of work, still feeling that thrill of anticipation during his morning prep work.

Gus paused for a moment and sipped on a steaming mug of coffee.

A shadow passed by the glass front door and tapped on the window. Gus raised his hand in greeting, not that Maddie Jackson could see him in the dark. She lived a few blocks down and grew some of the best raspberries and blueberries around. An early riser like Gus, she left several cartons of berries beside the door. She wasn't wearing her glasses, but she did have her cane, so Gus didn't worry about her getting hurt on her way home. He paid Maddie for her wonderful produce on Mondays, always giving her a little more than she asked for, knowing she was on a fixed income and how difficult the economy was making life for people like Maddie. Heck, it wasn't just her. It seemed like everyone was feeling the squeeze in Springerville. Well, at least those who'd called it home for most, if not all, of their lives.

The bread delivery would be next, in about fifteen minutes or so. Gus remembered when he was a kid and they had a milkman that delivered to the houses in the neighborhood. He wondered what had become of Mr. Keene, their local dairy man. Where did milkmen go when there was no more milk to deliver?

Gus put the biscuits in the oven and laid out three pounds of bacon strips on the flat top to get them going under the yellow hood light. His father used to deep fry the bacon, but Gus's wife, Annette, now gone ten years, had insisted he at least try to serve healthier fare. It didn't help that Gus's father and grandfather, the prior owners of the luncheonette who loved their cooking as much as their patrons did, had died too young of heart disease.

If Annette had been around now to see all of these horrid plant-based foods, she would have pressured Gus to add them to the menu (and drive his customers away). He never wanted to know how plant bacon tasted.

When the clock turned five thirty Gus threw on all of the lights, unlocked the door, and brought in the bread and berries.

Like moths to a flame, his early-morning regulars came ambling in five minutes later.

His good friend Chris Banks sidled up to the counter. Gus poured him a cup of coffee without his needing to ask. There was also Ron and Mike, best friends who used to own a restaurant in the next town but had shifted over to home security that paid more and involved a lot less stress. There was a sudden need for their services in Springerville and every other town in the county. Ron always took orange juice while Mike preferred his coffee black. In came Sarah Birch, who owned the launderette three blocks down. She opened at six for the folks who wanted to get a load in before work. Gus slid a mug of warm water and a box of tea bags her way.

"I'm feeling like blueberry pancakes today," Banks said.

"And just how does that feel?" Sarah asked. "I'm genuinely curious."

"Har har. And here I was ready to pay for your breakfast today."

"I'd rather you pay for my dinner. Preferably someplace nice with menus that aren't laminated with bad pictures of the food on them."

Gus smiled as he put some bread in the toaster for Ron and Mike. Sarah had been chasing after Banks for as long as he could remember. She may have been seven years older than Chris, but she was still a catch, at least in Gus's opinion. Banks couldn't get over her little sister breaking his heart back in high school.

"A little trip to Hilton Head would be very nice," Gus said as he cracked some eggs.

Banks shot him a warning look. Sarah concentrated on her tea, knowing when to back off.

"You guys hear what happened at the golf course last night?" Mike said.

"Someone arrived late for tee time?" Banks said.

"No, this is serious. A couple was attacked and mugged."

Sarah stopped stirring her tea. "What? At the golf course? When was this?"

"After it had closed," Ron said. "I heard it was Randy and Ashley Early. They're both in the hospital. It sounds like they're hurt pretty bad and Ash . . ." His eyes flicked over to Sarah.

"Go on, I'm a big girl. I can take it."

Ron cleared his throat and spoke just above a whisper. "They believe she was raped."

Everyone shook their heads in quiet disgust. Gus gripped his spatula hard enough to whiten his knuckles.

What the hell was happening to his town? There was a time, not so long ago, when the biggest crime was the occasional drunk driving, shoplifting on a very small scale, and the usual domestic dispute.

Muggings and rapes did not happen in Springerville. Never.

"Sweet Jesus, that's terrible," Banks said. "That Randy is gonna be fit to be tied the moment he gets out. The cops have any leads on who did it?"

While other people listened to the radio or podcasts while they went about their day, Ron and Mike stayed glued to the police band. Until a couple of years ago, there wasn't much chatter to warrant spreading a potential warning, like that time back in eighty-seven when there were all the car break-ins that turned out to be the work of seventeen-year-old Jimmy Yannick who had a thing for stealing radios. He never did anything with them. Just stored them in a couple of ratty boxes in his old man's garage. Jimmy was always a little off, and when he got caught, the whipping by his daddy stopped the rash of broken windows and empty dashboards.

No one in the luncheonette would have ever dreamt of hearing the news Ron and Mike were sharing.

"Right now, it's just four men wearing hoodies and those medical masks," Mike said, pushing his coffee away. "So far, no other descriptions."

"I never liked those masks," Gus said. "They didn't seem to help any, unless you're a criminal and need to hide your identity."

Gus leaned against the counter, suddenly thrown out of his comfortable routine. It almost didn't feel proper making breakfast right now. Randy's parents lived around the corner from him. He remembered when Randy was born and the big welcome-home party that was thrown for him by everyone in the neighborhood on account of how difficult the pregnancy and delivery had been on his poor mother.

When Randy brought that beautiful young bride of his to Springerville, he'd practically busted down the luncheonette's door to show her off to everyone. Gus was glad as hell to see him return and hoped they'd settle down for good. Nowadays, young people itched to leave small towns like Springerville, using college as a springboard to find roots elsewhere. It appeared the military had taught Randy to appreciate this place.

"Someone will have to keep an eye on him," Gus said. "Before he gets to something that'll land him in more trouble than the animals who did this to them."

"This would never have happened before the locusts," Sarah said, idly stirring her tea.

"Damn straight, it wouldn't," Ron said.

The true citizens of Springerville referred to the unending tide of big-city transplants as a plague of locusts that had brought plenty of change, and none of it good. Gus liked to remind folks that at least locusts eventually left. It didn't look like that was going to happen here. So now they were stuck with rising prices and crime and lowered quality of life.

"I'll hold off on the pancakes," Banks said. "I suddenly don't feel so good." He scratched at his dark, bald head, staring off into space. "I know a lot of people who'd help Randy find them. Hell, I'm one of them. People like that, they don't deserve to walk around like it's a quiet Sunday afternoon."

"Shouldn't we just let the police do their job?" Gus said.

"I'm happy to. I'm not sure about Randy, though. And I wouldn't blame him."

Sarah slapped her hand on the countertop. "Can we

please stop dreaming up gathering a posse and think about those poor kids and their parents? I'm going to call on George and Anne later this morning. See if there's anything they need."

"That's smart thinking," Gus said. "I'll whip them up a few meals. I'm pretty sure they won't be doing much cooking for the next few days. Think I'll stop by the hospital after lunch, too."

"I'd come with you, but I have a busy schedule today. Too many cars to fix and not enough time," Banks said. He used to have an assistant, but with the cost of parts and his rent rising, and his refusal to pass them along to his longtime customers, he'd had to let Frankie, his young mechanic in training, go a few months back.

"We'll keep our ears open and let you know anything else that we hear," Ron said when Gus served him his toast with a side of bacon and eggs.

"And keep your eyes open for anyone walking around with a hoodie. Especially if there's more than one of them together," Mike said, not bothering to touch his plate.

The sun had just started to rise, bathing the street in shades of pink and orange. Gus and his friends looked out the big front window, as if expecting to see a hooded figure at any moment. What should have been a beautiful morning was marred by the awful news.

Gus knew in his gut that this was just the beginning of very bad times for his hometown.

# CHAPTER 3

Braden Stranger listened to the chimes gently ring, signaling the end of his morning meditation. He took a deep breath and slowly opened his eyes, gazing upon the rock garden he'd installed in his backyard.

His phone rang before he extracted himself from his lotus position. He answered it, feeling all of his peace and calm dissipate when he saw who was on the other end of the line.

"It's a little early to do the whole screaming and threatening routine," he grumbled.

"I wouldn't have to call if you'd answered my text last night," his ex-wife, Susan, growled.

He had seen the text but wasn't in the proper frame of mind to type a reply. He'd been deep into a bottle of Caymus red Cabernet and feeling mellow after a solid day of Zoom meetings. His ears had felt clogged from hours upon hours of wearing earbuds, and he was just plain sick of interacting with people. Transitioning his position of chief communications ambassador to his successor, Siti Agarwal, felt like more work than the actual duties of the job itself. Bringing in the disabled Indian transplant had been his idea, and the company was already receiving great press. That and his plans to reduce the company's carbon emissions and restructure their facilities to adapt to renewable energy had increased their ESG score, which made them more attractive for investors and the stock market. The move had earned him an extra million-dollar payout as part of his already massive separation agreement. Not that he needed it, but who was he to turn his nose at a million dollars? Just because he came from money and was able to make a considerable amount on his own merits—whether dubious or not—didn't mean that he didn't crave more.

"Did you ever think I might have been indisposed when you sent it? It's six in the morning, for Chrissake. Patience was never your forte."

He could practically see Susan's lip curling. "I prefer to rain on your Buddhist parade. Are you taking Aiden next week or not?"

"Next week isn't a good time. You know that."

"Do you even care about your son? I didn't see you hesitate when you decided to move seven hundred miles away from him."

*Poor befuddled Susan*, he thought. *If only she knew why I'm here.* It was enough to make him smile, a shield against her slings and poison-tipped arrows.

"Of course I do. But I won't have any time for him. I'm handing over the reins and starting my campaign. A little busy, you know?"

There was a long, angry silence. Then Susan said coolly, "Fine. You're going to be the one to tell him when he gets home from school. I refuse to be the bad guy."

Braden poured himself a glass of pomegranate juice and took a long sip. He added a spoonful of protein powder to the rest and downed it in preparation for his workout. "Considering how hard you fought for full custody, I would think you'd be happy I can't take him."

"And considering what a jerk his father is, I should be. Unfortunately, children need their parents, no matter how unfit they are."

He felt his muscles tense and his stomach clench. Susan played the unfit father card whenever she wanted to really stick the knife in him. Granted, even he knew he would never win a father-of-the-year award. Sacrifices had to be made so they could all live the lifestyle they'd become accustomed to. Braden had made sure that could continue for his son. One could have financial security *or* a constant, loving presence. There was no in between. Aiden would thank him when he was old enough to understand, just as Braden had silently thanked his black-hearted father, at least once he'd passed.

This time, he wasn't going to let Susan push that button.

"How about three weeks from now? Meeting with the local Podunks won't exactly be heavy lifting."

"They'll run you out on the rails," she replied sharply. "What makes you think the people in that backwater town will elect a rat like you?"

Braden grinned. "You of all people should know, I can be very persuasive."

"Your charms wear thin, quick."

He walked to his office and shuffled the papers that revealed the latest demographic data for Springerville. The numbers were what had convinced him, along with the backing of his benefactors—men and women with money, power, and resources that would boggle the average man's sensibilities—to run for mayor. For them, when money was no longer an obstacle and power was a ho-hum fact of life, one could say all that was left was the need to possess souls. Not just of people, but of nations. Stranger wanted to be that soul stealer, and to do so, he would need to stake his claim here in South Carolina.

Change had already taken place in town. He was just here to usher in the final stages. His brother Steven had laughed when he'd told him his plan, saying the whole big-fish-in-a-small-town thing was not his game.

Braden didn't see it that way. Springerville was just the first step. There was a whole state up for grabs. Playing the long game was just what he excelled at.

"I remember them working on you for quite a long while," he said.

"I was young and stupid. If you win, I think the state's attorney general will appreciate a call urging him or her to take a good long look at your books."

Flicking her jab away, he replied, "Well, if you and Aiden want to move into a one-bedroom apartment in Mount Vernon, be my guest. I hear the buses run fairly regularly there."

There was no sharp-tongued reply to that. She knew he could pull the plug on the stream of money that came her way just as easily as ending the call, which he did with a tap of his thumb.

Booting up his laptop, he spent several minutes looking over the designs the company he'd hired in Los Angeles had sent him for his campaign logo and signage. It was nothing flashy, but he was sure it would be more eye catching than anything that current, past-his-sell-by-date rube of a mayor could come up with.

Uprooting his life to Springerville was exactly what he'd needed. People down here were polite enough to his face, but he knew they all chattered like washwomen about the influx of outsiders like him the moment his back was turned. He was aware that they all referred to him as The Stranger. Not very creative on their part. Too on the nose for his taste.

If they only knew what *he* called *them*.

Springerville was a beautiful town, a perfect escape from the city with its congestion and foul-smelling air. It was one of many similar towns in the South that had been on the radar of powerful men and women for quite a while. Behind the scenes, they had set about changing the country, one small bit at a time. Stranger considered himself an emissary with a much higher purpose than simply being the mayor of a one-horse town. The goal here was to re-create the mindset of a city like New York, only with a much nicer landscape to relax and enjoy. To expunge stale and outdated values with those of a more progressive mindset. Springerville was just one of many seeds cast about the country, waiting to flourish.

If Stranger knew his backers well enough, what didn't flourish would be used as invaluable fertilizer for a grander movement.

He was about to go downstairs to his home gymnasium when his phone rang again. It wasn't Susan, thankfully, but his assistant, Roger Anson, who had lived in Springerville until he was two when his parents moved to Boston. Roger had worked for Braden for close to ten years now. He'd been Braden's eyes and ears since he'd moved back to Springerville ahead of him. No one was aware that he and Braden had worked together in New York. For all they knew, Roger was a computer programmer working for a big tech company in Silicon Valley.

"Big news," Roger said.

"In Springerville? This early? Did someone tip a cow and it landed on them?"

"Much bigger. A couple who were out screwing at the golf course last night were attacked. They say the woman was raped. Both of them were beat up pretty bad."

"Where are they now?" Braden stared at his Peloton, knowing it would have to wait until later.

"Admitted to the hospital. Might be a good opportunity for you to show your face, make a statement. I'm sure someone from the local paper will be there all day."

A couple attacked and the woman raped. This would be very big news. Braden didn't need a crystal ball to tell him that this had been the work of some of their recent transplants. While plenty of people came here of their own volition, others had been sent just as Roger had, to scout the town. Along with other, more serious things.

The trick now was to cast doubt on who the perpetrators could be and focus on the locals. His mind worked the problem over.

Braden headed for his bedroom and opened his closet, deciding which suit to wear. He'd skip the tie. The locals didn't wear ties and he wanted to at least appear he was trying to blend in. "You're right at that. What are their names?"

Roger shuffled some paper on the other end of the line. "Um, Randall and Ashley Early. His family has been here for generations. He left to serve in the Army and came back with a new bride. I'll do some digging on her."

A military man. Braden Stranger had no taste for the military. His uncle, who had lived off Braden's father's riches, had been a marine who'd toured Vietnam. The man had been abusive, shiftless, and unable to provide for his family. Braden's aunt and cousins had had plenty of bruises to show for his version of tough love, at least until she ran off with another man. The state took the kids away and his uncle had moved into their pool house, working solely on drinking his liver into oblivion. Luckily for them all, his uncle had hanged himself in the garage less than a year later. Braden had been the one to find his body. He hadn't felt remorse then, nor did he now.

Randall Early was more than likely a blind follower. A sheep. Bad things happened to sheep. Predators had a taste for lamb.

"Good job, Roger. Can you clear my morning calendar? The transition can wait."

"You got it. If I find anything else out, I'll call you."

"Please do."

Braden practiced his smile in the bathroom mirror as the water heated up in the shower.

# CHAPTER 4

Gus shut the luncheonette down early as word got around about what had happened to Randy and Ashley. To say people were unnerved was a gross understatement. It was all they could talk about. His luncheonette buzzed all day as people lingered longer than usual to talk about it.

Walking down Main Street to his truck, he couldn't square what was going on with what he saw. It still looked pretty much the same as when he was growing up, though many of the storefronts had changed in the past year. Behind the library down the block was the parking lot that was used as an unofficial Wiffle ball stadium for all the local kids. Wiffle ball seemed a thing of the past.

More people filled the streets now, people he didn't know from Adam or Eve. The structure of the town itself still held, though it seemed as if it was being destroyed from within, bit by bit, day by day.

When he arrived at the hospital to check in on Randy, he was intercepted by the boy's parents, George and Anne. She looked about ready to collapse. This was the last thing the poor woman needed, considering everything she was facing. They said Randy had been in such a state, the doctor had to sedate him. He had a few fractured ribs, along with some severe contusions and bruises on his arms and legs. They were going to keep him overnight as a precaution. Gus told George and Anne he'd drop a care package of food on their porch later that day.

He was about to leave when a commotion at the other end of the waiting room caught his attention. A red-faced man, with his wife clinging onto his arm, started raising holy hell as he spoke to the doctor.

"That's Ash's parents," George whispered to Gus. "Man's been fit to be tied since they got here. Can't say that I blame him."

The doctor tried to settle the portly man down.

"Don't you dare tell me to calm down! I want to know who did this to my daughter. Where the hell are the police? I want someone guarding her room."

The doctor maintained his composure, keeping his voice low and calm.

Ashley's mother was a waif of a woman who, Gus would guess, was normally manicured within an inch of her life. The plane ride here and the emotional toll had her fraying at the edges.

Tears streamed down her cheeks and she tried to pull her husband away. He wasn't budging so much as an inch.

"I need a real doctor. Who is your boss? Or your boss's boss? Jesus, I've heard how the medical system is down here. We should bring her back home and get some qualified care."

"Your daughter sustained a head injury. She shouldn't be flying. We're taking very good care of her."

"I'll drive her home. I'm sure this town has a pickup truck I can rent." The man turned to his shocked wife. "I told you something like this would happen. What can you expect of rednecks when someone smarter than them comes to a place like this to live?"

If he was trying to get the doctor's goat, it wasn't working.

Though Gus felt a slight twinge in his gut.

If he'd overheard this down at the bar or in his luncheonette, harsh words would have been exchanged. Considering what the couple was going through, he let it slide.

"He doesn't know what he's saying," George said to Gus.

"I think he does," Gus replied.

"His daughter is nothing like he is. She's such a sweet, loving girl. We were so happy when they decided to move back here, even though I know it's been tough for them both having to share the house with us." Anne raised her voice for the next part so she could be heard across the room. "But I couldn't ask for a better daughter-in-law."

The harried couple looked her way for a moment, the doctor using the distraction as an opportunity to slip away. There was nothing to be gained by engaging with Ashley's father any longer.

"If it wasn't for your son, this would never have happened," Ashley's father said, wagging a finger at them.

The accusation had a physical effect on George and Anne. Gus couldn't help himself from intervening.

"I think that's about enough for now," he said. "I understand you're upset. We all are, sir. But this is still a hospital and there are some very sick people that we need to respect. Going off on everyone you see isn't going to make things any better. In fact, it will do the opposite."

The man's wife looked to be in agreement, though she held her tongue.

"And who the hell are you?"

"Just a friend of the family. You can believe me; our police aren't going to stop until they catch who did this."

Waving his arms in exasperation, the man said, "Just great. Andy and Barney are on the case. I don't know why I was worried."

Gus stepped closer, his imposing frame dwarfing the angry Chicagoan. "Your insults only make you look foolish. Why don't you take a walk for a bit, then go to your daughter. I'm sure she needs you."

"You've got nerve talking to me like that."

"If being polite and rational is nervy, I'm okay with that. Now, I'm preparing some meals for the Earlys. I'd be happy to do so for you as well."

Ashley's mother finally spoke up. "That's very kind of you."

"You'll find that in Springerville, we tend to rally around each other. It's the Christian thing to do. I'll swing by around five, if that works for you."

"Thank you."

Her husband could only manage an impotent glower.

Gus turned to give George and Anne a gentle squeeze of their shoulders. "Call me if you need anything."

"We will. Thank you," George said.

Gus was relieved to see that Ashley's parents were heading for the door and taking his advice to get some air. He avoided them as he went to his Jeep. The day was sunny and warm, with a mild breeze that cooled everything it touched. He mused that no matter how perfect a day seemed, there were millions of imperfections being suffered around the world. If the weather matched the mood, it would be cold, dark, and rainy.

He kept his radio off as he headed for his luncheonette, occupying his mind on what he'd cook.

\* \* \*

An old Gretchen Wilson song played on the radio while Gus slipped a tray of meatloaf in the oven. He looked out the window and across the way at the new cybercafe that had opened six months back. It was full, every chair and couch and love seat, none of it matching, hosting a person attached to their laptop. Giant white mugs of coffee or tea were by most of their sides.

He'd gone in there when it opened, shocked to see the prices they charged. When he recovered, he got himself a cup, just to see what the competition was brewing. It didn't even taste like coffee. More like Christmas dessert in a mug. He didn't see it as a threat to his two-dollar coffee.

Besides, he had no desire to fill his place with zombies and their technological overlords.

People talked with one another in his luncheonette. They shared news and retold old stories.

A few of the new folks had stopped by asking him for gluten free waffles or quinoa breakfast bowls. When he told them those items weren't on the menu, they usually settled for a muffin, picking at it while they gazed at their screen, refusing to integrate themselves with the townies who, to their credit, did occasionally try to strike up a conversation.

"Their loss," Gus would tell his regulars.

He remembered the time Sarah asked a couple what church they belonged to. You'd think she'd asked them if they liked to murder puppies in their spare time. The woman went on and on about the idiocy of all religion and how people like Sarah had been brainwashed by the great machine designed to keep the drones in line.

Sarah took it all in, and then flashed a wide smile. "Thank you for that, dear. But remember this, if I'm wrong, when I die, nothing happens. But if you're wrong, well, I think you'll have some serious regret."

The woman's mouth dropped open and she stormed out, barking at her husband to follow her. The regulars had a good old laugh. Gus had bagged up some biscuits on the house for Sarah.

Speaking of biscuits, Gus had to finish whipping up a batch of cathead biscuits that would go with the meatloaf, roasted garden potatoes, and garlic-fried green beans. Maybe after eating his dinner, Ashley's father would be too bloated to be a blowhard.

The bell chimed on the front door and in walked the most captivating creature in Springerville, at least to Gus.

"Something smells good," Emma Botin said as she settled into one of the round seats at the counter.

Gus leaned against the counter and planted a welcome kiss on her cherry-red lips. "I think you smell even better."

She let her bag slide off her shoulder and onto the floor. "Did you hear what happened to the Earlys?"

"Mike and Ron told me first thing this morning. That's what all this fine-smelling cooking is for."

Emma rested her elbows on the counter and brushed her golden hair from her face. She taught seventh grade English at the middle school. Gus told her innumerable times that he never would have made it to eighth grade if he'd had a teacher as gorgeous as her. In retrospect, he'd lucked out with Mrs. Kotcher, who looked a tad bit like an aardvark and had the disposition of a bobcat.

"You're a good man, you know that?"

"I'm just doing what's right."

"That's becoming a lost art," Emma replied, casting

her gaze at the cybercafe. The parents of some of her new students were most likely in there, and according to Emma, a few of them had deemed it their life's mission to make her life and all the teachers' a living hell. As Emma told it, these select parents believed their undisciplined hellions could do no wrong. Whenever Emma tried to punish their precious progeny by giving them extra assignments or sending them to the principal's office, there would be the inevitable meeting and scolding the next day. Not scolding of the child! Heavens no. Emma had to learn that these children were special and should be treated like Fabergé eggs.

It didn't help that the former principal, Mrs. Jameson, had passed away in her sleep a year ago and been replaced by Alexandra Morales, a young transplant from San Francisco who had less experience in a classroom than anyone who taught at the school. The city by the bay was a shell of its former self thanks to the progressive policies of folks like Ms. Morales. And now here she was, replicating failure.

Gus could still feel the impact of Mrs. Kotcher's yardstick on his posterior. He'd earned those whacks the few times he got them and had to face a few more when he came home with a note from his teacher. A lot of people didn't agree with the spare the rod, spoil the child theory nowadays, but it was effective at stopping the shenanigans of a hormonal thirteen-year-old boy.

"How was school today?" Gus poured a diet soda for Emma in a chilled glass with ice.

"Don't ask. Grading these theme papers will take up most of my night. Then I'll sit back and wait for the outcry when certain students don't get an A. I know for a fact that quite of few of my darlings let their parents write their homework for them. I've gotten some papers that would hit the *New York Times* bestseller list." She looked tired but her laugh lit up the luncheonette.

"Well, it's a good thing I made extra. After I do my rounds, I can stop by your place. Is this a red or white wine kind of night?"

She thought about it for a moment. "Better make it white."

Emma got up and stretched, walking toward the big window overlooking Main Street.

"You notice something missing?"

Gus slid some chopped potatoes into a roasting pan. "Nope. Can't say that I do."

"The flag outside Al's is missing. Again."

Al's barbershop had boasted both the standard red-and-white pole as well as an American flag that he put out each morning. Gus looked over and confirmed it was missing.

"Why on earth would an American flag be such a problem for some people?" Emma rolled the cool glass against her neck.

"Because some people don't know how good they have it here, and the sacrifices it took to make it that way."

Whereas Al had always sported a smallish flag, the one outside Gus's could wrap up at least three proud Americans. So far, no one had bothered to touch it, but he knew the day was coming.

"Do you think he'll just keep getting new ones?" Emma asked.

"Yep. He told me he'll buy a flag a day if he has to. I suggested he get one of those security cameras, but he wants to catch them red-handed himself."

"Al couldn't hurt a sick cat."

"Maybe so. But you never know what an angry man is capable of."

Neither of them said anything for a spell, both worried about what Randy Early would do when he was released from the hospital.

# CHAPTER 5

Wallace "Wally" Sturgis was just plain tired. As two-time mayor of Springerville, he could no longer afford to be a laconic overseer of a small, beautiful, and quiet town. His parents had moved here a hundred years ago from Savannah. His father was a carpenter, and his mother could sell whale oil to Moby Dick. While dad was out swinging a hammer, his mother went door to door selling everything from Bibles and magazine subscriptions to cosmetics and Tupperware.

Even though he'd turned eighty a few months ago, he still missed his parents. He wished his father was here to lend an ear and give some advice.

His office had been flooded with calls from the locals wondering what it was he and his police chief were doing about finding the men who attacked the young Early couple. There was outrage, fear, and the usual "something like this has never happened here before."

They were right.

Springerville was changing. And it was all under his watch. The weight of the guilt was oppressive, as was the tug of the upcoming mayoral race. He had planned to step aside and let someone else take his place on the ballot. So far, no one of any real note had risen from the ranks. If they thought running against The Stranger was going to be like shooting fish in a barrel, they were wrong. Wally was very afraid that there were enough newbies, or locusts as he heard folks call them, who didn't give a spit about the traditions of Springerville to get the slickster elected.

That would be a disaster.

Did he have it in him to run again against an opponent he was sure would take him to task every step of the way? Stranger and his ilk had fast-talked Wally into allowing quite a few "updates" to their community. At first, Wally had thought the influx of people and their money would be good for the town. There were a lot of projects that needed to be undertaken just to keep the infrastructure from crumbling. Those projects needed money, and money is what these interlopers had in abundance.

In just one year, they'd repaved most of the main roads, got a new fire engine, revamped the playground, put a fresh coat of paint on all the schools and installed too many computers to count. When looked at from above, they were all very good things.

Wally had seen enough *Twilight Zone* episodes to know that no good deed went unpunished. Springerville was no longer his town . . . or the town he knew and had lived in all his life.

*My fault. My damn fault.*

He should be dreaming of retirement. Instead, he was wondering if he had the strength to stop what he'd allowed to start. Wally pounded the desk.

A little birdie had told him Braden Stranger had been to the hospital to visit Randy Early and his wife and wouldn't you know it, the press was there to take a statement. From what Wally had heard, The Stranger had blamed the act of violence on what were probably disenfranchised youth who were victims of systemic nonengagement that came from a society that allowed the myth of dying in a small town to pervade from generation to generation.

In other words, it had to be someone local. Don't blame the locusts.

And what the hell was systemic nonengagement?

Wally was going to pay a visit to George and Anne Early later at their house, without prying eyes around. Anne Early had volunteered to make phone calls on behalf of his campaign for reelection if he decided to run. This wasn't a photo op. He was genuinely worried and angry.

Carolyn, his part-time assistant, knocked on his door, saving him from his pity party.

"Come on in."

She was white as a sheet. "Someone broke into your car!"

"What?"

She clutched the doorknob and stammered for a bit. "I . . . I was stepping outside for a little fresh air when I saw that your side windows were . . . were broken. I didn't check to see if anything was taken."

With some effort, Wally disengaged himself from his plush leather chair. He wanted to run, but his legs, with two knees that Dr. Brown had told him needed to be re-placed someday soon, allowed him only a slow waddle out of his office, down the town hall corridor and the front steps. There were a few lookie-loos standing around his Chevy Tahoe, looking at the broken glass all around. He didn't recognize a single one of them. But he did perceive the look on their faces. It wasn't concern. More like a morbid curiosity.

"Son of a . . ."

Sweat popped out along the back of his neck as he opened the driver's side door. His radio was still there, but the change he kept in the center console was gone. He took his time looking through everything as the crowd grew.

When he was finished, he was red-faced and damp. Four windows broken. Maybe three bucks in change missing. Why?

*Because there are some bad hombres around here now*, he thought. He was smart enough not to cast a wide net and think every transplant was the same. There were some very fine folks who had chosen to call Springerville home.

But there were others that came here itching for trouble. Why they would settle here with a chip on their shoulders and hatred for a town they didn't really know was beyond him. Maybe it wasn't the town. With all of the American flags that had been stolen or desecrated, he had to think there was something else bigger and deeper at play here. These people despised the country, and what better place to take your aggressions out on than Springerville, a town that had been a poster child for truth, justice, and the American way.

This was just another erosion of their values.

He didn't wonder how no one hadn't heard the breaking glass. It was a hot day, and everyone was inside, their hearing dulled by the steady hum of air conditioning.

"Did they take much? Did you have anything valuable in the car?" Carolyn asked, nervously tugging at the hem of her skirt.

Wally looked around at the strange faces. For all he knew, one of them was the culprit. A couple looked mighty suspicious, especially the guy with the neck tattoos who appeared to be enjoying the spectacle. He wiped the sweat from his brow with the blue bandana he always kept in his back pocket.

"Nah. Just left me with a lot of broken glass. Can you call Chris Banks and let him know I'll be stopping by his shop shortly?"

Carolyn, who was by nature nervous as a bird in a cat corral, nodded and hustled back inside.

"Anyone see anything?" he asked the crowd.

He got a lot of shaking heads in return.

This didn't feel random.

Someone was sending him a message.

Was this over the Early case?

Or maybe a disgruntled resident who didn't like what he'd allowed to happen to their town?

Was there a chance this was from The Stranger himself? He wouldn't put it past the snake charmer. Now there was a man with the devil in his eyes. Oh sure, he looked the part of the lifetime politician and smiled at everyone when he was out and about. But that smile never came within a football field of reaching his eyes. Wally didn't trust him as far as he could lift his truck off the ground.

Normally, he would think this was all just paranoid thinking brought on by the shock of seeing his property vandalized.

*Trust your gut*, his father had told him time and time again. *There're times you need to follow your heart, but your gut will save you more than once in your life.*

Wally was going to take his father's advice.

Which meant he was going to run for re-election because he knew what he was dealing with. And if the stress killed him in the process, so be it. At least he'd go down swinging.

A man like Stranger had to have enough skeletons in his closet to fill a family plot. The trick was unearthing them.

# CHAPTER 6

Chris Banks closed his shop early on account of he was tired and had no other cars to work on since he'd gotten the mayor's new windows installed. The act of vandalism bothered Banks as much as it had old Wally. He'd only charged the mayor half of what he should have. He would have liked to do the work for free, but he did have to keep the lights on and beer in the fridge.

What he needed right now was to get in his pontoon boat and commune with nature. Or better said, just get away.

Walking down Main Street toward Gus's luncheonette, he passed by a couple who at first looked like they were considering crossing to the other side of the street. The woman tugged hard on the man's arm and when they passed within feet of one another, the man, a young guy with one of those ridiculous man buns, raised a fist, and said, "Black lives matter."

Banks would have just kept on going, but he was feeling ornery and couldn't let it go. "What did you say?"

The white couple looked stunned. The woman, whose red hair came from a bottle, said, "We just wanted to let you know that we care."

"You don't even know me."

"But we know what you've been through. Especially in a place like this."

Bristling, Banks said, "Do you actually believe the words coming out of your mouth? You don't know anything I've been through. *A place like this* is my home. It was my father's home and his father's home. We've all had a good life here. I'll bet what I've been through is a lot better than where you came from. Because I'm still here, happy. I didn't run from my home."

The man said, "Look. I'm sorry. I just . . . I just . . ."

"You just keep on walking and stop saying any stupid thing the media has fed into your head."

They double-timed it in the other direction. Banks watched them retreat.

"I never thought I'd see the day. Black lives matter. No kidding. So does my cat's life," he mumbled as he made his way down the street. He'd bet dollars to donuts that if he or any Black man stood outside that couple's property for five minutes, they would call the cops, whispering in their phone that there was a dangerous person loitering about the neighborhood.

Gus stepped outside his place, wiping his hands with a towel. He saw Banks and nodded.

"Done for the day?"

"Yep. You don't have your overalls on, so I assume you decided to make it an early day."

"Want to go on over to the boat? I just have to make a pit stop at Food City to grab a twelve-pack."

Both men watched the comings and goings at the cybercafe. It was busier than usual today. Everyone either had a laptop in hand, or a laptop bag slung over their shoulder. Banks could only imagine the horse manure those folks were subjecting their brains to. Why did they come all the way here if they just wanted to be plugged into their devices? There was a beautiful day to enjoy, yet there they were, an army of robots.

"What kind of beer you thinking of?" Gus asked, turning his back on the café. Banks was sure he was having the same thoughts.

"Busch is on sale."

"Works for me. I just have to lock up. Meet you at the store. I need to grab a couple of things from home."

Banks went up the block and crossed the street to walk across Food City's parking lot. Not a lot of cars right now. It was too late for the older shoppers and too early for the working stiffs. Inside was colder than a well digger's hind quarters. A chill ran through him as he found his way to the cold case and grabbed a cardboard half case of Busch.

At the front of the store, there were only two open lines. One register was manned by Muriel Sheen. She'd been working at Food City since before Banks was born. The woman on her line had filled every square inch of the conveyor belt. She texted on her phone while Muriel went about scanning and bagging everything. Old Muriel wasn't known for her speed. That could take a while.

The other line was the brand-new do-it-yourself nonsense. The store's manager, Hector Jiminez, had told Banks over beers one night that the self-checkout was the result of a campaign drummed up by the locusts that went all the way to corporate headquarters. They saw it as a convenient and fast way to get their groceries. Jiminez and Banks saw it was one fewer job opportunity.

"Guess they don't like waiting for Muriel," Jiminez had said, tipping back a cold Budweiser.

"These people can't even wait for their own funeral."

As much as Banks hated the self-checkout, he wanted to be on his boat as soon as possible. It was his happy place, his center of calm. If he didn't get some of that happy calm soon, he felt like he was going to explode. The past few days had made him suspicious and angry. As much as he detested the locusts, he didn't want to take it out on them (even if they deserved it).

The machine gave him trouble checking out, which didn't help his mood. He caught Muriel's eye and asked her if she could help. The look of irritation on the woman's face when Muriel shuffled over to his aisle gave him a small measure of satisfaction.

"You're a life saver," he said to Muriel with a wink. "Don't let that woman rush you."

Muriel grinned. "The rush gear in my clutch burned out a long time ago."

As Banks exited out into the heat, Gus was walking across the lot. A woman pushing a metal cart was headed for the door the same time as Gus. She had a bandana on her head with long strands of red hair spilling out of the back. Her head was down, looking at her phone as she made for the automatic door.

Even though she smacked the cart into Gus's thigh as he tried to sidestep away from her, he was the one to apologize.

"Sorry, ma'am. You first."

Her head snapped up from her phone. "What did you say?"

Confused, Gus said, "Sorry I got in your way."

"Did you call me ma'am?"

"Yes. And again, my apologies."

"Well, I don't appreciate you assigning a gender to me."

Now even Banks was confused. Gus rubbed his chin, and replied, "Excuse me? I'm not sure I understand."

"I go by they."

"They?" Gus said. "Are there more of you I can't see?"

If looks could kill, Gus would be dead on the ground. "You know, it's rude to assume someone's gender and throw whatever pronoun you deem appropriate around. That's the problem with people like you."

"People like me?" Gus took a step back and lifted his hands in surrender. "I didn't mean any offense. I just assumed . . ."

"Don't you touch me!" the woman . . . or man . . . or they . . . shouted.

"I can assure you, I had no intention of doing any such thing."

"I bet you're upset that you left your MAGA hat at home."

Gus and Banks exchanged a look, each flummoxed by the turn of events.

"Filthy caveman."

Gus had to practically pirouette out of the way to avoid being run down by the cart.

"What just happened?" he said to Banks as the door closed. "And what's with that *they* business?"

Banks scratched his head, wondering if he should open the case and have a beer right in the parking lot. "Beats the hell out of me."

"One thing is for sure, I'm not going in there. I think it's best to avoid coming across each other again in the aisles." They walked side by side across the baking asphalt. "Was I wrong? I mean, that was a woman, right?"

"I don't know anymore. I'm not sure the pronoun police do, either. Welcome to our bold new world." He ripped a corner off the case and dug out a beer for each of them.

"I never thought I'd see the day when using the word ma'am would be an issue. Remember the eighties and the guys in our school with long hair?"

"I sure do. I was envious. I dug heavy metal, but my afro would just get higher and wilder."

Gus laughed. "That would have been a sight. I recall those guys getting called ma'am all the time by mistake, especially if someone was behind them. They never blew their tops. They just laughed it off."

Banks tipped his can of beer against Gus's. "Being offended wasn't a point of pride then." He took a long sip. "Better days, my friend. Those were much better days."

# CHAPTER 7

Braden Stranger had officially thrown his hat in the ring two months earlier and his confidence was already beginning to waver. That old pain in his ass Wally Sturgis had announced he was going to run for reelection, throwing a bit of a monkey wrench in Stranger's plans. Sure, Stranger had prepared for Sturgis to run again, but he'd been sure a private meeting would convince him otherwise. The carrot-and-stick approach had worked wonders with the man before. Now, all of his attempts to meet with the aging mayor had been left unanswered. It made Stranger wonder just what the heck was going on in Sturgis's sluggish brain.

Word around town was that Wally blamed him for vandalizing his precious truck. That was the stick approach, and one he had thought of taking if Wally had refused his entreaties. But this was a random act, and it was costing him.

The man may have been next to useless, but everyone in town knew him and was familiar with him. Name recognition could not be discounted. Plus, the people of Springerville seemed to genuinely like him. Being the out-of-towner, Stranger couldn't harp on the fact that

Wally had laid down like a good dog and allowed Springerville to . . . adapt. That would just fan the flames of the townies to come out and vote to keep the *carpet-bagger* from winning.

Sure, he'd have the vote of the vast majority of new-comers who loved the small town but craved all the luxu-ries of the cities they had left. They wanted a big-box store, Starbucks, craft breweries with restaurants attached, and access to entertainment a little more refined than a local cover band at Iron Works Bar and Grill. And once recreational marijuana was legalized, the town would need the right man in place to cut through the dispensary red tape.

He could get all that for them, given time and their vote.

Sturgis, despite his age and having all the vitality of an old hound dog, posed a serious threat to all of his plans.

That and the attack on the Early family, along with the recent spike in crime, all factored against him. Braden Stranger sensed a tipping point was near. The influx of residents was on the verge of wearing out their welcome, but they also weren't ready to leave. Some of the select others that were sent here were going off their leashes a bit too much. What could he expect of poorly bred dogs? His inquiries into who had attacked the Earlys and wrecked the mayor's truck had come up empty. That frustrated him to no end. When he did find them, they would wish their mothers had insisted their daddies get a vasectomy.

The man who was his primary benefactor had told him to stand down and find a proper hill to die on. As much as Stranger wanted to push his point, he had to acquiesce. There was a lot of power and money up in New York that he needed, especially for the future. So, for now, he had to suck it up and let it go, which was not something he was accustomed to doing.

The question now was, could he steer things in his favor? It was a big ask, but when had a high level of difficulty ever stopped him?

"What's on the agenda today?" he asked his assistant, Roger.

"It's a light one. I scheduled an appointment at the gun range at three."

Stranger, wearing an expensive robe cinched tight along his narrow waist, arched an eyebrow, and asked, "Gun range? You trying to get me killed?"

"You're going to take lessons. It's not a photo op." Roger scrolled through his phone as he sat on a stool along the kitchen island.

"Why on earth would I do such a thing?"

"To show that you're not a gun-fearing liberal from New York."

"I've never touched a gun in my life."

"I wouldn't say that, if I were you."

He wanted to fight Roger, but the man had a point. When in Rome . . .

"We need to redirect our focus," Stranger said as he fiddled with his espresso machine. Caffeine kept him sharp, and he liked the process of making the perfect cup of espresso.

"How so?"

He posed a simple question. "If the election were held today, do you think I would win?"

Roger put his phone down, paused, and said, "I think it would be close."

Stranger slammed his fist on the counter. "Not good enough!"

"But that's if it were held today. We have months."

"Yeah, well, if we can speed up time and make me a resident for at least a quarter of a century, that might do it. Do you have a time machine?"

Roger looked at him as if he'd lost his marbles. "What?"

"Do you have a time machine?" he repeated, louder this time, his tone dripping with irritation.

"Of course not." Roger's hand instinctively went to his phone. His fingers grazed the protective cover but pulled away nervously.

"Exactly! Which is why we need to think outside the box. If it's just me and that ancient geezer vying for the affections of the people who already live here, we're treading on some very shaky ground. And all it will take is another incident like what happened to that couple at the golf course to sink me for good." The espresso machine hissed and gurgled as Stranger worked the controls like a mad scientist.

Stranger poured himself a cup of steaming espresso without offering one for his assistant. "So, if we can't get the majority of the vote from the current population, what do we need to do to guarantee a victory?"

"Bribe some of the people on the board of elections?"

"There is that. But I want more. I want to run a town that realizes its full potential. Not one that will fight every little improvement tooth and nail so it can cling to some ridiculous bit of good old American nostalgia."

Roger grew pensive, tapping his finger against the cleft in his upper lip. Stranger knew exactly what they should do, but he also wanted Roger to come to the same conclusion on his own, so to speak.

"What do I need, Roger?" He sipped his espresso, savoring the warmth that filled his mouth and chest.

Lost in thought for a moment, Roger straightened on his stool and grinned. "People. We need more people."

"Bingo."

"But how are we going to get them, and where are we going to put them? Last time I checked, there are only two houses on the market in town."

Stranger paced the kitchen. "Two houses that are on the market and ready to move in. But what about that mostly empty trailer park?"

"The Pennsylvania?"

"Yes, that's the one," he said, snapping his fingers. "And I've seen at least a dozen or more houses beyond fixer-upper. I'm sure there's plenty of land for sale, too. When I drive around, I see a lot of empty spaces. Look into it."

Roger tapped at his phone. "If we managed to find out-of-town buyers for all of the distressed properties, there isn't enough time to build houses on them. Construction is still lagging behind everywhere."

Tipping back his small cup to finish the espresso, Stranger winced, and said, "I don't care if anything ever gets built on them. It doesn't matter if the owners live in a tent on the property or a condo in the Cayman Islands. I need them to be registered residents and voters with the town. Capisce?"

"I understand. All we have to do is find the people willing to come down here."

"Don't you worry about that. I know exactly who to call to make that happen. They've allowed a few to trickle through until this point. It's time to turn on the spigot. You find the places for them to call home. I'll take care of the rest."

"Got it." Roger jumped from his stool and headed out of the house, presumably to pay a visit to the local real estate office. Stranger knew it would raise suspicions and there would be talk. There was always small-town gossip.

In the end, it wouldn't matter. Just as long as Stranger had the support of the new majority of Springerville.

# CHAPTER 8

Garth Brooks blared from the jukebox, drowning out the clacking of pool balls at the three tables beside it.

"Who played Garth Brooks?" Banks complained, looking around for the culprit. The crowd at the Iron Works Bar and Grill was larger than most Wednesday nights.

"I think it was that dude over there," Don Runde said from behind the bar. He was pulling a beer for a customer. Don and his brother Dennis owned the Iron Works and did everything from barbacking to cleaning the toilets. Don also relished the role of bouncer. A former lineman for the Seahawks—he got to start four games until his neck snapped in a very bad way on a *Monday Night Football* game against the Broncos—his size alone was enough to settle people down, right quick.

Banks looked over at a young guy with a scraggly beard wearing a beanie. "Yeah, that looks like the kind of guy who would. Wants to get some of that Southern authenticity."

"Garth Brooks is fine," Gus said. "His wife ain't so bad either." Gus noted that wool beanies, even in this heat, outnumbered trucker caps and cowboy hats. When he was just old enough to drink and the bar was called The Time

Out, he recalled how there were mostly well-worn Stetsons from one end of the bar to the other. Yet another sign of how times had changed.

"Once you do a cooking show, you're out," Banks said.

"If Trisha Yearwood walked in and started singing, you'd be giving her a standing ovation by the end of the night."

Banks tipped his beer bottle back to drain it, looked at Gus, and said, "Do you even know me?"

"More than you think," Gus replied, slapping his best friend's back.

A voice behind Gus and to his right said, "Incoming."

Dennis Runde winked and nodded his head at the door, where Emma was making her grand entrance dressed in tight blue jeans with a tucked in white blouse, it's top two buttons undone. Gus watched men stop talking mid-sentence to check her out from head to toe. An insecure man would have been jealous, maybe itching to prove his manhood and stake his claim.

All those heavy gazes just confirmed that he was one hell of a lucky man. When Annette passed, he didn't think he'd ever be in a relationship again. For the first five years after her death, he never once thought of dating another woman. Then Emma got her first teaching job at the middle school after quitting the phone company and started coming into the luncheonette for coffee in the morning. It took a lot of coaxing from the regulars who spotted the flirting way before he did to ask her out two years into their dance. Emma liked to joke that getting him to ask her out was like coaxing a frightened deer out of the brush.

Emma squeezed between Gus and Banks, and all those leering eyes snapped away.

"One Bud Light coming up," Don said before she could ask.

Emma kissed Banks on the cheek and Gus on the lips. "How are my two favorite fellas?"

"Someone's grumpy over the choice of music." Gus signaled to Don to get him another beer.

"I can fix that."

Emma ran over to the jukebox and starting inserting dollar bills. Gus watched her tap the buttons on the jukebox. Every now and then, his eyes slid to the door.

"Waiting on someone?" Banks said.

"Not really. Or hoping someone doesn't come here."

"You talking about Randy?"

"Yep."

"Be a good place to work off some steam."

Gus swept his arm across the expanse of the wood-paneled bar. "And lots of people I'm sure Randy would suspect to take his aggressions out on."

Banks looked around. "These folks? Nah. Whoever did that terrible thing is hiding in the shadows."

"Hiding in plain sight sometimes works even better." Gus sighed and took a drink. He counted seven men wearing hoodies, just like the men who had attacked Randy and Ash. It could be any one of them, or none of them. The longer the mystery went on without someone in custody, the more uneasy folks felt. "Randy's more than likely home taking care of Ashley. I heard from George that his new daughter-in-law isn't doing so well. I mean, physically she's recovered. It's the other part that's harder to heal. If it ever truly can."

"What about her parents? They still around?"

"Staying at the Highland Inn." The old bed-and-breakfast was the only place in town for visitors to lay their heads. It was run by Ceil Murphy, a no-nonsense woman who worked day and night to keep the place tidy. Ceil was a transplant from Fort Mill who, after her divorce, took some of that settlement money and opened the B and B, a lifetime dream of hers. It was a ton of work, which suited Ceil just fine. She had no desire to marry again and the more work, the merrier.

Banks smiled. "I'll bet she just loves having Ashley's father around."

"Knowing Ceil, if he acts up, she'll put him in his place faster than a woodpecker's drumbeat."

Emma was still at the jukebox, which meant she was planning on being the unofficial DJ of the night. Gus sure loved watching her from behind, but not as much as when her face lit up the room.

Dennis cleaned off a table behind them, and called out, "Hey, Wally, you eatin' or just here for a nightcap?"

The mayor slicked his thinning gray hair back and eyed the crowd. Gus noted how tired Wally looked. Judging by the signs all over town and the appearances noted in the paper, he'd never had to campaign this hard before. It mustn't have been easy.

Garth Brooks stopped crooning and things went quiet for a moment.

"Come on over here and I'll buy you a drink," Gus said, waving the mayor over. Wally's face lit up and he waddled his way over to them. The man never could say no to a free drink.

"Evening, boys," he said, settling on the stool next to Banks. Then to Don, he said, "Two fingers of Jameson. Neat."

"How you been?" Gus asked, seriously concerned now that they were up close. Wally's skin was pale, and he had dark circles under his eyes.

"I've been up to my rear end with work. What I should

be doing is planning a fishing trip in Tennessee, but it looks like that's not going to happen."

"You really think The Stranger can beat you?" Banks asked. "That city huckster is about as transparent as cling wrap when he thinks he's being slick. There's no way he'd take you down."

Wally sipped his Jameson and swept his arm across the bar crowd. "Take a look around. You see a lot of Wally Sturgis supporters?"

The man was right. Gus didn't recognize half the people in the bar. Just a year ago, he would have fallen off his barstool if so much as one unfamiliar face walked in that door.

Dennis nudged him with his shoulder. "I'll bet most of these folks wouldn't even bother going to the polls. That would mean time away from their cell phones."

Even the ones playing pool were checking their phones if they weren't shooting. It was strange behavior, indeed. Why come to a bar with your friends if you weren't going to talk to them?

"Yeah, well, I can't take a chance. Imagine what would happen to this town if Stranger were in charge?"

What no one dared say was it would probably mean just an acceleration of what was already happening. Wally had enough on his plate. He didn't need to have a platter of crow with his whiskey.

Emma returned with a bounce in her step. "All done. Chris, you'll have nothing to worry about . . . for at least a dozen songs." She saw Wally and the state of him and rubbed his arm. "You look tired. You taking care of yourself?"

Wally lifted the glass of amber liquid. "I am now."

Banks checked his watch. "A dozen songs? I'll be in

bed after six at most. I have a lot to do tomorrow. Cars can't fix themselves."

"Yet," Gus said. "Give that Musk fella some time."

They sipped their drinks and caught up with one another until "Goodbye Earl" came on the jukebox. Emma raised her arms and whooped, "I love the Dixie Chicks!"

A woman sitting beside them turned to Emma and said with visible contempt, "They're called The Chicks now."

Emma's smile didn't waver. "I know that. But they'll always be the Dixie Chicks to me." She danced close to Gus, brushing the comment off like flicking a fly off her shoulder.

Gus watched the woman turn to her friends, three men and another woman, all probably in their late twenties, and realized they weren't going to let it go. They were drinking Moscow mules out of copper mugs, a new addition to the bar's menu. Don and Dennis had told him they got so many requests, they invested in the mugs and practiced making the cocktail so they could both give their new customers what they wanted and charge them an insane markup to boot.

"They had to change the name because even they knew it was offensive," one of the men, the blond with the man bun, said.

Banks swiveled on his stool to face them. "Unfortunately, we live in a world where most music is consumed by the young, and any word that makes them shudder in their safe space needs to be erased. If the word Dixie offends you, son, I believe you're living in the wrong place."

"Now, Chris, just ignore them," Emma said.

Gus overheard man bun say to his friends, "See? You can't deal with these knuckle draggers."

"What did you call me?" Banks said.

"Chris!" Emma said, latching onto his wrist. There was a meaty fist at the end of it.

"Listen to your woman," the woman who started it all said with a smirk.

Gus tensed. Don ignored waving hands for drinks and slowly wiped a glass, keeping a close eye on the proceedings. He didn't appear to be inclined to intervene . . . yet.

Wally got up and wedged himself between them. "Maybe we should call it a night? What do you all think?"

"I'm not getting chased out of my bar," Banks said.

One of the men got off his stool, expanding to his full height of a little over six feet, and stared at Banks. "I think it's past your bedtime."

Banks and Gus stood, and now they were looking down at him. Gus spoke as calmly as he could muster. "I think we can all just settle down now. We're just here to have a few drinks, shoot the shit, and listen to music. I'm sure you're here for the same thing. No sense going off half-cocked."

"Are you threatening us?" the woman said. She pulled her phone up and started recording them.

Gus rolled his eyes. "You have a good night." He stopped from calling her ma'am. He didn't need a repeat of the exchange at Food City.

Gus had to exert a lot of pressure on Banks's shoulder to get him to turn his back on the gaggle of locusts. There was nothing to be gained by remaining engaged with them. Well, if he was younger, he could see the value of knocking some sense into them, but the days of barroom brawls were well behind him.

Banks, maybe not so much.

Getting thrown in jail for fighting was far less glamorous when you were north of forty.

"Go back to drinking your Bud . . . ," the guy with

the man bun said. Then, to his friends, "It's probably champagne to them."

"Enjoy your bougie girl drink," Banks said offhandedly, giving them a salute with his bottle of Budweiser before finishing it.

Gus was relieved when Banks turned away from them and smiled. "Thanks for kicking up some drama, Emma," he said jokingly.

"I'll just have to remember to keep my mouth shut from now on," she said.

"That I don't see ever happening . . . dear." Gus put his arm around her. "We can always take this to my place and sit on the back porch. I just fixed the screen and I believe I have some cold ones on the lower shelf of the fridge. And there's pie."

"There's always pie," Emma said. She looped her arm through his. "Let's go."

Don yelled, "Hey!"

The man bun had cocked his arm back and was about to clock Banks in the back of his head. Instead, his footing slipped in the sawdust on the floor and his aim went wild. His fist glanced off Wally's shoulder, sending the elderly mayor to the floor. His drink flew out of his hand and landed behind the bar.

Before Banks could react, the locust was ready to try again.

Unfortunately for man bun, Don's massive fist found his face first. He stumbled into a table seven feet away and flipped over it. Dennis came running from across the bar and dropped to his knees beside the mayor.

"Any of you think of trying anything and I'll put you right next to your friend," Don said. The look in his eyes begged them to disobey his order.

Gus, Banks, and Emma joined Dennis in trying to get Wally back on his feet.

"Are you hurt?" Emma asked.

Wally's eyes squeezed shut and his mouth opened and closed rapidly as he fought for air.

"Don't move him," Gus said as he removed his denim shirt and balled it up, placing it under Wally's head. They were immediately surrounded by dozens of curious patrons. Gus undid the button at Wally's collar and said to the crowd, "Everyone get back! We need air. Don, get me a cold water and an aspirin and call an ambulance."

The woman who had instigated the disaster looked on in horror, and said, "But he only hit him in the shoulder."

Gus checked Wally's pulse at his neck. His skin was cold and clammy, and his pallor was fish-belly white. "He's not hurt. He's having a heart attack."

# CHAPTER 9

Chief of Police Dawn James stepped out of her car and walked to the luncheonette with a slight limp. The humidity did her gimpy leg and hip no favors, thanks to an IED detonating ten feet away from her back in the early days of the Iraq War following the tragedy of 9/11. She still carried the shrapnel around, a souvenir she'd never wanted and a constant reminder of the worst year of her life.

She looked up and down the street at a town she thought she knew better than anyplace in the world. Almost a quarter of the stores were new, most having opened in the last year. The locals smiled and waved when they saw her. She thought about the mound of paperwork waiting for her back at the station. Petty crime had been on the rise for some time now, and it was rubbing her nerves raw. Not to mention what had happened to the Early family. The fact that she had no potential suspects weeks later made her feel as if she was failing her community.

Or what had used to be her community. With the recent changes taking place, she was beginning to wonder if a transfer to a different town was in order. Although from what she'd been hearing on the grapevine, what was happening in Springerville wasn't unique.

"Guess we're not exactly a snowflake," she muttered to herself and chuckled.

The bell chimed when she entered. James spotted Ron and Mike tucking into their lunches and a few other regulars. She removed her hat and sunglasses and sidled up to the counter.

"Afternoon, Gus," she said.

The lunch crowd paused their chewing and offered her varying types of greetings. She responded with a smile and a head nod.

"Hiya, Chief," Gus said as he looked up from wiping down one of the round tables set by the rack of magazines and big bags of potato chips. "How's Jimmy been? I haven't seen him in a while."

Her husband's parents, who normally didn't have a sense of humor, had seen fit to name her husband of the past fifteen years Jimmy James. Most folks called him JJ. Gus was one of the few who referred to him as Jimmy. No one called him James James.

"He's been on the road a lot. Some new corporate training course they rolled out has him on planes, at conferences and hotel rooms more than home lately. He's just about done with his tour of duty. You know JJ, he'll be here for breakfast as soon as he gets a chance."

There were no menus at the luncheonette. Everything was written on a blackboard that hung above the counter. James didn't need to read it. The menu hadn't changed much since Gus's father ran the place, back when her father and grandfather were steady patrons.

"That's good to hear. Turkey club or cheeseburger today?" Gus asked.

"I'm feeling like a cheeseburger," she said, knowing it was not what the doctor ordered. Her cholesterol was up, as was her blood pressure, which was no surprise considering what she had to deal with lately.

"You got it."

Gus disappeared into the kitchen. It was an open kitchen, so they could talk while Gus put her burger on the flat top and dropped some home-cut spuds in the fryer.

"You hear anything about Wally?" Gus asked over the sizzling burger.

"He's out of the ICU," James said. "I'm stopping by to visit him this afternoon, unless something ruins my day. Which is entirely possible."

"God doesn't want him yet, that's for sure," Gus said as he wiped his brow with a towel. The air conditioner had been on the fritz for about the past twenty years. A row of ceiling fans did their best to cool the place down, but they couldn't combat the heat and humidity today.

"That Wally's a tough old bird," Mike said. "You gonna arrest the man who hit him?"

"The mayor doesn't want to press charges, so no."

"But he gave Wally a heart attack!" Ron protested.

"As the doc put it, it was bound to happen anyway. Too much stress, he said. Maybe it was better it happened around people who could take care of him and get him help. That was smart to get him the aspirin," James said to Gus.

Gus's face reddened. "It was just common sense. My father use to carry an aspirin in his pocket every day after he turned sixty."

After shoveling some fries in his mouth, Mike said,

"Old Gus is the town's number one Boy Scout. Always prepared. And handier than a pocket on a shirt around a grill."

"Gee, thanks, Mike," Gus said as he brought out James's lunch.

The police chief lifted the top of the bun and put some ketchup and mustard on her steaming hot burger. "I'm here for more than just lunch, Gus." She took a big bite and chewed, letting the tension build.

"I'm all ears."

After swallowing and taking a sip of iced tea, James said, "Wally called me this morning before I headed for work. He's going to have to drop out of the race. Doctor's orders. And even more than that, he said he's not up to the task."

"I suspected as much," Gus said.

"Which means we have to find a replacement. And fast."

"Well, Wally's earned some rest. Plenty of good people here that can take his place."

James wiped the corner of her mouth with a napkin and pushed away from her plate. "Wally thinks you'd be the best candidate."

Gus shook his head. "Wally's on a lot of meds in the hospital. I can make a list of fifty people that would be better, and that's just for starters."

"Your humility is one of those very things that makes you a natural choice. I can embarrass you and list all the other reasons in front of everyone here if you like."

"No need to do that," Gus replied, holding up his hand. "You're overlooking the fact that I'm not a politician."

"Neither was Trump," Mike said, stabbing a French fry in the air for emphasis.

"And you see what happened there," Gus said.

"Yeah. The country prospered while fools in New York, Chicago, and Los Angeles lost their damn minds. They have no say about what happens in our town."

Gus refilled Ron's soda. "Thank Wally for thinking of me, but I'm not your guy."

James took another bite of the burger. After she swallowed, she addressed the crowd of ten people in the luncheonette. "Who here would vote for Gus if he ran for mayor?"

Ten hands shot straight up without hesitation.

James looked to Gus. "I'll bet dollars to donuts I couldn't find a single person who has called Springerville home for as long as we have that *wouldn't* vote for you."

Shaking his head deprecatingly, Gus said, "I'm not the mayor type."

James stood and wrapped the remaining burger in a thick napkin. "Nobody is, until they are. Just think about it, will you? It's not about you. It's about Springerville. It's about our home. Your home. We need someone smart and strong and honest who will get our house back in order. You see what's been happening. It'll only get worse if Stranger is elected."

James wasn't going to let this go. Sad to say, Springerville needed cleaning up. To do that, she needed a strong man in the mayoral seat to back her up. Wally had gotten soft and let people like Braden Stranger and the locusts walk all over him. He'd thought the influx of their money and promises would help the town. It wasn't entirely his fault that he couldn't see this coming. And when he'd gotten some fire in his belly, it was too little too late.

Gus was the right man for the job. What he needed was some coaxing in the right direction.

"I'm just a grill cook."

"You're much more than that," James said. "And we all know it."

# CHAPTER 10

Because it was test week, Emma hadn't been able to see Gus until Friday. He'd told her about Dawn James's offer from the mayor. She'd been quick to tell him he should do it. The gossip tree had spread its branches to the teacher's break room an hour after the police chief had walked into the luncheonette. Gus said this was something better discussed face to face.

Now Friday was here and he'd closed up shop. He sat in the wicker rocking chair his grandfather had made, reading the paper and enjoying the shade the awning provided. The soft breeze was cooling things a bit and there were more people cluttering the sidewalks on both sides of the street than usual. There was a line outside of the cybercafe, as well as the place that sold handmade jewelry and craft soaps for prices that made him blanch the first time he and Emma had taken a gander inside.

"A ten-dollar bar of soap ought to keep you clean for a month at least," he'd whispered to Emma. The middle-aged blonde woman who was the proprietor had been giving them the stink eye as soon as they'd walked inside.

"You can't put a price on beauty," Emma said with a hint of sarcasm.

He held up the black bar of soap. "Says this is made of lava. You ever hear of someone bathing in lava?"

"Not someone who survived."

He put the soap back and introduced himself to the owner, welcoming her to the town and wishing her the best. She still looked at him as if he were a virus caught under a microscope.

"Well, she seems pleasant," he said when they left the boutique. It had taken the place of Art's stationery store, a staple of the town for almost sixty years. Art sold newspapers and magazines, along with cigarettes, chewing tobacco, soft drinks, beer, and lottery tickets. Art had fallen while stocking a high shelf with fresh cartons of Marlboros and broken his hip. Things got worse for him in the hospital, and he had to be moved to assisted living over in Charlotte. A few months after he had to close the shop, the boutique that would have been better if it were somewhere in a rich New England town seemed to come out of nowhere overnight.

Emma looked at Gus's battered and sweat-stained trucker cap, and said, "I think it's the hat."

"If she sells one just as nice for under a hundred dollars, I'll be sure to replace it."

Gus thought of bringing the owner over some food one day as an official welcome and then decided against it. No sense wasting good food on someone who most likely wouldn't appreciate it. She was thinner than a starved bird. He'd bet she was one of those keto dieters or some other fad eater.

Gus spied a lot of people going into the boutique and coming out with small brown bags. Two women and one man who had just exited the store walked to his luncheonette and tried to open the doors.

"Sorry, closed for the day," Gus said as he folded his paper.

"But it's only three o'clock," the redheaded woman said with a slight whine. She tugged on the door again.

Gus pointed at the sign in the window displaying the hours. "I close up shop after lunch."

"Yeah, but we just want something to drink. Maybe a quick appetizer," the man said. Well, he looked more like a boy pretending to be a man. He tried to open the door again.

Gus wondered if there was something mentally wrong with this bunch. Did they not know what CLOSED meant? Or how locked doors worked?

"That door isn't going to unlock just because you yank on it," he said. "And I don't sell appetizers."

The brunette woman who had been peering inside had the audacity to say to him, "It doesn't look like you're exactly swimming in money. We'll pay you. Just open for us for a little bit." She took some bills out of her purse and flashed it in front of him.

Gus felt the back of his neck grow hot. "You think you're special?"

The brunette smiled. "I *know* I'm special." Next came a wretched fake southern accent that put his teeth on edge. "Now why don't you be a dear and *make* us something special."

Gus got up from the rocker and the trio stepped back a bit in surprise. Were these people drunk? It seemed a little too early in the day for that, but you never knew. Most of the locusts worked from home and did whatever they pleased. From what he could tell, there was not much work being done by the telecommuters of Springerville.

"I think it's time you all just went your way," Gus said in a measured tone.

The man tugged on the door again.

"Hey!" Gus barked. "You do damage to my door, you'll pay for it. And I'm not talking about money." He said this part while staring daggers at the rude brunette.

"Whatever," the redhead said. She took a tiny bag out of her pocketbook and pulled out what looked like gummy bears, doling one out to each of them. "There are better places to eat."

The trio sulked away, chewing on their candy. Gus jumped when something touched his back. Emma covered her face as she laughed.

"I didn't mean to scare you," she said.

"You didn't scare me. You startled me. Two different things. You see what I was dealing with?"

"I'm pretty sure they were high as kites."

The thought had never occurred to him.

"I don't think those were their first edibles of the day."

He had no idea what an edible was. Emma explained.

"So, there was marijuana in those candies?"

"Most likely. And they call it weed now."

"What is this world coming to when even candy will get you high?"

"Come on. You're not that old and out of touch."

"Well, I do remember pot brownies back in the day. I saw a lot of people eating them at a party once when I was on leave after basic training. And I also saw how they acted later. It's why I stick to cheap beer and good whiskey."

They walked arm in arm down the busy street. Gus noticed all of the flags in the local storefronts were gone yet again. He'd taken his down for the day and stored it inside, but he knew his time was coming. Unless they could nab the idiotic flag thief . . . or thieves.

*Better they catch the people who battered the Earlys,*

he thought. Though with so much time passing, he didn't hold out hope.

He and Emma turned left on Grand Street to get away from the crowd. Down this way were mostly older houses with large front and backyards. Even though the sun was in full bloom, crickets chirped all around them.

"Have you thought about it?" Emma asked.

"Thought about what? Putting my size eleven in that guy's ass?"

Emma slapped his arm playfully. "I'm talking about running for mayor."

Their boots crunched on the gritty sidewalk. Wind chimes tinkled on a wraparound porch. Gus sighed, and said, "I don't think I can do it. It's nice of them to think of me, but being in the spotlight just isn't my thing. What do I know about running for office? Or running a town for that matter?"

Emma beamed at him. "You already run a business. Just be yourself. That's why they want you to run. There's only one side to Gus Fuller. And that's a very good side, I might add."

Two cars passed going the other way. Rap music blared out of the speakers in both. They were packed with young people, maybe college age. The cars were going too fast, and their tires squealed as they turned the corner. None of the passengers were familiar to Gus.

"They'll kill someone driving like that," he said.

"Or go deaf. Whichever comes first."

"We're starting to sound like old people," Gus said with a laugh.

"More like people who don't like what they're seeing lately. And we are not alone. Which is why folks want you to run for mayor."

"You're not going to let this go, are you?"

Emma smiled. "Nope. Sometimes, getting out of your comfort zone is a good thing. Like the day you finally asked me on a date. I think that turned out pretty good." She beamed at him. "You serve people every single day. I know you look at it as only food, but you also provide a comfortable place for people to sit for a while and connect. And think about all the free meals you've given out over the years. If anyone is hurt or sick or just down on their luck, there you are, keeping them fed and providing your friendship. That's what being a mayor is all about. It's not about the town. It's about the people. You care about people, Gus. It's one of the many reasons I fell in love with you."

He pulled her closer as they walked. "You're buttering me up thicker than one of my biscuits, little lady."

"Is it working?"

He didn't answer for a while. What he wanted to do was appreciate the moment with Emma, away from the hustle of downtown, which no longer resembled his hometown.

As they walked, they passed by men and women in their yards or getting into their cars. All of them knew Gus by name and waved or asked him how he was doing.

At the bend in the street, they heard a woman screaming and the squealing of tires. Gus let go of Emma's hand and took off running, advising her to stay where she was. Naturally, she followed close behind.

He came to Aileen Wuhrer's house, an octogenarian widow who spent most of her days out tending her garden at a snail's pace so she could be in the fresh air. She was on the other side of her white picket fence that needed a fresh coat of paint, her arthritic fingers gripping the triangular-tipped posts.

"Help! Help!"

She was looking down at the ground. Gus followed

her gaze and found a young girl lying in the grass. Gus dropped to his knees, making a visual inspection of the girl. She was unconscious and a bit of white foam leaked from the corner of her mouth.

"What happened?" he asked Aileen.

"I . . . I don't know. I was clipping some roses and this car stopped right outside my gate. Next thing I know, the back door opens, and some boy comes out carrying her. He dropped her in the grass like she was yesterday's garbage, jumped back in his car, and it took off."

"Oh my God, it's Gina Cordry," Emma said. She got next to the prone girl and took her wrist, feeling for a pulse.

Gus knew Gina Cordry, but it had been some time since he'd seen her last.

"She has a pulse but it's weak," Emma said. Tears brimmed in her eyes. "Gina, honey, can you hear me?"

Several other neighbors gathered around. Gus pointed at Pat Demerest, and said, "Call 9-1-1!"

"I'm on it." Pat pulled his phone out of his pocket and was talking to a dispatcher in seconds.

"You think she's had a seizure?" Emma asked in a shaky voice.

Gus tapped the girl on the shoulder. "Gina." When she didn't respond, he tapped her harder and repeated her name. She gave a slight groan, but that was all. More froth spilled from her now open mouth. He checked her from head to toe, searching for any wounds or signs of a broken bone, hoping for some kind of reaction from the girl.

"Does Gina do drugs?" he asked.

Emma's eyes grew wide. "Why would you ask such a thing?"

Even though it was against protocol for this type of situation, Gus lifted the girl until she was on her feet, though he had to bear all of her dead weight. "I think she overdosed."

"What?"

"Not that poor, dear girl," Aileen said, clutching her hands to her chest. Gus silently prayed that the excitement wouldn't impact the woman's frail heart. "I used to watch her from time to time. She's a sweet, smart kid."

"Even the sweet and smart ones get into trouble," he said. He kept saying her name and forced her to walk. She didn't respond at first, but he thought he felt some of her weight fall from him.

"Maybe you shouldn't be moving her," Emma said.

"Ambulance is on its way," Pat said. "Should be here in a few minutes."

Gus wanted to thank him, but he had to get Gina awake and moving, despite Emma's concern.

He'd seen this before when he was on his second tour in Iraq. For some men and women, the need for something to take the edge off, or fill the downtime, caused them to seek relief in drugs. They flowed from Afghanistan like the waters of the Mississippi River. Except whatever they were taking was often designed not to give them pleasure or escape, but a one-way ticket to a pine box. In his time, he'd witnessed three overdoses. Fortunately, all had survived, though one came out of it with brain damage and the loss of the use of his left arm.

Experience told him this beautiful young girl who wasn't even in high school was fighting off something her body couldn't handle. He had to keep her moving until the paramedics got there and administered Narcan or at least kept her stable until they could pump her stomach.

"Come on, honey. I just need you to walk a little with me." Her head slumped forward, and Emma gently lifted it by her chin. Someone in the crowd handed Emma a bottle of water. "Splash a little on her face," Gus said.

When she did, Gina's eyelids fluttered, and she muttered a soft protest.

"Attagirl. Tell her not to splash you again," Gus said encouragingly. He nodded at Emma to do it again. It seemed to wake the girl up a bit more.

Gus felt her body stiffen moments before she threw up. He held her up with one hand while patting her back with the other. "That's right. Get that poison up."

They heard the sirens, and the ambulance tore around the corner. People parted to make a path as two EMTs rushed out and took Gina from Gus.

"She's starting to come to and she threw up," Gus told them. They asked him and Emma a few standard questions while checking the girl's vitals. In no time, she was on a stretcher and headed for the hospital.

"I'll go with her and call her parents," Emma said.

"That's a good idea. Call me with any updates."

Emma's tears had streaked her mascara over her face. She gave Gus one last, worried look before the rear doors of the ambulance closed. The neighbors watched it depart in stunned silence.

It was Aileen who spoke first.

"I've never seen anything like it. How did you know what to do?"

The adrenaline running through Gus's system had him feeling jittery. "Unfortunately, I have."

"But never here," Aileen said.

"No. Never here."

"I may be old and not long for this world, but I don't want to leave knowing the place I love and raised my family is going to hell. I hear they want you to run for mayor."

Gus gave a slight nod. Aileen grabbed his forearm.

"Then you best do it and take back our town before there's nothing left worth taking."

# CHAPTER 11

The Pennsylvania was a hastily put together trailer park on the outskirts of Springerville, abutting some swampland to the left and a sea of cattails higher than the tallest person in town. It had come to life in response to Hurricane Katrina, meant to be temporary housing for the downtrodden from New Orleans who had suddenly found themselves homeless, battered, and broken. The mayor at the time had made an offer to take in any and all lost souls in need of a place to mend their broken lives.

Most of the people who had come to The Pennsylvania—named so because many of the trailers had been donated by a South Carolina businessman, now deceased, who had originally hailed from the Keystone State—had stayed for about a year or so before settling back to their new homes near and far.

With so many empty trailers, and always a need for affordable housing, the park became a rental property, open to all. People of little means came and went, and the trailers fell into various states of disrepair, as will happen in a place of transience with poor management.

Where there had been over fifty gleaming new trailers a month after Katrina, there were now around forty still serviceable. The entire property was in desperate need of decent landscaping and, if you asked Braden Stranger, a tidal wave of bleach.

Stranger paced within the entrance to The Pennsylvania in the dark of night. A few lights were on in some of the trailers in the distance, the few residents being confined to a particular section closer to the swamp, where the chorus of frogs at night was akin to torture.

"If you have time, I can show you some of the homes we have," Shane Varrick said as he checked his light-up digital watch.

"That won't be necessary," Stranger said, trying to keep any notes of disdain from his voice. Varrick was a tried-and-true local, but with all the business Stranger was throwing his way, he just might win his vote. Every vote counted, even with Wally Sturgis out of the way. Stranger kept waiting to see who would take his place. There was a lot of buzz going around about the man who ran the luncheonette. If that was going to be his competition—a hash slinger—Stranger just might go from underdog to favorite.

Stranger looked over at Varrick, with his stained trucker hat and lump of dip in his cheek. Wow, could he be any more on the nose? With the influx of new residents came an increase in the trailer park manager's pay, thanks to the donors who were funding this operation. "I'm sure they're just what we need. I have faith in you." It hurt just saying the words while maintaining a straight face. The truth of the matter was, Stranger wouldn't trust Varrick to feed a goldfish.

Bats flitted overhead, causing Stranger to duck every now and again. He had no idea if they came close to his head, but he wasn't taking any chances.

"Seems like a weird time for folks to be moving in," Varrick said.

"I was told they experienced a long traffic snarl up around DC, and then one of the buses broke down," Stranger said quickly to avoid Varrick's suspicions. Traffic snarls around the DC corridor were common and easy to believe. "The actual process of moving in I hear will unfold in the coming week. Right now, we just need to greet them and show them to their new homes."

"Well, I made sure all the electricity was running properly. The trailers are furnished, though some a little better than others."

Stranger could only imagine said furnishings. He wondered how many critters had slept on the mattresses and made nests in dark corners, cabinets, and ovens. If he'd had the time, he would have found a way to spruce things up. But the important thing was getting these people down here so they could register. Housekeeping could and would come later. He'd set aside funds for a one-time top-to-bottom cleaning. His plan was to employ as many local cleaners as Roger could find. They were to be paid triple their normal fee and made aware of who their employer was, in the hopes a few more votes would come his way.

He thought he heard the deep bass rumble of an approaching bus. There was a flash of lights in the distance. His heartbeat accelerated slightly in response.

The moment of truth was near.

"If only they knew what's coming," he muttered.

"What'd you say?"

"Nothing. You have all the keys?"

Varrick tapped a plastic bag bulging with keychains. "Two sets for each trailer. And I used your campaign keychains just like you asked. They are pretty nice. I hope you don't mind that I took one for myself."

Braden smiled, but there was no mirth in his eyes. He clapped Varrick on the shoulder. "Mind? I'm happy you like it. Lots more swag to come, Shane. You just keep a welcoming home for these people, and you'll want for nothing."

It was a big boast, but Stranger was sure Varrick was a man of little means. It wouldn't take much to keep him satisfied.

The first bus arrived and Varrick hustled into its headlight beams, waving his arms and directing it to an empty parking space to the left of the entrance. When the second bus came right on its heels, he guided it to park alongside the trailer that served as his home and office. The bus's lights brightened up the park considerably. Stranger hoped the noise would drive the bats away.

As if rehearsed, both doors opened simultaneously. Mostly young people in their twenties came streaming out of the bus lugging backpacks, some of them carrying sleeping bags.

Branden Stranger beamed as they gathered before him. They were a ragtag bunch of every race, creed, and color. He saw many women with brightly colored hair, nose rings, and an array of tattoos. The men were no different. In appearance alone, they were truly outsiders. Sprinkled in were some others that were clearly ex-convicts. He could see it in their eyes, that dead glare that was as much an offensive as well as defensive weapon. The presence of every single person on these buses would be jarring to the people of Springerville. A sign of great changes to come.

A young man dropped his backpack, reached into his pocket, and inserted a joint in his mouth, which he quickly lit and puffed on.

This would have to be addressed.

Stranger opened his arms, and said, "Thank you all for coming! My name is Braden Stranger and as you can tell from my accent, we all have a little something in common." He paused for a reaction, getting a few titters. "I know you've traveled a long way and you're probably tired. I just wanted to introduce myself and let you know that you can come to me for anything while you're here. I have cards for each of you with my information."

The cards in fact had Roger's phone and email. Varrick would distribute them along with the keys. After today, the next time Stranger wanted to be before this group was at the polls.

He strode over to the man smoking the joint and gingerly removed it from his fingertips. "Unlike up north, recreational use of marijuana is illegal down here. They will arrest you for using it publicly. But, with your help, hopefully we can change that soon." There was a round of applause for that.

*Not shocking*, Stranger thought.

The man, whose eyes were already a sheen of glass, nodded meekly. Stranger pinched the lit end with his finger to snuff it out before stuffing it in his pocket for later. Taking a few puffs always did wonders for his meditation. He reached into his pocket and handed the man a twenty-dollar bill. "For your loss."

Again, the crowd laughed. All except the hardened men and one woman who stared through him as if he weren't even there. He made it a point to avoid their steely gazes.

"To my right is Mr. Shane Varrick, the manager of The Pennsylvania. He's prepared your new homes for you and can address any needs you may have in terms of maintenance. Also, we have some special surprises coming your way in the coming days and weeks, including one hell of a Southern barbecue lined up for Saturday night. I promise you won't leave hungry or thirsty."

He smiled while they clapped. Again, he'd assigned Roger the task of organizing the barbecue. Stranger knew he should attend, but now he was having second thoughts. Yes, they came here to serve a purpose, and their votes were already determined. Of all the places to campaign, The Pennsylvania wasn't one of them. But he did need to keep them happy. It would be too easy for them to simply up and leave if they didn't feel engaged or appreciated.

A few of the trailer park's full-time residents had sauntered over to the gathering, no doubt curious about the commotion. A family of five, all the children under ten, scanned the crowd of new neighbors and looked frightened. The mother whisked the children back while the father, his beer belly barely contained by his shirt, crossed his arms and eyed the arrivals suspiciously.

"I'm sure you just want to settle in and call it a night," Stranger said. "But for those that don't, we have a little welcome-home gift." He nodded at Varrick who winked back and scurried over to a blue tarp. He whipped the tarp away to reveal two beer kegs sitting in metal tubs of ice. Next to them was a picnic table piled high with buckets of KFC that Roger had procured from the fast-food chain over thirty miles away. Springerville had so far denied access to chain restaurants and stores. That would change, very soon.

Stranger could see the hunger in most of their eyes. The others locked onto the kegs.

"Mr. Varrick will be happy to serve you all. Eat up, drink up, and welcome to Springerville!"

There followed a final round of cheers and applause. Seconds later, Varrick was pumping the keg and people were loading plates with fried chicken, whipped mashed potatoes, and corn.

Stranger shook a few hands and did a mental headcount. Just over a hundred and twenty. That was a nice haul for one night.

And there were more to come.

# CHAPTER 12

The luncheonette's doors may have been locked for the day, but the interior was packed to the gills. Luckily, the thermometer had dipped a bit, so it wasn't hotter than one of Gus's ovens. He still needed to keep the overhead fans on high. Sarah Birch had distributed hand fans to some of the women. When they folded them out, Gus saw red, white, and blue along with the words

## GUS FULLER – OUR TOWN, OUR MAYOR.

It made him cringe, but Emma reminded him repeatedly that he would have to get used to it. He'd had some of his own money set aside that Emma used to make some promotional materials. After today, when he made his official announcement, she assured him that his supporters would happily pay for the rest. Braden Stranger signs were all over town. Gus wouldn't have to match him sign for sign, but he did need to make his presence in the race known.

He still couldn't believe this was happening. The drug overdose incident with young Gina Cordry, who was released that same day and sent home with her relieved parents, had made up his mind. She had told the doctors that a cute boy she had been talking to over the past few weeks had met her at the park. They spent some time talking, and then kissing. At one point, she thinks he put something in her bottle of water. Next thing she knew, she was waking up in a hospital. She gave a description of the boy and police were on the lookout. Aileen Wuhrer had said there was more than one boy in the car that dumped her in front of her house. Dawn James was sure she'd find him. He wasn't a local, but she was sure he was lurking around. She had to catch the boy who had drugged Gina as well as the scum of the earth that had brought drugs like that into town. This wasn't New York where criminals had more rights than victims. At least not yet.

Gus never wanted another child to experience Gina Cordry or Ashley Early's horror. There was a sickness in Springerville, and it was spreading. If being mayor was one way to stop it, so be it.

When he'd closed after the lunch crowd dispersed, Gus had gone home to shower and change into a new blue dress shirt, his good jeans, polished boots, and tan pinched-front Stetson. The hat had been a gift from his father after he'd come back from the service. Gus wanted a piece of his father with him today.

Emma had met him outside his house, wearing a lovely dress that was conservative enough not to raise eyebrows but hugged her ample frame quite nicely. It was obvious she'd been to the beauty parlor. Her hair was done up in golden ringlets that spilled across her shoulders.

"It looks like we're the oldest attendees at the prom," Gus had joked.

"It pays to look our best."

Gus grazed his fingertips against the curve of her jaw. "I don't think anyone could ever look better than you do right now."

Emma beamed. "Remember to say that to all the ladies.

You'll make 'em swoon. Just make sure you only mean it with me."

His face reddened. "I don't think I'll be doing any such thing."

"What kind of politician are you?"

"I keep telling you and Banks and everyone else behind this madness that I'm not."

Emma turned and walked down the porch steps. "Well, learn to fake it, just a little."

When they'd arrived, there was already a gathering outside the luncheonette. All of his regulars were there, as well as some folks from the local paper that used to be daily but was now weekly and just slightly larger than a pamphlet. There was also a woman who Emma said was from WKLU, the radio station of choice in their parts. The whole idea of a local man who ran a modest luncheonette running against a New York interloper who reportedly came from big money at a time when crime was on the rise and quality of life was dwindling was too enticing not to cover. Gus knew just about everyone in that crowd except the radio woman. There were gawkers across the street and at the periphery who were definite strangers. He was pretty sure they were not going to be among his constituency, but you never know.

There was a thunderous round of applause when he and Emma got out of his truck. He looked over at the cybercafe, noting the odd looks they were getting.

Gus leaned close to Emma's ear, and said, "Well, here we go."

And now here they were. If smiles could be converted to power, there was enough amperage in the luncheonette to light up the town for a week. Wally Sturgis was nowhere to be found. Gus had heard that he wasn't feeling up to being out and about today. Gus wished he was here to lend him a hand on how to run something like this. Emma had said he should make his official "hat in the ring" announcement outside city hall, but he thought the place he loved and served the town would be better. For once, she conceded that he was right.

Things settled down after some back slapping and hand shaking. The back of Gus's neck was on fire, as was his face. He was truly a fish out of water at this shindig.

A young woman he didn't know or recognize tapped him on the shoulder. "How can I help you?" he said.

"I'd like to use the bathroom," she said. She had her phone in her hand, tilted up toward him. He couldn't help feeling she was recording him.

"Sure thing. They're right there." He pointed to the small hallway to the right of the candy racks.

"Don't you have any gender-neutral restrooms?" the girl asked. She had her wild hair barely contained under a bandana.

He wasn't quite sure what to say. "Well, you can take your pick. Whatever makes you comfortable."

"Neither makes me feel comfortable," she shot back. She looked like she was either going to cry or scream. At that moment, he knew he was being set up. His eyes flicked to her phone and the awkward position she had it in. She was most certainly recording.

"Well then, my apologies. Gender-neutral bathrooms are kinda new here. Maybe you can help me figure out the best way to address it. At another time."

For a nonpolitician, he was pretty proud of his solution.

"So much for inclusion," she said.

"Excuse me?"

"I can see I'm not wanted here." She didn't turn to leave. Just kept the phone trained on him.

"Please, stay. We can find a, uh, bathroom that works for you after I do my thing here. That sound good?"

"It sounds to me that your platform for mayor is as outdated as you. Have you ever even heard of diversity and inclusion?"

Gus caught Emma's eye and sent a silent plea for help. She came rushing over.

"Do you think you could help this lady find a gender-neutral bathroom?" he asked Emma.

Emma's eyebrow rose.

"I'm not a lady," the girl said.

Gus felt like he was outside Food City again being scolded for his pronouns. He wanted to say, *You are correct, you sure aren't a lady.*

"I think I can help you," Emma said. "Just follow me."

The lady huffed but finally followed Emma. Once she was out the door, Emma turned back inside and locked it, giving Gus a thumbs-up. The girl stared at them through the window for a bit, then walked away. He could practically see storm clouds hovering over her head.

The noise in the diner made sure no one heard the exchange. When the crowd started chanting Gus's name, he shook off the strange encounter and painted a big smile on his face. He ducked his head and waved for them to settle down.

Don and Dennis Runde must have closed the bar for the afternoon because they were by the front window whistling and giving four thumbs-ups. Don was wearing a Panthers baseball cap while Dennis favored his beloved Falcons.

Chris Banks, who was looking pretty dapper himself, got onto a stool and addressed the crowd. "All right, everybody. Knowing Gus, if we don't give him a moment to speak, he'll just go back there and start whipping up some biscuits." The crowd laughed and Frankie Martin said from the back, "Speech!"

Gus removed his Stetson, paused for a moment to take in all these fine friends and neighbors, and finally said, "Well, I guess I should first thank you for coming." Emma rubbed his arm encouragingly. "I'm not really one for speeches. I'm also not one for politics, yet here I am." That got a round of applause. When it died down, he continued. "I don't think it's much of a secret that I'm going to run for mayor." He nodded at Sarah who was fanning herself with one of the campaign fans. "Not sure who I have to thank for this privilege, but I'm pretty sure she's standing right over there." A few people clapped Dawn James's back. She was dressed in full uniform and had a few of her men with her. Not to restore order. But to show that the police department was behind Gus's candidacy.

"I'll be the first to admit that I have no idea how to run a political campaign. Heck, I'm not even sure what all the duties of a mayor even are." There was a round of lighthearted chuckles. "What I can assure you is that I won't let you down. This town . . . our home . . . has seen a lot of changes in a little amount of time. If they were for the good, I'd gladly be back there whipping up some country fried steaks. Seems most of this world is always fighting *for* change. If you ask me, we've had it pretty damn good here for as long as I can remember. Which is why I'll fight *against* change. Or, at the very least, change that is not for the common good of our town. For you."

The roar of approval was deafening. Ron and Mike rushed forward to shake his hand, as if they didn't see him every single morning. Gus had a few more prepared lines to say, though it didn't seem necessary at this point. Banks turned on the radio he'd brought from home and "Born Country" by Alabama blared from the speakers. That got people to raising their hands in the air and swaying them about.

Emma reached over and squeezed his hand. He gave her a wink.

Someone held up a sign over near the racks where he kept bags of chips and popcorn. It showed a cowboy boot stepping on a rat with New York written on its pink tail, black *X*'s drawn over its bulging eyeballs. When the sign moved, Gus saw that Randy Early was the one holding it. He remembered that Randy had had some artistic talent when he was young. Apparently, that skill had not diminished over time.

Gus and Randy locked eyes across the excited crowd and Gus mouthed, *This is for you*. Ashley was not in attendance. She hadn't left the house in months after being released from the hospital. Randy had laid low as well, which was a relief to Gus and Banks.

As much as he was no fan of all this attention, Gus made it a point to always keep Randy and Ashley at the forefront of his mind. Whenever he complained about the whole shebang, and he would, he'd have to remember there was a very good reason for doing this.

He wasn't able to linger long on that thought as it seemed everyone wanted to shake his hand. Emma said, "I'm so proud of you."

Banks wedged his way through the revelers and slapped Gus's hat back on his head. "Stand tall, cowboy. You got this. I'll be with you every step of the way."

"You better be."

"There's work to do, but for today, just enjoy this."

An excited Muriel Sheen pumped his hand as if he were going to draw well water.

"Oh yeah, you know how much I enjoy stuff like this," he said to Banks.

Muriel grabbed him by the back of his neck and planted a kiss on his cheek that left a lipsticked imprint on his skin. "Give 'em hell," she said.

Alabama faded into Toby Keith. Gus had prepared several sheet cakes and other refreshments. "I'll get the spread," he said to Emma, turning toward the kitchen.

"Oh no you won't . . . Mr. Mayor." She nudged him back to facing the crowd. More people were streaming through the door. "Leave that to the help. You have work to do."

He was about to insist when the crash of glass brought everything to a halt.

And then the screaming started.

# CHAPTER 13

As soon as the front window exploded, Banks jumped in front of Gus as if he were his appointed secret service agent. Women and men ducked for cover, while Police Chief Dawn James and her men tried to make their way outside the luncheonette.

They weren't faster than the Runde boys, who had been right by the window. They leapt out of the now empty frame and went running. Gus heard the squealing of tires as he struggled to get around Banks, but not before he grabbed the bat he kept behind the counter. He thought he heard Emma plead, "Gus, don't!" but he wasn't going to stop.

Banks was right behind him as they carefully stepped around the panicked crowd. Once outside, there was no guesswork as to where the perpetrators had gone. All heads up and down Main Street were looking in the same direction.

Down the block, stopped in midturn at the intersection, was a motorcycle, one of those imports that looked to be made of plastic and was built for speeds most inadvisable for a bike. Don Runde had one man in his grasp and was shaking him like a rug taken out for spring cleaning.

Dennis stood in front of the motorcycle with his hands on the bars, trying to knock the rider off his mount.

The police were almost at the scene. Chief of Police James shouted at Don to just hold the man.

The rider wore a black helmet with a tinted visor. He jerked the handlebars enough to knock Dennis to the side. A second later, the motorcycle peeled off, leaving the smell of burnt rubber and exhaust lingering in the air.

"You scumbag!" the man Don now had in a headlock screamed as he watched his cohort leave him literally in the dust.

"Look what I caught," Don said with a delighted grin as the man fought to break free. James's men coaxed Don into letting him go so they could drop him to the ground, pull his arms back and slap a pair of handcuffs on his wrist.

"You get the license plate?" a breathless James asked Dennis.

Dennis adjusted his Falcons cap, his expression one of intense irritation. "I checked and I didn't see one. But I can tell you the make and model of the bike."

"Probably stolen and they chucked the plate," Don said. His shoulders heaved as he regained his breath.

"Can you turn him over?" Gus asked.

"Sure thing," one of the officers said.

The frightened man was young, maybe in his mid-twenties, with muttonchops that would have made Elvis blush. His clothes were askew thanks to Don's manhandling, and one side of his face was already puffing up. That face was completely unfamiliar to Gus.

"Just who are you?" Gus asked.

"Your mother," the man shot back with a decidedly Northern accent.

"Looks like yours failed you," Banks said.

The man tried to get up, incensed. He was easily held down.

Gus heard a commotion behind them. It seemed the entire town was making their way to the spectacle. Leading the pack was Emma, holding something in her hand.

"It was a brick," she said, offering it to Gus.

Police Chief James intercepted it with a gloved hand before it touched Gus's hand. "I wish you would have left it where you found it," she said to Emma.

"I . . . I'm sorry. I wasn't thinking straight."

James sighed and shook her head. "It's not your fault. We're all a little excited just about now."

Gus squatted so he could be at eye level with their captive. "You mind telling me why you chose to throw a brick through my window?"

The man laughed dismissively. "I didn't throw no brick."

"I saw him," someone in the crowd said. A few other people were quick to add that they had as well. Gus registered the fact that they were not Springerville tried-and-true. At least they had the sense to speak out against a crime.

"You could have hurt someone real bad," Gus said, hoping that in fact no one was back at the luncheonette nursing a wound. He did see some blood on the back of Don's thick neck, assumed it had been by the spray of glass. "Those were my friends and neighbors in there. I don't take kindly to people who hurt my friends. So, I have to wonder, do you have something you need to square with me, or do you hate luncheonettes in general?"

"I don't have to talk to you," he said with a sneer.

"All right, get up," James said. The cops yanked him to his feet. "You and I have a date at the station." To Gus, she said, "I'm sorry something like this had to happen today. If you want, stop by later and we can talk."

"I definitely will."

The trio of police marched the thug through the parting crowd. Gus watched them load him into the backseat before they made a U-turn and headed for the police station on the other side of Main.

Emma slid her arm around him as he turned to face the crowd. "Anyone recognize him or that bike he was riding on?"

All he got was a lot of headshakes.

"Well, I guess this means the party's over," Gus said. "Or, we can choose not to let some two-bit punk spoil our day. I'm not of a mind to eat all that food myself."

Smiles broke out among the worried faces, and a few claps turned into thundering applause. Even some of the cybercafe folks were cheering on his sentiment.

"Okay, let's go back to my place. But before you go inside, let me sweep up that glass."

Hours later, Gus, Emma, and Banks sat in the now empty luncheonette, exhausted as they listened to Randy, Ron, and Mike put a piece of plywood in place over the window frame. Even though it was still light outside, inside was mostly dark. Gus got up to flip on the lights. He also went to the pantry and dug out a bottle of Wild Turkey Rare Breed whiskey.

"Anyone care for some?"

Banks reached over the counter and procured three yellow plastic cups. "Make it a healthy pour."

Emma held her cup up and Gus gave it three fingers worth. He did the same for Banks and himself and sat between them.

"That was an event," he said.

After regrouping at the luncheonette, the party miraculously went back into full swing. The crowd spilled into the street as more and more people came to see what had happened and just why folks were having such a good old time after being the target of an attack. Don and Dennis Runde had stood watch outside, but Gus thought it wasn't necessary. What was done was done and at least someone was going to jail for it.

Gus had spoken to the reporter and then the woman from the radio station, both of them seemingly impressed by the way he'd handled the whole situation. He made sure to get in his talking point, lovingly drawn up by Emma with an assist from Banks a few nights before. He found it hard to stay on script because he'd never had to follow one before, other than his time in the military, and that was just obeying orders. Somehow, he'd made it through, saying as much as he could in as few words as possible. Those two interviews wore him out more than anything else so far.

Emma tapped her cup against his. "It sure was. Nothing like a little levity, vandalism, and terror to kick off a campaign."

"That guy is lucky the cops were here. No telling what state he'd be in if Don had been left alone with him."

"I'm just grateful no one got hurt and Don and Dennis were able to catch at least one of them."

The drilling on the plywood stopped and there came three sharp knocks, signaling they were done. "Thanks, guys," Gus boomed so he could be heard. Ron and Mike had said they were taking Randy to the Iron Works for a couple of drinks when they were done. The kid needed a little time to blow off some steam after disappearing from the crowd and scouring the town for the motorcycle. He came back apologetic that he wasn't able to find it. Gus was glad he hadn't because he saw the look in Randy's eyes and knew if he had, he might be in jail next to the punk Don and Dennis had caught. Ashley and his parents needed him home, not behind bars.

"I was worried that Wally's little assistant would have a heart attack," Banks said as he knocked back his drink. "Carolyn is wound up pretty tight on a calm day. I didn't know a human could scream that loud. She missed her calling. She could be a star in one of those horror movies."

Gus poured him some more. "I was more concerned about people like Aileen or Muriel, but they took it in stride. Thank God."

"You know that wasn't random, right?" Banks said.

Gus nodded as he stared contemplatively at his drink. "That's more than likely."

"But who would do such a thing?" Emma asked. She reached for the bottle. The woman could hold her whiskey better than just about anyone in Springerville.

"Take your pick," Banks said. "A lot of senseless things going on in this town lately. Those guys were definitely not from around here. Or at least until recently, I'd bet."

After a long silence, Gus said, "I think it might have been The Stranger."

"You think he'd sink that low?" Emma said.

"I can't be sure because I don't know the man at all," Gus said with a shrug. "But it makes sense. Wally suspected he was behind the vandalism of his truck. Maybe it could have been one of his overzealous supporters. Dawn might be getting to the bottom of it as we speak. If I was a Magic 8 Ball, I'd be flashing 'All signs point to Stranger' either way."

"Or *strangers*," Banks said. "Way too many of them around now. Shane told me The Pennsylvania is all booked up. Two busloads came filled with Northerners. He said a few of them were downright scary. And guess who was there to greet them?"

"Stranger," Gus said.

Banks pointed at him and winked. "Give that man a prize."

"Just what the hell is he up to? And what did I get myself into?"

Gus got up, walked across the luncheonette, and pressed his hand against the wood. The boys had done a solid job. Getting the glass replaced would be a task best suited for tomorrow. He was grateful for how quickly they had patched it all up, insisting he take a load off while they did the work.

"If Stranger is really behind this, then it's a good thing you're running instead of Wally," Emma said. "This isn't a job for a man of his age. And health. This needs someone more . . . immovable."

Scratching a bugbite at the back of his neck, Gus walked back over to where he'd left the whiskey. "Is that your way of saying I'm stubborn as a mule?"

Emma grinned. "I'm much more polite than that."

"The only thing I wonder now is, how bad are things going to get between now and Election Day? If this is Stranger's doing, this isn't politics. It's a street brawl."

For the first time since the brick throwing incident, Banks smiled. "Or a bar brawl. You keep saying you're not a politician. But you were one hell of a fighter back in the day."

Even Gus had to smile. "That was a lifetime ago, though I get your drift. A fight is something I can wrap my head around better."

Emma grabbed his arm just as he was about to sip his whiskey. "Please don't tell me you're going to start throwing fists. You can't be mayor when you're in jail for assault."

He pulled her close and finished his drink. The whiskey was doing a fine job of calming his nerves and clearing his head. "Babe, that's the furthest thing from my mind. I *am* thinking that I need to pay a visit to Mr. Braden Stranger so I can get the measure of the man. For some people, it's easy to be a bully from a distance. You look them in the eye, things suddenly change."

Banks got off the stool and hitched up his jeans. "If you're going on a field trip, I think I should join you for another visit."

"And where's that?"

"We need to see what's going on at The Pennsylvania. I don't like anything Shane told me. If we want to know what Stranger's up to, that's a good place to start."

After Gus collected their cups and put them in the sink and the empty whiskey bottle in the trash, he donned his Stetson and laced his fingers within Emma's. "Sounds like a plan to me. Think I'll knock on Stranger's door tomorrow afternoon. Maybe we can drive over to The Pennsylvania after dinner. By the end of the day, I'll know exactly what this town and I are in for."

# CHAPTER 14

Never one to put off what could be done today, Gus closed up shop the following day after lunch and headed over to Braden Stranger's house. Everyone in town knew where the man lived. He'd moved into the old Corbin place, one of the oldest and most expensive homes in town. The Corbins had built the five-bedroom plantation house in the mid-1800s. It gave shelter to generations of Corbins, until the passing of Margaret Corbin several years ago. She was a reclusive but amiable spinster who had never had children and was last of the Corbin line. Tales were told by kids that the old woman was a witch who would cast a hex on anyone who dared step onto her property.

Gus used to bring her meals from time to time, and she was always a grateful host. The poor woman was just awkward in social circles, and in later years, with her health failing, getting out and about was difficult.

The place had been spruced up quite a bit since Gus has last been there. The exterior was freshly painted, and the front garden was immaculately kept. There was a new fountain with statues of little Buddhas around it. Gus scratched his head. You didn't see many Buddhas in

Springerville. He wondered what Mrs. Corbin would have thought of the gaudy fountain. Probably would have had it removed and chucked in the old quarry a couple of miles away.

When Gus rang the bell, he remembered the first time he'd stood on this porch, bag in hand, dressed like a fireman with "trick or treat" at the ready on his lips. Back then, Mrs. Corbin was famous for giving full one-pound chocolate bars to every ghoul, hobo, and princess that rang her bell.

Banks had wanted to come with him, but Gus thought it best he do this alone. Later, they would do a little recon at The Pennsylvania.

"Coming," a man's voice echoed from inside. A moment later the door whisked open, and Gus was met with a look of harried irritation. "Can I help you?"

Braden Stranger was tall and lean and had the quaffed blond hair of a news anchor . . . or career politician. He wore blue slacks, striped dress shirt, and what looked to be very expensive shoes.

Gus extended his hand. "You Braden Stranger?"

Stranger looked Gus up and down as if he were appraising him for an auction. His demeanor quickly changed, and he gave a wolfish grin. "You must be Gus Fuller. I recognize you from the paper."

"I am. Or at least that's what my parents told me."

He opened the door wider. "This is a pleasant surprise. Please, come in."

Gus stepped into the house, knowing full well by Stranger's tone that this surprise was anything but pleasant.

The interior of the great house had been as revamped as the exterior. The design was best described as modern antiseptic. It had all the homey feel of a hospital waiting room. Every wall was white, and the sparse furniture was colorless, cold, and uncomfortable-looking. Stranger led him to the living room and waved for him to take a seat on the leather couch. "Can I get you something to drink? Water? Coffee?" He looked at the clock on the wall over the fireplace that hadn't seen a burning log in quite some time. "Or something with a little more bite?"

"I'm good, but thank you."

Stranger shrugged. "I just got off a three hour Zoom call, so I hope you don't mind that I have a little something to unwind." He went over to a well-stocked wet bar in the corner of the living room. Gus noted some bottles of pretty expensive whiskey. At least the man had good taste. A little rich for Gus, but the man knew his whiskey.

"Go right ahead. Nothing wrong with kicking back after a long day." He couldn't imagine how difficult it was to sit on a video, but everyone had their perceived struggles.

Ice tinkled in Stranger's glass as he took a seat opposite Gus in a white leather chair that looked like it was designed to torture a person's back. "So, what can I do for you? I had assumed our first meeting would be at a debate or on the campaign trail."

"I can't remember there ever being a debate for mayor around here. As far as campaigns, they've mostly been a few signs and some speeches at a few local establishments. This isn't exactly an election for president."

Stranger took a sip and nodded. "I'm sure that's the way it's been in the past. The difference here is that I'm not one of you." Did Gus detect a note of disdain? This man was trying real hard to hide his true feelings and not doing a very good job of things. "I need to get out there more than candidates before me just so people can get to know me."

"Then by all means, you should do that." Gus couldn't recall seeing Stranger in town or talking to anyone, other than the media when he saw a quick photo op. "Folks around here like to look their mayoral hopefuls in the eye and have a conversation. Signs don't account for much, until it comes time for our fall bonfire."

Gus held back a smile. Stranger had signs seemingly on every corner. It was more like littering than campaigning. This year's bonfire would be bigger than ever.

"Yes, well, maybe I overdid it a bit with the signs. I have to keep telling myself this isn't New York where political hopefuls spend money like it was water." He eyed Gus keenly as he sipped his drink.

"You said you recognized me from the paper. I'm sure you read how someone crashed my little coming-out party, no pun intended."

"I did. Completely senseless. I'm glad no one was hurt. The person who was caught, has he said why he did it?"

Gus didn't know Stranger from Adam, but he knew when a man was lying. The man in custody—Jim Lukas from Perth Amboy, New Jersey—had shut up tighter than a clam since he'd been brought into custody. All he did claim was that the man riding the motorcycle had been the one to throw the brick and that he had no idea why the man would do such a thing. That man was unidentified, because according to Lukas, he'd hitched a ride with him into town because his car was out of service. Police Chief James checked it out herself and confirmed that the old Ford was indeed a junker that wouldn't start. Lukas had purchased the plot of land where the crumbling Larson house stood being devoured by nature for a good decade. He didn't look like the kind of guy who would have the money or credit to buy land, even if it were the size of a hopscotch board. Unfortunately, James had to let him go, but promised her force would keep an eye on him.

The leather chair creaked as Gus adjusted his weight and leaned forward to rest his forearms on his knees. "Nope. He hasn't said word one. Cops know he's lying, but for the moment, there's nothing they can do."

"It's a shame. I came down here to get away from crime. I guess it's everywhere you look, nowadays."

"It seems that way. Though I don't have to think far back to remember when it wasn't."

There was an uncomfortable silence that Gus just let hang there. Stranger put on his poker face as he rolled his crystal glass in his hand.

After a while, Stranger said, "It's a little disconcerting to me. I mean, if something like that happened to you, a longstanding pillar of this community, I wonder what might be done to me, a complete outsider."

*Oh, I think you'll be just fine*, Gus thought. He came here to see if Braden Stranger would be the kind of man to hire some two-bit goons to intimidate him. The man sitting opposite him was a reptile in expensive clothes, sipping on expensive whiskey. Gus didn't like to paint people with a broad stroke. Not every person from up north was a slick son of a biscuit eater with an agenda.

But Stranger was.

"Is that why you came?" Stranger said, getting up to refill his glass. "To warn me?"

"The thought actually never crossed my mind. No, I thought it best for us to meet in person before things get rolling. And seeing as I never spot you in town, I thought I should just pop on by. I wanted to say good luck and hope that we can do this whole dog and pony show fair and square."

"I think that goes without saying. I see no reason to run one of those slash-and-burn campaigns. Springerville is a town of civility. I plan to keep it that way."

Gus slapped his knees and stood up. He figured he had about four inches on Stranger, enjoying how the man had to tilt his head up a bit to look him in the eye. "That's good to hear. I agree. Springerville is a great place. A special place. And lately, civility and order are slipping by the wayside. Not all change is for the good."

He headed for the door. Stranger walked beside him. Gus wanted out of this stark, soulless place.

"Growing pains come with change," Stranger said. "Just ask my son who is growing like a weed. Most nights, his legs hurt like hell. But in the end, it's the way of nature."

This didn't look like a house with a child living in it. Gus figured Stranger must be divorced. He'd have to sit with Emma and find out what they could about the man.

Stranger opened the door, and said, "Thank you for coming by. I know we'll be seeing a lot of each other over the next few months."

He didn't offer his hand.

"Can I ask you just one question?" Gus asked.

"Shoot."

"Why here?"

Stranger smiled, revealing his too-white, too-perfect teeth, and replied, "Because a town like Springerville is the heart of America. What better place is there to be?"

Gus could think of many other cities better suited for a man like Stranger.

As he stepped back onto the porch, they locked eyes, their gazes saying much more than they'd speak aloud.

This was going to be a fight, that was for sure.

Gus may not have been all that enthused to run for mayor before.

Now, things were different.

He not only *had* to run.

He had to win. For the sake of everyone who truly called Springerville home, he had to win.

# CHAPTER 15

They headed to The Pennsylvania trailer park in Banks's beat-up Wrangler. He'd taken the top and doors off, and Gus had to hang on for dear life as it bounced down the uneven road.

"If this keeps up, that beer I bought Shane will only be good for spraying suds ten feet high," Gus said. It was going on dusk with a purple haze hanging over the distant tree line.

"I don't think Shane's all that picky," Banks said. "You have to add fixing this road to your to-do list when you're mayor. I'm going to have to replace my shocks after this."

"I'm not mayor yet. And if Wally didn't fix it, there might not be any money in the budget for it."

A particularly deep pothole whipped them from side to side as Banks fought the wheel. "Yeah, well, find it."

"Talk to my secretary and we can set up a meeting."

"Meeting my ass," Banks grumbled.

On the way over, Gus had told Banks about his one-on-one with Braden Stranger and how his head had chimed with millions of alarm bells. Banks had suggested some very old ways of running the man out of town, none of them pleasant, but Gus let him blow off his head of steam. If Shane was right and The Pennsylvania was now host to what he claimed it was, those alarm bells would grow into ear-splitting claxons.

They came to the gated entrance, sans the entrance gate that was lying rusted in the weeds, and pulled up outside of Shane's trailer. As soon as Banks cut the engine, all they could hear was blaring music and loud voices. Gus saw people milling about in the encroaching darkness. It smelled like someone had started a fire pit. That was mixed with the skunky scent of cheap weed.

Banks knocked on Shane's door. He answered it wearing camouflage cargo shorts and a shirt that had more holes than a sponge. "Hey Chris, Gus. Good to see ya. Come on in."

Gus peeked inside Shane's trailer and got a whiff of body odor and clothes that needed to be washed around the time Obama was president. He held up the case of beer, and said, "Why don't you give me a tour?"

Shane took a quick peek into his trailer, scratched his head under his baseball cap, and grinned. "Uh, yeah, that's probably a good idea. The maid has been out sick lately." He broke out in a big grin that put Gus and Banks at ease. Gus hadn't had much interaction with Shane. The man mostly kept to himself. At least this proved he had some modicum of self-awareness.

Banks looked around, and said, "Looks like you have a full house on your hands."

"I'll say. It hasn't been like this since it opened after Trina. Except I liked those folks a whole heck of a lot better. I haven't locked my door in years. Now, I not only lock it, I put a chair under the handle."

Shane ripped the cardboard case open and handed them

each a beer. It was this side of tepid at this point, but Gus didn't want to be rude. They walked a bit, staring down the long stretch with trailers situated on either side of the dirt walkway. A lot of people were out and about, with a good gathering around the roaring fire pit. This was definitely a ragtag bunch. Gus spotted a lot of tattoos, which wasn't that big a deal. These days, it seemed everyone had one, even grannies looking for poundcake at the Publix. Emma had a small butterfly tattoo on her ankle. But there was quite a bit of neck art in the crowd, which always seemed a step too far to his liking.

What he didn't spy were any children. That was a good thing, considering all of the pot being smoked out in the open. He considered calling Dawn James to bring a handful of uniforms to crash the little party. But she had enough on her plate right now. No need to tie her up pursuing petty crimes.

"You get to know any of your new neighbors?" Gus asked.

Shane shook his head while he gulped his beer. "I steer clear of them. And so far, they steer clear of me. The trailers are in pretty bad shape, but I got just about everything working before they came. Though I suspect they're doing a good job breaking most of what I put together. I hear a lot of fights out here, things getting tossed around. There're a few real bad eggs calling this shithole home." He tipped his head toward a muscular man wearing a leather vest with no shirt underneath. He had a fat joint jammed in the corner of his mouth as if it were a cigar. His hair was long and wild and when Gus saw his eyes, two dark points in a face scarred by childhood acne, he knew the man was trouble. Those were the dead eyes of a convict, and not one who had been put away for swiping a few things from a store.

"He got a name?" Banks asked.

"I hear people call him Sniper. I haven't spoken to him myself." Sniper glanced their way for a moment, as if taking their measure, before heading into an open trailer. "That trailer is where this girl is living. She looks like one of those rich kids who exists just to piss her parents off. Not sure of her name. I don't think her daddy would be too happy if he could see her now."

"Taking a walk on the wild side," Banks said as he crushed his can.

"Might be too wild," Gus said. He tried to study the face of everyone out and about without staring and causing suspicion. He was sure a lot of them were wondering who the two men with the park manager were. "Everyone but Sniper seems to be about in their twenties."

Shane nodded. "Pretty much my guess, too. That's usually the age that has the time to cause trouble. There are others like Sniper around. Bikers who have seen some stuff. Bad stuff. They come and go, but from what I can tell, they take orders from him."

"How many you think there are?" Gus asked.

Shane closed his eyes for a moment. "Hard to tell. They all look the same to me. Dressed in leather, riding bikes, lots of tattoos, dirty and nasty-looking. I'd say there are around a dozen of them. Could be more. Doubt it would be less. Believe it or not, the bikers keep pretty quiet. It's the young ones that wake me up at all hours of the night with their partying and shouting and nonsense."

Gus wondered who he had to be concerned with more. He had watched so-called protestors turn cities into dumps in no time, setting up filthy encampments and looting at will all in the name of . . . well, he was pretty sure most of them didn't rightly know. They were young and angry, whipped up by the news and social media. There had been a lot of chatter that behind many of the protests, some lasting almost a year, was a master puppeteer—some rich, wealthy overlord who enjoyed the spectacle all in the name of politics. The bikers could well just be opportunists, going where hell was to be raised. South Carolina's new governor had grown soft on crime over the past couple of years, kowtowing to a loud minority. Men like Sniper knew when a place was ripe for picking.

What Gus was seeing in The Pennsylvania had him thinking all conspiracy theories weren't wrong or the work of tinfoil-hat loonies. Stranger was behind this, that was for sure. Shane had told Banks so. But who was behind Stranger?

And speaking of Stranger. "When's the last time you spoke to Stranger?"

"The night the buses came. He said he had maids lined up to come clean the trailers, but like mine, they never showed. I don't think this crowd really care much. Normally, his butt boy, Roger, does his talking and meeting for him. Haven't seen hide nor hair of him either."

"You know anyone named Roger?"

Banks shook his head.

Gus patted Shane on the back. "Thank you for cluing us in. I'm glad we came out here to see what's going on."

"This ain't all of it," Shane said, tipping his hat back with his second beer can. "I heard Roger talking about bringing more. They better not come here, because if I had one, there'd be a no vacancy sign hanging out front. Unless they run the three trailers I have with regulars out. I wouldn't blame them if they beat feet."

"Forget locusts. This is more like cockroaches," Banks said. He kicked a rock into the weeds.

"Maybe we should turn a light on and see if they scatter," Shane said.

"Wish it was that easy."

Before they left, there was one more thing Gus wanted to do. He took out his phone and zoomed into the crowd around the fire. He thumbed the picture icon and snapped as many close-ups as he could, hoping they wouldn't be too blurry. Dawn James might be interested in taking a look and seeing if any popped up on a wanted list. Half the crowd looked just like Shane had said, rich kids who dressed like bums in search of a cause and some dangerous fun. The other half just might have a mug shot or two on file.

The question was, which cities housed those prisoner pics?

"You a photographer?" a gravelly voice said from behind them. Shane literally jumped. Gus and Banks slowly turned around.

Sniper stood with his arms crossed, the muscles in his forearms like coiled rope.

Gus looked back to the trailer where they had seen the man enter moments earlier. He must have gone out a back door or window and circled around them. The thug looked primed for a fight. He was an ugly son of a bitch, complete with battle scars to complement his acne scars.

Gus recovered quickly. With a smile, he said, "Only if you like most of your pictures with a thumb in front of them."

Sniper remained stoic. "Do I know you?"

"Nope, most likely not. But I am running for mayor. Can I count on your vote?"

Sniper spit on the ground.

"How are you enjoying South Carolina?" Banks asked, sounding as if he were part of a welcome committee. Gus knew his friend. If he let him, Banks would bait the man into throwing the first punch. "I can tell you're not a Southerner, so this must be new for you."

"What gave it away?"

As if being called a Southerner was akin to being called a rat in a prison.

Banks rubbed the back of his neck. "Well, your accent is what? Somewhere in California?"

"It's none of your business where I'm from." Sniper turned his attention to Gus. "He your boy or something?"

Gus could feel the charge in the air as Banks bristled.

"What did you just say?" Banks grumbled.

Gus put a hand on his friend's chest. "That was impolite. Most people new to a town want to do what they can to ingratiate themselves."

"What?" Sniper's hard exterior twisted into an expression of confusion.

With a wave of his hand, Gus said, "It's neither here nor there. I'm just wondering what brings you all here to Springerville? I like to take little personal polls when I'm out and about. Helps me understand the people better, you know what I mean?"

It looked like the man had had enough. His hands balled into fists. "Why don't you two piss off? I don't like people coming around taking pictures like some kind of sneak. In fact, maybe I should take that phone of yours. I don't remember giving you permission to film me."

Gus took a moment to look at his phone before casually slipping it in his back pocket. "That phone cost me a pretty penny. If you were willing to buy it off me, I'm sure we could come to some sort of agreement."

He hadn't realized it until that moment, but Shane had slipped away and was currently walking into his trailer. No doubt locking the door and wedging a chair under the knob.

Sniper sneered at them. Gus could practically hear his teeth grinding. Several other toughs had pulled away from the fire pit and were now walking toward them.

Well, the civil act was wearing thin quickly, which, if Gus was going to be honest, was not a surprise. As much as he'd enjoy a chance at going one-on-one with Sniper (or two-on-one when Banks inevitably and rightly joined the fray), it looked like it was going to be six-on-two in a few seconds. Sometimes, a tactical withdrawal was best. This was one of those times.

"You have a good evening, then. I may not be much of a politician, but I can tell when I'm not wanted. You know what Democrats say. Vote early and vote often."

Gus started to walk away, keeping one eye on Sniper and the other on the approaching men, all of them looking as if they were part of an outlaw biker gang.

Banks stood his ground. Gus had to tug him to get him moving.

Then Gus took a chance. He turned his back to Sniper and casually walked away.

"Keep walking. And make sure your boy doesn't get off his leash. I'm sure you don't want something to happen to him."

"Just give me the word and I'll make sure his jaw won't work right for the rest of his miserable life," Banks whispered.

"Now's not the time. Just stay cool. I have a feeling we'll get our chance. Whiskey at my place?"

"I may need a whole bottle just to calm the hell down."

"Whatever it takes."

They were climbing into Banks's Wrangler when Sniper let go with a parting shot.

"Good luck with that mayor thing, Mister Photographer. Maybe we'll see each other again. Maybe when you least expect it."

As Banks pulled the Wrangler back, Gus called out, "I always expect the unexpected. Looking forward to it."

# CHAPTER 16

The next few weeks were a flurry of activity. Gus still worked the luncheonette, spending his afternoons and evenings campaigning, which mostly consisted of stopping at various places around town like the nursing home over on Chestnut, the library where he spoke a bit before a book club meeting, a bean supper on Sunday to help restock the Baptist church's food pantry, and the high school, where he spoke with seniors, many of them eligible to vote for the first time.

Behind it all was Emma, who designed his signs and pointed him where to go and helped him with what to say. He tended to wander away from his talking points, realizing that he knew most of these people and they knew him. The exception was the high school, where Emma had told him to regale them with tales of his military experience.

"It's not exactly a glamorous story," he'd said.

"These kids spend more time playing video war games than talking face to face with one another. Trust me, they'll eat it up."

"I'm going to have to be very selective then. And clean things up a bit."

"Just tell them how you got your Purple Heart."

"I'll do you one better. How about I offer a free fried chicken sandwich for every one of them that comes to my place and shows me they registered?"

Emma clapped. "That's perfect! A way to a teen's heart is through their stomach. You better up your weekly order of chicken."

He did (after working really hard not to glamorize war) and a few kids came in each day, flashing their proof of registration and rumbling bellies.

As Emma had promised, folks reached out to him looking to donate money toward his campaign. He used a very small portion of it to print up some signs. Emma did the designing and Banks and a few others put them up around town. It was nothing compared to the explosion of Stranger posters that blighted just about every telephone pole and tree. The man didn't have many lawn signs because very few residents agreed to let him put one on their property. When Gus saw a sign in a yard, he knew it was a house inhabited by a newcomer.

After a few weeks, he stopped accepting money. Springerville wasn't exactly a wealthy town. They had better things to spend their money on. He used the rest to buy food, which he prepared and distributed for free to those who needed it most. It did him good to take care of them more than he usually could. Every single recipient of a meal was grateful, pledging their vote come Election Day.

Those were the positives.

As predicted, his flag was stolen. He found it in the trash bins behind his luncheonette, smeared with something best left unexplored. He'd cleaned it, put it back up, and saw someone had torn a hole in it two days later.

Chief of Police Dawn James stopped by from time to time, letting him know that small crimes were still on the rise. There were no leads in the Randy and Ashley Early attack and there probably wouldn't be at this late stage. "We can only hope that someone we catch for a completely different crime knows who did it and squeals on them to save their sorry butts. I do have some good news. We did catch that boy who dosed Gina Cordry. He's a junior, just moved here from Philadelphia with his rich parents. Claims he thought he was giving her a Molly so they could *get closer*," she said, making air quotes with her fingers. "I asked him if she was aware he was giving her a Molly. He wouldn't answer that. Lawyered up real fast. His attorney did allow him to give us a description of the biker who sold it to him in exchange for not pressing charges. Problem is, the description matches more than half the bikers who have been prowling around here lately. We're keeping a close eye on The Pennsylvania. Seems to be their hangout. It doesn't take a genius to realize something bad is happening there. But it has to practically blow up before we can do more than catch and release. Until then, we're seeing more overdoses than ever. Gina has been the only true resident so far. But even the locusts don't deserve this. It's gotten to the point where we're running low on Narcan. Before this nonsense, I think we might have needed to use it once every couple of years."

Gus put bacon, egg, and cheese on a roll together for Freddie Powell. "Makes one wish we had some Charles Bronson types around."

"And on that note, I advise you to keep away from The Pennsylvania. That place is bad news, and it can only result in worse news for you."

Gus changed the subject while sticking to the topic. "You find anything from those pictures I sent you?"

She nodded with a serious look in her eyes. "There are

some real pieces of work out there. That guy you said they called Sniper? He's got a rap sheet long enough to wallpaper this place. Spent a few stints in prisons in different states. They've got him for everything but murder, though he's been a suspect in a few cases but managed to wiggle free. Real name is Tyler Conroy."

"Tyler?" Gus couldn't stop himself from smiling. "I can't see him as a Tyler."

"Well, his momma did when he was a cute little baby. How was she to know he'd turn into a monster?"

"I know it sounds crazy, but he seems a lot less imposing to me now."

"Don't let his name fool you into a false sense of complacency. Just keep thinking of him as Sniper and you'll do right by steering clear of him. Just like the others out there, he's suddenly a registered voter and will most likely blow out like the wind when the election's over. If he can read the ballot. I'd take odds on that."

At first, Gus had wondered if the rabble that had come to the town on buses had been brought down to intimidate him. Then he sat a while and thought and figured Stranger had pointed the way for one reason and one reason only— to gather a false constituency so he could win the mayoral race. It was dirty pool at its best. Bordering on criminal at its worst.

Braden Stranger may have been in some social circles that put him in touch with the disenfranchised twenty-somethings out for a little rebellion. He was not the kind of man who associated with the Sniper types.

"You got anything on our boy Stranger?" Gus asked.

He and Emma couldn't find anything public about the man that would place him in criminal circles. For all they could see, he was just another rich huckster in a suit who had been on the boards of some very successful companies in New York. Yes, he was divorced, but his profile was too low to make the news. They found out he had a young son. Gus wondered what would become of a boy with a role model like Stranger. Probably carry on the tradition of attaining C-level positions, making a lot of money at the expense of others, and wishing he could take it all to the grave with himself.

"Just a few moving violations over the past few years. He has a thing for fancy cars and opening them up on highways. I thought there'd at least be one DUI. He's associated with a lot of exceedingly wealthy people. Blue bloods that go way back with his family. None of them from the South, which makes his move here all the more suspicious. Stranger and whoever is behind him is up to something. I'm sure of it."

"Intuition?"

"Cop and woman's, as well as just being able to read the tea leaves."

"Looks like we're of the same mind." Gus looked over James's shoulder. "Speak of the devil."

Braden Stranger pulled up to the curb outside the luncheonette in a white Porsche Boxster. A black BMW slid right behind it. As if the whole spectacle had been coordinated ahead of time, the doors to both cars opened at the same time. Out stepped Stranger from the Porsche. A man Gus thought he'd seen around town a few times climbed out of the BMW carrying a briefcase. They wore suits without ties and shiny dress shoes without socks. Both wore aviator sunglasses. They paused for a moment to stare at the luncheonette, then walked in lockstep to the door.

"Those fellas look like they watch too many movies," Gus said.

"I wonder what kind of entrance music they have going through their pea heads."

"Any chance it's that clown music they play at the circus?"

James grinned.

All heads turned when Stranger and his lackey stepped inside. One didn't see many suits around town at lunchtime. Hell, just about any time.

Stranger locked eyes with Gus and broke out in a wolfish grin. "Just the man I wanted to see."

"Not sure if I should be honored or not," Gus replied, getting a few titters from his patrons.

Stranger waved at the man to his left. "This is Roger Anson. He's my . . . ah . . . campaign manager."

*Toadie is more like it,* Gus thought.

Gus stuck out his hand. Roger had the grip of a wounded monkey. "Nice to meet you," Roger said. The man was in a full sweat, no doubt from catering to Stranger all day in a climate he was not accustomed to.

"Same here." Gus turned to Dawn James. "This here is my head of security, but on the side, she's the police chief, Dawn James."

James rolled her eyes and stood up, shaking both men's hands. "Good to finally meet the man behind the placards. I see your face so much; I feel like I already know you."

Gus had to stop himself from laughing over her little dig.

Stranger played it cool, never allowing his smile to falter. "A pleasure. I know what you mean. I think we may have gone a little overboard. But my intentions are good. I know I'm the outsider. Just takes a little more work."

Gus saw that Robbie Maleck's coffee mug was almost empty. He scooted behind the counter to grab the pot and topped him off. All eating and conversation had stopped.

Robbie didn't even so much as touch his mug. He had a bit of cheese in his beard.

"Speaking of intentions," Gus said. "I was wondering what yours were."

"And that's exactly why I'm here. I wanted to stop by and offer you a chance to set up a debate."

"Uh-huh."

"So that way the residents can get to know both of us and where we stand."

"We'd be happy to set everything up at the location of your choosing," Roger said.

Emma had found out that Stranger had been a lawyer before becoming a corporate executive. The man could probably talk the Pope into shoplifting.

"Is that so?"

"Absolutely," Roger replied. "You name the day, time, and place."

When Gus didn't say anything, Stranger said, "So what do you say? I mean, it's only right that everyone hears both sides before making a decision. Plus, it will be fun. None of that mud dragging you see everywhere else. Let's just discuss the topics that matter. We owe it to the people of Springerville, don't you think?"

"You mean topics like crime becoming an everyday thing?" Gus said. He couldn't see Stranger thinking he owed anyone here anything. Best to leave the remark alone.

"Exactly. I'm sure you have ideas on how to tackle it. So do I."

"I've got a way," Chris Banks said. Everyone had been so fixated on Stranger and Gus, Banks had waltzed inside unnoticed, which wasn't easy for a man his size. "Rent a few buses to take the people who are ruining Springerville back to where they came from. I'll be happy to foot the bill. I'll even give your car a tune-up, free of charge."

Stranger's poker face dropped for a moment. "Yes, this town has a lot of new residents, but they came here to find a better place to live. To raise a family. To experience life the way it should be. Why, look at me. I love it so much, I want to dedicate my life to helping it thrive."

"I didn't see any families at The Pennsylvania," Gus said. "Or any of the other places folks are popping up in lately. You'd think we were giving away free iPhones or something. You wouldn't happen to know why *they're* coming here, would you? And I can tell you with absolute certainty that Springerville was thriving just fine until a year or so ago."

Braden's lips pulled into a tight line as he looked to measure his response.

Sarah Birch, who had been sitting at the counter, chirped up. "He's right about that. Looks to me like this influx of people looking for life the way it should be have turned it into life the way we wish it wasn't."

A murmur of agreement filled the luncheonette.

"If you need any proof, I can lay it out right now," Banks said. He turned to Dawn James. "I just called your department to report a stolen car. I was fixing to work on Myrna Baxter's Impala this afternoon after I got done with Buster Gage's old Ford. When I went to bring it into the garage, it was gone. Someone must have swiped it during the hour I was under Buster's car."

"Have you called her yet? Maybe she came by to take it back for some reason," James asked, suddenly standing and concerned.

"First thing I did. She's pretty upset. That Impala was her late husband's. It means a lot to her." Banks shook his head, using a grimy rag to wipe the sweat from the back of his thick neck. "In all my years, I never had anything like that happen before." Now he fixed his attention on Stranger. "That's what you people have brought to this town."

Roger Anson stepped between them. "You can't possibly blame us for a stolen car."

"Not you specifically. But what you represent, absolutely."

Stranger finally spoke up. "I think we need to take a step back. I'm sorry and upset that this just happened to you. Officer, can you see to it personally that this gets top priority?"

Dawn James looked at him as if he had unicorns struggling to get out of his ears. She turned to Banks, and said, "Let's go to your shop and see what we can see."

"Right."

They left in a hurry.

"That was very unfortunate," Stranger said.

Gus ignored him. Instead, he went over to Robbie Maleck and asked, "You still have that old Dodge?"

"Under a tarp in the yard."

"Does it run?"

"Might need a jump."

"I'm closing soon. How about I meet you at your house and we get her started. I don't think you'd mind loaning it to Myrna for a bit." Myrna had been Rob's babysitter, and then sixth grade teacher. His Dodge Intrepid had been his errand car for years until he'd gotten his new Ram truck.

"Sounds like a plan to me, Gus."

"Lunch is on me. Part of the Good Samaritan package." Gus gave him a wink and asked everyone if they needed anything else. All declined, knowing he wanted to get going. He turned off the burners and fryer and stuck his apron on the wall peg.

"Before you leave, did you want to discuss the debate?" Stranger said, visibly perturbed. Gus stopped what he was doing. "Not particularly, no."

"I see. It's more fun to play the hero in front of a crowd."

That got Sarah's ire. "And that's exactly why you don't belong here. If you knew and loved this town as much as you say you do, you'd understand that this is what we've always done for each other. If Gus and Robbie weren't here, it would have been someone else. You want a debate so people know where Gus stands? The folks that matter already do. I'm talking the people who have built their lives here and will be buried out at Forest Hills Cemetery one day, hopefully well in the future. What you want to do is try to talk circles around people. Actions speak louder than words, son."

Gus pulled a baseball cap on and checked to make sure he had his keys. "Thank you, Sarah. You think you can lock up for me? I'll stop by your place to get the keys in a little bit."

She held up her hand and he tossed them to her.

Gus pulled up a couple of feet from Stranger. The man had entered the luncheonette brimming with confidence. Now he looked tongue-tied.

"The people have spoken," Gus said. "Looks like the answer is no. Feel free to have Sarah get you each a biscuit on your way out. You look a little peckish."

He left the stunned men behind, walking out of his luncheonette to the sound of applause.

Before he jumped into his Jeep, he turned back to see Stranger and his assistant emerge. Stranger looked fit to be tied. Roger said something to him, but he brusquely brushed Roger off and got in his car.

A debate. What would have been the point? Everyone knew where each vote was coming from. Gus just hoped there were no new arrivals anytime soon, because at this rate, the locusts just might outnumber the true-blue people of Springerville.

# CHAPTER 17

"Morning, Ash."

Randy Early brushed a stray lock of hair from his wife's face and set the serving tray on her night table. "I thought some bacon, eggs, and toast would be a good way to start your day."

Ashley pushed herself up into a sitting position. "You don't need to bring me breakfast in bed every morning. I need to get up more anyway." She looked at the plate, the eggs still steaming. "You didn't make this, did you?"

"I learned my lesson. I did help my mom, though."

She settled the tray over her lap and took a bit of crispy bacon.

"How are you feeling?" Randy asked.

"Fuzzy."

"Well, you did just wake up."

She shook her head. "No, it's those meds the shrink gave me. I don't think I want to take those pills anymore."

Randy sat on the edge of the bed. "But the doctor said it was important for now, you know, to help lessen the pain."

Before she'd been given the prescription, Ashley had had terrible nightmares and difficulty sleeping. The fear of being impregnated or contracting a social disease by one of those animals had passed, but not the fresh scar of what they had inflicted on her physically and mentally. At least with the pills, she could sleep and heal.

Ashley grabbed his hand. "There comes a point where you have to lean into your pain. I think I'm ready now. As long as I know I have you here with me, I'll get through this. *We'll* get through this. We can't let some scumbags ruin our lives just when we were getting started."

Randy had to take a deep breath and lower his head for a moment, feeling a tear coming on. He had to be brave for his wife. He already felt as if he'd failed her. It would not happen again.

"Okay. No pills today. But if you feel like things are getting worse, you promise me you'll reconsider."

"I will."

Randy stayed with her while she ate breakfast, marveling at her strength and courage. Ashley was a fighter. He'd learned that quickly in the service. With her getting healthier, he had one last item on his wish list.

To find the men who had attacked them. Hopefully before anyone else did.

Gus and Emma sat on his porch on a lazy Sunday drinking coffee and reading the paper. Some traditions died hard. Gus refused to get his news online. The luncheonette had always been closed on Sundays so Gus's family could attend church and take a day to rest. He was in no mind to change that. A squirrel scrabbled along the porch banister, its puffy gray tail twitching. It stopped for a moment when it spied the humans, then hopped off and headed for the birdbath to drink.

"You almost done with the sports section?" Gus asked.

"Almost. You know the Panthers are underdogs today? That makes no sense."

"Nothing much does these days."

He grabbed the local news and opened up to a one-page ad taken out by none other than Braden Stranger. In the ad, he listed the so-called improvements he wanted to make to the town. Gus read them over twice before handing it over to Emma. "He's pretty ambitious," he said.

Emma was aghast. "If even half of these things happened, we wouldn't recognize the town. He wants to open strip malls and big-box stores all in the name of job opportunities. If that happened, we don't have enough people to fill them, or the roads to handle the traffic. And bail reform? That just sounds like he wants to keep the people who came down here to vote for him out of jail. You see how well that's worked in other big cities." She tossed the paper onto the porch with disgust. "He didn't come here to get away. He came here to remake the cesspool where he came from. And I'll bet as mayor, he'll make sure his pockets are overflowing from all these deals he intends to broker."

Gus retrieved the local section and turned the page. "Looks like he wants to re-create Springerville into a mix of New York and New Jersey. Anyone from here that was on the fence about voting will make the effort now."

"But will they definitely vote for you? We have a lot of unemployed folks here. The promise of a job might get them to vote for Stranger."

"The people out of work here are primarily skilled workers. I don't think making minimum wage as a cashier or stock person will be all that appealing."

"It isn't until your unemployment checks run out.

With the election two weeks away, what do we do to counter it?"

He took her hand, leaned over, and kissed her softly. "We have to trust the good sense of our town. Stranger took that ad out to rattle our cage. If you ask me, I think he just stepped in something he'd rather not have on his expensive shoes."

Emma got up and started pacing. "I keep seeing new faces in town, but no new kids being registered for school. If Stranger pulls this off, we have a major news story. He's packing the voting booths with transients!"

"Whoa, whoa, whoa. It's Sunday. The Lord said this is the day to relax and I plan to do just that. How about we get ready for church. We'll know Stranger's desperate if we see him there."

"We'll know it well in advance from the lighting." Emma's worry deflated a bit, and she took both of their empty mugs.

As they walked inside, with Gus holding the door open, he said, "Besides, there's a plan that the Rundes and Dawn cooked up that might burst Stranger's cockeyed bubble."

"Oh. What is that?"

Gus rubbed his chin, feeling it was in need of a shave. "I can't take credit for it, but it should be fun to watch. It's scheduled to go down on Saturday."

"Just tell me what it is."

Walking upstairs to the bedroom, Gus said, "Well, I guess you could say it's fighting fire with fire."


Saturday came just as sure as Gus's biscuits rising with the sun each morning. Emma arrived at his house to find him on the porch with Chris Banks. They drank from cold bottles of Budweiser.

"You boys pregaming?" she asked. She was dressed in her weekend going-out clothes, which included cowboy boots and jeans with strategic rips up and down the legs.

"I don't think there'll be much game at the Iron Works tonight," Gus said.

She put her hands on her hips, staring up at them from the bottom step. "You've been so mysterious all week about this. Why?"

Gus tilted the bill of his baseball cap back with the mouth of his beer bottle. "It's a little tricky."

Banks cut in. "What he means to say is that it scoots right around the ethics line. At least that's what he thinks."

"Now I'm really concerned."

"If it helps, I'm completely onboard with it."

"Call me doubly concerned."

Gus got up, set his bottle down, and closed and locked his front door. He'd never locked that door before. The past few months taught him it was better to be safe than sorry. "We need to take separate cars, honey."

"Why?"

"Because you're not staying. In fact, I shouldn't let you go at all."

When he ambled down the stairs, she looped her arm through his. "We both know that's not going to happen."

They got into separate cars and headed downtown. The lot to the Iron Works was so full, they had to park two blocks away.

"Are they giving out gold bars?" Emma asked when they parked.

"You could say that," Gus said.

"Okay, spill it. What the heck is going on?"

Banks leaned against his Jeep and laughed. "This is all the Runde boys' idea. Well, I might have helped a little."

Gus put his arm around her, making no move to walk up to the bar. "Seems our man here had a late-night session with Don and Dennis. As my assistant campaign manager, he voiced his concern that there were increasing numbers of locusts that were brought down here to vote for Stranger. I think it was Dennis who figured out how to thin the swarm a bit."

"Dennis *is* the brains," Banks said. "Pairs well with Don's brawn."

A police cruiser stopped beside them. Dawn James was sitting in the passenger seat. "Looks like we've got ourselves a full house."

"You think you have enough people on hand?"

She grinned from ear to ear. "Everyone is on duty tonight. I don't think I could have stopped them if I tried."

"We were just going to head inside and look around. Make sure good fish don't get caught in the net," Gus said.

"Good idea," James replied. "This might get a little crazy. You need to be careful. You have a target on your back."

They all looked at the cars trying to find a space in the lot and spilling into the street.

"I'll be fine. I brought my muscle," Gus said as he pulled Emma closer.

James gave them a finger salute. "We'll tuck in out of sight for now. This might be the most fun I've had all year."

Gus tapped the roof of the car as it rolled down the block.

When he looked back at Emma, he saw she was

steaming mad. "If you don't tell me everything now, I might punch you."

He held up his hands in surrender. "Okay, I'm sorry for dragging this out. After I tell you, you might just want to get back in your car and head home."

"I'll be the judge of that."

"Well, Banks, Don, and Dennis all decided it would be best if a lot of these folks just went away. But we all know that's not going to happen. None of these new locusts seem to work, but they have plenty of money for booze and drugs and food. Someone is paying them."

Emma didn't hide her irritation. "Speed it up, buddy. I already know this."

Banks interjected. "We found a way to make them go away. At least for a little while, with the election just a few days away. Remember when Gus gave Don and Dennis back their campaign contribution money?" Emma nodded. "They used it to stockpile on a few extra kegs of beer."

"So?"

Now Gus said, "That beer is currently being offered for free to everyone who walks in the door. I've been telling folks I know who like to frequent the Iron Works on Saturdays to find something else to do. Hopefully they listened to me."

"I still don't get it."

"We're gonna let them get nice and drunk and find ways to get themselves arrested," Banks said with a triumphant grin. "From DUIs to a good old bar brawl. The idea is to let them hang themselves and have the police grab them and stick them in a cell for a few days."

Emma tapped her boot and studied both of them as if she were searching for visible signs that they had lost their minds. Gus held his breath.

He didn't have to hold it for long. A wry smile went all the way to her beautiful eyes. "That's downright diabolical. You could almost call it entrapment."

"Or just giving the new citizens of Springerville a warm welcome," Banks said. "And three hots and a cot for as many as we can."

"Is this even legal?" Emma asked.

"Arresting people when they hit the road drunk or cause a public disturbance? Dawn sure thinks so." Gus started walking, a nervous twitter starting in the pit of his stomach. He'd had the same reservations as Emma at first, but like Banks had said, this was a bar fight now. Literally.

Emma took his hand. "I get it. Let's go see who we can save before the hammer falls. I can't say that a lot of those people don't deserve what's coming."

"That's what I'm talking about," Banks said.

They made their way to the Iron Works. When the door opened to allow more patrons anxious to partake of free beer, Kid Rock's gravelly warble filled the streets. The place was more packed than he'd ever seen it, even on the night before Thanksgiving and New Year's Eve. Gus was suddenly overcome with concern that if a fight broke out, the bar, filled wall-to-wall with imbibing bodies, would be destroyed.

Until he saw Don Runde's mischievous grin from behind the bar, flashing him a thumbs-up as he filled another beer mug. At least half a dozen were lined up at the bar.

"Don seems happy," Gus said.

"That's because he knows there's gonna be a fight,"

Banks said. "And if it doesn't start on its own, he'll be sure to light the match."

"Good Lord. I didn't know this many people lived in town," Emma said.

"They don't. Let's go look for friendlies."

# CHAPTER 18

It was difficult squeezing through the press of drunk or well-on-their-way-to-inebriated bodies. Gus held tight onto Emma's hand. All he wanted to do was make a quick circuit and get her the hell out of the bar.

Dawn James was sure going to have her hands and jail cells full tonight if everything went according to plan.

Dennis popped out from between a couple, both white people in their twenties with dirty dreads. "Heya Gus, Chris, Emma. Can you believe this?"

"Actually no," Gus said. He glanced over at the pool tables and saw there were no games being played. There wasn't enough room to maneuver around them. Dennis had smartly put the covering on the felt tops. People were using the pool tables as a resting spot for their beers. One had already spilled, amber suds forming a pond in the center of the table. "How much beer have you gone through?"

"Hell if I know. We got two kegs of some high-octane IPA. Don started serving it about ten minutes ago. We figure that should push things along."

Gus scanned the crowd, looking for any familiar faces. Dennis caught on, and said, "I manned the door for a while, quietly letting the regulars know it was better they drank at home tonight."

"I think you have your first victims," Emma said, pointing at two men stumbling out of the bar, most likely heading for their cars.

"First of many," Banks said eagerly. Gus could tell there was no way he was dragging his friend out of the bar. He was here until the bitter end.

"Y'all want a drink?" Dennis asked.

"I think it's better if we keep a clear head," Gus said.

"I'll go grab a beer from Don," Banks said, plowing through the crowd like a bull.

Dennis nodded his head toward a spot to the right of the long bar. "Those are the ones I'm worried most about. Been pounding them down for a couple of hours now. They look like they know the inside of a prison better than a house."

Gus spotted Sniper in the crowd of outlaws. He was surrounded by a raggedy bunch of men, presumably his entourage from The Pennsylvania. "It'll be nice if we can offer them some complimentary accommodations."

"I'm heading behind the bar," Dennis said. "It'll be a nice barrier when things get rough."

"I don't like the look of them," Emma said, staring at The Pennsylvania gang. "They're kind of scary."

"That's what the look is for," Gus answered, having to bend close to her ear to be heard over the revelry. "Stops most people from messing with them. Others see it as a challenge."

"Others such as yourself?"

"Perhaps."

"I don't want you getting yourself hurt tonight . . . or worse."

"I'll be fine. I'm not going to say their bark is worse than their bite, but I know how to handle angry dogs."

The atmosphere in the Iron Works was this side of euphoric as people drank as if it was their last night on Earth. Gus caught some men giving others a bit of side-eye as they were bumped into, or a gaze lingered a little too long on their woman. It wouldn't take long for folks to start flexing their beer muscles.

"I think it's time I walked you to your car," Gus said.

"And what if I refuse to leave?"

"I guess I'd have to put you over my shoulder."

Emma looked torn. She'd told him tales of dustups when she was younger, but she was a respected teacher now. It wouldn't look good to come to class with a black eye.

"Fine. But you need to call me every half hour, so I know you're okay."

Gus led the way out of the crowd and toward the door. "Yes, mother."

"I'm serious." She hopped to look over the heads of the crowd to her left. "Is that Sarah?"

Sarah Birch had just walked in. She gazed at the hard-drinking throng with bewilderment.

"We better hustle her out of here," Gus said, diverting their course.

When they got to Sarah, she said, "What in the name of all that's holy is going on in here tonight?"

"I forgot you were sick this week and didn't get the memo. Emma will explain."

They made it outside without incident, which was a huge relief for Gus. "Emma, can you drive Sarah home?"

"I only live four blocks away," Sarah protested. "But I think I saw Chris in there. You think he could be my escort?"

"I can make that happen, but not tonight. I just need you to trust me. Okay?"

Her eyes bounced between Gus and Emma for a moment, and then she sighed and straightened her back. "Okay. Emma, you can clue me in on the drive. If you talk fast or drive real slow."

"I can do that." Emma pulled Gus's collar and pulled him down for a kiss. "Good luck, soldier. And don't forget to call me."

"Promise. That's one fight I want to avoid tonight."

Emma and Sarah walked away, leaving Gus with his misgivings about the plan. There were just too many people. Things could go sideways real quick. Maybe it was best to have Dennis and Don announce that the kegs were tapped.

"Gus!"

He turned toward the bar and saw Banks waving him over. Gus ambled to the doors where more people were streaming in than out.

A man in raggedy jeans and a dirty T-shirt bumped into Gus, staggered to the sidewalk, threw up, and then pulled his car keys out of his pocket. Gus walked over to him and easily took the keys from his hand. "You're in no shape to drive, son."

"Who the hell are you? Give me my keys back." The man feebly swiped at Gus's hand and missed.

"Let him go," Banks said.

"He can't even see straight."

"That's the idea. Let Dawn's people grab him."

"He'll kill someone if he gets behind the wheel. I can't let him go."

The man tapped Gus on the shoulder. "I want my keys."

Gus tucked them in his pocket. "They'll be here when

you sober up. Take a nice long walk. Maybe sit a spell on that bench over there."

The punch came looping and slow. Gus took a step back and instinctively raised his fists. The drunk spun and hit the ground, knocking himself out. Gus and Banks picked him up by his arms and walked him to a bench.

"Problem solved," Banks said. Several people paused to watch them. "Now come inside. I think trouble's brewing."

Gus clipped the keys to the man's back belt loop so he couldn't get them and followed Banks inside. Some song Gus didn't recognize blared. A female rapper said things not spoken aloud in most company. "Since when did the Rundes have that kind of garbage on the jukebox?"

"It's hooked up to some cloud-based music server. We just never had someone here play that nonsense. Now check that out over there."

"By the way, I may have promised Sarah that you'd take her out one night and escort her home."

"Gee, thanks."

"I think it's time you settled down. I know Sarah would do everything she could to take care of you."

"Stick to biscuits and figuring out how to be a mayor."

Banks pointed at a mass of people by the pool tables. Three of the men, all of them looking in need of a haircut and shave, were wildly gesticulating as they spoke, or rather, shouted at one another. The women around them had to duck to keep from getting hit.

"It's all gonna start right there," Banks said. "Sooner or later, one of those drunk fools are going to connect with the wrong person. Second that happens, it'll be like dominoes."

Gus scratched his chin. There was an electric charge in the air that he could practically smell over the beer. Banks was usually right when it came to spotting trouble. When he wasn't causing it. He flicked a glance at the toughs from The Pennsylvania and was relieved they were keeping status quo . . . for the moment. Don and Dennis worked the bar like a couple of hummingbirds, though Don seemed to have spotted the potential brawl's ground zero. His eyes kept shifting toward them as he filled endless beer mugs.

"Now I wish I had a beer," Gus said.

"It's not too late."

That's when one of the men by the pool tables lifted his elbow right into the chin of a woman holding hands with a much larger gentleman. Her hands flew to her nose. The gentleman, if he truly was one, grabbed the drunk by the collar. The drunk's two friends rushed to his defense. There was blood seeping from between the woman's fingers.

The first punch got the drunk square between the eyes. He staggered but didn't fall, lashing out with a wild right that hit his buddy instead.

Banks nudged Gus. "See. I told you!"

A full-on fight broke out between the three drunks and the man with the wounded woman. As they pulled back to punch or missed one another, they managed to clip everyone around them. Now the circumference of the fight was in expansion mode. Men and women shouted, mostly egging on the combatants.

Gus and Banks were rocked on their heels as the crowd tried to shove away from the brawlers. Don Runde jumped on top of the bar, leaping off of it like a wrestler with a wild gleam in his eyes. He landed shy of the fight but plowed through everyone in his way. As people scattered, they bumped into others, some who took offense and started lashing out.

"Oh boy," Banks said. "Don's in. Things are about to get nuts."

Dennis stayed behind the bar and was on the phone, hopefully calling Dawn James.

In the time it took to holler that supper was on the table, it seemed that every man was in the fight. And quite a few women, too. The jukebox went silent as a body knocked it sideways. The sound of shattering glass was everywhere. A chair flew over the crowd.

*What the hell have we done?* Gus thought.

Someone took a wild swipe at Banks. He missed. Banks hit him with a sharp jab to the ribs and he folded like an omelet.

A pair of men attempted to jump over the bar. Dennis thwacked them with the Louisville Slugger he kept under the bar.

Some folks made for the doors, hands over their heads to protect themselves from projectiles.

Gus felt an arm wrap around his neck. He leaned back and felt his head connect with a face. When he spun around, a kid who had to be just barely of legal age to drink stared back at him with glazed eyes. He was pulled in by the swirling melee of bodies.

"Coming up behind you," Banks said. "We better watch each other's backs."

They did so by standing back to back, fending off all comers . . . and there were plenty. Gus did his best to push them away while Banks made sure he'd have to ice his knuckles when this was over.

Where the hell were the police? If this kept up much longer, the Iron Works was going to be demolished.

"Look, it's the mayor!"

Sniper's throaty roar laced with sarcasm rode herd over the madness. He was flanked by a pair of men with bloody faces. They looked as if they had just crawled out from under a pile of thrashing bodies, which they probably had.

"Trouble is headed our way," Gus barked to Banks. A beer mug flew past Gus, just missing his face. It fortunately hit the wall and not someone else.

"This should be fun," Banks said. "I owe him one."

Sniper wore a leather jacket with the sleeves torn off. He locked onto Gus like a bull at a red cape. His two pilot fish charged first. They came at them like wild animals, one of them actually roaring. There was fine white powder under his nose.

A stray barstool caught the one on the left on the side of his head.

That was one down.

The other didn't even see his buddy was knocked out.

He charged at Gus and Banks with his right arm cocked back.

"Knees," Gus said.

Just before he could let his punch loose, Gus and Banks stomped his right knee with the heels of their boots. That took wind out of his sails. He lay on the ground cradling his knee and trying to avoid getting stomped on by the brawlers around them.

Sniper pointed at Gus.

"I think he wants you," Banks said.

"Always nice to feel wanted."

Sniper was just as undisciplined as his friends. Gus bet seeing Sniper in all his scary regalia and wild eyes was enough to finish most fights before they started.

What Sniper didn't know was that Banks and Gus had seen far worse in the Middle East.

Sniper pulled his punch at the last second and bent low, tackling Gus to the floor. The breath exploded from Gus's lungs. He threw a series of rabbit punches at Sniper's kidneys, followed by a headbutt into his nose. Blood sprayed Gus's face.

Sniper snarled. "You mother . . ."

Banks hit him in the temple with a hard right. Sniper slid off of Gus.

Sniper was far from down. He kicked at Banks, catching him in the calf. Gus got back to his feet and was elbowed in the skull, just behind his ear, by someone fighting next to him. He saw stars for a moment, which was all Sniper needed to recover and deliver a hammering blow to his solar plexus.

Gus doubled over, searching for his breath yet again. Out of the corner of his eye, he saw Banks was busy with one of Sniper's goons. The goon wasn't faring too well.

Sniper flexed his fingers, goading Gus to come at him. "Let's see what you got, cowboy."

After getting small sips of air, Gus ran the back of his hand against his jaw, and said, "I'm not a . . . cowboy. Just a small . . . town redneck that's about to . . . kick your ass."

He tottered on his heels and blinked hard, as if trying to shake the cobwebs out of his brain. Gus hoped the ruse would telegraph to Sniper that the fight was mostly out of him.

Sure enough, it worked. Sniper came at him, looking to land a whopper of a roundhouse. Gus caught his arm and used Sniper's momentum to flip him over. As soon as he hit the deck, Gus showered him with body blows. Back in the military, when he used to box to let off steam, his fellow soldiers had nicknamed him Bricks on account of his heavy hands. His hands lived up to their name as he walloped Sniper. When Sniper's eyes rolled up a bit as he struggled to breathe, Gus finished him off with an upper-cut to his jaw.

Sitting back on his heels to catch his breath, Gus heard the sirens and saw the red-and-blue glow of lights filtering in through the window.

"I was just coming to help," Don Runde said. He came toting a man in a headlock.

"I think you've had enough fun for tonight."

At the sound of the police, most of the fighting stopped and people tried to scatter. They were blocked at the exit by a phalanx of police officers.

Banks dropped Sniper's goon. He collapsed in a heap. "We have to do this again."

Gus flexed his hands and hoped he had enough ice in the freezer back home to get the swelling down.

He had to admit, a part of him felt good. When he looked around at the destruction of the Iron Works, he felt guilty.

"In your dreams," Gus said, dusting himself off.

They watched the police zip-tie as many people as they could. Dawn James approached them, clearly enjoying the moment.

"I might have to commandeer the B and B to hold all these folks," she said.

"You're a dead man."

All eyes turned to Sniper. His face was a bloody mess and several of his front teeth had chipped. He wouldn't take his eyes off of Gus, even as James personally cuffed him.

"I'm gonna come for you. And you ain't gonna have your friends around to save you," he said, pointing a stubby finger at Gus.

James shoved him forward so one of her men could take him out of the bar and into a waiting squad car. Sniper glared at Gus all the way out the door. If a look of hate was a weapon, Gus would have been vaporized.

"Looks like we just pissed in Stranger's Corn Flakes," James said.

"We did what we had to do," Gus said, with a note of resignation. Unfortunately, he was in a position to win at all costs. He just hoped he could cover the cost of the damage to the Iron Works.

# CHAPTER 19

The plan at the bar had worked. Quite a few of the people Dawn's force had rounded up had warrants for other offenses large and small in other states. Most of the men and women in the cells in Springerville and the neighboring counties were filled with what they learned were wealthy kids looking to make mommy and daddy angry. It was no shock to Gus. He'd watched what had been going on in the country with a close eye and saw the type of people filling protests and encampments across America. At the time, it made him wish they'd reinstate the mandatory draft so these wayward children could be brought back into the fold of reality.

It was a lost generation.

Gus chuckled as he fiddled with his tie.

Wasn't that how Gertrude Stein had described Ernest Hemingway's contemporaries?

What was old was new, and things just went on in an endless circle, lessons never learned, just repeated.

"You almost ready?" Emma called from the living room.

"Just figuring out the intricacies of this tie," he replied, undoing his failed knot and trying again.

Emma came storming up the stairs. She wore a new dress and looked like a movie star. Just seeing her took Gus's breath away. "Here, let me help you."

He dropped the tie. "Be my guest."

Her perfume filled the air between them as she got his tie in presentable order. What he wanted to do was skip the formalities and spend the rest of the day with her in the house.

She patted his chest. "There. You look pretty darn handsome, Mr. Fuller."

Gus pulled her close and kissed her. "I think I look like I'm outkicking my coverage next to you."

She grabbed his hands and kissed his red and swollen knuckles. "I'm a sucker for tough guys."

"They don't look so good, do they?"

"They look like they belong to a man who will do what it takes to save our town."

"Is that why people have been leaving twice what they owe at the diner?"

"Just a small token of appreciation."

He plucked his Stetson from the bedpost and squared it on his head.

"I plan to give all that extra cash to Don and Dennis."

Emma kissed him. "God, I love you." She brushed some lint from his sport coat. "You ready to make nice and show people what they're voting for today?"

"Yes, ma'am."

They were headed for the luncheonette where everything was free for the day. Gus had agreed to relinquish his spatula to Sarah Birch and Ashley Early, who was coming out in public for the first time since she'd been attacked. Randy would be there as well. He'd been laying low lately, spending his time taking care of his wife and parents. It filled Gus's heart when Randy and Ashley called him and said they wanted to take the reins for the day.

Gus couldn't find a place to park for the first time ever. It seemed every tried-and-true citizen of Springerville was up and out. Some applauded when Gus and Emma got out of his Jeep several blocks from his place. He spotted a lot of "I Voted" stickers on display.

"You got this, Gus!" Abner Aberdine cheered when Gus helped Emma out of the Jeep. "I got up at the crack of dawn and waited outside the school to vote. And I wasn't alone."

Gus shook his hand and thanked him. "If you're hungry, there's pancakes waiting for you."

Abner rubbed his belly. "Already had my fill. You might want to hire that pretty girl when you win, since you won't have as much time to run the luncheonette."

Gus grinned and tipped his hat. He'd never thought of how much of his time being mayor would take up.

*Guess I might have to take on some help. It'd be nice to give Ashley a chance to fill all these bellies,* he thought. He also wanted to do a little taste test to see just how good her pancakes were. Maybe he could learn a thing or two.

As he and Emma walked up the block, folks stopped to shake his hand and tell him how they supported him.

"You got this," Emma whispered to him.

"Don't go counting your chickens," he warned her.

"I'm counting chickens, eggs, and chicks," she said, bursting with confidence.

They walked hand in hand into the luncheonette. It was packed to the rafters. The savory aroma of pancakes and hot maple syrup got his stomach grumbling. The place erupted in applause and backslaps the second they walked in the door.

Gus felt his cheeks and the back of his neck grow hot.

He shook a lot of hands and hugged his fair share of women and men. Slowly, he made his way to the counter. Sarah Birch was busy refilling cups of coffee while Ashley, wearing a red bandana to keep her hair back, worked the griddle that was filled with rising pancakes. Randy hustled behind her, mixing the batter under her rushed instructions.

"Got a few of the new people in here today," Sarah said with a hot coffeepot in her hand. "Said they voted for you."

"Is that so?"

"Yep. Guess you're more charming than you think," she said with a wink.

He patted her shoulder. "My mother always did say I had charisma. She also would say I had a bit of the devil in me, too."

Emma waltzed amid the crowd, pressing the flesh and simply being radiant.

"Hey, Ashley," Gus said,

She looked up from the griddle. There was flour in her hair. "Hiya, Gus! I never thought there were so many mouths to feed."

"Nothing slows down the appetite of Springerville," he said with a wide grin. "Word is, your pancakes are top-notch."

She flipped a stack and dropped them on a plate. "I think people are just being nice."

He went behind the counter and gave her a fist bump. "This is no place for modesty. Thanks again for feeding the masses. We should talk when this is all said and done."

There was a look in her eyes that reminded him that she'd been to hell and back. The wide-eyed girl from Chicago was gone. But at least she looked as if she was enjoying what she was doing right now. "If I make it through today."

"You will." He called over to Randy who was grabbing a carton of eggs from the cold case. "Looks like you're making a pretty good sous-chef."

Randy put the eggs on the counter. "I don't even know what that is. I just do what Ash tells me."

"That's what makes for a happy marriage."

Gus turned when he heard a chorus of boos.

*I should have guessed*, Gus thought.

Braden Stranger was dressed in a suit that Gus assumed would have cost him a year's salary to buy. Stranger smiled at the crowd and raised his hands. "I understand, I'm in enemy territory. Gus, can you spare a moment to talk outside?"

Gus took a list out of his shirt pocket and passed it over to Randy. "Can you and Ash prepare these in to-go containers. Thought I'd spend the day delivering food to the folks who can't get out and about. Beats sitting around waiting for news."

Randy grabbed the slip of paper and tacked it to the corkboard wall. "You got it."

"Just call me when it's ready." Gus found Emma within the throng. She gave a slight nod, and he could see in her eyes that she wanted to know if he needed her to tag along. He shook his head and addressed his patrons. "Eat up, everyone. And let's be a little more hospitable to our guest here."

He stopped beside Stranger and swept his hand toward the door. "After you."

You could have heard a pin drop in the luncheonette as Gus walked out. "We should probably take a walk," he said.

Stranger turned to the faces gathered at the door and new window. "I think you're right."

The sun was out, and the heat had given the town a break. There were a few fat clouds in the sky that brought almost chilly moments of shade. The smell of pancakes followed them down the street. A slight gust of wind wound down the alley between two buildings. Gus secured his Stetson to his head.

"That was some pretty dirty pool you played at the Iron Works," Stranger said.

"I've never been much of a pool player."

Stranger looked down at Gus's bruised hands. "So that was just another night in Shitkicker, USA?"

Gus squinted at the library two blocks down. Mrs. Donovan, the head librarian, was outside handing out what looked to be flyers. He remembered getting his first library card, printed on a square of cardboard, from Mrs. Donovan when he was in fourth grade. It looked like the library would have to run itself this morning.

"I would say it was a bit more rambunctious than usual. I was surprised I didn't see you. There appeared to be quite a few of your . . . constituents on hand. Then again, no sense preaching to the choir, I guess."

They stopped at the corner. Stranger stuffed his hands in his pockets. The sunlight glinted off his capped teeth. "It was a nice try, Gus. You don't have enough jail space to even the odds, my friend. There are big plans for Springerville. Plans that you and your pals can't stop. Hell, this is just a small piece of a much bigger pie. You should have stuck to *making* pies. When this is over, maybe you can sell them online from your home. Because I already have plans for the street your little luncheonette is on, and they don't include biscuits and gravy."

What Gus wanted to do was wring the smug slimebag's

neck. Instead, he returned the phony smile. "I've heard your plans. Speaking of pie, I think you might have bitten off more than you can chew this time. This kind of nonsense works in big cities run by liberals and progressives. Feel free to find a safe haven when this is over and try again."

"You think you're only running against me?" Stranger chuckled. "This isn't David and Goliath. Back then, David only had to face one man. You're up against something you can't begin to comprehend."

Gus resumed walking. After a few steps, Stranger hurried to catch up. Gus said, "I think I have a pretty good idea of who you and your backers are. Oh, I may not have names, but I understand the mold you all come from. You may be rich, but I'll bet someone, or some group that makes you look like a street beggar, has you on their puppet strings. You think they're on your side and you share a vision, but they'll jerk you around any way they like, just like they'd impose their will on this town. If progress means selling your soul for greed and some twisted political ideal, it can go play in traffic."

Stranger never once looked his way as Gus spoke. The man's gaze was somewhere else. Maybe in one of the boardrooms where this whole cockamamie plan had been drawn up.

"But there's always a silver lining," Gus continued. "If and when you lose here, you can just pick up and go to the next place, fully financed by your puppet masters. Or maybe they'll cut you free. If that happens, I'm sure you'll land as a CEO of some company that does no public good but engages in plenty of virtue signaling to hide its sins."

"You think you've got it all figured out, don't you?"

"No, but I think you think you do. Or did. We'll see what happens at the end of the day."

They stopped again and Gus almost snickered when he saw the irritation in Stranger's face.

"You better go back to your greasy spoon and enjoy it while you can."

"I plan to enjoy it for a long time."

The edges of Stranger's lips ticked up in a disturbing smile. "Whatever happens today, this town will belong to me."

"Is that so?"

"If I were you, I'd pray that I simply lose at the polls. I don't think you'll like the alterative."

Gus tensed. "Are you threatening me?"

Stranger shook his head. "I never make threats. Only promises. You seem like a good guy. And that's your major flaw. I'm not a good guy. And neither are the people I'm working with. We've prepared for you, Gus. Oh, we've prepared for you." He stuck out his hand. Gus looked down at it as if he were offering a fresh dog turd. "Well, I'm off to vote. Enjoy your little pancake party."

Stranger turned and walked back toward the center of town.

Mrs. Donovan spotted Gus and waved to him. He did his best to force a smile, but inside, he was in turmoil.

What in the blue hell was that all about?

They'd prepared for him?

There was a click-clack of heels behind him. He spun around and saw Emma with her brow creased in concern. "Everything okay?"

Gus shook off his concern. "He was just wishing me good luck."

"I'll bet." She obviously didn't believe him.

"Well, in his own way."

"Uh-huh. Randy and Ash have your deliveries ready. You want to go make some house calls?"

He slipped his arm around her waist. "Yep. I need to keep busy today."

They walked back to the luncheonette. Cars honked when they spotted him, and he waved. He didn't see many locusts out and about today. That worried him, too. It felt as if a trap had been set around Springerville. Gus couldn't stop wondering what was going to be the thing that sprang it into action.

# CHAPTER 20

The Iron Works became *Gus Fuller for Mayor* headquarters at around four. Gus noticed far fewer barstools and tables. Don and Dennis had done a good job cleaning up the mess, but evidence of the melee was everywhere, from chunks taken out of the walls to the almost empty pool cue racks.

"It's the man of the hour," Don said. He had a bandage across the bridge of his nose and a black eye.

Banks was with Don at the bar, along with Ron and Mike and Wally Sturgis. Wally had lost some weight and was pale, but it was good to see him up and out of his house.

"Should you be drinking?" Gus asked Wally, tilting his head toward the glass in the man's hand.

Wally chuckled. "Swapped out whiskey for cola. At least for now. Not a chance I'm going to give it up for good."

"You want something stronger than Mr. Pibb?" Don asked Gus.

"Mr. Pibb sounds just right."

Banks grabbed two barstools and slid them next to

him. Emma and Gus took a seat and Emma said, "Unlike the boys, I'll have some Jack with my Coke."

"There's a lot of buzz out there," Ron said.

"Good buzz?" Gus asked.

"Hell yeah. People have been impressed with the way you handle things. More than a few locusts I've talked to said you won them over."

"I've been hearing the same thing," Mike said. He was uncovering a tray of potato salad. It was his specialty. It looked like he'd made enough to feed an army. The bar was closed to the public for the night. Gus wondered how many people Emma and Banks had actually invited over to wait for the results.

Gus turned to his best friend. "You're awfully quiet."

Banks took a pull from his beer. "I talked to Shane over at The Pennsylvania. He said that everyone staying there left first thing in the morning and went straight to the school to vote. I think their plan was to hang around and intimidate people from going inside. Luckily, Dawn was one step ahead of them and had her people stationed around the school."

"I noticed that," Gus said.

"I never saw so many people come out to vote before," Banks said. "Before I got here, I swung by the school and saw a line out the door. Can you believe such a thing? I didn't see too many friendlies on that line."

Dennis came out from the back room with a remote control in his hand. "What I can't believe is that none of our TVs got damaged on Saturday. Let's see if there's any update." He changed the channel to the local news station. It was still rebroadcasting the news at noon. When the interview Gus had done earlier that day popped on screen, he had to turn away.

"You did such a good job," Emma said as she rubbed his back.

"Wake me when this part's over. I have a face made for radio."

"If you did, I wouldn't be with you."

Gus looked at her with mild shock and amusement.

"That's right. We can be superficial, too," Emma said.

Wally piped up. "It'll be a while before we hear anything of substance. Right around five, they'll go live and give a lot of anecdotal observations. It's not like we have exit polling here. So, I suggest until then, we tuck into some of this fine food and just try to forget everything for a while. I know how tense this day can be, son. Take a breather. You earned it."

Gus waved at Sarah Birch when she walked in the door and felt the knot of tension in his shoulders.

It wasn't waiting for the results so much that wound him up. It was wondering what Stranger's contingency plans were, should Gus win.

*We've prepared for you.*

More of Gus's friends came to the bar over the next hour, everyone bringing a platter of food or a cake holder. The potluck table looked like a Thanksgiving feast on steroids by the time all was said and done. At Emma's urging, Gus had a couple of whiskeys and felt his nerves settle down some, but not enough to wipe away the anticipation and unease that ran up and down his spine.

"Maybe we should have just gone out fishing," Gus said to Banks at one point.

"I'm all for it now, but I think Emma would skin you alive."

"I just don't like all this waiting."

"We spent a lot of time hurrying up and waiting in the desert. Don't forget your roots," Banks said jokingly.

"I was going to say the end of this waiting isn't as potentially deadly as it was back in Afghanistan, but I think that might be underestimating what's going on here."

Banks poked his chest with his beer bottle. "You have a lot of cleaning up to do when you win, buddy. Don't think for a moment you have to do it all on your own. Just look around. There's no shortage of people willing to lend a hand."

There must have been fifty people in the bar. They'd gone through the food and dessert and now had gathered in clusters, watching the news. The tension in the Iron Works was palpable.

Gus looked around for Emma. She was talking with Ashley Early who had swapped out her apron and bandana for a nice skirt and flowery top. He didn't want Emma to hear what he had to tell Banks. "Stranger came to see me today."

"I heard. A little birdie told me it looked like you wanted to pop his fool head off."

"If only. He did say something that's been rolling nonstop through my head." Gus spilled the beans.

Banks took it in, sipped his beer, and said, "He's playing mind games. Don't let him mess with you."

"Look, I know the man is a liar. I wouldn't trust him to ask the time. But when he said that, I could see plain as day that he was telling the truth. No matter what happens tonight, I'm going to be on high alert."

"Maybe we should call a few of our buddies and talk to them about a little security detail tomorrow."

"That would be too straightforward. No, whatever

Stranger and his cronies have in mind will be something we can't fight with fists."

"Or more."

"Or more."

Gus spotted Emma walking toward them. "Guess we just need to wait and see."

Banks clapped him on the back. "That we will. Until then, let's see if we can make this an all-night party."

Gus spent the next two hours making small talk with everyone and snacking on Sarah Birch's blueberry pie, which was this side of heavenly.

He was standing near the front door when it opened and someone he didn't recognize walked inside. He had longish hair tied in a ponytail and wore cargo shorts with sandals. Someone else was with him, but Gus couldn't make them out because they stood off to the man's left, just outside the door.

Randy had been keeping an eye on the door. "Sorry, we're closed for a private party."

"You serious?"

"Yep. Waiting for election results. It'll be open as usual tomorrow."

Someone spoke behind the man. He turned, and asked, "Yeah, what about her?"

Gus saw Ashley, who was standing beside her husband, go pale as a bedsheet. Her eyes went wide, and she staggered back a step. For a second, Gus worried she was about to pass out. He excused himself from talking with Wally and his assistant Carolyn and made a beeline for Ashley.

When he got there, she said, pointing, "It's him."

Randy's head swiveled between Ashley and the man at the door. "Ash?"

"He was one of them," she said, steadying herself. "I'd know that voice anywhere."

The man with the long hair spun and tried to get out of the bar, but the person who was with him blocked his quick exit. Randy pounced on him, driving him to the floor. Gus got to the door, but whoever had been there was sprinting across the parking lot and into the darkness.

When the man tried to wriggle out from underneath Randy, Ashley drove a knee into his back and landed a fierce right hook at his cheek.

The commotion caught everyone's attention.

"What's going on here?" Don said, making his way toward them.

Ashley drove her knee deeper into the man's back. "He's one of the men who . . . who attacked me!"

Now everyone was standing around. Gus made a motion to pull Ashley away, but one savage look from her had him standing his ground.

"Are you sure?" Randy asked her as the crowd pushed closer.

"I hear that voice all day, every day." She punched him again.

Gus was alarmed by the burst of fire in Randy's eyes. Randy nodded at Ashley, and they pulled the man up.

"You s.o.b.!" Randy snarled a split second before doubling the man over. Ashley kept him from hitting the floor by driving her knee into his chin. Randy spun him like he was a child's doll, one with most of the stuffing taken out of it, and hurled him onto a pool table. "You wanna know how it felt? Huh?"

Randy snatched a pool cue from the holder on the wall.

Gus had to stop him. If he didn't, Randy, Ashley, or the both of them would kill the man.

"Randy, no!" Gus shouted.

Randy paused just long enough for Gus to grab the pool cue from his grip. Ashley leapt toward the pool table, but Don caught her midair by her waist and held onto her as she struggled like a pissed off catfish. She screamed incoherently, but the message was clear. She wanted to take out all of her rage and pain on the man on the pool table.

Banks came and helped Gus keep Randy at bay.

The man on the pool table was out like a light. Dennis, Ron, and Mike held his arms and legs down anyway while Dennis asked for someone to call the police.

"Just give me a minute with him," Randy said as he tried to shake Gus and Banks off. He was close to succeeding.

"So you can go to jail and leave your wife alone?" Gus whispered in his ear. "Settle down, son. We have him. Let's use him to find the rest and stick them all in a deep, dark hole."

Ashley's screams turned to cries as Emma and several other women gathered around her, trying to calm her down. Don still kept her in his beefy arm.

Two patrolmen burst into the bar a couple of minutes later. There was a lot of frantic chatter as too many people tried to explain what happened. Even with the police on hand, Randy still tried to get his hands on the unconscious man.

Sweat flowed down Gus's face. It was like trying to rein in a charging bull. He needed the police to cuff the man and get him the hell out of the bar.

As the police tried to make some sense of the chaos, a lone voice rode herd over the commotion.

"Gus won!"

All heads turned to Aileen Wuhrer, who had been smart enough to stay away from the fray, keeping her eyes on the big-screen television. She was beaming. "Thank the Lord! Gus, you're our new mayor!"

# CHAPTER 21

Braden Stranger chose to be alone while he waited for the election results. Roger had asked if he wanted company, but he'd told his assistant to get some rest and be on standby, no matter how things shook out.

The crawl at the bottom of the screen said:

"GUS FULLER – 62%, BRADEN STRANGER – 35%.
FULLER IS PROJECTED WINNER
OF SPRINGERVILLE MAYORAL RACE."

Stranger threw his glass of Macallan 25 against the wall. The high-priced whiskey splashed everywhere. Drops of it cascaded down the wall-mounted television.

He picked up his phone, made to dial, then put it down.

There was no need to make any calls. Anyone who was of any importance in this endeavor already knew. No sense being the town crier.

For a moment, he considered going out to his Zen garden and meditating. There would be calls and texts coming his way, and he needed to be in a proper headspace.

Or, better yet, he could pour himself another whiskey. Yes, that was a better plan of action.

As three fingers worth of Macallan splashed into a fresh glass, he examined the brown stain on his white wall and carpet. Let the cleaning woman take care of it tomorrow. If the stains were stubborn, he could always hire a painter to touch up the wall and have the carpet replaced. Even though he'd lost, he was far from done with Springerville. This house still had to be home to him for some time.

He sank into his couch and crunched the numbers in his head. Even after Fuller's little stunt at the bar, the percentages didn't add up. They were close to fifty-fifty before that. He may have shaved a few points off by throwing those drunken idiots in jail, but it wasn't enough for him to get over sixty percent of the vote.

*Face it, you had traitors in your midst.*

Stranger gripped the crystal glass until his knuckles turned white.

His phone buzzed. It was a text from his ex-wife.

*Saw the news. Good thing to know there are still people with common sense. Oh, sorry for your loss.*

There were a great many replies circling around his head. Instead, he tossed the phone onto the cushion next to him. *No sense getting involved with that woman*, he thought. If anyone could push his buttons, it was Susan. His nonresponse would irritate her more than anything he could text.

When the phone buzzed again, he almost ignored it, figuring it was Susan getting another dig in.

He was glad he picked it up.

*We need to talk.*

For a brief moment, his heart fluttered. He'd never once had a good conversation that started with We Need To Talk! He knew the phrase well. He'd used it to unnerve underlings at work or women in his life more times than he could count.

Rather than waiting and letting his nerves get the better of him, he dialed the number right away. As soon as the other end picked up, he said, "Not exactly what we were hoping for."

"That's one way of putting it."

Stranger ground his teeth. He could feel a dressing down coming. His ego made him believe that he was too smart and successful for such a thing. But his brain reminded him that the man he was talking to could buy and sell him a hundred times over without needing to look at his bank account.

"No matter, we'll make this work to our advantage. Don't make any plans to leave town."

"That was never my intention," Stranger said.

"Set aside your afternoon tomorrow for a debrief. In the morning, you are to give no comment to any media that reach out to you. You will also not concede. They may think they've won, but the worst is yet to come. The problem with small people is that they can't see the bigger picture. They revel in a short win but are unaware of the long game. There's still plenty of work to do, Braden. You may not be mayor, but you have much work ahead of you."

Stranger swallowed his whiskey. "I understand. These Southern nuts are a little tougher to crack than I'd thought."

"Not to mention a good many of the transplants that appear to find you . . . *unsuitable* to run Mayberry. We'll take these lessons learned so the same mistakes are not repeated. Until then, we've shifted to plan B."

This was news to Stranger. He'd never been told of an alternate plan. "What would that be?"

"That would be for me to know. Let's just say that trust is an enormous commodity in this world. Gaining it, as well as degrading it, are filled with tremendous power. Even when used to destroy, that only paves the way to rebuild . . . correctly. Do you understand?"

After pulling the phone away from his face to take a deep breath, Stranger coolly replied, "I understand."

"Good. I'm going to send something to you tonight. We'll call this our fresh start and talk more about it tomorrow. Consider it the first shot across Mr. Fuller's bow. We'll map out the next steps from there. There is a contingent of, let's say, *fresh blood* that is being gathered. I'd suggest you try your best to get a good night's sleep, Braden. Your real work is about to begin."

The line disconnected before Stranger could reply.

He turned the phone off. No other calls of more important meaning would be coming tonight. Sleep would not come easy. He refilled his glass and rewatched the news, seething when the crawl announced Gus Fuller the winner.

Things were never going to be easy down here. He knew that from the start.

But Gus Fuller and his redneck disciples were in for one hell of a ride now.

"They'll wish they'd elected me," he said, toasting the television.

As angry as he was, he couldn't help the slight tremor in his hand as he brought the glass to his lips.

# CHAPTER 22

The fact that he was going to officially be the mayor of his hometown never entered Gus's mind as he woke up early as usual, prepared everything for breakfast, and opened his door to Chief of Police Dawn James.

"Congratulations, Gus," she said, shaking his hand with a wide smile.

"Thanks. Not sure it's set in yet. How are things with that fella we caught?"

More like the Earlys pummeled.

"That's what I came to tell you." She took a seat at the counter. "That and have some waffles with strawberries. The good news is that he's singing like a little canary. His name's Jack Meyer, a petty thief from Philadelphia. He named all three of the other assailants. Unfortunately, only one is still here. The other two have presumably crawled back to some sewer in Philly. We picked up his accomplice last night and are working with Philly PD to get the other two. Thankfully, Ash allowed the doctor in the ER to administer a sexual assault evidence kit. Believe it or not, not all victims of assault do. At that moment, they're too traumatized. What we gathered that night should be enough to put them away for some time."

Gus had sauntered into the kitchen and was pouring batter into the waffle maker. "Amen to that. I'm sorry this had to happen to Ashley, but I hope this can give her some kind of closure. You should have seen her face when she realized he was one of the people who had attacked her and Randy. I'll never forget it." He slid a cup of hot coffee her way and she blew on it.

"Don't quote me on this, but I'm glad they were able to get a few shots in. Hope it helps the healing process."

The door opened and Mike and Ron took their seats with a nod toward Dawn.

"They get the right guy?" Ron asked.

"I was just telling Gus here that they did. We have two now. Hope to get all four soon."

"God does answer prayers," Mike said. He looked very tired and kept rubbing his eyes.

Gus got to work whipping up Ron and Mike's usual while plating Dawn's steaming hot waffle and sprinkling it with some of Maddie Jackson's strawberries. It came with a side of hot maple syrup. "Hard to believe it was just two days ago. Feels like a few hours ago at times, and weeks at others," Gus said.

Before James took a bite, she said, "There's something else I need to tell you. Since election night, petty crime is getting worse. Mostly stuff like vandalism and shoplifting. But I can't stop feeling as if this is all just a sampling of something bigger to come."

"That should slow down some when the folks who Stranger brought down here for the election go back to wherever they came from," Gus said. "And then we find a way to take care of the rest."

"I drove by The Pennsylvania and spoke to Shane. So far, no one has left. Same with the other properties that were mysteriously purchased over the past few months.

There's something else going on at The Pennsylvania, but Shane has been too squirrely to come right out and say it. I'm going to send a steady patrol out there to keep an eye on things."

"If you're looking for a powder keg, that's the place," Gus said.

James took a bite of her waffle and spoke with her mouth full. "My intuition is getting pretty itchy, and I can't scratch it away."

Outside the luncheonette, the street was bathed in the first pink rays of the sun. It was hard to believe there was a dark underbelly to Springerville. Gus hoped James's intuition was wrong.

Deep down, he felt it too. Stranger's threat had not been an idle one.

Speaking of which.

"Any sign of Stranger?" Gus asked.

"He hasn't reached out to you yet?" James replied.

"Not a word."

"Guess they don't teach folks about how to lose gracefully up in New York."

"Guess not."

He should have been feeling good about James rounding up the animals who had assaulted Ashley and Randy, but ever since election night, he'd been waiting for the other shoe to drop. Maybe he should pay Stranger a visit. There'd be no need for phony politeness now.

More of his morning regulars came streaming in and busy hands silenced his busy mind for a spell. Dawn James shook his hand before she left, congratulating him again and telling him they should set up a meeting soon to discuss their plans to clean up the town.

When the lull between breakfast and lunch came, Gus called Banks.

"What are you doing around two?"

He heard the thrum of a compressor in the background. "If possible, getting my hands even greasier. I have to replace the gasket around Ines Rosalez's oil pan."

"You think you could take a quick break?"

"What's going on?" Banks asked.

"I was thinking of dropping in on Stranger."

"I'm in. Not gonna miss that."

"Great. I'll swing by your shop after I close up here."

"Should I stop home to, you know, pick anything up?"

Gus knew exactly what he was inferring. "I don't see this as a showdown in the town square. I just don't trust him and would rather have a witness."

"Okay. Fine." There was disappointment in Banks's voice. "Who knows what this guy is up to."

"See you at two."

Gus felt better knowing he was going to take some action. He hated sitting back and waiting for things to happen.

Lunch came and went, and Gus kept busy right until he took his flag in and locked the door. A car alarm whined down the street. He waited until someone popped out of the barbershop to turn it off.

When he pulled up to the bay doors of the repair shop, Banks came out in his stained overalls wiping a large wrench relatively clean with a greasy cloth.

"You plan on bringing that wrench?"

Banks tossed it on a table and pulled the door shut. He made two fists and pounded his chest. "These are the only tools I need, brother."

Gus laughed. It felt good to laugh. He hadn't even smiled so much since his win, something that concerned Emma. He decided at that moment that he best tell her what Stranger had said. "Hop in."

The drive to Stranger's house only took five minutes. This time around, Gus stopped his Jeep well short of the turn to the driveway. A trio of motorcycles were parked at the head of the driveway as a kind of roadblock.

"Looks like he doesn't want visitors," Banks said.

"It appears he has a new security detail."

"Well, that Roger guy didn't look like he could stop a ten-year-old."

"Those bikes look familiar?"

Banks leaned forward and squinted. "Yep. They were at The Pennsylvania."

"I'll bet you a case of beer, one of them belongs to our pal, Sniper."

"I'll pass on that bet. So, what do you want to do now?"

"Same as I did before. Just need to do a little more walking."

He locked his Jeep and they trudged to the driveway. Gus kept his eyes and ears pealed, sure that the owners of the motorcycle blockade were close.

"Maybe they stopped by for afternoon tea," Banks said as they got closer.

"Don't forget the biscuits."

As Gus and Banks angled past the motorcycles, sure enough, two burly men wearing battered leather jackets appeared to spring up from nowhere. They must have been laying low, waiting for someone to dare pay a visit to Stranger.

"This is private property," the one with the long beard and blue bandana on his head said. He wore leather gloves with holes around the knuckles. The other one, a mite shorter with a jean jacket with the sleeves cut off and his long hair tied in a ponytail, had his hands in his pockets, which concerned Gus more than the sneering tough guy.

Banks must have shared his misgiving, because he stayed silent and put all his attention on jean jacket.

"We just wanted to pay a quick visit with Mr. Stranger. I hadn't seen or heard from him since the election."

"I know who you are," the bearded one said.

"That puts me at a disadvantage then. You wouldn't mind us passing by to ring the bell, would you?"

"I would." He flexed his fingers, the leather of his gloves creaking.

Gus wasn't ready to give up. "Well, maybe one of you could let him know I'm here then."

The bearded man shook his head. "He don't want to see you."

"You know that for sure?"

"I do."

Gus put his hands on his hips, flicked a glance at the quiet one, then called out, "Stranger! It's Gus Fuller! I just want to talk. Your, ah, security guards won't let me through!"

The bearded guy took two steps toward Gus. "I said he don't wanna see you."

Gus refused to give the man any ground. "I'd prefer to hear that from Stranger himself." He looked over the man's shoulder to see if there was any activity by the house.

"Why don't you just get the hell outta here before you get hurt?"

Gus called out to Stranger again.

The bearded guy nodded toward jean jacket. Suddenly, his hand shot out of his pocket, and in it was a pistol.

Banks also had his hand in his pocket. He brandished a hefty wrench and brought it down on the man's wrist with a sickening crunch of bone quicker than a hummingbird's heartbeat. The man and the gun both fell to the ground.

The bearded man froze for a moment in shock. Gus used that moment to punch him in the throat. His hands flew to his neck as he struggled to breathe, toppling onto his back like a felled tree.

When jean jacket went for the gun, Gus stooped down and swiped it.

"We don't like having guns pointed at us, as you can see. Best not to try it again. In fact, I have a mind to bring this to the police, though I'll bet it's untraceable."

"You're dead men," jean jacket said, his face pale from the pain in his limp wrist.

Gus looked down at the gun. "Well, not exactly at the moment." He looked to Banks, and said, "I thought you left the wrench at the shop."

Banks winked. "I always keep a spare one on me."

The bearded man retched for a bit as he caught his breath. Gus listened for any movement in the nearby brush. He tapped Banks on the arm and pointed at the house. Banks nodded, and they both moved out of the sightline should anyone be there with a gun pointed at them.

"Now, which one of you wants to get Stranger for us?" Banks said, still gripping the wrench.

They heard crunching on the driveway.

"There's no need."

Braden Stranger came alone, wearing a light gray linen suit without a tie. He had an air of confidence about him that told Gus he'd made sure his back was covered.

"Any reason why you have thugs guarding your house?" Gus asked.

Stranger grinned wolfishly. "You've said it yourself before. Springerville isn't exactly as safe as it once was. I need to protect myself and my property."

Gus eyed the men who had managed to get to their feet. "I think there are probably better ways to go about it."

Stranger shrugged. "Apparently. It appears the wrong men are on the ground. So, what can I do for you?"

Not wasting any time. Good.

"I'd like you to clarify what you said to me on Election Day."

Pausing for a moment and thrusting his hands in his pockets, Stranger said, "I'm not sure what you mean. I spoke to a lot of people that day. To no avail, it appears."

Gus saw through his lie as easily as peeking through a lace curtain.

"So, you don't want to man up and talk straight with me?" Gus asked.

Stranger's gaze drifted to the gun in Gus's hand. "Are you planning to shoot me if I don't?"

"What I'm planning to do is keep this illegal weapon before your goon hurts someone with it."

"I believe I saw you arrive with that gun. I have quite a few people who were watching who will attest to that."

Gus bristled. "I'm sure they're all of impeccable reputation. A field of bull crap like that won't fly down here."

"We'll have pictures to prove it."

Which meant if needed, Stranger would have someone editing any photos or video they'd taken. Gus was undeterred.

"Accept your loss and move on. You and your . . . friends . . . aren't needed. You know what Mick Jagger said. You can't always get what you want."

Stranger turned his back on them. "You forget. He also said if you try sometimes, you get what you need. And we will get just that, Gus. Now, head on home before I call the police. I still have that right."

Banks watched the retreating Stranger and said to

Gus, "I should have wrenched him, too, while I had the chance."

The wounded thugs followed their leader back to the house. Gus didn't see anyone else around or in the house when the door opened and closed, but he knew there were eyes everywhere.

"I'm starting to think you should have."

# CHAPTER 23

Now that the election was over, all talk was about putting on a parade.

Gus lobbied for the parade plans to be canceled, but he was resoundingly outvoted. He knew he could get Emma on his side if he told her of his misgivings about Stranger, but he didn't want to worry her.

He did win on one thing. Since he wouldn't be sworn in as mayor for another month or so, the parade's theme was more about the holiday season than a hometown man getting his first crack at politics. There would be a small float for Gus and Wally, but Gus made them promise it would be right in the middle of the procession so it was, in a way, lost in the festivities.

It was amazing how quickly everything had been put together. Props that had been in storage from previous parades were dusted off and the children from Emma's school went to work creating the artwork and decorations that would adorn Gus and Wally's float along with dancing Christmas tree costumes, huge empty boxes wrapped in shiny paper, and even a papier-mâché Frosty. Gus was pretty proud of what all the kids and adults had accomplished and despite his misgivings, looked forward to the big day.

That day, a Friday where the schools had been closed just for the event, had arrived.

"You want to dress as Santa?" Gus joked with Banks as they inspected the float parked in the high school lot.

"I don't think the world is ready to see me as Santa, yet."

Banks was nervous. Gus had seen that look in his eyes before, except then, they were in a foreign land where everyone and everything was out to kill them. Banks's eyes never stopped surveying the area, searching for trouble. All Gus saw was a lot of kids and smiling adults getting in place for a special day. It made him uneasy. If Stranger simply wanted to play mind games with him, it was working.

Emma was directing her class, helping them make the final touches on their amazing work. She hot glued a silver ornament on a felt Christmas tree outfit (with Ron inside it) and turned to give Gus a million-watt smile.

The weather was being exceedingly cooperative, with temperatures in the upper sixties, which was pretty good for early December. Gus even felt a little sweat building under his armpits.

"You see Wally?" Gus asked Banks.

"Nope. Running late as usual."

"I hope he's okay."

Wally Sturgis had been recovering nicely, but Gus worried about the stress, even the good kind, an event like this would have on the current mayor.

Emma strode over in her red velvet dress with a white half-sweater and adjusted Gus's tie. "I really have to set some time to teach you how to do this right."

Gus undid the knot and put it in his pocket. "I like it better this way. Helps me breathe."

She rolled her eyes. "You sure you don't want that trucker cap you got from Publix?" she said sarcastically.

"I do, very much, but I fear my girlfriend would never forgive me if I wore it on such an auspicious day."

Emma kissed him lightly on the lips. "Good call. Are you ready to take the stage, so to speak?"

"I'm actually waiting on Wally."

"He's not here yet?"

"I have eyes on him," Banks said, pointing beyond the crowd as Wally's truck pulled into the lot by the baseball field. Wally and Carolyn exited the vehicle and hurried toward the float.

Gus cupped his hands over the sides of his mouth. "No running in the halls, Wally! Take your time." The last thing he wanted was for Sturgis to have another heart attack. He wasn't sure he'd be able to save him a second time.

Wally didn't listen. By the time he got to the float, he was red-faced and sweating. Carolyn was right behind him looking more nervous than usual.

Banks rushed over to Wally and put an arm on the man's elbow to steady him. "You all right?"

It took a moment for the mayor to collect his breath. Carolyn answered for him. "We drove by the parade route and saw media everywhere."

"Media?" Gus said. As far as he knew, only a reporter from the local paper was scheduled to be there.

"I counted five news vans," Wally said.

"Why would there be *any* news vans?" Emma asked.

*I know why*, Gus thought. Stranger wasn't bluffing. What in the name of all that's holy were they about to walk into?

"That's not all," Wally said. He dabbed his sweat with a handkerchief. "The sidewalks are packed. I know there are a lot of new people I don't know from Adam, but this is on another level. Looks like every single person in the neighboring two counties is out there."

Banks's lips pursed. "I don't like the sound of this. Maybe we should cancel the parade."

"Because there will be a lot of people and news coverage?" Emma said. "That's usually a good thing for a parade."

Gus knew it was time to come clean. He told everyone what Stranger had said to him on Election Day and his recent visit to the man's house. Emma looked ready to bite his head off.

"I don't know what that sewer rat has up his sleeve, but I say we don't let him spoil all the hard work everyone has done here," Wally said, sweeping his hand around the collection of people and cars in the school parking lot.

Gus held out his hand to help Wally onto the float. "You're right. There are a lot of kids here who will be mighty disappointed if we call it off. Whatever Stranger has in mind, I can deal with."

"What about his goon squad?" Banks said.

"Even he . . . or whoever controls him . . . won't hurt a bunch of children in front of the media. No, let's do this and then deal with whatever he's come up with later."

"Fine, but at least let me get some other people to get on the float with you. The kids will be fine, but I want you protected."

"Can I stop you?"

"Not a chance."

Banks ran off in search of a makeshift security detail.

"Do you really think you need protection?" Emma said, her brow creased with concern.

"No. But whatever keeps the man happy, I'm fine

with." He turned to the mayor. "You ready to get this show on the road?"

Wally took a quick nip from a flask that he'd pulled out of his sport coat pocket. "Carolyn, can you please pass the word that it's time to go wheels up?"

"Yes, sir." His assistant scurried off to let everyone in the line know.

Five minutes later, they were off and running . . . at a very slow pace. The high school marching band led the way. Don Runde was dressed as Santa. He'd added a pillow under his shirt and had a huge sack of candy that he planned to toss to the kids along the parade route. The turn onto Main Street was several blocks away. Several times, the car motoring the float hit a pothole, jostling Gus, Emma, and Wally. He had to grab them both to keep them upright.

"I'll give this whole Stranger mess one thing," he said.

Emma held tightly onto his hand. "What's that?"

"It's making me feel like less of a horse's rear end, standing here on this float. My mind has other things to chew on."

As they turned onto Euclid, Banks came jogging to the float, along with Randy Early, Joel Hernandez, and Freddie Powell. Freddie had a shaved head lined with scars from the time he'd spilled off his motorcycle. He was a full-blooded Cherokee who looked dangerous but was as docile as a puppy, at least until you made him angry. Don Runde had had a tough time throwing him out of the Iron Works one night after Freddie had found out his girlfriend was cheating on him. Not many men made Don break out in a sweat.

All three men had served in the military and were roughly the same age.

"Permission to come aboard," Banks said, holding out his hand.

"Permission granted." Gus hauled him up, and they helped the other three onto the float.

"Nice try, Randy!"

They looked over to see Ashley Early catching up. She made it onto the float with no assistance. She smiled at Gus, and said, "Hope you don't mind."

Gus cast a glance at Randy. The boy didn't look all that enthused, but he had to learn sooner or later—happy wife, happy life.

"Happy to have you. Though I think this is a little overboard. I don't see what can happen during . . ."

That's when the float made a right onto Main. And that's when Gus saw the throng of people lining the street. It was like looking at Fifth Avenue during the Macy's Thanksgiving Day parade on television.

Seeing all those people put a little pep in the band's step, and the music got louder. The kids were eating up the attention.

Not so much for Gus and his companions.

Because by and large, the crowd was silent.

News vans with their raised satellite dishes were peppered throughout the gauntlet.

The air here was completely different. It was almost an absence of air, all of it having been replaced with coiled tension. Gus had felt that same air in the streets of Jalalabad on more than one occasion. When it felt like this, things never ended well.

# CHAPTER 24

Gus heard the cheers, but even from a slight distance, he could see it was coming from a minority of the crowd. He suddenly wished he had left Emma and Wally off the float.

Wally squinted at the crowded streets, then fumbled for his glasses. "Are you sure that's our town?"

"I'm sure, Wally," Gus said. "It's not. At least not most of it."

Randy Early leaned toward Gus. "Ash and I had a hard time finding people we know before along the parade route. I heard a lot of chatter and didn't hear a single Southern accent."

"I'll bet if we hit the road, we might catch up with a few departing buses," Banks said.

"Why would anyone go through all this trouble for a small town like Springerville?" Emma asked, clutching Gus's hand for dear life.

"Because we're dealing with people who don't like to lose on any scale. Especially to some nonpolitician yokel like myself. You saw how they reacted when Trump won. That appears to have set the mold. No such thing as losing with dignity. Now, if you don't get what you want, you throw a tantrum, destroying everything in your path."

It seemed as if all eyes had turned to the float. Gus saw a good share of smiling faces.

But he saw more expressions of anger and something bordering on hate.

At first, there were cheers. Sarah Birch waved an American flag and blew a kiss their way. Ron and Mike were with her, heads on a swivel, clearly confused about who surrounded them.

"I think that kiss was for you," Gus said to Banks.

"From what I'm seeing, I'll take that kiss over this."

The residents of Springerville turned to their strange neighbors with mild shock. Why would anyone come to a parade to jeer?

Gus spotted an incoming egg. At least he thought that's what it was. He stepped in front of Emma and took it in the chest. It exploded, spattering his shirt and chin in slimy yoke.

That first egg was a signal for others to let fly.

"Get down," Gus barked at Emma. It was just in time because mixed in with the eggs was a beer can. Luckily, it was empty.

Banks grabbed Wally and tucked the mayor behind him.

Something zinged right next to Gus's ear. It sounded and felt like a rock.

It didn't take long for the float to be covered in eggs. Banks and his impromptu crew formed a circle around Emma and Wally, taking on all the flack tossed their way. They batted away eggs and more cans and red plastic cups as best they could.

The boos changed to shouts and chanting. Gus had a hard time making out what they were saying over the cacophony. Despite it all, he made sure to stand tall on the float. Stranger and his people were watching. Hell, as they passed by the first television crew with their cameras trained on the madness befalling the float, the whole country might be a witness. But to what end? How could egging a float carrying a mayor and mayor-elect benefit Stranger?

No matter the endgame, Gus wasn't going to give Stranger the satisfaction of seeing him cower.

Some folks in the crowd turned on the people hurling objects. Scuffles started to break out in various pockets. The uplifting sound of the marching band was replaced by police sirens. Don Runde pulled down his beard and shot a look at Gus while mouthing, "What's going on?"

And then Gus saw the first sign. It was crudely hand drawn on a piece of white oak tag paper.

It read **RACIST!**

Another one popped up out of the crowd, suspiciously right in view of a television camera.

**WHITE SUPREMACY HAS NO PLACE HERE!**

He tapped Banks and pointed at one of the signs. "What the hell does that mean?"

"I haven't a clue." A full can of soda hit at their feet. A small hole sprayed fizzy cola everywhere like a smoke bomb.

Punches were being thrown in the crowd as the townies reacted to the angry protestors. Gus wanted to jump into the fray. That might be just what they wanted. Have Gus caught defending his neighbors and misconstrued as assault.

He looked back at Emma. "You okay?"

She tugged on the leg of his jeans. "Don't worry about me. You need to get down before you get hurt!"

Wally looked scared. When an egg hit his leg, the terror turned to anger.

They had to get out of here. But how? The float was locked in a sea of quarreling people. The television cameras were catching every livid moment of the madness. People cried out, screamed, shouted each other down.

A man tried to climb the float while carrying a metal garbage can. Banks put his boot to the man's chest before he could hurl it at them. He fell back and was swallowed by the crowd.

His brazen act only encouraged others to do the same.

Banks, Randy, Ashley, Joel, and Freddie did their best to repel the rioters. This had gone past a protest. Because they had to break their tight circle to patrol the edges of the float, it left Emma and Wally exposed.

A rock hit Gus in the back of his head. Bright sparks filled his vision for a moment. Then an egg broke over Emma's face.

Gus saw red.

He made to push a ponytailed man from getting on the float but was stopped by Banks, who did it for him.

"He's Black," Banks said.

"So?"

"Those signs! If the cameras see you do that, God knows what will become of it. Leave that for me."

A white man who looked like one of the bikers from The Pennsylvania scrambled to get on the float. He had a fire extinguisher raised above his head.

"This one's mine," Gus said.

"Have at it."

Gus delivered a precise kick, catching the extinguisher with the heel of his boot and sparing the man. It did unbalance him, and he fell onto his side. The fire extinguisher rolled off the float and into another man's hands. He looked down at it as if it were manna from heaven.

The man's eyes were wide and glassy. Gus was pretty sure if he asked him where he was, he'd get a head scratch at best.

The crowd had run out of eggs and projectiles. Or maybe the protestors were just too busy squabbling with the townies to pay Gus and everyone on the float any mind. Don had lost his Santa hat and was pushing several men back onto the sidewalk as if he were tackling a sled back in football practice.

When Gus looked down at the man with the extinguisher, he noticed the nozzle was pointed at them. "Don't do it, son."

His words fell on deaf ears. An instant later, a cloud of white foam shot out of the wide-mouthed nozzle, forming an artificial snowstorm that dropped onto the float. Gus hopped off the float and pulled the extinguisher from his grasp. The man took off into the crowd before Gus could introduce him to his fist.

Hands reached for Gus in anger. Others tried to pull them away from him. He felt his collar rip. A young woman with wild hair got in his face, and shouted, "You racist pig! Go back to whatever cave you came from!"

"He's a TERF!" another woman wailed. Others started chanting, "TERF! TERF! TERF!"

Gus wasn't sure if he was hearing them wrong. What in the name of God was a TERF?

A throng of men and women, all looking fresh from college, blurted, "This election was a fraud! Cheater! Cheater!"

There was no trying to rationalize with them. Not with

the red fever in their eyes and a swarm of jostling bodies around him.

Red-and-blue lights flickered to either side of him. Someone kicked his leg. He felt a warm spot on his neck and realized someone had spit on him. There was no greater way to get any man hotter than a barn loft in July than to send some expectoration his way.

Gus twisted amid the groping hands and angry faces, searching for the person who had done such a demeaning and cowardly thing. He no longer cared about cameras or his public persona. Someone had to pay for what they did.

Air horns shrieked above the din. It was enough to make most people stop what they were doing long enough for a phalanx of police to break through the crowd. One of them got ahold of Gus's arm.

"Are you okay?" It was Joe Iacovo, one of the younger men on Dawn James's force. When he was in high school, he used to stop by the luncheonette every afternoon for a basket of fries that he'd lather in mayonnaise.

Gus knew how he looked, covered in eggs and foam, his clothes ripped and disheveled. "I'm fine."

"I'll get you out of here."

The rioters that had been so anxious to get a piece of Gus knocked into everyone to beat a retreat.

"Not without my team," Gus said, nodding toward the float and his disheveled friends and girlfriend. "If it's all right by you, I'll wait with them until things settle down."

Joe looked torn. Finally, he said, "I'll wait with you all."

"That'd be just fine."

Emma rushed to him when he clambered back onto the float. She looked a little worse for wear, but unhurt, which was all that mattered.

There were tears in her eyes. He wiped them away with his thumb.

"I know, honey, I know."

"How did this happen?"

"When there's a snake in your garden, you need to be more careful where you step."

# CHAPTER 25

Back at the police station, Dawn James had given Gus and his crew bottles of water and towels so they could clean up. The spit shine did little to change their mood.

Gus, Emma, Banks, and Wally sat in James's office after things had settled down. Randy, Ashley, and the others were told they could go home, but they refused to leave, happy to stay until Gus was ready to go.

"Looks like you have yourself some bodyguards," James said as she closed the door behind her. "What's your payroll look like?"

Gus leaned back in his chair. "I guess it'll depend on how much they eat."

Normally that would have gotten a laugh. Everyone, including Gus, was in too much shock to so much as smile.

James opened her file cabinet and pulled out a bottle of Jack Daniels. "Anyone interested?"

All hands went up. She had a stack of plastic cups by the filtered water dispenser on the counter next to the cabinet. She gave everyone a healthy portion and settled into the leather chair behind her desk. There were no toasts. Just eager sipping to settle their nerves.

"I wish I'd sent everyone sooner," James said. "Maybe things wouldn't have gotten so out of hand."

"You couldn't know it would have come to that," Wally said.

"True. But I did have a heads-up." She opened her laptop and typed for a moment. "Did any of you see this?" she asked as she swung it around so they could see the screen.

"What is it?" Banks asked.

"A little video that came out this afternoon."

"Was it on TV?" Emma asked.

"As far as I know, no. But it did hit quite a few social media sites."

Gus couldn't get the smell of raw eggs out of his nose. "We were kind of busy today before the parade."

"Emma's probably the only one of us that looks at anything on social media," Banks said.

She nodded. "One of us has to keep up with the times. I refuse to be outlapped by my students. But, I didn't have time to check anything today."

James took a deep breath. "You'll know why today happened once you watch this."

On the screen was a YouTube video. Gus leaned close and saw it had over one hundred thousand views. That sounded like an awful lot to him. Not that he knew what a good number was for a YouTube video.

James pressed play. On the screen was a very pretty young lady dressed in a black shirt with a white button-down sweater. She stood across the street from city hall. It looked to have been shot a few days ago when they had cloudy skies.

"Hi, my name is Jennifer Posada and I'm down at Springerville, South Carolina. Not long from now, the whole town is coming out to watch a Christmas parade that's actually a celebration of the election of one of their own as mayor. Why is this new mayor essentially hiding within the festivities? It might be because he's a known racist."

There was a dramatic pause. The wind blew the girl's hair into her face.

It then cut to a Polaroid picture that had been blown up to fill the screen.

"What the hell?" Gus said.

It was a picture of him when he was eighteen. He was in his driveway standing next to his prized possession, a 1969 Dodge Charger he'd bought when he was seventeen and rebuilt with painstaking care. When that was done, he'd brought it to Charlotte and paid a pretty penny to have it painted just like the General Lee from his favorite TV show, *The Dukes of Hazzard*. Standing next to Gus was his best friend, Mike Gilligan. They each sported terribly embarrassing mustaches and mullets.

The camera slowly zoomed in on the picture until it focused on the Confederate flag on the car's roof. The woman, now off camera, narrated what came next.

"They say a picture tells a thousand words. We've come a long way, trying to right the wrongs of the past. Do we really need to go backwards now? *This* is the America that so many people have been longing to get back to. *We* can't let that happen."

Gus remembered when that picture had been snapped. Banks had been the one to take it and was the one who had poured an equal amount of blood, money, and grease into that Charger as Gus had. That car had been the reason Banks had become a mechanic.

"This is ridiculous," Gus said. "Name me one person who watched *The Dukes of Hazzard* back then and didn't want their own General Lee."

Dawn James paused the video. "You don't have to convince me. There's one more bit." She clicked the play icon. It showed a side-by-side picture of Gus now (this one taken on Election Day when he was at the luncheonette) and then, next to his General Lee. Stamped across the screen in bold red letters was RACIST.

"So that's what riled them up."

"The Confederate flag has been a hot button for a few years now," James said.

"That's the *excuse* for getting riled up," Wally said, shaking his cup for some more Jack. "That crowd wasn't just the regular locusts. They came here to start trouble. That video is simply their justification. That Reverend Al Sharpton used to bus rabble-rousers all over the country back in the day. The liberal-progressive machine has just adopted his playbook. Look what they did to cities like Portland and Seattle."

Gus got up and paced the room. "I don't appreciate being called a racist. You can call me a lot of things, but that's not one of them. Look who's my best friend! They think just because a replica of a car on television had a Confederate flag that I'm some kind of racist? I get that times have changed, and we view the past through eyes of the present. And sure, many times, innocence is lost, or ignorance is revealed. I was a kid. You don't see anything but an American flag outside my luncheonette, do you?"

James put a calming hand on his shoulder. "This has nothing to do with reality. It's all optics and what you can do with them to make your point."

Banks kept shaking his head, staring at the laptop screen. "Who the hell is this girl? Why would anyone listen to her?"

James swiveled the laptop around and closed it. "I looked that up. She's one of those social media influencers.

Has a few million followers. Mostly models clothes and tarts herself up to promote female empowerment."

Gus looked to Emma. "What's a social media influencer?"

"Someone with a lot of followers who hang on their every word or picture. It's a weird kind of fame these days. The successful ones make a ton of money from it. She is pretty enough. They usually don't get involved in politics, though. At least not small-town stuff."

"Which means there's been a considerable deposit into her bank account recently," Wally said. "Or she's related to someone involved in this whole Stranger nonsense."

"Aside from being a racist, they were accusing me of stealing the election. And some of them were calling me a TERF. Anyone know what that is?"

Everyone shook their heads. Emma went to her phone. "You learn something new every day. It means you're hostile toward gender identity issues, specifically transgender people."

Gus and Banks exchanged a look. "Food City?" Gus said, remembering the one-sided heated exchange with the man, or woman, at the supermarket.

"Probably."

"Jesus." After finishing her whiskey, Emma said, "I wonder where they found that picture."

Gus felt a tingle at the back of his neck. "That picture was in my house. It was a Polaroid, so it's not like there are a bunch of copies out there." He looked to Banks. "You didn't have one, did you?"

"Nope."

"Dawn, would you mind coming with me to my house?"

James got up and put the Jack Daniels bottle back in the cabinet. "Let me grab someone and I'll meet you at your house. The rest of you will have someone drive you to your cars. I don't want you walking the streets alone right now, even if they do look empty and quiet."

No one argued with her.

"We can't let him get away with this," Banks said.

Gus said, "I don't plan to."

As they were about to leave the station, one of James's officers came over to her, and said, "I just heard from the hospital that Maddie Jackson died."

"What? How?" James said.

"Looks like a heart attack. She was at the parade and when things went sideways, she collapsed. They tried to save her, but I guess it was just too much."

Gus pounded his fist into his palm. It may have been indirect, but the misguided cretins who had flooded Springerville had, in essence, murdered a wonderful, innocent woman. Emma squeezed his hand. She had tears in her eyes. Gus's anger overrode his anguish.

"Oh. Gus," Emma said.

He was too angry to speak.


Gus and Emma arrived at his house a few minutes before James and one of her officers, Guy Hernandez, a veteran on the force. Guy was born to be a cop. He looked the part and even acted it when he was off duty.

At the door, he checked the lock to see if it had been tampered with recently. It looked fine to him. Until a year ago Gus had never even thought of locking his door. That changed when the wave of crime washed over Springerville. Now, even that wasn't enough to keep evil from invading his home.

Inside, he should have felt at home. Now, it felt different—violated, no longer his safe haven. Stranger had tainted it, and he didn't know what it would take to get it back to normal.

"I'm going to check all of the doors and windows," Guy said. "I'll start with the basement."

"Thanks, Guy," Gus said.

"Where did you keep that picture?" James asked.

"All of his pictures are in a pile of shoeboxes in his closet," Emma said. "I've been bugging him to get them into photo albums for some time now. Forget about digitizing them."

They made their way upstairs. Gus kept waiting to hear a floorboard creak that shouldn't creak or see a shadow lurking behind a corner.

"Now I just wish I'd put them all in a safe-deposit box at the bank," he said.

He opened his closet door and pulled his clothes aside to reveal the shoebox stack.

"That's not right," Emma said.

"What do you mean?"

"They're in the wrong order."

Gus stared hard at the boxes. For the life of him, he couldn't remember there being any order to the stack.

"Are you sure?" James asked.

"Absolutely. That pink box on top was in the middle."

The pink box had been Gus's deceased wife's, once containing a pair of high heels she'd bought for a wedding they'd gone to. She'd gotten quite ill a couple of weeks after that night, the start of her slow and painful end. It made him sick to his stomach knowing some thief had touched one of the last things Annette had purchased.

"You have gloves?" Gus asked James.

She handed over a pair and he snapped them on, careful to barely touch the boxes and lids. Inside the top three boxes was a messy pile of photographs. Gus had carefully placed them in those boxes.

"Looks like they rifled through them like raccoons," Gus said. "Hope you can find some prints in there or on the boxes. Not sure which one had the Polaroid they took."

Heavy footsteps came bounding up the stairs. Guy burst into the room, and announced, "Looks like they jimmied one of the basement windows. I can even see where they stepped inside."

Dawn James motioned toward the boxes. "Dust these boxes and pictures for prints when you're done downstairs."

"Will do." Guy headed back to the basement.

Gus, Emma, and James went to the kitchen for coffee. As they sat around the breakfast table, Emma said, "Do you think you'll get a print and catch who did it?"

James took a deep breath and pushed a stray lock of hair behind her ear. "My gut tells me the only prints we'll find are yours, Gus's, and maybe Annette's. Most breakins, the perp uses gloves. But you can't discount them being dumber than a chicken. We'll just have to wait and see."

James's radio squawked. The alarm at Al's barbershop was going off. It appeared not everyone had headed for the hills. She got up and put her mug in the sink. "I have a feeling this long night is just going to keep going and going. You know where to find me."

Gus shook her hand. "Thanks. Looks like we're going to have our work cut out for us."

"And you haven't even been sworn in yet. I'm going to be busy putting out fires. I need you to think of a way to stop them from starting."

"No pressure."

"Nothing you can't handle. It looks bad now. Real bad. Think of it as a wrestling match. The bad guy always gets the upper hand at first. But in the end, he's ass down on the canvas being counted out."

Gus and Emma walked James to the door. When he opened it, two news vans were pulling up to the curb. *Of course*, Gus thought.

"You can have Guy set boundaries with them if you want," James said.

"He's got enough to do. We're just going to pretend they aren't here."

"This is the first wave. It'll get worse until something else catches their attention. Lay low for now. Maybe consider keeping the luncheonette closed for a few days."

Emma shook her head. "Fat chance of that, if I know Gus."

"Which you do," he said.

"I'm sure going to miss Maddie Jackson's berries," James said.

"I'm already missing Maddie," Gus said. "When I was about twelve, she once whupped my behind for stealing a bunch of her strawberries. When she called my father, I got another whupping. I went back and apologized the next day. Once I started at the luncheonette, I saw her just about every day. I'm not looking forward to doing my morning prep without seeing her."

"Maddie's still with us," James said. "We just can't see her."

James waved and left, breezing past a reporter who was still trying to get her hair and clothes in order. Gus turned off the porch light and locked the door while Emma closed the blinds.

"Welcome to our prison," Emma said.

"It won't be for long. I can promise you that."

Gus peeked out of the blind and saw several people walking up to his porch. Seconds later, the bell starting ringing.

He poured a fresh cup of coffee and brought it down to Guy while Emma went upstairs to wash the foulness of the day off.

# CHAPTER 26

Gus had had a restless night. Sleep eluded him until around three in the morning. A couple of hours later, his alarm went off. He normally was up before the alarm.

"You really should consider what Dawn said," Emma said with her back still turned to him. He thought she was asleep.

"I'm not letting people scare me out of my home or place of business." His knees cracked when he rose out of bed. "Besides, Ron and Mike can't feed themselves. Someone has to do it."

He took a quick shower and shaved, slipped into jeans that were older than all of Emma's students, and kissed her on the head. "I'm just glad it's Saturday so I don't have to be your lead blocker to get you to school."

"I will need to go home at one point today."

Gus ran his fingers down her cheek. Emma in the morning was a joy to behold. It always made ambling off to work difficult, more today than ever. "Just wait for me to take you, even if the coast is clear. Okay?"

She took his hand, hers warm from being under the covers, and kissed his still-bruised knuckles. "Sir, yes sir."

"That's a good girl." He smiled for the first time since

the parade fiasco. "And see what's with the whole social media hubbub for me. I'm sure I'll get plenty of the regular news from my customers." He was also certain it would be more than he wanted to hear.

"It'll probably be even worse today than yesterday," Emma said. "Social media whirlwinds build up quick, but die even quicker. Love you."

"Love you, too."

The news vans were still parked outside his house. He didn't see hide nor hair of anyone milling around.

*Must be taking a siesta in their vans*, he thought.

He was tempted to lay his foot on the gas and make a tremendous racket when he started his car just to startle them, but he didn't want to upset his neighbors any more than he supposed they were with the extra attention he was getting.

As he pulled away, he spotted someone's head pop up from the driver's seat of a van. Gus was happy to leave them in the rearview mirror. At some point during the day, he'd have to come up with something to say to them. Maybe he should talk to Wally after he got the latest from Emma.

It took some effort to push all of his troubling thoughts to the back of his mind. What he needed now was the ritualistic comfort of running his luncheonette and filling bellies.

A quick glance at his rearview mirror revealed a pair of headlights in the distance.

Wonderful. He knew that had to be the news vans. He rarely saw anyone else on the road at this hour. There'd be no way to keep reporters out once he opened for business.

Maybe he should close down for a spell and wait for things to settle down.

All thoughts of being open or closed ceased when he pulled up to his luncheonette.

Gus cut the engine but didn't get out of his Jeep. He stared wide-eyed at the business that had been in his family for three generations.

One hand gripping the wheel so tight it might break, Gus extracted his phone from his pocket and called Banks.

His best friend sounded hoarse when he answered. "Gus? What's wrong?"

"Sorry to wake you, but there's a big problem. Meet me at the luncheonette as soon as you can."

"I'll be there in five."

Gus hung up and stared at his place. The headlights of the news vans swept along the empty street. He stayed in the Jeep, unsure of what he would say or do if he got out.

A minute later, three cameramen were stationed at the front of his luncheonette. A reporter, a youngish woman with cherry blonde hair and a sensible pants suit, knocked on his window. He kept his eyes straight ahead, not wanting to encourage her to talk to him.

When Banks arrived, he motioned for the reporters to stand back so he could open his door.

"Sonya Rivera, News 14. Do you care to make a comment about what's happened?"

She was short, so much so that it almost hurt his neck to look down at her. "There are a lot of things I'd care to comment about. First of them being, where were you all when this happened? Looks like I needed you here, not camped out in my front yard."

Before she could open her mouth, be breezed past her and walked over to Banks. His best friend saw the luncheonette and ran his hand over his face.

"Jesus, Gus. Just . . . Jesus."

Gus swallowed hard. "I know. I'm kind of numb right now." His back molars hurt from clenching his teeth.

The new front window was gone. Pebbles of glass glittered under both the streetlight and the lights mounted on the cameras.

Inside, it looked like a herd of bulls had been set loose, destroying everything in their path. Tables and chairs were scattered everywhere, most of them broken. Food was tossed all about. It looked as if someone had taken a sledgehammer to his counter. Gus could only imagine what things looked like in the back.

Two more reporters came over, but Banks kept them at bay. "I just need you to back off. Have some compassion, please."

Gus walked into his luncheonette, glass and other debris crunching under his boots. The cameramen backed up, but only so they could get a better shot of him inspecting the damage.

Everything was in pieces.

He couldn't feel his legs. It felt like one of those dreams where you just float from place to place, eyeing the impossible. Only this horror show was very much possible.

His flat top was pocked with dents and scratches. Whatever had been used to break apart his counter had drummed down on the flat top. The floor was awash with oil.

The storage room door was wide open, as was the cold case. The shelves were empty. The vandals were also thieves, making off with all of his supplies.

A hand on his shoulder caused him to spin around, ready to deliver a punch that would contain every ounce of his rage.

"Whoa, whoa. It's only me," Banks said with his hands

up. "This is insane. One crazy person didn't do all this, that's for sure."

"What they didn't break, they stole."

Banks peered around Gus to look into the storage room. Most of the shelves had been torn off the wall and lay in a heap.

"Whoever did this won't get away with it," Banks said. "I called the police. They'll be here any minute."

Gus barely heard him. He was busy staring into the past, watching his grandfather whip up a patty melt at the grill, or his father taking time to talk to everyone who came inside. He even saw himself when he was just a teen, helping decorate the luncheonette for Christmas while Bing Crosby played on the radio and his father doled out free cups of eggnog.

So much of his life had been spent in the luncheonette. Almost all the memories contained with its four walls were good, so many of them cherished. His first date with Annette had happened here. His father had closed up shop and Gus snuck the keys so he could make a special dinner for two. One of the broken tables in the front was the very one where they had dined on that night, two young kids struck by love, unaware of the life they would build together, only for it to be cut short.

It was gone. Ground under the boots of a bunch of devils that didn't belong here.

A reporter traipsed into the ruins, nearly snapping her ankle when she stepped on a sugar bowl. Banks stopped her before she could get to Gus and crossed his arms. At least she was bright. She twirled her finger at her cameraman and they both went back outside without a word.

"Insurance will help you rebuild," Banks said.

"But it won't be the same, will it?"

"Don't know. It could be better than before. That's up to you, I guess."

"I want to hurt someone, Chris. It's been a long, long time since I felt that way."

"Whatever you do, you can't go off half-cocked. You know that, right?"

Gus nodded, his eyes flicking over the damage, his brain assessing what was trash and what could be saved. There wasn't much in the latter category. The flat top that had made innumerable pancakes, burgers, and bacon was beyond repair. He wanted to take the people who had done this and bash their skulls against its dented surface.

"Gus?"

He spun around and spotted Sarah Birch at the entrance.

"Best you stay there, Sarah. I don't want you to lose your footing and hurt yourself."

She brought her quivering hands to her mouth. "How could someone do such a thing?"

Gus came to her. She wrapped him up in a hug and cried against his chest. "I'm so sorry, Gus. I'm so sorry."

He saw the cameras zero in on them and wanted to swat them away as if they were houseflies.

"It'll be all right," he said, not feeling the words himself.

"It's just . . . just . . ."

Gus rubbed her back until her crying subsided. Ron and Mike pulled up seconds before a pair of squad cars.

Office Joe Iacovo was quick to ask the reporters and cameramen to step back.

"Who did this?" Mike asked.

"That's the million-dollar question," Gus replied as two

officers, both regulars at the luncheonette, approached him.

As he recounted everything to them, he thought he saw a white Porsche turn the corner two blocks away.

Stranger coming to inspect his dirty work?

As much as he wanted to jump in his Jeep and tear after him, he had to tamp his impulse down and go through the motions. A time for revenge would come.

Oh, it would come.

# CHAPTER 27

Braden Stranger finished his workout on his Peloton when the bell rang. He knew the person at his door was a friendly because he still had his shabby crew of guards out front. He hated having them there, but there was no choice in the matter.

It was especially galling to have them in his house. At best, they belonged in a pig pen. Not that he was going to tell them that.

Wiping sweat from his face with the towel around his neck, he opened the door.

"Did you see it?" Roger asked as Stranger stepped aside so he could enter.

"Of course I did."

"On the news?"

"Earlier."

The local news channel ran the thirty second story on a loop all morning. Intercut with the footage of the ruined luncheonette were scenes of fighting at the parade and the picture of Gus with his redneck car.

Stranger couldn't have edited the story any better

himself. He suspected someone *not* from the station had a hand in it.

Roger looked around the living room. "Are we alone?"

Stranger sighed. "For the moment. I'm sure one of Sniper's band of merry miscreants will need to use the bathroom or get a snack soon." The injustice of having to host the criminals chafed Stranger to no end. Especially when he knew that a detail of legitimate guards could have been dispatched at any time. This was a punishment for his not getting the job done.

Lowering his voice, Roger asked, "Did you know this was going to happen?"

Stranger fought the smile and lost. "Whatever gave you that idea?"

"The police are at an all-out search for who did it. I even saw cop cars from other towns in the street just now."

"Well, I'm sure Mayberry's finest will have their man in no time."

"They're going to come here," Roger said. "And I think it's best if you told Sniper to make his men disappear for a while."

"Any cop with three working brain cells knows I wouldn't do such a thing."

"Not with your own two hands, no. But they're not idiots. They'll suspect that you were behind it."

Stranger went to his kitchen to get a glass of cold filtered water. "Good luck with that. I actually had nothing to do with it. As I've been told, I'm supposed to sit tight for now and keep my head down. Besides, there are plenty of angry people out there knowing a racist was just elected mayor."

Roger pinched the bridge of his nose. "It's getting out of hand. I didn't sign on for this."

Setting his glass down carefully on the counter, Stranger stared deep into Roger's eyes. "As a matter of fact, you did. I wouldn't get cold feet now, Roger. It could be bad for you."

"Are you threatening me?"

Stranger broke his gaze and turned his back on his assistant. "I'm not, but I know who will if you get a case of a guilty conscience. There's no bailing out now. In fact, pretty soon, we're going to have more work ahead of us."

Roger stuffed his hands in his pockets, looking like he was deciding whether to pop off at Stranger, storm out, or take his medicine.

"I'd give you a talk about being in this together and weathering the storm, but it's such a waste of oxygen," Stranger said as he settled onto his couch. "Pep rallies were never my thing."

"And you'll say I knew what I was getting into." Roger poured himself a glass of scotch even though it was ten in the morning. This was new. The man never so much as helped himself to a bottle of water without asking before. Stranger would let it slide for now. Roger was upset and needed to show some act of rebellion, even though he knew there was nothing he could do about his current situation.

"There is that."

"I'd appreciate it if you at least gave me a warning before the next disaster hits."

Stranger looked out the sliding glass doors into his manicured yard and saw Sniper smoking a cigar and leaning against his Buddha statue. Sniper terrified him. He wondered if there was any way the thug could choke to death on that cigar.

"You talk as if I knew exactly what was going to happen," Stranger said, getting up to put his empty glass in the dishwasher. "I was simply told things were going to be put in motion and to remain in the house. I can tell you with certainty that it's not over."

Roger downed his drink and sank into a chair. "I don't like this. The bit with the picture was fine. That's politics. But demolishing a man's business? I'm sure we had Gus reeling. Now, we've given him a reason to keep fighting."

"You need to see the bigger picture. Mr. Fuller needs to find out there's nothing for him in Springerville."

"You're not going to scare him off. I saw him talking to the cops. He didn't look like a man who was afraid. You know his history, his military background. This is not a man who can be chased off."

Stranger waved Roger's concerns away with a flick of his hand. "Every man has a breaking point. It just takes a little longer to get there with some. Gus Fuller is not unbreakable. I've yet to meet the man or woman who is." He motioned for Roger to join him at the back door. Sniper was still puffing on his cigar, now with his back to them as he stared at a pair of squirrels chasing each other up a tree. "Even he can be broken. In fact, in a way, he already is. I'm sure he'd rather be at some bar raising hell, selling drugs for pocket money, and hurting someone for fun. Yet here he is, watching squirrels like a bored child. Somewhere along the line in his sorry excuse for a life, he crossed a line and is still paying the price. You think Gus is a tougher, wilder man than Sniper?"

Roger spun away quick enough to make his neck crack when Sniper turned back to the house. "No, I don't think that."

"Then there's the answer to all your worries."

"But what we did before wasn't illegal. Sure, it skirted the boundary of ethics, but it wasn't anything we could go to prison for. Breaking into Gus's house to find dirt, vandalizing his business, and whatever else is on the agenda, that's the kind of stuff that could come back to bite us."

Stranger guided him back to his stark white living room. "It will, but only if we don't do exactly what we have to do. The minute you decide to walk away, you lose your protection. You don't want that, do you?"

Roger looked as if he were going to be sick. His shoulders slumped and he sighed. "What do you need me to do?"

"Right now? Nothing. Keep away from Main Street. Did Gus see you before?"

"I don't think so. He was very focused on the cop he was talking to."

Patting him on the back, Stranger said, "Go home. I'll call you when I need you. It won't be long before I do, so don't get too comfortable. I think I'll ask Sniper to send someone to watch over your house as well. Better to be safe than sorry."

*And better to keep an eye on you and make sure you don't do anything stupid*, Stranger thought. Bravery had never been one of Roger's strengths. But he looked like a cornered man, and Stranger didn't trust him. Maybe they'd have to do something about Roger sooner rather than later. He added it to his mental to-do list.

Roger left without saying another word. Stranger went out back and told Sniper he'd need to send someone to Roger's place. The criminal nodded and walked away in a cloud of smoke. He could be heard barking at one of his men from all the way in the front of the house.

Stranger poured himself a scotch and considered calling his ex. The little repartee with Roger had him in the mood for a good fight.

It would be welcome practice for so much more to come.

# CHAPTER 28

Gus woke up with a pounding headache and sand in his mouth. The sunlight stung his eyes. When he could focus, he saw two bottles of water and two Tylenol on his bedside table along with a note from Emma that read, *Take the pills and drink both bottles as soon as you wake up. I'll call you on my break. We'll get through this together. Don't ever forget how much I love you. Emma*

He groaned as he sat up, opened the first bottle and downed half of it. He washed the Tylenol down with the next large swig, rubbed his scalp and winced as his headache spread to his temples.

Yesterday had been a rough day. After dealing with the police, insurance company, going to the lumberyard and boarding up his luncheonette along with some help from Banks and Randy Early, he came home to a meal cooked by Emma and a fresh bottle of Knob Creek 12 Year. Over the rest of the night, he consumed more whiskey than food, asking Emma not to tell him anything she may have seen on social media or the news. He'd had enough to deal with. The rest would have to wait.

After showering and changing, Gus drank the second

bottle of water, looked at himself in the mirror, and said, "Well, today's the day."

The paper was on the porch. It was little more than a pamphlet these days. Not many people bought a physical newspaper anymore and it showed in the final product.

That didn't mean there wasn't enough page space to dedicate an article about his questionable past, the possibility that there was election fraud, and a small piece on the vandalism of his beloved luncheonette three pages back.

He immediately called Wally. "Did you read the paper?"

"At the crack of dawn, as always." Wally sounded tired, even though he must have been up for several hours. The sun was out in full force and Gus felt strange being home at this time of day.

"Have you heard any proof about actual election fraud?"

"Not yet, but I suspect they'll point to our little roundup before the election."

"And I'm sure they won't mention the intentional influx of so-called new residents brought down to tip the election."

"I wouldn't hold my breath waiting for it. Only way to get that side of the story is to put it out yourself. But I wouldn't say anything until they come out with something specific."

Gus's head was feeling a little better. He paced around his living room, the scent of Emma's perfume lingering in the air. "I need to get ahead of this. Today."

Wally sighed into the phone. "I've been asked to provide a statement. How about we meet at city hall and put our heads together? We have to be careful with this. Maybe I can call some folks I trust and respect, get their input. It's not like I ever had to deal with anything like this before. I see this kind of cow manure play out in other places, but it's different when you're in the thick of it."

"If you have people you trust, I trust them, too. I'll take whatever help I can get."

"Good man. Meet me at my office at eleven. Oh, and there's one more thing."

Gus thought he knew what was coming next. "What's that?"

"Stay away from Stranger. I know you're madder than hell. It won't do you any good going there to have a chat . . . or more."

It took a lot of whiskey to wash the images of him throttling Braden Stranger from his troubled mind last night. Right now, he didn't have the energy to indulge his fantasizing.

"Scout's honor," Gus said.

"I'll have Carolyn order us lunch, too. Bring a notepad and a number two pencil, son. We have work to do."

That left Gus with an hour to kill. Emma had cleaned up the house while he slept (or passed out to put it more accurately). First, he made a quick call to Randy Early and asked a favor of him. Next, he decided to drive by the luncheonette and make sure the plyboard was holding up. Not that there was much more that could be done to the place to make it worse.

As he turned the corner onto Main, he saw a small crowd outside his place.

"Now what," he grumbled, his teeth instantly on edge.

He parked across the street by the cybercafe and got out. He had to weave through a few bodies to see what held their attention.

Overnight, someone had spray-painted RACIST and SEXIST on the plywood over the door, as well as ELECTION THIEF and his new favorite word, TERF.

They'd also stapled multiple copies of the picture of him with his old replica General Lee.

Behind him, he heard someone say, "That's the guy."

The hairs on the back of his neck sprang up.

What he wanted to do was ask if anyone had seen who had defaced his luncheonette. But seeing the sea of unfamiliar faces, he knew there was no point.

"Karma's real," a woman at the back of the crowd said. That got a few murmurs of agreement.

The young man next to him, relatively clean-cut but slight as a reed, said, "Do you at least regret it?"

"Regret what?"

The man turned to face the crowd and threw up his hands. "He doesn't even realize how wrong he is. This is who you elected to be mayor? Oh, I'm sorry, you didn't because the election was rigged!"

Folks started shouting at Gus. This rabble-rouser, who looked like he'd blow away in a medium wind, was simply here to stir up trouble. He looked Gus in the eyes, as if daring him to do or say something that would get him in deeper trouble. Out of the corner of Gus's eye, he saw quite a few phones held aloft, presumably recording the event.

With some difficulty, Gus wriggled his way out of the crowd, careful not to push too hard or step on anyone's foot. By the time he made it to the curb, a police cruiser was pulling up, a voice on the loudspeaker telling everyone to keep moving.

None of them did.

The passenger window rolled down and Chief of Police Dawn James reached out to unlock the back door. "Want a ride?"

"That's right, take him to jail where he belongs!" someone blurted.

Gus's frustration was at a boiling point. It was better to get away than wait for his temper to blow. "Thank God for the cavalry. Only this time, a retreat is best." He slipped into the back seat as people clapped and cheered.

"Boy, do they love you," James said, looking out at the crowd with thinly veiled contempt.

"It's my boyish charm."

Before they could drive away, James told Officer Iacovo to stay. "I'll just be a sec."

James got out of the car and hooked her thumbs in her duty belt. Gus couldn't remember the last time he'd seen her wear it.

"Since you're all such concerned citizens of the world, would any of you care to join me at the station and have a little talk about the string of robberies that happened here last night? I mean, seeing as you've all camped out looking for trouble, I would assume you would have seen it when it walked on down Main Street last night."

Their cheers for Gus's so-called arrest died quickly. Suddenly, dozens of sets of eyes looked furtively around, and once-open mouths pressed into tight white lines.

James pressed them. "No takers? I mean, if you're so hopped up on being social justice warriors, you should want the owners of the businesses around here to get justice as well." She took out her phone and snapped a picture of them. "For the scrapbook. If anyone wants to do some real good, come on and see me at the station anytime. It's just a few blocks away. Can't miss it. It's the building with a bunch of cars that look just like this one parked out front. Well, thank you for your vigilance." She tipped her cap and got into the car.

As they pulled away, Gus leaned forward in his seat, and asked, "What was all that about a string of robberies last night?"

James pulled up the picture she'd taken and zoomed in on the faces. "This has the potential to be the biggest mass mugshot in South Carolina history. Last night was a busy one. Just about half the stores on Main got hit last night. A few others show sign of an attempted break-in. Looks like it all happened at around the same time, just after we had a car patrol the area. Which means it was a coordinated effort by a lot of people. I assume the alarm going off in Al's scared them off."

Gus clenched his fists. "Why would anyone break into a barbershop?"

"That's a good question. Thing is, the businesses that got hit were all owned by locals. The cybercafe and those boutique shops were spared. Makes you wonder."

"But not for long."

They pulled up to the station and got out. Iacovo asked, "You need me for anything?"

"Yes. Help get all those reports completed."

His shoulders slumped a little. Paperwork was a necessary evil. Gus had yet to meet a cop who relished it. He nodded and went through the double doors.

"Why don't you come inside for some coffee?" James said. "And file your own report about the latest set of vandalism."

"This is getting to be a bad habit."

"Never been a habit that can't be broken."

They stepped inside to contained chaos. He'd never seen it so packed before. Al from the barbershop was talking animatedly to a young female officer that was relatively new to Gus. Al saw Gus and called out, "Can you believe this, Gus? What the hell is happening to us?"

It would be easy to say he knew exactly what was happening, but that would open a can of worms that was best sealed for the moment. "I'm sorry to see you here." All eyes turned to Gus, eyes in faces that belonged to friends and neighbors. Mrs. Wallace from the real estate office had streaks of tear marks through the makeup on her cheeks. Without even opening their mouths, they were all saying the same things.

*Why?*

And, *Is there anyone that can make it stop?*

He took a deep breath and thought about his meeting with Wally later. Then he said, "It's clear to see the buck stops with me. I think we've all had enough of this. Give me until the end of the day. I'll find a way to make it right."

James whispered out of the side of her mouth. "Kind of a bold statement, don't you think?"

Gus followed her to her office. "Not if I can help it."

# CHAPTER 29

Gus's meeting with Wally at city hall had to be changed because of the protest outside. A gathering of about forty people were making a scene, though peacefully for the moment. Wally suggested Gus come to his house, away from the madness. When Gus saw the text at the police station, he winced.

"You okay?" James asked. They were on their second cups of coffee that were so strong, he was sure he could use it as paint thinner.

"Just more nonsense. Normally, I would walk to my car, but I don't want my mere presence to cause any more of a scene today. Do you think someone could drop me off at my car?"

James punched a button on her phone and asked Officer Hernandez if he was free. He said he'd be able to drive Gus in five minutes.

Gus used the time to talk to his fellow merchants and simply let them vent. They had all noticed that only long-standing businesses had been targeted. They blamed everyone from Braden Stranger to the locusts, the New York Progressive Party, and shadow money men who were hell bent on redesigning the American political system and life as we know it.

He heard them all out, wondering if maybe they were right on all counts.

"You ready?" Guy Hernandez called over to him. He looked worse for wear after a morning of taking statements and filing reports.

"Yes. Thank you."

As they walked out into the calm, Hernandez said, "I should be thanking you for the break. I'm both exasperated and royally pissed. This is Springerville, not Seattle, for Chrissake."

"In that, we're simpatico."

They got in the cruiser and Hernandez took a longer way to get to Gus's car. Random people walking by his shuttered luncheonette were taking pictures of the latest defacement. He detected quite a few smiles as they walked away.

"We're losing the war on human decency," Hernandez said as he looked in the same direction.

Gus popped the door open. "Wars are just a series of battles. We're not done just yet."

He kept his head low as he got into his Jeep and headed to Wally's modest house a mile out of town. The elderly mayor was on the porch waiting for him, dressed in a denim shirt and blue jeans.

"I can't remember the last time I didn't see you in a suit," Gus said.

Wally shrugged. "It feels like a down and dirty kind of day. Not a suit day. Come on inside."

It took him a bit to extricate himself from his Adirondack chair, refusing Gus's helping hand. Inside, his house was immaculate. Nothing much had changed since Wally's wife Darcelle had passed years ago. Pictures of the two of them were on the walls and mantel above the fireplace. Darcelle hadn't been able to have children, but they'd never let that get them down. They'd simply enjoyed the time they'd had together.

Wally led Gus to his study, which was just a converted guest room with a desk he'd found at an estate sale and three leather chairs on casters. There was a wide bookshelf on one wall and more pictures of Wally and Darcelle during happy times on the other. They took seats opposite one another. A heavy silence stuffed the room as they each contemplated what to say.

Gus took in a deep breath, and said, "I've made a decision, Wally. I'm going to drop out."

Wally rocked back in his chair. "And here I was making plans to fight back. Gus, you can't do this. Not when the town needs you most."

"If I don't, there won't be a town to run. Look at what they're doing to us. I can't let it continue like this."

"You're making a mistake. You think your stepping aside will slow the tide of locusts and crime? Think again. It will open the floodgates for even more. And the people who have called Springerville home for decades, or even generations, will leave. They'll have to, or be stuck living in a place re-created in Braden Stranger's own image. That's not much of a choice."

Gus got up and gripped the top edge of the chair hard enough to make the leather creak. "If I stay, for all I know, they'll burn the entire place down before I'm sworn in. Then everyone *has* to move anyway. Hell, I had to call Randy and Ashley to ask them to watch my house while I was out because I don't know what's going to happen to it. We're dealing with someone with the mentality of a spoiled child who will destroy his toys before he has to share, only this is a child with lots of money and secret backers who not only indulge his tantrums, they encourage them. How am I supposed to compete with that?"

Now Wally was on his feet. His cheeks reddened. "How? With honor. And integrity. And bravery in the face of adversity. All things that you not only stand for but are part of your makeup."

Seeing the steel in the older man's eyes filled Gus with shame. Here was a man that was unwell and at an age where fighting was just a thing you watched other people do. Wally looked like he was ready to take on all comers, while Gus was talking about walking away.

They stared at one another for an uncomfortable span of time. Gus's mind went in a thousand different directions, working out scenario after scenario, trying to find a way out of the predicament they all found themselves in.

"You have a plan?" Gus asked Wally.

A grin tugged at the edge of Wally's mouth. "I have a few. Care to sit and chat?"

Gus took his seat. Wally did the same.

"I forgot my pad and number two pencil," Gus said, feeling very much the student.

Wally opened a drawer and dropped the supplies on his desk. "There you go. We have a lot to go over, and none of it will involve putting up the white flag. I suggest what you said earlier never leaves my office."

Feeling bolstered, Gus nodded and said, "Time to kick some ass?"

"More than that. Time to get the exterminator to clear out our infestation."

And with that, they began to talk, and plot, and estimate outcomes. They breezed past lunch, and then dinner, neither feeling the slightest bit hungry. Saving their town was enough to fill them up.

Gus had phoned Randy at one point in the afternoon to let him know he'd be late, and he and Ashley could knock off if they wanted.

Randy and his wife were there waiting for him when he got home just before eight. So was Emma's car.

"All quiet on the Western front?" Gus asked.

"Yes, but we saw quite a few suspicious characters checking out your house throughout the day," Ashley said. "Almost makes me think it's going to need round-the-clock surveillance."

"Well, there's no way I'm going to put you or anyone in that kind of imposition."

"It's not an imposition at all," Randy said. "I'll see who I can round up."

Gus put a hand on his shoulder. "I can't afford 24/7 protection."

"Who said anything about money? Just give me a day and I'll work out the logistics. You've got a lot of people who would drop everything for you. This town owes you big-time. So don't you worry."

Randy headed off to his truck with the glow of a man on a mission.

Ashley said, "Emma looked upset when she came over. She tried to hide it, but women know."

"Thanks for the heads-up. And thank you for today. You two are really something special."

Gus watched them drive away and swept the area around his house. There were a lot of dark corners where anyone could be hiding. He couldn't believe he was thinking such a thing. This is what it must be like to live in New York or Chicago. No wonder Ashley was happy to uproot her life and come to Springerville. It was a shame that she had to come at the worst time in the town's history and pay such a heavy price.

When he opened the front door, he locked it behind him and called out, "Emma?"

"In here," she replied from the kitchen. He could hear from her tone that something was off. The house smelled like her homemade sauce and meatballs.

"If I knew it was spaghetti night, I would have been home sooner."

She was stirring the sauce with her back to him. "How did things go with Wally?"

He caressed her shoulders and kissed the back of her head, inhaling the sweet scent lingering in hair. "It was . . . different, that's for sure."

When she turned to face him, he saw the puffiness around her eyes. Her makeup had been wiped off.

"What's wrong?" he said.

Emma looked to be struggling to hold back what was bothering her, but she lost the battle. "I . . . I was suspended today."

"You were what?"

He had to make sure he didn't crush her arms with his hands as he held her close.

A lone tear escaped her left eye. She let it roll.

"Principal Morales buzzed me during my last period to come to her office. I didn't think it was a big deal. Stuff like that happens all the time. Getting called to the principal's office has far fewer foreboding connotations for teachers than students. As soon as I walked in, I knew something was wrong. She had this look on her face. It's hard to describe. She was stern, yet I thought I caught her repressing a smile. It had me on edge immediately."

More tears came and she slumped into a chair. Gus took a knee and held her hands within his own.

"What could you possibly do to get suspended? You're the best teacher in that school."

Sniffling a bit, Emma said, "Apparently not to the parents of one student. Morales didn't even ask me to sit down. She just came right out and asked me, 'Did you assign *Harry Potter* to read in your class?' I couldn't understand why she was coming at me the way she was, but I told her yes, I had it as part of my curriculum every year. The class would read the book and then I would show them the movie to open up a discussion on what was better and the challenges of adapting a book into a movie. It's always been fun for the kids and so many of them told me years later it's their favorite book."

"You're not alone there. Far as I can remember, isn't it one of the best-selling children's books of all time?"

Emma looked at him with watery eyes. "Any chance you ever read it?"

"I was more into *Hardy Boys* back when I was a kid. And I liked some of those H.P. Lovecraft paperbacks they had at the drugstore rack. Not sure I understood what was going on. I think I liked the covers more than the stories." He pushed her hair back and wiped away her tears. "So, what was the big deal about having your kids read a book? It's a challenge to get them to read anything nowadays, even comic books despite every movie being about superheroes."

"Well, it appears the book offended the parents of a student, Chad Lutzke, who just transferred to the school. I think his family is from Boston. Morales said to me, 'Considering who you're dating and what's going on around us, did you really think a book promoting witchcraft written by a woman who bashes trans ideals was the smart and right thing to assign? Honestly, Emma, I'm as livid as the parents. You're suspended until further notice.' She didn't even give me a chance to speak. She just turned her back to me and started organizing her desk. I've never been so shocked or felt so humiliated."

"She can't do this. You need to reach out to the teacher's union or the school board." Gus's heart felt like it was being squeezed in a vice. The last thing he wanted was for Emma to get hurt . . . and potentially lose the job she loved more than anything in this world. It seemed like there was no avoiding watching those he loved getting caught up in the madness.

Emma blinked away her tears and sat straight. "I would if I thought it would make a difference. Most of them are just like Morales. They'll side with her no matter what I say."

Gus was tempted to find a bottle of whiskey, but he'd learned last night it didn't make any of their problems go away. "All over a book. What is this world coming to?"

"It's been like this all over the country for years. We were just insulated from it. Now the ideological fervor that has been threatening to tear the country apart has come to roost in our home."

"Is there anything I can do?"

Emma opened her arms. "Yes. Hold me."

He was happy to oblige.

"What do you think will happen next?" he asked.

"I honestly don't know."

"Could you lose your job over it?"

"Maybe."

"Damn."

"I would say you could hire me at the luncheonette, but it looks like both our worlds have gotten a little bit smaller."

Gus hugged Emma as if he were the only thing keeping

her from being flung off the edge of the world. He wanted to ease her pain. He desperately needed to help not just her, but everyone in Springerville that had suffered losses over the past few days.

He and Wally had come up with one way to potentially get things rolling in their favor.

But there was much more that needed to be done.

After he and Emma ate in relative silence, he made a call to Chris Banks. Thankfully, Emma was exhausted, so she turned in early.

Gus had a beer on the porch and napped for twenty minutes until Banks pulled up in front of his house.

Banks was dressed in all black, right down to his service boots whose shine he'd dulled. "Showtime, brother."

# CHAPTER 30

They parked two blocks from Main Street where the streetlight was out. Gus checked his phone.

"Don's outside my house."

"I feel bad for anyone that wants to mess with it tonight," Banks said.

"Crazy that I can't leave Emma alone in the house anymore. At least not until we get this under control."

"Silver lining is that the news vans are gone."

There had been seven news vans parked along Main, grabbing anyone walking by to ask them about their opinion on the newly elected racist mayor. Banks had said they miraculously only selected nonlocals who were happy to televise their disgust. Gus was sure any townies who had a counter opinion had their interviews erased.

"Why shouldn't they be gone?" Gus said with exasperation. "This was only the scene of mass robberies and vandalism last night. Why would they possibly want to be here to get the scoop if it happens again? Damn sons of biscuit eaters."

Banks nudged him. "Don't demean biscuit eaters. I'm the son of one, and if I ever make a son of my own, he will be, too. I used to think that the whole fake news, controlled narrative media was a little blown up, you know? Man, was I wrong. I don't think I'll ever believe anything I see on the news after this."

"All you need is the weather report so you know when we can go out on your boat."

"That's very true. I'd like to be on it right now doing a little late-night fishing."

"What do you think we're doing now? We just need someone to bite."

From their vantage point, they could see the pizza parlor and the used bookstore. They were both owned by longtime residents and were the only two merchants not targeted the night before. When they'd pulled up, Gus noted how it appeared someone had knocked out the nearby streetlight. Whoever had done it was practically telegraphing their intention.

A patrol car rolled slowly down the strip, the officer at the wheel shining his spotlight on both sides of the street.

Gus had thought of calling Dawn James and letting her team take down whoever was planning on hitting the two stores. But after the past few days, he needed to take out some of his pent-up aggression.

Banks handed Gus a thermos of coffee. "Think we might need this."

Gus yawned. "It's past my bedtime already. Though I don't have anything to get up early for now."

"You will. If I have to get everyone in town to lend a hand, your place will be back in business before you know it."

"It's going to take some time for insurance to get through everything."

"To hell with that. We take care of our own. You know that. It's why we're sitting out here in the dark."

Gus sipped his coffee, watching for any movement. He

was tired of sitting back and waiting for the next shoe to drop. That wasn't in his nature.

He told Banks the plan he'd concocted with Wally.

"There's the Gus I know. You ever think of dropping out again, call me. I'll knock that thought right outta your head."

"Why, thank you for promising to beat some sense into me." Gus squinted as he peered into the alleyway between the pizza parlor and a new nail salon that had been untouched by the previous night's criminal activity. "You see that?"

Banks leaned over the steering wheel. "I see someone. Maybe another behind them in the alley."

"Any reason they should be there this time of night?"

Banks grinned. "Oh, plenty. One of them being getting their butts whupped."

They donned black ski masks, a relic from the time they went skiing at Snowshoe Mountain in West Virginia ages ago. Neither of them were very adept on the slopes. Now, Gus was just glad they'd kept the wool masks.

They crept out of the truck, careful to leave the doors open rather than make any sudden noise.

Sure enough, three men popped out from the alley. One of them had a brick in his hand. Hunched low, Gus and Banks hustled across the street and rested behind a parked Ram truck. Gus took a quick peek over the flatbed and confirmed it was just three men. They were dressed in jeans and T-shirts, one of them wearing a beanie cap. Gus pointed to the front of the truck, then himself, and then the back. Banks nodded. Gus made a fist, and they broke off in different directions.

Banks jumped up from his hiding place, and shouted, "Y'all got the munchies or something?"

He clearly startled the men. The one with the brick held it aloft, ready to launch it at Banks.

"I wouldn't do that if I were you," Banks said.

While their eyes were on Banks, Gus crept up behind them. There wasn't a face he recognized. They didn't even look like the crew staying at The Pennsylvania.

"You a cop?" one of the men asked.

Banks rolled his neck. "When I'm done with you, you'll wish I was."

The brick went airborne. It was a bad throw. It clanged off the front quarter panel of the pickup. The alarm blared to life.

When Banks charged them, they turned to escape.

Gus was waiting for them.

He hit the first one with a savage jab to the center of his chest. All the air exploded from his lungs and he took a knee, clutching his chest. The one behind him got an uppercut to the jaw that set his teeth clacking.

Banks tackled the third one around the waist and used all of his weight to crush the criminal against the unyielding sidewalk. Gus thought he heard a bone crack and hoped it didn't belong to his best friend.

In seconds, it was all over, unlike in movies where fights went on and on. Once you hurt a man, which wasn't hard to do, he generally lost all the wind in his sails.

Despite that, Gus was breathing hard as adrenaline pulsed through his veins. The one on the receiving end of the uppercut was out cold.

The man holding his chest wheezed, "I think you stopped my heart, you psycho." He said this while keeping his eyes fixed on the ground.

"Well, it seems to be beating just fine now. Never known a man with a stopped heart being able to insult the man who stopped it."

Banks pulled a couple of zip ties from his pocket and wrapped them around his man's wrists and then turned him over. None of them could have been older than twenty-five. Right around the same age Gus and Banks were fighting for their lives in a desert thousands of miles away.

"What the hell do you think you're doing?" the man asked Banks. "You can't go around assaulting people." He had a Northern accent.

"Just like you can't go around breaking store windows and whatever else you were planning," Banks spat back.

"Yeah, but we're not the ones dressed like ninjas with masks on," the one Gus had hit said.

Gus grabbed him by the collar and lifted him to his feet. "I'm going to give you two choices. You can continue to piss us off and we'll hold you down until the cops get here. Or, you run back to whatever hole you're living in and tell everyone we're not sitting idly by anymore. You want to wreck our town? You're going to have to get through us . . . and I mean all of us . . . first. And we won't come to the fight with bricks."

When the man finally looked up at Gus, Gus made sure to squint his eyes to make it even harder to make out who was behind the mask.

He felt him sag in his grasp. "Fine. Don't call the cops."

"And then what?"

"And then we'll tell everyone not to mess with the town anymore."

Banks got up from his man and snapped the zip ties with a flick of his hunting knife. "This is a one-time warning, fellas," Banks said. "We put on kid gloves with you tonight. Next time, with the next person, it won't be so nice."

Both men were in obvious pain and looked like they

didn't want to deal in any further agonies. They picked up their unconscious coconspirator by his arms. He started to come to once his feet touched terra firma.

As they turned to go back down the alley, Gus said, "We'll be watching. And not just us. Make sure everyone knows that."

The trio limped down the alley and out of sight without looking back.

Gus rubbed his knuckles. "Good thing that kid had a glass jaw."

"I was hoping they'd have a little bit of a fight in them."

"They weren't street punks. You can tell it in their voices. Just some misguided fools with nothing better to do. Guess you can only play video games in your parent's basement for so long."

They walked back to Banks's truck. "You think they'll do what you said?"

"I don't know," Gus said. "They may just pick up stakes and head out of town tonight. I don't think there's much allegiance among their ranks."

"Unlike ours."

"Yep. Maybe we should hang tight a little longer just to make sure there isn't a second wave."

Banks took his coffee cup off the dash. "One can only hope and dream."

# CHAPTER 31

Sarah Birch called Gus first thing in the morning to let him know that yet another crowd was growing outside of city hall. This time, it looked like it was going to be much larger than the one from the day before.

"There're a lot of people holding signs and they keep looking around as if they're waiting for someone to tell them to get things started."

Gus missed the days when his morning interactions with Sarah involved watching her flirt with Banks and getting her caffeinated.

"I'll tell Wally to make today a work from home day," Gus said.

Emma was just putting eggs in a skillet when Gus asked her if she wanted to take a quick ride into town. "Just to see what's brewing."

"Let me finish these scrambled eggs so we can heat them up later."

After the eggs were done, they quickly changed and hopped into his Jeep. Sure enough, there was quite the gathering outside the city hall steps. New today were the tents that had been set up in the grassy square across the street from the municipal building. He did a quick head count as he scanned the crowd.

"Looks to be around sixty or so," he told Emma.

She pointed to the side roads. "With more coming."

Indeed, they were. They came on foot, car, motorcycle, and even a few skateboards. There were signs for Gus to resign and other more colorful depictions of his character. Among the growing mass were multiple news vans, including a few new ones with logos for CNN and MSNBC plastered across their sides.

"Looks like we're about to go national," Emma said.

Gus punched the wheel. "Stranger isn't taking his foot off the gas, is he?"

"Or whoever controls him. Let's go back to your place. Looks like today is going to be trying to say the least. You can't face it on an empty stomach." Gus was about to contradict her. Then, he thought of how many times he'd come with a homemade meal and said the very same thing to so many of his neighbors over the years when they faced hard times.

Breakfast was a solemn affair, and Gus had to force down every bite so he didn't upset Emma. It wasn't until they were loading the dishes in the sink that she noticed his knuckles.

"What did you do last night?"

"Stopped the pizzeria from being bashed up."

"You didn't hurt anyone, did you?"

He looked down at his hand. The redness from the brawl at the Iron Works had just started to lessen before his latest tussle. "Not permanently, no. Last night was a chance for us to send a message. I'm not sure if it got as far as Stranger, but Banks and I are hoping some of his minions will think twice before causing any more damage to the town."

"What if you got caught being a vigilante? You think these people are riled up now? This will look like a bean supper compared to how it will get."

"We wore ski masks." He could tell she was not amused. "Look, we had to take a chance. And we may have to do it again. Dawn's force can do just so much, and almost everyone they arrest is out in no time. Sometimes you have to fight dirty if you want to win."

Emma hugged herself as if she'd gotten a mighty chill. "I understand what you mean, but that doesn't mean it makes me any less nervous."

"The best thing for nerves is to find something to distract your mind. And I have just the thing, especially now that you have the time." She gave a slight wince when he said it, and he wished he'd worded it better. Being on suspension with no end in sight was like being thrust into purgatory. It had to be eating her up inside.

"What is this distraction you have in mind?"

"Just something Wally and I came up with. Time to rally our troops. I need you to make calls, ring some bells, whatever it takes."

He explained the plan and told her he'd make sure someone stayed with her to keep her safe.

"I can't even go through my own town without a bodyguard now?"

"Not for the moment. I'll feel better knowing you're safe."

After chewing on her thumbnail for a bit, she said, "Fine. I need to go to my place to change and get my laptop."

"I'll see if Randy can cover." Since the attack on the Earlys, Randy had taken a remote job so his days were flexible enough to care for his wife. He hated telecommuting, but it was a means to an end for now. And poor Ashley, just when she was ready to work and Gus was going to ask her to help out at the luncheonette, everything went sideways.

"And where are you going?" Emma asked him as he shrugged into a light jacket.

"Out to meet my adoring public. Let's agree to check in with each other every hour, okay?"

"Please be careful."

"I always try."

Gus called Banks and Don Runde on his way to town. Both agreed to meet him a couple of blocks from city hall. When he got there, Banks was in his overalls and Don was wearing camo shorts and a Lynyrd Skynyrd T-shirt.

"Holy cow," Don said, eyeing the angry mob.

There had to be a couple of hundred angry protestors, many waving their signs, and someone on a bullhorn shouting, "No place for racism! No place for Gus!" over and over. When they tired of that, they went with, "Election thief! Cisgender TERF!"

"At least I'm on a first-name basis with them," he said. "And yes, I now know what cisgender is. I looked it up. I liked things better when I'd never heard the word."

"I love a good fight, but I'm not crazy about the odds," Banks said.

"We're not fighting. At least I hope not. Too many cameras around."

"Sometimes morons like this wait for the cameras to really start acting out," Don said. "They want their fifteen minutes of infamy."

Banks cracked his knuckles. "So, what's the plan?"

"I'm kinda winging it here. But I thought maybe it's time I spoke publicly."

"Didn't Wally tell you not to do that?"

Gus shrugged. "He did want us to work on a joint statement. I never was one for speeches. I know I'll look the fool if I have to read off some cards. Besides, how much worse can I make it?"

Don laughed. "A hell of a lot, Gus. But I know you, and I know whatever's about to come out of your mouth will at least be honest."

"And twisted by these dummies and the press," Banks added.

Gus squeezed Banks's shoulder. "I thank you for your vote of confidence. Let's go."

A few of the protestors turned around as they approached but didn't appear to recognize him. In fact, he'd bet his grandmother's china that if he stood in a lineup of two, most of the people here wouldn't be able to pick him out. They were here simply for the party. According to Wally, there was a mix of professional rabble-rousers who just liked to make trouble wherever they went, others that were bleeding hearts with little else to do, and some that were more than likely paid to be a nuisance. It was quite the collection, for sure. Gus couldn't imagine being in any of those camps at any time in his life. Being without direction, bored or just plain stupid were not part of his character.

It was the reporter for the local news who noticed him first. She tapped her camerawoman on the shoulder and got her to swivel around from the lady with the bullhorn.

Word spread faster than ants at a picnic. Soon, everyone had turned around to face him, letting out a chorus of boos and what they must have assumed to be stinging epithets. Gus responded with a smile as they parted for him so he could make it to the steps. That was a surprise. He thought they would make it difficult. Considering he, Don, and Banks towered over almost all of them, they were probably taken aback.

As soon as he got to the fourth step, the bullhorn lady started again, and the sign waving went into a furor. Gus couldn't make out what anyone was hurling his way, much less his own thoughts. Banks and Don were on either side of him on the third step, eyeballing the protestors with calculated menace.

Gus waved his hands to get everyone to calm down for a moment. It only riled them up more. He thought he spotted Sniper somewhere to the left of the mob. The thug wasn't jeering or holding a sign. He was just there, taking it all in with a look of smug content.

"Can I just say a few things?" Gus shouted. He wasn't sure anyone was able to hear him.

For the first time in his life, Gus wished he had a microphone.

"If y'all can just calm down for a moment, maybe we can talk like adults here."

A few women at the front of the gathering stopped shouting and turned around to tell their neighbors to quiet down. It was a wave of shushing that eventually reached the back. Things weren't library or church quiet, but at least Gus could get a word in.

"Thank you," he said, looking straight at the folks in the front. "I understand you're all pretty upset . . ." A roar exploded and died as quickly as it had come. "And I understand why. When we look back at our past, all of our pasts, things don't always look the same as we remember them. A picture of me with a very popular car on television some forty years ago surfaced last week. I can't honestly think of a boy my age back then who didn't want one of his own."

That did not make the crowd happy. It took a bit for them to settle down again. "The Confederate flag is looked upon much differently now than it was back then. As a kid, what really mattered was having that Charger and working hard to restore it and make it look like the real thing. My intentions were never based in any sense of racism." A swell of boos washed over him. When they settled down, he said, "In fact, the person who helped me, my best friend since I was ten years old, is right here." He motioned toward Banks, who nodded.

There was a stunned silence.

"That car belonged to the both of us. We may not have exactly looked like the Duke boys on TV, but we had fun pretending we were."

Someone in the middle of the crowd blurted, "Token!"

"Whoever you are, your ignorance is showing," Gus said. "My friend here has been a part of this town, and my life, for decades."

"He's probably an actor. Liar! Racist!"

"Did he help you steal the election?"

"I heard they both attacked someone at the supermarket!"

Attacked? Gus had to grit his teeth to stop himself from saying something he might regret.

That got the mob worked up again.

"*You're* the actors and racists," Banks shot back. "I mean, who the hell are all of you? Until recently, I've never seen one of you before. You come here like mindless sharks sensing blood in the water, tearing up our town. If you're going to fight for something, at least have some understanding of what you're fighting for."

The crowd settled down.

"What you should all do is go back to your real homes, and leave our town alone. We were doing just fine until you got here," Banks said.

"I wouldn't necessarily say that," a man called out from Gus's left.

Braden Stranger, dressed in a sharp suit and carrying a briefcase, ascended the steps to stand alongside Gus. "Springerville has been a town in decline during my time here. It's why I ran for mayor. I want to preserve small towns like this, not watch them degrade into dens of crime and faltering morals."

The resounding cheers were deafening. Stranger smiled at the crowd, taking it all in. Gus narrowed his gaze, staring at the side of Stranger's head.

"Crime has been steadily on the rise over the past year," Stranger said when they settled down. "Mr. Fuller here is just an extension of the good old boy establishment that's been in place here for far too long. The world has changed, but not the core of Springerville or its leaders. The decay of this town has occurred under the watch of Mayor Sturgis. How are we to believe things will get better under the auspices of the very man that Sturgis hand selected and connived to get elected? How can he respect your rights if he doesn't even respect you?"

Fists went in the air and the posterboard signs swayed back and forth.

Gus couldn't stand by and watch this continue. He shouted above the cacophony. "Have you had a chance to look over the crime statistics *before* you arrived? You came in with the first wave of transplants right when big cities were emptying out. I think you'll find a distinct correlation with the unacceptable rise in crime."

Stranger spun on his heel and looked Gus in the eye.

"So, what you're saying is, you don't appreciate having outsiders in your little town? I'll bet you're not the only one who thinks that way. A lot of these crimes have gone on without an apprehension. That is a direct criticism of your law enforcement. Maybe it's people of your ilk preying upon, what have I heard folks in town call us? Oh, yes, *locusts*. Perhaps the police here don't feel it necessary to arrest their own for committing crimes. That doesn't feel like Southern hospitality to me. It feels like something else very Southern from decades ago. Is that the America you want to return to? I refuse to let that happen." He turned to the mob. "*We* refuse to let that happen!"

The uproar was loud enough to nearly knock Gus back on his heels.

He knew his ears were burning red. He cursed himself for falling into Stranger's trap. The crowd surged forward. Banks and Don did their best to keep them at bay, but even they couldn't battle a crowd this big.

What he wanted to do was press Stranger on who the victims of those crimes were. From what he'd gathered from James and Wally, it was almost exclusively longtime residents.

The problem was, he knew whatever he said would be turned around by Stranger. And with people and cameras locked on them. As much as he hated to admit it, he, Banks, and Don had to leave.

The crowd went wild as they made to exit the scenario. Gus felt something hot and wet hit his neck and knew someone had thrown a drink at him. He thrust his hands in his pockets and balled them into fists.

"Walk away," Stranger said to them. "Not just from these steps, but from the position you stole from me in the election. Your time is over, Gus Fuller. Nobody wants your version of the great American town."

"Permission to knock his head clear off his pencil neck," Don whispered as they walked away.

"Only if he gets in a bar fight at your place, which is something he'll be very careful not to do."

# CHAPTER 32

The next day, Gus and Emma were with Banks, Wally, and Sarah Birch at the Iron Works. Dennis had turned to CNN and they saw the replay of the previous day's debacle.

"You sure do know how to get a crowd going," Wally said.

Gus was still seething. "Well, I did tell all of you that I'm not a politician."

"However, Dawn James confirmed with me this morning that there were no new break-ins last night. So, on the one front, you did pretty darn good."

Gus had looped Wally in on his and Banks's excursion at the pizza parlor. Wally said off the record, he didn't . . . couldn't . . . approve. But as a lifelong Springerville resident, he was grateful.

"Dennis, turn that nonsense off," Don said. "I sure as hell don't want the cable company thinking we watch CNN."

"You're right about that," Dennis said, flipping to a replay of a college basketball game and turning the sound on low.

"Funny how none of these networks have shown Chris here shutting everyone up," Don said.

"I'm too handsome for TV," Banks said.

"Shows you how calculated everything is," Wally said. "And one-sided. It's not necessarily fake news. Just . . . tailored." He turned to Gus. "James also told me there were two more overdoses last night. One of them was Bobby Cantrell. The other was a recent transplant. She was found slumped in front of the recycling center."

"Are they all right?"

Wally nodded. "Both saved by Narcan. Appears Bobby got hooked on painkillers after breaking his leg senior year. You remember that game?"

"That was a few years ago," Gus said somberly. "I knew he was going through some troubles. When you lose the means of your scholarship, your whole life takes a turn. Poor kid."

"Let's hope this was his rock bottom."

Gus recalled Dawn James telling him they were running low on Narcan. It was almost impossible to wrap his head around. For the first time since they had passed, he was glad his parents weren't here to see what was happening to their home. Gus made a silent prayer for Bobby and the other woman.

With every fiber of his being, Gus knew that Sniper's gang had to be behind the majority of their drug epidemic. James had told him she'd been advised to keep it on the back burner for now, considering the overall state of Springerville. What fool would do such a thing? Someone at the top was allowing the pot to stir, and for the rot that had come to town to fester. They both would bet their lives that Stranger's puppet master . . . or masters . . . was behind it.

Sarah flicked a tear from her eye. She was a big supporter of the high school football team and had worried about Bobby since the on-field accident. She sipped her wine, and said, "I made all the calls on my list. Didn't get a single no."

"Same here," Emma said. "Now the problem is, how do we get everyone there without *them* finding out?"

The headline in the Charleston newspaper had read:

*The Town That Dreaded Locust Sundown.*

The ensuing article now painted Gus and the town with a broad brush, decrying them as backwards and an affront to the modern-day South. A woman was quoted as saying, "We've spent generations overcoming the stereotypes folks have of us. What's going on in Springerville has set us back decades." Who the woman was didn't matter. The words helped build on the narrative.

"I just brought one of those old church vans back to life," Banks said. "Tinted the windows this morning. I'll use that to pick people up from their houses and make as many trips as I can."

"And Ron and Mike have their minivan they can use," Wally added. "That should keep things low-key enough."

Gus nursed a glass of seltzer. "Are we sure the old sugarhouse is even safe?"

Dennis gave a thumbs-up. "I had my friend Sharper check it out. He's a structural engineer. It won't collapse on anyone. At least not tonight. It's a little dirty, but that won't be an issue. A few volunteers are there now sprucing it up."

The derelict Amboy Sugar House has stood untouched and decaying for close to twenty years. When the last of the Amboy line had passed, there were no interested suitors to take over the business. It was tucked well away from any main roads, now surrounded by trees that seemed to be growing to protect its anonymity. Wally had thought it would be the perfect spot to have their town hall. Their goal was to keep any and all lookie-loos well away from the empty building.

"What about tables and chairs?" Banks asked.

"Dropped them off this morning," Don said. "We won't have chairs for everyone, just those that need them. Like Wally here."

"Very funny," Wally said.

Everyone was trying to break the tension, but for Gus, it was an impossible task. His mind went over a thousand scenarios and how things could go wrong, in the hopes of devising ways to prevent them.

Emma, sensing his unease because she was closer to him than anyone on the planet, rubbed his back. "We've got the logistics covered, honey. You just worry about what you're going to say."

"I know. I know. I'm just frustrated."

"We all are. Which is why we have to take action."

"And security is covered," Banks said. "Between me, Randy, Ash, and a few of their buddies, no one is getting near there . . . well, not without a little trouble."

Gus pushed his stool away from the bar and slapped his hand on the top. "Let's get this show on the road."

Anyone who happened to drive down the path into the woods where the Amboy Sugar House resided would have seen very little. The few cars and trucks around were parked in the back. The wood façade still peeled paint in great ribbons and the roof was as bowed as ever.

But for the first time in over two decades, there was light.

It wasn't very bright because the main electrical line

had been out of service since Clinton was president. The flicker of candles seeped out of the makeshift shades that had been tacked over the windows for the night's events.

Chris Banks pointed out the windows that needed some adjusting. "Secure those corners so nothing gets out," he said to Freddie Powell.

Freddie, who was tracing the scars on his head with his fingertips, said, "On it."

Ron and Mike's alarm company minivan trundled down the rutted road. Banks waved them to the back where they would discharge the last of the participants.

"How's it looking?" he said into the walkie-talkie.

"Quiet. A few people just went into the Iron Works, but that's about it," replied Ashley Early. She was keeping an eye on the center of town. Dennis ran the Iron Works while Don was somewhere in the dark outside the sugarhouse.

"What do you say, Dennis?"

There was a moment's pause, then Dennis replied, "No regulars, of course. Just locusts looking to get drunk. I can help them with that."

Mike came over and tapped Banks on the shoulder. "Time to rock."

As Mike ran to the back door of the sugarhouse, Banks whispered, "Knock 'em dead, Gus."

Gus was relieved to see that no one had brought their children. There were some husbands and wives in attendance, but never both if they had kids. The floor of the sugarhouse was packed.

"You'd think we said Toby Keith was the opening act," Gus said to Emma.

"Maybe you're just as popular."

"You have everything prepared?" Wally said. He was dressed in a suit with a vest and pocket square. Emma had insisted he take one of the few chairs they had, despite Donald's joke earlier.

"Got it right here," Gus replied as he tapped the side of his head.

Wally shook his head and rolled his eyes. "That's what got you in trouble over at city hall."

"Yeah, but now I'm in friendly territory." Gus smiled and it felt genuine and good. He wasn't one for public speaking, but back before he'd joined the military, he wasn't one for shooting at another person. When desperate times came to the fore, he was not one to back down.

"Just give me a minute," Wally said. "I'll get the crowd warmed up."

It was odd seeing so many people Gus had known most of his life standing in the glimmering candlelight. If he hadn't known better, he'd have thought this was a public gathering from another era, though this intent was the same as so many.

They had to save their town, and their way of life.

After Wally came out and introduced Gus to a wave of applause, Emma had to push him onto the makeshift stage.

His reception was as humbling as it was discomfiting. Gus's face blazed as he waved his hands up and down to get everyone to settle in.

"I'm sorry there's no microphone," he said at the start. "I'll do my best to talk loud."

"Just pretend you're calling an order up!" Muriel Sheen cried out, eliciting titters.

"That I can do. I can't thank you all enough for coming out tonight. I wouldn't have done this if I didn't feel it was an emergency."

Heads nodded and sober faces were locked on him.

"What we're dealing with isn't pretty. In fact, it's ugly as hell. I never thought I'd live to see the day when my hometown turned into . . . into what it has. I ran for mayor when Mayor Sturgis pulled out of the race to restore order and peace to the place we love. And thanks to you, despite Braden Stranger's efforts, we won."

Another round of applause thundered in the abandoned building.

When they settled down, which didn't take long because everyone knew the seriousness of this clandestine meeting, Gus continued. "Since the election, things have only gotten worse. So many of you have been hit hard with losses. Losses that the news is now blaming us for because they've managed to twist my words. Which brings me to this. I felt the right thing to do would be to step aside in hopes that it would end the wave of violence and crime that has swamped our streets and homes." There were gasps and heads shook in disapproval. "I spoke to Mayor Sturgis, who advised me to see this through. What I need to do is ask you. If you think I should walk away, please raise your hand. Don't be shy and don't feel like I'll take it personally. I ran for mayor to represent *you*. I need to make sure that everything I do is in *your* best interest. Consequences to myself don't matter. It's you who matters."

What followed was a long, uncomfortable silence. People looked about as if waiting to see who would be the first to raise their hand. Gus held his breath, scanning the crowd, making sure not to lock eyes with anyone lest he sway their vote.

After a while, he said, "I promise you, it's okay. When I get my luncheonette back and running, I'll still serve my biscuits and gravy to you." There were some titters, but still no hands in the air. "Not one?"

Mike, who was standing in the back, said, "Not a chance, Gus!"

Sarah Birch, who was just a few feet from Gus, beamed as she clapped. Then others joined her. Gus's chest felt so full, he thought it would burst.

"Thank you," he said once he'd composed himself. "You have no idea how important this is to me. You elected me to fight and fight I will. In fact, I wanted you all here to tell you that we'll have to fight this together. How do we do that? By changing the way we live our lives until this is over. And I promise you, this will end. The people who have come to our town are not here to stay."

A lone hand went up. It belonged to Aileen Wuhrer. "How can an old gal like me fight back?"

Gus smiled. Aileen would be ninety in a couple of years and here she was ready to pitch in. "What I'll suggest is for any age gal. I know a lot of you don't like to even think about it, but if you're not doing it already, lock your doors whether you're home or not. If you see something or someone suspicious, call the police right away." Springerville's finest had been left out of the night's proceedings because if they were somehow caught, he didn't want James and her force implicated in any kind of collusion. "For you business owners, get a security camera. I know none of us like the whole Big Brother concept, but capturing these thieves and vandals on video will go a long way to helping the police. If you can't afford one, come to me. I have money left in my campaign fund and a little extra to help with the expense. I'm sure Ron and Mike will be happy to figure it all out."

"It sounds like you want Springerville to be a prison," Mr. Fernandez, who ran a successful HVAC company, said.

"This is all just temporary. We're not done. You need to write to the paper. Write to the television stations. Write to our governor even though I know she's not the most popular person down here. Make your voices heard."

Frankie Martin strode up to the makeshift stage and stood beside Gus. "We can protest these damn protestors! They think they're loud? We can be louder because this means everything to us!"

There were a lot of words of encouragement and clapping. Gus had to interject. "I would prefer if you didn't protest. The people who had invaded our town are, for a large part, professionals. If you come there in peace, they will find a way to twist things their way. Same with the media, who will be more than happy to film it all and spew whatever message they choose. Plus, I don't want anyone hurt."

"We can take care of ourselves," someone said.

"I know you can," Gus said. "Lord knows, I'm aware of the spirit within all of you. But we can't fall into their traps like I have. Things may get worse before they get better. Their interest won't last long. They'll find another place to ruin. Or *try* to ruin. You've seen what mobs like this have done to cities all across America over the past half dozen years. That won't happen here. It simply won't."

The roof nearly came off from the round of applause.

What Gus didn't say was that he and Banks had worked out a team of trained men and women who would be on patrol every night in the hopes of stopping terrible things before they happened. He'd even kept it secret from Wally and Chief of Police James. The fewer people who knew, the better. He was done mopping up the latest disaster while keeping a smile for the cameras. These interlopers—since locusts had lost its shine—were going to learn just exactly who they were messing with . . . and they weren't going to like it.

He was about to tell everyone to avail themselves of the beverages that had been provided when Randy burst through the door.

"They're coming!"

"Who?" Gus replied, feeling his blood pressure rise.

"The news!"

Christ. That was the last thing he wanted to hear. Dealing with one of the thugs or progressive airheads that had somehow gotten wind of the meeting would have been simple.

They couldn't manhandle and threaten a news crew now, could they?

Banks and Freddie Powell cut through the crowd and grabbed Gus and Wally by the arm. "Time to go," Banks said.

Gus shrugged him off. "I'm not going anywhere."

Banks got hold of him again. "Oh yes you are. If the press gets ahold of you holding a secret meeting along with Wally, we're toast. In their eyes, all that's missing are some torches and hoods."

As much as he wanted to, Gus couldn't argue with his logic.

"Come on, Emma," Gus said.

"Can anything go our way?" Emma said, taking Gus's hand.

"If it's easy, it's not worth pursuing."

As they walked past everyone who had gathered there, he got dozens of pats on the back and words of encouragement.

"We've got this," Sarah Birch said.

"What are you going to say?"

Sarah flashed a wicked smile. "We could tell them we're just out here worshipping the devil." She grabbed ahold of Bank's hand. "Or better yet, this is just a quirky engagement party."

Banks rolled his eyes and shook his head.

"I think that sounds better than the devil thing," Gus said.

"It doesn't matter what we say. All that does matter is that you and Wally aren't here. Now go!" Sarah said.

Banks and Freddie led them out a side door where Randy and Ash were waiting. "Here's my keys," Randy said, tossing them to Gus. "You know how to get out, right?"

"With my eyes closed," Gus said, snatching the keys in midair. He opened the doors for Emma and Wally and started up the new Dodge Charger. The irony wasn't lost on him. He was going to thank them all for the warning, but Banks, Freddie, and Randy had all slipped back into the dark.

It took him a bit to find the control to keep the headlights from going on. Seconds later, they were creeping down the busted road that once led to the truck depot. He drove through the old lot, remembering when he was a kid and seeing it full of sugar trucks and swearing, sweaty men. His uncle had worked there for fifteen years before a stroke put him on permanent disability.

"Shouldn't you slow down?" Emma said when he popped out of the lot and onto another much disused road.

"Moon's nice and bright tonight and I know the way. But you might want to put your seatbelt on just in case. You okay back there, Wally?"

He was expecting the mayor to be pale and sweaty after being hustled out of their meeting. Instead, the old man was all smiles. "That was a close one, wasn't it? That'll put hair on your chest."

"No, thank you" Emma said.

When Gus got out of the trees and onto the main road, he still kept the lights off.

"Shouldn't you be going that way?" Emma asked, pointing out the back.

"I just want to check on something."

"Gus, hon, we're supposed to be getting out of trouble, not back into it."

"This is going to be trouble no matter what."

When he was at the turnoff that led to the sugarhouse, he pulled to the other side of the road and parked the car thirty feet into the tree line where it couldn't be seen. "Keep the motor running. I'll be right back."

Before Emma could protest, he kissed her on the mouth and slipped out of the car. He did hear Wally say, "He knows what he's doing."

Gus hoped he lived up to Wally's words.

He ran in a crouch across the empty road. Up ahead, he could hear people talking and saw the faint light coming from the sugarhouse through the trees. A bright spotlight flared to life. Must have been from the news crew.

Staying within the trees, Gus made as little noise as possible.

At the bend in the road, he saw a dark shape parked

astride the cracked asphalt and grass. A tiny orange spark within it came and went, just like a July firefly.

Gus had expected to see a motorcycle or two, assuming Sniper and his cronies had somehow gotten the drop on them.

The black BMW was a surprise.

Gus got close enough to see a man in the driver's seat sucking on a vape pen, the thin smoke curling out of the partially open window.

Wasn't that Stranger's crony's car? Roger something or other. Word was that he had lived briefly in Springerville when he was a young child. It wasn't long enough to make an indelible impression. He should have stayed away.

Gus snuck around the back of the car, keeping low enough not to be seen in the rear or side-view mirrors. When he got to the driver's side door, he slipped his fingers under the handle. Roger sat idly smoking his vape.

In one swift motion, Gus ripped the door open, grabbed Roger by his collar and yanked him out of the car, throwing him onto the hardpack. The vape pen bounced from his hand and skittered under the BMW.

"What? Whuh?"

Roger squinted, trying to make out who had attacked him in the dark. Gus spun him so he was on his stomach and drove a knee into the small of his back. He jerked one of Roger's arms back hard enough to elicit a pained yelp. Gus used his other hand to hold the man's head in place, which meant he was eating dirt.

Doing his best to disguise his voice, Gus barked, "Who told you?"

Roger feebly struggled to turn around. "Told me what?" He sounded on the verge of tears.

"To bring the media here."

"Son of a . . ."

Gus's head whipped to the right. Banks was there pushing a wool hat from his face. Gus put his fingers to his lips. He didn't want to give Roger a chance to ID either of them. Banks must have been on patrol and spotted the BMW that certainly didn't belong.

When Roger tried to jerk his head to the side, Gus almost lost his grip. He doubled down on the pressure. "Don't move."

"Okay, okay."

"I'll ask you again, who told you?"

"Nobody told me."

"Then why are you here?"

"To . . . to make sure it happened."

"How did you know?" Gus knew he had to work fast and get back to the car. Pretty soon, folks would start filing out of the sugarhouse and heading home.

"I don't know what you're talking about."

Gus delivered a savage rabbit punch to Roger's kidney. He almost felt bad for beating on a man who would never have a chance in a fair fight.

Almost.

Banks clearly didn't share the same feeling. He pressed his boot onto Roger's shoulder, applying more and more pressure until Gus heard bones start to crack. Banks had his hat pulled all the way down to his chin, but there were eyeholes so he could see exactly what he was doing.

"Ow! Jesus, you're breaking my shoulder!"

Gus rabbit punched him in the kidney to knock some of the wind out of him. "I'd keep it down if I were you. How did you know what was happening here?" Gus repeated.

Huffing dirt with every forced exhalation, Roger said,

"We have people tailing certain people from the town. Please, let me go. I can't breathe."

"You're breathing just fine. Who's being tailed?"

"I don't . . . I don't know. I was just told to go here tonight and wait."

Gus didn't bother asking who told him.

So, they were being followed. They would have to be more careful from now on. He wondered which of them had eyes on their backs.

Gus got close to Roger's ear, and growled, "You might want to think about leaving town. That boss of yours won't have your back. If you want to see this through, you could get hurt."

"I'm hurt now."

"This is only a love tap."

Gus punched Roger in the back of the head. His struggling stopped immediately.

"Good work," Banks said as he ripped off his hat and wiped away the sweat from his face.

"Had to be done."

"I wouldn't have been so nice."

"Trust me, I'm aware."

Gus and Banks lifted Roger like a rag doll and set him back behind the wheel of his BMW. He patted his head, and said, "Let's hope you remember this when you come to and let Stranger know. We're onto you."

Banks scribbled on a piece of paper he had in his pocket.

"What's that?" Gus asked.

"Directions to the interstate. And a little incentive to follow them." When he was done, he slipped the note into Roger's shirt pocket.

"You coming with me?" Gus said.

"Nah. I'll work on damage control here. Get Emma and Wally home. We're getting old."

"Maybe you are."

"That's not what I mean. We've been followed and didn't even know it. Kinda burns me up."

"Me, too. Though now we know. And we're going to put a stop to it."

They bumped fists. Banks had a mile-wide grin. "Damn straight we will."

Gus slammed the door and sprinted back to the Charger.

"What happened?" Emma asked.

"Just doing a little information gathering." The Charger rumbled to life. Gus eased it back onto the dark road.

"You find anything?" Wally asked from the back seat.

"I sure did." Gus left it at that.

When Emma turned on the interior light, her eyes went wide when she saw his knuckles. "Again? We're going to have to tape boxing gloves on you."

Gus's eyes kept sliding to the rearview mirror. "Not just yet. There's plenty more to do. Don't want to soften any blows."

# CHAPTER 33

That night, Gus made sure no one was outside Wally's house before dropping him off. He completely bypassed his own house. Odds were high that a news van would be parked outside. They went to Emma's place, and he told her to lock the door until he got back. Then, he drove Randy's Charger back to his house and walked the half mile to Emma's. By the time he got back, he was exhausted.

Emma had a bag of ice for his hand and a glass of whiskey for the rest of him.

"Well, that was . . . exciting," she said as they lay in bed sipping from jelly jars.

"Can't wait to see what Sarah ended up saying."

Gus got up to put the plastic bag of ice in the bathroom sink. When he came back, he sank into the bed. "That's a disaster for tomorrow. Right now, I just need to shut my eyes."

"Are you sure?"

Emma pulled the sheet down. She'd managed to remove every strip of clothing she had on during his trip to and from the bathroom.

Sleep would have to wait.

* * *

The news the next day wasn't good. No one from town was interviewed. Reporters told the tale of a town's clandestine meeting to work out a way to "deport" the influx of new citizens to Springerville. They were compared to the ex-president, which was all designed to get a certain portion of the population foaming at the mouth.

Gus watched it all unfold while he and Emma ate a light breakfast.

"At least they got it mostly right," he said. "Anyone who thinks we're wrong for wanting to get rid of them should invite them into their own town. They'll be singing a different tune. At least the ones with a brain."

"Some places are pretty short on brains," Emma said before taking a spoonful of yogurt.

His phone buzzed on the kitchen table. "Yeah."

"You see the news?" Banks asked.

"I think I'm on the fifth cycle of the story."

"They interviewed about a half a dozen people, but conveniently left all that out."

"What did they say you were all doing there?"

Banks chuckled. "Having a square dance. I don't think they liked our answer."

"On another note, we have to deal with the eyes at our backs."

"You don't have to tell me twice."

"Maybe later today, we can shake our shadows."

"Sounds about right to me. But first, I have a transmission to fix when I get to the shop. Call me if you need anything."

"You bet." Gus's phone buzzed again. "Yeah."

"It's real bad out here," Chief of Police Dawn James said. "And there seems to be a direct correlation between that little stunt last night and this shit show. We'll talk about last night later."

Gus didn't even try to pretend he didn't know what she was talking about. "What's happening now?"

"Downtown is overrun with fools. It's like a jumbo jet parachuted them in overnight. Word to the wise, stay wherever you are."

"I'm supposed to meet my insurance adjuster this morning."

James sighed. "There's been more damage to your place overnight. We caught three men and two women tearing down the boarding and looting it."

Gus gripped the phone tighter. "There wasn't much left to loot."

"That's what frustrated them, so they decided to add to the damages. One of them spray-painted some nasty things all over the walls. We have them locked up right now."

"I'm still meeting him."

"Not a good idea. We're dealing with enough without my worrying about protecting you."

"I don't need protection."

"Against an unruly mob? Yes, you do. Not to mention these ass hats with the media. Please, stay put."

Emma saw the look on his face when he hung up and came over to him. "What's going on?"

"They hit my place again last night. And Dawn says it's a nightmare in town right now. I have to check my house, then I'm going to the luncheonette. I'll be back in a couple of hours."

"If you think I'm sitting here like some damsel in distress, you're gravely mistaken. In case you forgot, school's out for me and I'm just as mad as you are. Let's get changed and go."

He didn't argue. Fifteen minutes later they pulled up in

front of his house. Toilet paper hung from the branches of the tree in his front yard. One of the second-floor windows had been broken and dog excrement had been smeared on his porch and front door. At least he hoped it was dog excrement. He and Emma walked around the house, looking for more damage. Luckily, the so-called peaceful protestors had stuck to the front.

"That smell," Emma said, fanning her nose.

"Nothing a hose and some soap can't fix." Gus checked his watch. "The adjuster should be at the luncheonette about now. Come on. I'll patch up that window later. Getting to be an expert at it."

Gus hit the brakes just before they made the turn onto Main Street. It looked like the road had been closed for some kind of fair. The streets and sidewalks were filled with people, almost all of them under thirty and looking for trouble. There was no way he could drive down to his luncheonette. He was pretty sure his adjustor wouldn't make the attempt to wade through the crowd of angry protestors.

There were tents erected haphazardly on every patch of grass. Rolling down his window, Gus was hit by a wave of weed smoke and body odor.

How did things degrade so quickly?

"They must outnumber the total population here by two-to-one," Emma said.

"Where the heck did they all come from?"

"People like this are moths to a flame. Right now, Stranger and the media have this place glowing like a thousand-watt lightbulb at midnight." Every now and then, different chants would ring out. Gus had the windows closed and couldn't make out what they were saying. "The professionally offended."

"What's that?"

"We have a whole generation of people that are professionally offended. They want to be offended because it then makes them survivors of some great tragedy that they can trade on. You're not with the in-crowd if your sensibilities haven't been assaulted to the point where you can say you're both a victim and a survivor," Emma said.

Gus couldn't take his eyes off the crowd. "Is that what drives all of this?"

"I'm around children all day. Being a victim is very important to them, at least when they get older and exposed to social media. Mix that with the concept of 'adulting' as something to avoid, and we have millions of wounded souls who refuse to grow up. It's a very dangerous concoction. Let's go back to my place."

A young man pulled away from the crowd and urinated against Al's barbershop. The shop was closed.

"They're going to destroy every bit of our town if this keeps up."

Emma patted his thigh. "This flame's burning too bright to last very long. Once they realize there isn't a Starbucks or McDonald's for miles, they'll find somewhere else to muck up."

"I don't know." Gus wanted to strap a cattle catcher on the front of Emma's SUV and drive the herd into the Atlantic Ocean. "Or I can get rid of the one that brought them all here."

He put the car in drive and slowly headed for Oak Street.

"What did you say?"

He didn't realize he'd thought out loud. "Just working on a solution. Let's just . . ."

A rock hit the windshield, taking a chunk out of the

glass, a spider's web of cracks branching out from the dent. A dozen or so protestors who had been on the way to join the raucous party recognized Gus. Before he could make a U-turn, they ran to the SUV, two of them jumping on the front hood.

Gus hit the brakes and one of them slipped off the side.

Emma's door flew open. A woman and man reached for her.

"Don't you touch her!" Gus said.

Emma elbowed the man in the nose. Blood sprayed the interior of her car and he fell back onto the street. The woman curled her fingers in Emma's hair and tugged. Emma grabbed her wrist to try and stop her.

"Redneck garbage," the woman screamed. Her eyes were wild. Gus was certain she was on something. "She's a racist, too!"

Gus reached over to extricate the woman's grasp from Emma's hair but fell short. He had to get out of the car.

When he did, it felt like high school football all over again. He was the man with the ball, and everyone wanted to get a piece of him. Gus shrugged off two men and clambered atop the SUV, sliding over the roof so he could land next to the woman assaulting Emma. He pinched the bones of her wrist hard enough to make her let go. Emma unclipped her seatbelt and kicked the woman in the stomach when she tried to reach for her again.

Gus's own stomach dropped.

They were surrounded.

People screamed incoherently. Some were close enough for their spittle to hit Gus's face. He had to fight himself from lashing out. Members of the unruly crowd were recording the incident on their phones.

"If you back up, we can turn around and get out of here," Gus said to the encroaching mob. He kept his body in front of Emma and wasn't surprised she hadn't gotten back in the car. She had her dander up and she wasn't done if they weren't done.

"Go back to whatever cave you came from!" a woman shouted.

"Get the hell out of South Carolina!"

"Racist pig!"

"Your America is dead . . . just like you!"

He didn't like that last one a bit. That was a threat. Gus didn't take kindly to threats.

"I can't go back to my cave with you in my way."

He turned to Emma, and said, "Please get in the car."

Her jaw was set. He looked down to see her hands balled into fists. She softened a bit when she locked eyes with him and slid onto her seat. When Gus went to close the door, it was stopped by a meaty fist.

A burly man wearing a denim jacket loaded with different patches refused to let Gus close the door.

"Hand off the door," Gus said.

"Yeah? Or what?" He was probably in his late twenties with a week's worth of beard and food stuck in between his teeth.

"I'm asking you nicely."

He added his other hand to the door. "Make me."

"I'm not looking for a fight," Gus lied. Right about now, that's exactly what he wanted.

"Looks like you found one."

The shouting had died down. Now, everyone had a phone in their hand recording the exchange.

If there were no phones, Gus could end the standoff with a jab to the bridge of the man's nose. In two seconds, he would be able to close the door and get back in the driver's seat.

Unfortunately, he'd fallen into their trap. He should have listened to Dawn James and stayed at Emma's place. His penchant for ignoring well-informed advice was going to be his downfall. That along with his under-estimating the level of insanity that gripped Springerville.

"Get your hands off the damn door," Emma spat. She went to punch the man's ham hand, but Gus caught her by the wrist.

"That's one wild cat you got there," the man said, eyeing Emma in a way that made Gus angrier, if that was even possible.

No matter what, he couldn't throw the first punch. He shouldn't throw *any* punch, but he didn't see this ending without a fist or two flying.

"Better be careful, big guy," Gus said in a gravelly voice. "She might just smack the ugly right outta you."

The man curled his lip but didn't say anything. Nor did he let go of the door.

"Though that might be a good thing," Gus continued. "Face like that, with all these cameras around, could end up breaking a few screens. And those things are expensive."

That did the trick. He finally let go of the car door so he could swing at Gus's face. Unfortunately for him, Emma was quick enough to kick the door so it thwacked him in the thigh, setting his aim off. He barely clipped Gus's shoulder, punching the side of the car with a painful-sounding crack.

The crowd around them gasped.

Then cheered when the man recovered in an instant and went for Gus again. This time, Gus sidestepped his punch. Emma was out of the car and hit him dead center in the gut.

"Nice try, hellcat."

He charged Gus, driving him into the SUV. Gus's back didn't appreciate the impact, but it didn't stop him from hitting the man with an uppercut. That did it. The man took a knee, holding onto his chin and jaw. Emma finished him off with a haymaker to his cheek. His head whipcracked to the side.

Gus used the moment where all eyes were on his attacker to dash around the SUV and go for the driver's side door. He felt a sharp pain in his forearm and saw a man holding a tree branch smiling at him.

"Are you out of your mind?" Gus asked.

The man swung the branch again, this time knocking off the side-view mirror.

"Get in, Gus!" Emma said, reaching for him.

Boy, did he want to wipe that smile off that man's face. Gus reluctantly got in the car and put it in reverse. Fists pounded on the car until he got away from them. Then came the thuds as they threw whatever they could find at Emma's car. Seconds later, they were out of sight.

"That was insane," Emma said as she flicked her wrist and examined her red knuckles. "Don't get me wrong, I did enjoy hitting that meathead. What are they all thinking?"

Gus tried in vain to settle his nerves. Every molecule in his body was screaming for him to fight. "They're not thinking. Not a one of them. When you talk about mindless drones, remember today." He punched the wheel in frustration. Sure, the media would love the phone video of him punching that moron. He was positive they would edit out the part where the man swung first. They probably wouldn't show Emma getting her licks in, either.

To hell with it. As if being a diplomat would have earned him any points in the world of public opinion right about now.

His town had gone mad, and he felt himself sliding into lunacy right along with it.

# CHAPTER 34

Braden Stranger had tried to drive downtown and found an impasse at every street. The mob had grown to epic proportions for a small town. The news of the townies having a clandestine meeting had everyone up in arms. Even though Gus Fuller hadn't been caught there, they all knew and believed he had been the catalyst. It called up dark memories of the very bad times in the South oh so long, or not so long, ago.

It appeared the ranks of the rowdy had swelled considerably. One couldn't accuse his side of not being organized.

Stranger couldn't have been happier.

Until someone threw a soda cup at his Porsche, splashing it all over his windshield and hood. He almost got out to grab the person who'd launched it.

His hand was on the door handle when a can filled with garbage popped out of the mass of protestors and landed in front of his car, missing it by inches.

When he looked to his left, he saw someone had made a fire with a cardboard box they must have pulled out of the trash. The wind blew the box, sending tongues of flame skittering into the crowd. People kicked it and whooped as if it were a game.

The steps of city hall were hidden beneath a throng of protestors. He could make out an array of different shouts and chants and was unsure if the half of them even knew what they were protesting.

Pulling away as fast as he could, he dialed Roger and got his voicemail. "Damn it, Roger, where are you? Have you seen downtown? Where did these new people come from? It's pure bedlam. Yes, it's exactly what we wanted, but even I don't feel safe here. Call me as soon as you get this, you hear me?"

He drove back to his house, where there were six motorcycles parked in the driveway. Sniper and a couple of his lackeys had been missing the past couple of days. It appeared they were back, along with the usual retinue of at least three thugs that kept an eye on him and his property.

As soon as he got out of his Porsche, Sniper walked out his front door smoking a cigar. "Looks like you need a car wash."

"Were you smoking that in my house?" Stranger said.

"Only for a little bit," Sniper said casually. "Well, this one. I finished another before this one."

Stranger's anger simmered. Not that he could do anything to Sniper. Not if he valued his health.

"Did you have anything to do with what's going on downtown?"

Sniper took a drag and exhaled a thick plume of white smoke Stranger's way. "Me? As far as I know, that's all you and your buddies. I'm just here to do a job. You don't like it, tell them."

The man had a look on his face as if he knew something. Stranger was painfully aware it was pointless to press him.

"How am I to assume authority if I can't even safely drive to city hall?"

"That's your problem. I never had an issue with authority myself. *My* authority, I mean."

Stranger strode past him and locked his door. He made a quick sweep of his house to make sure no other bikers were inside. When he knew he was alone, he made a call.

"Have you seen the news?"

"You keep forgetting, we *are* the news. Looks to me like things are progressing nicely."

Stranger paced around his kitchen. "It looks like a goddamn siege. Last I saw, they were starting fires . . . and playing with it!"

There was a slight chuckle on the other end. "That is what they tend to do. Is there a reason for this call?"

"Yes. How many more did you send overnight? I appreciate the help, but it's at the point where it's getting out of hand."

"Are you questioning me?"

Stranger gripped his kitchen counter, closed his eyes, and took a deep breath. "No, no, I'm not questioning you. I would have appreciated a little heads-up. I'm just concerned. Protesting is one thing. This looks like a prison riot. If this keeps going the way it is, there won't be a town left to run."

The long pause put a lump in Stranger's throat. He shouldn't have called when his emotions were cresting. But damn it, they sent him here to plant the flag in this little town with hopes of taking over the state. He had to be able to have a say!

"Do you want a town of slack-jawed yokels, or something entirely new and improved? You're to stay in your house and say nothing for two more days. Let them do what they need to do. When the dust clears, most of the locals who opposed you will be making plans to leave. We're not just replacing the mayor. If that was the ultimate goal, we could have made that happen quite easily. Braden, you need to step back and see the bigger picture. We're going to *redesign* Springerville, and it will be the roadmap for transforming not just the state, but everywhere in the country that needs an assist to the twenty-first century. It's in your best interest now to hang up, rethink questioning us again, and figure out your place in all of this. You're not invaluable. It's wise to remember that."

The line went dead before Stranger could cobble together a reply.

A quick glance out his back window revealed two bikers dressed in leather drinking beer by his Buddha statue. When they were finished, they left the empty bottles on the Buddha's head.

Heathens. He didn't even recognize them. It appeared everything had changed overnight.

Never before in this whole enterprise had he felt smaller and more insignificant. *Not invaluable. They* chose *him!* How dare they treat him like some ignorant, petulant child.

Stranger dialed Roger and got his voicemail again. Had they pulled Roger out of the project without telling him?

One of the bikers had stopped talking to his swarthy companion and was staring at Stranger through the sliding glass door.

Had one of them done something to Roger? But why?

This was spinning out of control.

Sit and wait. That was nothing but a show of weakness. Stranger had been picked because of his strength and conviction and burning ambition. He'd never sat back and let others run the show.

What would his benefactors think of him if he just cowered and waited now? How could he one day run the state if he couldn't handle the upheaval in a one-horse town?

He'd show them why he'd been chosen.


Gus needed to vent at least some of the anger coursing through his system. Which was why he got in his Jeep and was out driving late at night. He'd waited until Emma was asleep to call Banks and hit the road.

Driving down backroads and in the residential areas of Springerville, you would never know that downtown was a scene of complete chaos. All was quiet, save for the crickets and other night critters. He kept checking his rear and side-view mirrors, looking for his tail. Maybe they had clocked out for the day. Or were part of the party around city hall.

No. If anyone was being followed, it had to be him, and they wouldn't take a night off. Whoever they were, they were doing a very good job navigating the unlit side streets without the aid of headlights.

He drove past the winding road to the sugarhouse and kept on going in the direction of the town salvage yard, cruising on a mostly straight road surrounded by trees.

The pop and flash of gunfire behind him had him stomping on the brakes. He made a quick U-turn, heading back. His Jeep's headlights illuminated a black Honda. Banks and Freddie Powell were on either side of the car with their rifles pointed at the driver.

"Gotcha," Gus said before he got out of his Jeep.

"You want me to smoke him?" Freddie said. On a sunny day, Freddie was an imposing man. In the dark, with a high-powered rifle, he looked downright terrifying. He was playing it up to put an extra scare in Gus's shadow.

"I might," Gus said, ambling over to the driver's side window. He knocked on the glass. The man behind the wheel looked to be around thirty, scruffy, with a tattoo of a devil on his neck. His eyes bulged from their sockets. The window had been partially open which meant he'd heard what Freddie and Gus had said. He rolled it the rest of the way down.

"You a friend of Sniper's?" Gus asked.

"Wh-who?"

Gus looked him in the eye and saw he had no clue who Sniper was.

"You like following people?"

"I . . . I don't know what you're talking about. I was just out for a drive."

Banks kicked the passenger door. "Right. With your lights out on a pitch-black road. Let's finish him and leave him in the woods. The bears will have him eaten in a couple of days."

Gus almost grinned. There were no bears in Springerville, but the driver clearly wasn't aware of that. The ammonia smell of urine wafted from the car.

Despite the smell, Gus leaned closer. "Who hired you to follow me?"

"I don't know. Just some dude."

Gus thrummed his fingers on the hood of the car. "Just some dude. He have a name?"

"No."

Shots split the still night. Gus, Banks, and Freddie hit the dirt.

Another car was heading toward them. A man leaned out of a window, firing away with a pistol.

Recovering quickly, Freddie and Banks returned fire,

laying waste to the car's front grill. The hood flew up and the car swerved into the brush before hitting a tree.

"We got a two-for-one special!" Banks cried out as he ran to the wrecked car.

"Stay with him," Gus said to Freddie. His friend shoved the gun into the frightened man's cheek.

Two men were inside the smoking car. The driver was a bit woozy, but the shooter was up and ready to resume shooting. Gus was on him like a panther. He grabbed his wrist and slammed it against the car. The gun skittered over the hood and fell out of sight. "I don't like being shot at," Gus said, seething.

These two looked like they could have been related to the first one.

"You wanna die?" the man shouted.

Gus doubled him over with a punch to his solar plexus. "Judging by your skills, it wouldn't be by your hands." He punched him in the face when he tried to straighten up.

"Fuck you," the man said between wheezing breaths.

"Your days of following people are over. You understand me?"

Banks's captive tried to run away. Banks clubbed him in his back and sent him sprawling.

Gus whistled. They had to wrap this up fast. "Freddie, bring him over here."

The terrified driver of the first car came stumbling over.

"You tell the dude who hired you that you and everyone else quit. Pronto. Anyone else in my town gets followed, they don't make it to see another sunrise."

He shook his head vigorously.

"I believe you will," Gus said. He looked at the shooter. "You, I'm not so sure. So, looks like I have to put you on disability."

A sharp heel kick to the man's knee produced a pop

and crack that made Gus wince. That knee was good and broken. The shooter howled in agony.

"We're onto you now," Gus said. "And as you can see, we know our town better, and we have bigger guns. You're in over your heads, boys. Time to go home. Well, after the hospital."

"Please don't kill us," the one on the ground said.

"Don't give us a reason to," Banks barked. "Now, get in the car and keep rolling until you see the Pacific Ocean. You dig?"

It took some effort for the two men to get the shooter with the broken knee into the car. It peeled away and out of sight, this time with the lights on.

Freddie traced the scars on his head while he silently watched them drive away.

"You think that'll do it?" Banks said.

"Everyone knows what happens when you punch a bully," Gus said.

"Even so, we need to all watch each other's backs."

"I'll be happy to," Freddie said. "Haven't had this much fun in a while."

Even his grin was scary.

# CHAPTER 35

The town was overrun. Dawn James had called out to neighboring counties to lend a hand. Wally, who should have been home convalescing, was in a makeshift office at the police station manning phones and trying to find a way to get a handle on the situation.

Gus had boarded up the broken windows in his house and found graffiti on his back door. His neighbor Patrick hadn't heard or seen a thing, but that could be explained by his having to work from home because he couldn't get past the mob to his office. He apologized for having his headset on. Gus assured him there was no need to apologize or be the lookout for his house.

Emma had called her principal to see if there was any news about her suspension. The reply from Ms. Morales had been terse and discouraging. It looked like things were teetering on Emma losing her job. She was more angry than upset. Gus thought about the stages of grief and gave Emma as much support as he could.

Chris Banks came by around dinnertime. He had a grave look on his face.

"I had to close my shop hours ago," he said as he settled into a wicker chair on the porch. "Those devils broke every pane of glass in my bay doors. I was under a truck working on that transmission when it happened. There were at least a dozen of them with bricks. One of them nearly hit me. It was over as fast as it began. I'll never forget those faces. They were smiling, Gus. What kind of maniac smiles while destroying another man's property . . . in front of him?"

It was another blow to Gus. He felt responsible for everything that was happening to his friends. "I'm so sorry, man. I still can't wrap my head around all of this."

"It's not your fault. But it gets worse. They stole Mr. Santiago's car. I had it parked outside, and someone drove off with it while I was boarding up the bays. I can't get all woe is me because there are other businesses that have it worse. All the ones where the protestors are concentrated are in shambles. They started looting in the afternoon. I'll bet most of Main has been picked clean. The cops have had their hands full. It's impossible to catch them in the act because the crowds are too thick, and the looters are gone by the time the cops push their way through."

Gus abruptly got up from his chair. Emma came out to the porch, saw his face, and said, "What now?"

"They're looting and destroying everything in sight. When it was just my place, I could handle it. But enough's enough. I have to resign. Let Stranger and his mob win the battle. We'll just have to take a step back and plan how to win the war."

Banks accepted the cold beer Emma had brought out. "I hate to say this, but I agree. Give them what they want now before there's nothing left to give. Or, you can find me a net big enough to snatch them all up and I can dump them in the desert."

"I like your idea. You think they'll have one at Bass Pro Shops?"

"If they do, I'll mortgage my house to buy it if I have to."

Gus looked over at Emma. "What do you think?"

She was silent for a moment. Then, she took a deep breath and sipped on her beer. "I think Chris is right. If this goes on much longer, Springerville will be unrecognizable."

He slapped his hand on the porch railing. "Then it's settled. I'll call Wally in the morning. I'd call him now, but the man needs some sleep. Not that I think he'll get much with all that's going on."

A silent sadness passed through them as they drank beer and stared into the darkness. Crickets sang all around them and gnats swarmed around the streetlights.

Emma leaned forward in her chair, and said, "You smell that?"

"It's a little early for skunks," Gus said.

"But not for skunk weed," Banks said.

Several seconds later, they saw the source of the bitter smell as five men walked under the soft glow of the streetlight across the road from Gus's house. They were drinking and passing a joint around. They stopped and stared at Gus's house. He wondered if they could see the three of them on the porch since he hadn't turned on the overhead light. Even the living room was dark.

"What are they looking at?" Banks whispered.

"What I believe they were looking for," Gus said.

Banks and Gus slowly started to rise from their seats.

"Don't go starting anything," Emma said.

"Wouldn't dream of it, darling."

The first bottle came tumbling end over end. It landed in a bush to the right of the porch. The next one rattled feebly on the lawn.

But the third hit the steps and shattered. A shard of

glass pegged Gus in the cheek. He glanced at Banks. "Considering I won't be mayor . . ."

"Your chance to prove you can be an efficient street cleaner."

Emma sighed. "Oh boy."

One of the men was ready to launch another bottle when Gus and Banks stormed off the porch. By the time the group of bottle throwers realized what was coming, it was too late, though they did attempt to flee.

Banks left his feet and rolled into them like a wrecking ball, taking three out of the race to escape. That left two for Gus. He threw an elbow at one, clipping him on the side of the head. The shot reverberated up his arm. Another down.

"You like throwing bottles?" Gus called after the last man standing, who kept looking back with abject fear on his face.

Getting closer, Gus grabbed a garbage pail without breaking his stride. He heaved it at the man. The can barreled into his back and planted him face first on the ground. When Gus got to him and yanked his head up by his hair, he was greeted by a face covered in blood.

"Come with me," Gus growled, lifting him to his feet and practically dragging him along. The one he'd elbowed was leaning against a car, cradling the side of his head. "You, too."

"Huh?"

Probably had a concussion. Good. Gus grabbed him by the arm and brought both men staggering back to where Banks was stomping on cell phones. The three men were sitting cross-legged on the sidewalk. None of them could be much older than twenty-five.

"You can't do that!" one of the men protested.

"I think I just did."

"Jerry, Tyler, one of you has to record this."

Gus eyed his two captives. Neither reached for their phones. When their friends saw the state they were in, they tried to get up. Banks said, "Sit!"

They sat.

Lights flickered on in the nearby houses and Gus's neighbors came out to investigate.

"Everything okay out here?" Mr. Anders said. He was a widower going on seventy who'd lived across from Gus all his life.

"Just caught these fellas throwing bottles at us and Emma," Gus said.

"We didn't see you there," one of the men on the ground said.

"Oh, so that makes hauling bottles at houses all right in your book?" Gus snapped.

"I need a doctor," the one with the bloody face said.

"You need a good kick in the pants," Mr. Anders said.

"You're gonna pay for my phone."

"Like hell I will. You're lucky all I did was break it," Banks said.

"Need me to call the police?" Mr. Anders asked.

"They have their hands full," Gus replied, narrowing his eyes at the men, not a one of them with even a lick of a Southern accent.

"So, what are you going to do with us?" the one with the bloody face asked.

Gus got real close to him. "Tell you to hit the road. Your time here is done. You get me?"

He nodded.

Gus held out his hand. "Your phones, please."

"No."

Gus stretched his neck until it cracked. "That wasn't a yes or no question. Give me your phones."

Both men reluctantly pulled their phones out of their back pockets and handed them over. Gus gave them all one last look that he hoped drove his message to get out of Dodge home. "Now go. And don't let us see you around again." He chucked their phones in the sewer.

The men on the ground got up and helped the other two limp away.

"You can't just beat everyone up," Emma said, surprising Gus. He hadn't heard her sneak up behind him.

"Well, not everyone. But we can sure try."

Banks tapped Gus on the chest with the back of his hand. "Hey, I have an idea."

"Chris, no," Emma said.

"I'm all ears," Gus said.

"When I left, it looked like more people were pouring into the streets downtown. They must be coming in by car, bus, train, and plane."

"So?"

"Want to take a drive to a certain place where they nest?"

Gus knew what Banks was talking about. "And then what?"

"We stop by my storage lot and pick a little something up. Scratch that. We get something big. Really big."

A smile bloomed on Gus's face. "A little eye for an eye?"

"More like suburban renewal."

Emma's head went back and forth as she waited for one of them to expand on their idea. "You going to tell me?"

"I don't want you to get mad," Gus said.

"Too late. I'm already mad. But not at you."

Banks put an arm around her, and they walked across the street to lock up Gus's house. "I think you might get a kick out of this."

\* \* \*

Driving in Gus's Jeep, they stopped at a rise on Main Street so they could witness the mayhem downtown. Their town was in ruins. The streets were filled with people either drinking, smoking, screaming, or looking for something to destroy.

"I thought you both should see this first," Banks said.

Gus didn't see any patrol cars. He wondered if Dawn James had decided it was best to stay back, if only for the safety of her men and women.

"I don't know whether I want to cry or shout until my throat is raw," Emma said.

Gus backed up and took them to the lot that Banks had on the outskirts of town where he kept old wrecks that were either reclamation projects or valuable for their spare parts. Banks was out the door before Gus could stop the Jeep. "Just follow me," he said as he opened the gate and slipped into the rows of cars, trucks, and a couple of pontoon boats.

"This is crazy," Emma said.

"Yep. But necessary."

A few minutes later, they heard the heavy-duty truck before they saw it.

Banks's yellow bulldozer came out of the darkness and through the gate. Banks hopped out to lock up and gave them a salute.

"He looks like a kid on Christmas morning," Emma said.

"Except this time, he's Santa and we're going to deliver a whole lot of much-deserved coal."

Luckily, the distance between the lot and The Pennsylvania was short, because the bulldozer topped out at around five miles per hour. Just as Banks suspected, the trailer park was empty.

Save for Shane Varrick, who stumbled out of his trailer when he heard them pull up. He had a baseball cap on backwards and was holding a bowl of franks and beans.

"What's going on?" he asked Gus and Emma when they got out of the Jeep.

"Is anyone in the trailers?" Gus asked.

Shane scratched his stomach. "I don't think so. I've been grateful for the peace and quiet. The few folks that was here before everyone on those buses came up and left. I don't blame them. This used to be a quiet place to live. Not exactly the Ritz, but we all felt safe and could rest at night. That sure ain't the case anymore."

"We need to be sure. Do you have keys to all the trailers?"

"Yeah. Why?"

"I know this will put you in a bad spot, but we're fixing to level the place. Destroy the nest, so to speak."

"You're what?"

"Think of it as a fire sale," Banks called out over the deep thrum of the bulldozer. "Everything must go!"

Shane looked at the three of them as if they had just walked out of a spaceship and demanded he take them to his leader.

"I know that when we do this, you'll be out of a job," Gus said.

"That is a pretty big consideration of mine," Shane said. He set the bowl of food on the trailer step.

"Banks needs some help at the shop. And I'll need someone who can swing a hammer to get my place back in order. In the meantime, I know we can find something for you. You know we take care of our own. We need to drive these people out so we can get things right again."

Shane went inside his trailer without saying a word. Gus expected him to lock the door.

To his surprise, Shane came back out with four cans of cheap beer and a key ring. "Might as well toast the occasion. I'm sick of this place and the knotheads who live here anyway."

After popping open the beers, he, Gus, and Emma went about checking each trailer. Most of the doors were unlocked, and for good reason. If they were unkempt before, things had been taken to another level. Each trailer looked like it had been hit by a cyclone after a college frat party.

When they did come upon a locked trailer, Shane hesitated. "This is the one that Sniper and his buddies use. For what, I don't know. I heard they're basically camping out at Braden Stranger's place now. But I have my suspicions about what goes on in there."

"Let me open it," Gus said. "It might be booby-trapped." He'd had plenty of experience in Afghanistan carefully picking his way down streets and into seemingly abandoned houses that were rigged to maim and kill anyone who happened upon them. More men and women than he could count had lost limbs or worse. "You might want to step back," he said to Emma and Shane.

Carefully opening the thin door, he looked up and down the doorframe to see if there were any trip wires. Using his phone to see in the dark, his light fell upon wrapped up bricks of what looked like marijuana and possibly cocaine. A table was littered with scales and other drug paraphernalia. He also spotted plastic storage containers full of tiny, zipped bags filled with pills and white rocks. The source of so many of the town's recent problems was all there on ugly display. He thought of young Gina Cordry who had almost lost her life and felt his blood come to a boil.

"Bulldozer's not enough for this. You got any gas, Shane?"

"Plenty. Never know when the generators will need a topping off."

"Can you please fetch me one?"

"On it." Shane ran off to get the gas.

"What's in there?" Emma said, still keeping her distance.

"Things we don't want here."

When Shane returned with the metal gas can, Gus took it from him, stepped in the trailer, and doused everything. "You have your lighter, Emma?"

"You know I gave up smoking."

Gus rolled his eyes. "I know you still sneak one from time to time. You think my nose is broken?"

Shaking her head, Emma dug her cheap lighter out of her purse and tossed it to him. "Guess it's good I didn't quit entirely."

"For tonight. We'll talk more about that tomorrow."

Gus found a box of rolling papers and lit it up. He backed out of the trailer and tossed it inside. The flames erupted with a sharp *whup*! "Run," he said to Emma and Shane. There might have been some chemicals in there and he didn't want them close by if it blew.

They caught up to Banks who was ready to demolish the first trailer, which was well away from Sniper's burning drug den.

"Playing with fire now?" Banks said.

"Sniper's office. He had enough drugs in there to overdose every man, woman, and child in town."

Banks's eyes narrowed. "Once the flames die down a bit, I'll make sure there's nothing left."

"We should stay upwind of it," Emma said.

"You do that," Banks said. "Now, I've got work to do."

He put the bulldozer in gear and plowed into the nearest trailer. The screech of rending metal and crack of snapping wood hurt Gus's ears. The trio walked over to Shane's trailer and watched Banks level the entire trailer park. He saved Sniper's place for last, rolling over it again and again, pulverizing it to tiny bits.

"Shane, I want you to grab your stuff and stay at my place for now. We can't have you anywhere near here when Sniper and his friends come back."

"That's awfully nice of you. It won't take me long. I don't have much."

"It's the least I can do after"—he swept his hands around the demolished trailer park—"all of this. We have to keep you safe."

Banks rolled over to them with a giant smile on his face. "I have always wanted to do something like that. I don't know if it's the fumes or adrenaline, but I'm riding a big high."

"Probably both," Gus said. "Get your toy back to the lot. We'll meet you there."

The bulldozer rumbled out of the park and onto the road like a lumbering giant. Shane came out with a black garbage bag and a cardboard case of Budweiser.

"That's everything?" Emma asked, clearly concerned.

"Everything worth saving. When we get to your place, you mind if I use your shower?"

Gus took his bag and put it in the trunk. "Mind? I insist."

# CHAPTER 36

Braden Stranger tried Roger one more time and got a message that his mailbox was full. The man had clearly deserted him.

*Spineless coward*, Stranger seethed as he put on one of his best suits.

No matter. He didn't need Roger anymore. As of today, he was taking the reins. He was going to show his benefactors that he could take charge of a situation. Maybe then, they'd realize they couldn't push him around. He'd been too compliant in the past, too eager to do their bidding because he thought he saw the big picture. In doing so, he hadn't seen the forest for the trees. They had to realize he was their partner, not their puppet. It was time to cut the strings.

Snoring emanated out of the guest room. It was either Sniper or another of his miscreant posse. Stranger would have to make it clear that their presence was no longer warranted or desired.

Disgusted, he made his way to his kitchen and started up his espresso machine. The stench of lingering cigar smoke assailed his senses. Sniper was, in fact, sitting at the dining room table looking at his phone. A smoldering cigar sat in a tin ashtray the man always kept in his jacket pocket.

"Morning, sunshine," Sniper said cheerily, though there was no mirth in his eyes.

"Morning," Stranger said as he walked away.

"Busy night last night. I thought we put the fear of God into these rednecks. Definitely gave their little hometown a makeover."

Stranger tried his best to tune him out. There were plenty of other things jockeying for his mind's attention. He set about making espresso. To his dismay, Sniper followed him into his kitchen.

"Problem is, while we were out painting the town, someone came and wrecked The Pennsylvania."

Stranger arched an eyebrow. "What do you mean wrecked the Pennsylvania?"

"I mean totaled it. Flattened every square inch. Well, except for that weasel Shane's trailer. He's somewhere on the wind." Sniper's jaw muscles pulsed as he spoke. "I lost some very valuable stuff. Worth more than your stupid house."

Stranger was smart enough not to ask what the *valuable stuff* could be. He assumed it was drugs or guns or both. "You look at me as if I did it." His stomach quivered when Sniper stepped closer.

"I'm looking at you so you can see how angry I am. You tell your boss things are going to step up a bit today. I know he wanted a drawn-out process to wear everyone down, but I'm turning this Tupperware party to a full-on rager. Same results, just in less time. That smug redneck you're running against probably won't be around for long.

Oh, and if you hear anything about the whereabouts of Shane, you let us know. Pronto. We clear on that?"

"Quite."

"Good. I'm pulling my men from here. We have man's work to do. Think you can make it on your own?"

A mixture of elation and unadulterated fear coursed through Stranger's veins. He found it hard to stand. "I'll be fine."

Sniper turned and walked away. "I'm sure you think you will." He shouted up the stairs for whoever was in the guest room to get up and meet him outside. The door slammed behind Sniper. Stranger staggered a bit and leaned against the counter, taking deep breaths.

Who the hell had torn down The Pennsylvania?

It could have been anyone. There were plenty of angry people who called Springerville home. Just because they were the minority for the moment didn't mean they couldn't lash out.

Whatever. That was Sniper's problem.

Stranger called Shane but the man didn't pick up.

"Hope you're running as fast as you can," he said while he poured a cup of espresso.

Things were not looking up for Gus, either. Stranger was on the fence about it. His battles were in boardrooms, not with biker enforcers. Should he warn Gus? From what he'd heard, the man should already be on high alert after beating Sniper at the bar and now, potentially being behind destroying the psychotic's side business.

*That's his battle*, Stranger thought. *Not mine.*

He needed to compose himself before heading to city hall. Meditating couldn't cut through the roiling thoughts and emotions. He finished his espresso, popped an anti-anxiety pill in his mouth and headed for his car.

\* \* \*

Downtown looked like Woodstock—the original, not the phony one in the nineties. Stranger had to drive down five side streets just to find an available space. A police cruiser pulled up to him when he got out. A young officer rolled down his window.

"I'd advise you to steer clear for now," he said.

"I'm from New York, son. I see crowds like this on every street."

"I'm sure you do. But maybe not this riled up."

"Then maybe you should do your job and round up the worst offenders."

The cop was unphased. "My orders are to keep to the periphery, let the wind get out of their sails. All those cameras around, not to mention everyone having a cell phone and a grudge, makes for a volatile situation. It's not safe, Mr. Stranger."

"I'll take that under advisement."

What Stranger wanted to tell this young punk was that the people who had swarmed the downtown were there *for* him, not against him. But that would be playing his hand, not something he would ever do.

"Suit yourself. Good luck." The window rolled back up and the cop said something into his radio.

Stranger adjusted his suit jacket and walked downtown with his head held high. Sniper wanted to put the pedal to the metal. Stranger couldn't afford to let him do that. What would be the point of being mayor of a broken town? He had to take charge of the situation, show that he was the only man who could restore peace and order. Springerville *needed* him. It was abundantly clear that the current mayor and Gus were incompetent. Where were they when Springerville needed them most? Hiding in their houses, presumably.

That was the narrative Stranger was sure to push to the media. The world was tired of men like Wally Sturgis and Gus Fuller. They'd had their time, and they were stuck *in* time.

The new century called for new leaders with fresh perspectives. *Enlightened* perspectives.

As he turned onto Main Street, he walked past several tents that had been set up on a grassy area beside the hardware store . . . or what was left of it. Boards had replaced windows, but the door had been kicked in. Tools and parts lay all over the ground and littered the sidewalk. A burly man walked out with an armful of drills in boxes. He looked at Stranger as if daring him to say a word. Stranger averted his gaze.

Swiveling to avoid the looter, Stranger saw the Iron Works Bar and Grill across and up one street. Its windows were intact. Several men, one of them big enough to have been an offensive lineman, stood outside, urging anyone to keep moving. There was a big handmade sign in the window that said:

**CLOSED UNTIL COMMON SENSE RETURNS.**

City hall was four blocks away, but it may as well have been miles. The throng of protestors was thicker than cold peanut butter. Various offshoots were chanting their own slogans. Signs were everywhere, though just as many were underfoot and crushed. There were fires in trash cans and the unmistakable odor of urine and feces hung in the air.

It was an unmitigated nightmare.

Was this what they wanted all along? Why else would

they flood Springerville with so many rabble-rousers and downright criminals?

Stranger was beginning to reassess this entire plan. When he'd signed on, the end game was for intellectualism to replace decades of ignorance and conservatism.

This wasn't intellectualism. It was outright animal indignance.

He had to make it stop.

"Nice suit," a white woman with dreadlocks said to him as he jockeyed through the crowd. He ignored her.

For a moment, he feared he'd be swallowed up by the literally unwashed masses and considered turning back and locking himself in his house until everything blew over. Seeing as that's what his benefactors wanted him to do, he fought through his fear.

Feeling like a salmon swimming upstream, he pushed and elbowed his way toward city hall, one labored step at a time. Along the way, his head had been clipped by waving signs more times than he could count, his feet stepped on, his appearance mocked, and even had a cup of what he hoped was beer spill down his pant leg.

"Look at this rich rogue," a youngish man with a goatee said when Stranger accidentally bumped into him. "Looks like a lawyer or something." He nudged his friends who were sharing a bottle of liquor. "You here to defend that racist caveman?"

"The very opposite," Stranger snapped. "I'm the man who ran against him and *will* take his place when he's forced to resign."

The man laughed. "Yeah, right. You're the answer to what doesn't belong and why."

One of his friends pawed at Stranger's suit. "Real nice duds. Definitely not from around here."

Stranger wanted to remind him that neither was he,

judging by his accent and the fact that he was part of the uncontrolled crowd. "My name is Braden Stranger and you're here protesting because the election was stolen from me. Now, if you'll let me pass, I can set things straight."

"I don't know who Braden Stranger is, but I do know a wealthy SOB who probably doesn't care about people or the planet when I see one," the one with the goatee said.

Things were deteriorating quickly. Rather than try to convince them who he was, Stranger made as hasty an exit as possible. Something hit the back of his head and he heard their taunts, telling people to stop the rich guy.

Fortunately, their voices were swallowed up by the cacophony.

It took him five minutes to wriggle his way through the remaining one block to city hall. The doors looked to be locked, and there were two policemen standing on the inside, watching the madness.

Somehow, Stranger made it to the doors and knocked on the glass. "Do either of you have a megaphone?"

They stared right through him. This was outrageous! They knew exactly who he was. It wasn't as if he were asking them for protection. He simply needed a way to project his voice over the unruly din.

"Are you kidding me?" He slapped the glass. The larger of the two officers stepped closer.

"I need you to step back. Do not hit the glass again."

Was there a slight smile on his face? Stranger fumed.

Fine. The police weren't going to help.

A woman wearing a T-shirt and jeans was on the steps to his right shouting into a megaphone. She was whipping up the crowd, repeating over and over that Gus Fuller was a racist pig and a homophobe.

Sidling over to her, he tapped her on the shoulder, and said, "Would you mind if I borrowed your megaphone?"

She was quite pretty, in a crunchy way, with her cheeks reddened from shouting. "Who the heck are you?"

"The man you're fighting for. I was the one who ran against Gus Fuller. When he resigns, I'll run this town the right way."

She looked him up and down. "How do I know that?"

"Weren't you here for the election?" he asked, knowing the answer. She was most certainly part of the second wave.

"I don't need to vote to stand up for what's right," she said. When he made a motion for her megaphone, she jerked it away. "Guys in suits are behind everything that's wrong." She put the megaphone to her lips and said to the crowd, "Am I right? Can we trust white men in suits?"

The protestors, almost all of them white, yelled, "No!"

"You don't understand what you're saying," Stranger said to the woman, reaching out to her.

She edged away from him. "You all saw that? He's trying to touch me!" Her pretty face morphed into something out of a nightmare. "I didn't give you permission to touch me, whoever you are!"

"Get the hell away from her!"

"Abuser!"

"Take your privilege and your suit and go home!"

An empty beer can bounced off Stranger's arm. That was followed by a clump of grass that thudded against his chest. Bits of soil hit him in the face, went into his mouth.

The woman turned the bullhorn on him and screeched at the top of her lungs, "Get away from me! Get out of my personal space! Pervert!"

Pervert. Where had that even come from?

He searched for the TV cameras, but they were focused

elsewhere, interviewing people who no doubt had no real clue where they were. If someone from the media could just look this way, they'd vouch for him.

"Don't touch me!" the woman shouted again.

Stranger realized he was dealing with someone completely unhinged. More projectiles came his way. He turned his back to the crowd to make sure nothing hit his face. When he did, he came eye to eye with the two police officers behind the doors. The look of smug satisfaction on their faces told him that no matter what, they wouldn't lend a hand to help him. They blamed him for this disaster in their streets.

As much as it pained him to admit it, they were right to do so, even though he hadn't personally called everyone here.

There was no way he could fight through the crowd now.

He skirted the top step, climbed on the edge, and dropped to the ground ten feet below. The impact rocked him from his ankles to his hips, but he was at least on his feet. A few people stared at him, but because their view had been blocked by the steps, they weren't aware of what had just transpired.

With his heart thudding in his chest, Braden Stranger ran down the street, bumping into people as he passed, wondering how he was going to circle around and get to his car.

# CHAPTER 37

"They what?" Gus was sitting in his lounge chair, with Emma on the couch and Shane puttering around upstairs. "You mind if I put this on speaker?"

Gus tapped the phone and set it on the coffee table, atop a collection of newspapers.

"The officers I spoke to said the protestors ran him right off the city hall steps," Wally Sturgis said, his voice tinny but clear.

"I thought they were doing all of this for him," Gus said.

"Aw, hell, most of them have never seen or heard of him. They're doing it because they like to cause chaos. I swear, I recognize some of their faces from the news. I know they've been at St. Louis, Seattle, Portland, New York. These are pros, Gus, or as professional as you can get with being a drifter who adopts any cause that lets you vent your pent-up anger. Jesus, you want to bet most of them come from well-to-do homes? Now they hate mommy and daddy because they worked in a system that doesn't give all its profits to the poor or doesn't make every move based on whether it can harm a blade of grass. These jackasses sucked on silver-plated pacifiers until they were in college, and now instead of working, they tear things down that offend them. Well, it all came home to roost for Stranger. They said he was an absolute mess when he went running for his life."

Gus stared gravely at the phone. This should have been good news. Instead, it deepened his concern.

"So, what do you suggest we do?" Emma asked. Gus had called Wally to talk about the best way to get the word out that he was going to resign. Now, things had changed dramatically.

"First of all, like I told you before, you can stop that talk about dropping out. What's going on now is beyond me or you or even Stranger. One thing I've learned is that these nut jobs will move on to the next flavor of the month before you know it. Hell, there's not enough around here to keep them fed, especially with your place trashed. Once they get hungry and find out they've run out of booze and drugs, they'll move on, most likely to a big city that can cater to their needs better. Once that happens, you have to be here to put Humpty-Dumpty back together again."

"Wally, if this goes on for another week, there won't be anything left to put together." Gus got up and paced around the living room. Emma chewed on a nail.

"You're wrong. We'll be here. All of us who call Springerville home. Stores can be rebuilt. Streets can be cleaned. Lawns replaced. As long as we all work together."

Taking a deep breath, Gus said, "Too bad I didn't record that. We could use it in a campaign to get *you* re-elected."

"I'm too old and tired. The next chapter is going to take a very special man. If you're not that man, I don't know who the hell is." Wally said something to someone with what sounded like his hand covering the phone. When he came back, he said, "You hear what went down at The Pennsylvania last night?"

Gus and Emma locked eyes. Gus wasn't going to lie to Wally. But he didn't want to clue him entirely in on what they'd done so he had plausible deniability.

"Yep. I heard."

Wally paused for a bit, no doubt to see if Gus was going to admit his culpability. "I wish I could go by and see it, but Dawn James has me on lockdown in my house. Whoever did that deserves a medal, if you ask me. The place has been an eyesore for years."

Exhaling, Gus said, "Tough times call for tough measures. Glad to see we have some concerned citizens who aren't willing to just sit back and let the fight come to them."

He could almost see Wally's grin on the other side of the line. "We may have to find a way to reward those concerned citizens someday. Might want to add that to your to-do list when you take office."

When he hung up, Gus settled on the couch next to Emma. "That didn't go the way I thought it would."

She put his hand on her lap. "But he's right. This town will need someone strong if we're going to make it through all of this. Those people out there right now are just here to make a mess of things. They have no real vested interest. It's nothing like the protests in the sixties where people were fighting for equality or end the war. This . . . this is just a generation of bawling babies who don't want to grow up and face the real world."

"I know you're right. It just makes me sick that it's happening in our home."

She cupped his face and pulled him close until they touched noses. "Just remember, you ran to send Stranger packing and take our home back. Your job isn't done yet."

They kissed until Shane came clomping down the stairs. He was clean as a freshly bathed baby and wearing clothes with faded stains thanks to Emma having put them through the washer and dryer the night before. Gus almost didn't recognize him, especially because his head was hatless for once.

"Hey, guys, I can't thank you enough for taking me in last night. That was the best night's sleep I've had in a long while. I promise I won't overstay my welcome. I'll start looking for a new place today."

"There's no room at an inn in town," Gus said. "You'll stay right here until things blow over."

"You think they will?"

"No storm lasts forever. I need to keep you safe. I'm sure Stranger and Sniper are blaming you for what happened and wondering where you are. And while you're here, you can keep an eye on my house, keep certain vandals away."

Shane shook his head furiously. "Count me in, Gus. I noticed some spray paint on your house. If you want, I'd be happy to paint over it today."

"That would be fine. Just stick to the back of the house. I want your whereabouts to be a secret for now."

Gus let him know there were waffles and sausages in the kitchen. Emma picked up her phone and went to the porch for a few minutes while Gus tidied up. When she came back inside, she was in tears.

"They let me go," she said, her voice quivering.

"What?" Gus rushed over to her.

"I just spoke to the principal. She'd left a message for me, but I had my phone on silent. I've been terminated."

He wrapped her up in his arms as she sobbed. Teaching was all she wanted to do. Now a narrow-minded fool from San Francisco, the place where up was down and wrong was right, had taken that away from her. All for getting her students to read one of the most popular books in all the world. A book that inspired a love of reading in millions of children.

Gus could spit nails.

When Emma settled down, he asked her, "Would you have wanted to continue working under her?"

Sniffling, she replied, "No."

"Then consider it a blessing. You'll find a new school with a principal that doesn't have his or her head planted firmly up their rear."

Just as she was about to reply, Gus's phone rang with the ringtone Emma had set for Banks's number. It played a snippet of "A Boy Named Sue" by Johnny Cash.

"You see the news?" Banks said.

"I'm not sure I can handle much more this early in the morning," Gus said wearily.

"This time, it's good for a change. There's a big hurricane headed up the coast."

"In what world is that good news?"

"I'm at my shop now, making sure no one touches it. Dennis Runde is here with me." Gus heard Dennis say hello in the background. "He and Don have been doing guard duty, along with some others, to protect the Iron Works. Anyway, he was in the bar doing some paperwork just now and saw the news about the hurricane. You know what that means, don't you?"

Gus still had an arm around Emma, who was straining to hear the conversation. "Honestly, no."

"Those new vans have pulled out! They've got bigger fish to fry. And you know they're not coming back. After the hurricane, there'll be another story. No one wants rehashed old news."

Gus's relief was short-lived. "Okay, that's part of our

problem solved. Now, my concern is, without cameras around, will people settle down and leave, or were the cameras keeping them from really getting out of control?"

Banks sighed. "That's a real glass-half-empty way of looking at things."

"Or realistic. We have to be prepared for it to go either way."

"What we have to do is start some major street cleaning."

"No more bulldozers."

"Nah. More tactical. Like before. Unless the party's plain over and people start wandering out of town ahead of the hurricane."

"Should we meet at the Iron Works to talk things out?"

"Sounds good. Dennis and Don could use some paying customers. But make sure you walk. Your car won't get anywhere near it."

"See you soon."

When he hung up, Emma asked, "Where are you going?"

"Iron Works. Seems like a hurricane has gotten the full attention of our media visitors. We need to talk about next steps. I'm not even going to ask you to stay here. I want you with me."

Her eyes were red and bleary, but she managed a slight smiled when she punched his arm. "You're learning."

Gus went into the kitchen. Shane was rolling two sausages into a pancake dripping with syrup. "Not big on utensils, are you?"

"It's easier this way."

"Emma and I are heading out. Mind the store while we're gone. If anything happens, give me a call."

Shane gave him a greasy thumbs-up.

Gus handed Emma her light jacket. "We'll have to

hoof it. We can make some calls along the way, get the whole gang together."

She looked back at the house. "You sure Shane won't burn the house down by accident?"

Gus considered it for a moment. "Nope. We'll just have to take our chances."

# CHAPTER 38

Don Runde and Randy Early were outside the door to the Iron Works, each holding black baseball bats.

"Hell of a way to greet your customers," Gus said.

"Better to keep out the rodents. Seems to be working."

He was right. The Iron Works looked to be the only business without any damage to the exterior. Enough damage had been done to the interior when they set up the locusts.

Just down the street, people milled about, some of their fervor having been lost.

Two men Gus didn't recognize walked around the corner of the bar, also wielding bats. "Who are they?"

"Just some friends from college. They needed a job and I have the perfect one for them. Come on inside. The party's started without you."

Don and Randy followed them inside. Several tables had been pushed together. At the head was Wally Sturgis. Dawn James sat to his left and Dennis to his right. Ashley Early was there, patting the seat next to her when she saw her husband. Sarah Birch sat alongside Ron and Mike. Banks had a large Coke by his hand. "Saved you the best seat in the house." He gestured for Gus to take the seat at the other head of the table.

"Morning, everybody," Gus said.

Good mornings were exchanged. Everyone looked ragged and exhausted.

Gus looked across the tables at Wally. "So, what's the temperature of the town as you see it?"

"Going down a bit. Hope it continues that way as the storm gets closer."

"Maybe we need to pour some ice on it?" Banks suggested.

James tapped the table. "Was that ice or fire that was applied to The Pennsylvania?"

Banks tipped his chair back and shrugged, wearing a "who me?" expression. Gus remained silent, aware that James had fixed her gaze on him.

"I don't know whether we need to talk about how to clear *out* the town or clean it *up*," Gus said.

"Both," Don said. "I volunteer for clear-out duty."

James turned to him. "I want you on this side of a jail cell."

"I have plenty to do with putting my laundromat back together," Sarah said. "If I can afford to. Have to wait for the insurance people to assess the damage, if they can ever get to within ten feet of it. I saw people on the floor in sleeping bags this morning. They're using it as a campsite!"

"At least they haven't set fires in it like they did with the barbershop," Mike said. "Luckily someone with a clear head appears to have put it out quick. Has anyone seen Al?"

"He left to stay with his daughter and son-in-law in Greensboro for a spell," James said. "I called him and sent him pictures of the damage. He said he was going to talk to his family about whether he ever comes back or not."

Ron shook his head. "That's a shame. Al's been here since the day he was born. His father used to pal around with my grandfather."

"He's not alone," James interjected. "You'd be surprised how many people left for higher ground over the last week."

Wally said, "I've been making it a point to reach out to them, keep them abreast of what's happening and see how they're feeling. Quite a few don't want to come back."

Gus made a fist under the table until his knuckles whitened. "We have our work cut out for us, then."

"Which is why you can never mention resigning again," Wally said.

"Just don't take any pictures with the *Dukes of Hazzard* cast," Banks joked, breaking some of the tension in the room.

"It's getting dark outside," Emma said, looking toward the window. "We must have our own storm heading our way."

"Weatherman called for thunderstorms," Sarah said.

"Which should wash out a few more people by the end of the day," Dennis said.

"Or at least clean them up a bit," Don said. "These people got more funk than an NFL locker room."

"Mother Nature appears to be working on our side," Ashley said.

"But let's not forget that that hurricane is going to hurt others," Gus said. "I know we're down at the moment, but we need to think about ways to help folks if things get bad out there."

Everyone agreed, even though many of them were deeply affected financially.

James stood up, and said, "I have to go, but I want to address some whispers of vigilante justice, or in the case of The Pennsylvania, out-and-out shouts. I know you're all angry. But you need to let us take things from here. Even though TV cameras aren't around, we still have hundreds and hundreds of cell phones out there waiting for their gotcha moment. So, what I propose . . ."

A tremendous boom shook the Iron Works. Everyone went rigid before turning their eyes to the windows.

"Was that thunder?" Sarah asked.

Don's friends came barreling through the doors. "There was an explosion!"

"Where?" Don asked.

"A few blocks down. It looks like it might have been where you said the luncheonette was."

Gus's heart sank as his body rose from the chair. He rushed outside with everyone right behind him. Black smoke billowed up from what was once his luncheonette. People in the streets were panicking. Surely others were hurt or dead. Within the smoke were tongues of flame.

Dawn James ran past him, heading for the fire. The streets were clearing fast as people fled the scene.

Other explosions could be heard in the distance but not seen.

As Gus sprinted after James, he wondered what was going on. The protestors that had flooded Springerville were disruptive and vandals, but this was on another level. This sounded like a military assault.

A screaming woman ran into him and almost knocked him off his feet. Banks was right behind him, propping him up. A block away from the fire, Gus saw a blackened hole where his luncheonette once stood.

Several bodies lay scattered about the debris strewn around. Sirens split the air. James was on her knees, administering chest compressions to a young man whose shirt had been blown clear off. His chest was covered in burns and blood.

"Oh my God!" Emma shrieked behind Gus.

He counted eleven bodies before them. There were others walking about in a daze, but at least they were ambulatory.

Gus and Banks checked the people nearest them, going through a visual check of the bodies and seeing if they were conscious and breathing. The woman in front of Gus groaned when Gus asked her loudly if she could hear him and tapped her shoulder. Her pulse was strong, but judging by her head wound, she may have had a concussion.

Banks was giving the breath of life to another woman while Emma applied pressure to a stomach wound on an unconscious man. Don, Dennis, Ron, and Mike were all attending to the wounded as best they could while Sarah held on to Wally. The first ambulance came, along with the fire truck. It couldn't get too close to the fire because the street was filled with bodies and those working on them. The EMTs went to the man who was getting chest compressions from James. The firefighters hooked the hose to the hydrant across the street and carefully skirted the area of the wounded.

Another blast sounded off in the distance, back beyond the Iron Works.

It sounded as if the entire town was under attack, and Gus suddenly knew who had to be behind it.

"Over here," he said to another EMT that had arrived. Gus had moved on to a man who didn't have any visible wounds but was unconscious and barely breathing. He worried he might have massive internal injuries. Or possibly he'd had a heart attack.

More sirens rang out throughout the town. Dawn James barked orders into her walkie-talkie.

Everything they'd experienced prior to this moment had been nothing but a gentle prelude.

Hell had come to Springerville, and Gus knew the devil was in their midst.


It took calling in first responders from five different towns to get everything under control. At least they hoped so. There had been a total of what the police supposed were four homemade bombs, wiping out Gus's family business, one abandoned house on the other side of town, the old Baptist church that had closed its doors a year ago, and the junkyard. In fact, the bombings had taken place on each point of the compass. The assumption was that it had been planned to spread their resources as thin as possible.

Gus sat on an overturned garbage can and stared at the remains of his family's luncheonette. His hands and shirt were stained with blood, soot, and dirt. Every muscle in his body ached.

"Fires are all out," Banks said. He nudged Gus, who slid over to make room for him. He'd just come from making a round by the various disasters around the town. When he'd set out to go, Gus was too busy tending to the wounded and helping out Springerville's overtaxed fire department.

"For now." Gus sniffed the acrid air and cringed. He'd told Dawn James his suspicions about Sniper and his gang. They were nowhere to be found, which worried him to no end.

"If it was Sniper that did this, he's long gone. Guy like that doesn't stick around to gloat."

"A guy like that is as unpredictable as a reptile."

"Where's Emma?"

"She went with this girl in the ambulance. One of the protestors. Just a kid, really. Said she just graduated high school. She was hurt and afraid and asked Emma to stay with her."

Banks huffed. "Just a kid. When we were eighteen, I remember our fathers telling us we were men and to act like it . . . or else."

Knees popping, Gus groaned when he stood up. "That was a different time. Might as well have been a million years ago." Resting his hands on his hips, he stared at what was left of the luncheonette. "Not much to assess now, is there?"

"I think we can call it a total loss. On the bright side, having it just about leveled should make it easier to rebuild."

"If I can rebuild."

Banks got up and gripped Gus's shoulder. "You will. We all will. Come on, let me take you home. Get some rest before Emma calls you to pick her up."

"Hold on a sec." Gus spotted something completely unexpected in the blackened rubble. His boots crunched on debris as he made his way to where the soda case once stood. The case was now a lump of metal and broken glass.

Somehow, on the floor was the remains of Gus's flag. He always took it in before closing, fearing it would be vandalized. In a patch a foot or so long, some stars and red-and-white stripes crisped but still visible, it lay atop a pile of ash. Gus gingerly picked it up. "I'll be damned."

Banks was beside him, unable to take his eyes off the cloth that should have been burned to nothing. "You know

I'm not one for testifying or seeing signs and miracles. But . . ."

Gus carefully folded it up and put it in his shirt pocket. "Yeah. But." He looked around, as if coming out of a daze. "Where did everyone else go?"

"Home. Or the hospital. Or the morgue."

They walked on weary legs to Bank's Wrangler. Gus's hip barked as he pulled himself inside. There were no more words to say on the drive to his house. Neither had the strength to speak.

Closing his eyes, Gus let his head roll back and forth across the seatback, lulling him to sleep.

When he felt a tap on his chest, he thought he'd been dozing for hours, not minutes.

"You didn't leave your door open, did you?" Banks said.

"No."

Banks reached into his glove compartment and took out two pistols that had been hidden underneath a jumble of papers. One was a Glock 44, the other Smith & Wesson M&P. Banks handed the Smith & Wesson to Gus. "I went back to my place and grabbed these just in case, what with the whole town blowing up and all."

"Good call."

They got out of the truck without shutting the doors as to minimize any noise they might make. Pausing, crouched, they looked all around to make sure there were no hidden surprises waiting for them. When Gus felt they were clear, he waved to Banks to follow him. They crept up the steps and settled on either side of the open doorway. The lights were off inside. Gus strained but couldn't hear a sound.

"Flip the lights on and I'll go in," Gus whispered.

Banks reached inside and flicked the light switch. The

overhead light blazed to life. Gus scooted inside with the gun held before him, his finger hovering on the trigger.

Nothing appeared out of order.

They did the same with the dining room and kitchen. Once they'd swept the bottom floor, they stood out of sight of the windows and listened for any creaking floorboards overhead. Sweat rolled down the sides of their faces.

Keeping his voice low, Gus said, "Maybe Shane forgot to lock the door."

"Sounds like Shane. But then where the hell is he?"

"Might have left when he heard the explosions. He either went out to help or rubberneck."

Gus pointed up. "Let's check anyway."

Everything was normal upstairs as well as the basement. When they were satisfied nothing was amiss, they crashed on the couch.

"Paranoia is exhausting," Gus said.

"Your man Sniper's clearly out to get this town, so it's not exactly paranoia. Just called being smart."

"You want a beer?"

"How about six? I'm beat, but I don't think I could sleep."

Gus had a difficult time opening the refrigerator door because he still had the gun in his hand. He put it on the counter and took out two cans of beer. His stomach grumbled. He and Banks hadn't eaten since breakfast, and now it was dark outside. After grabbing a box of crackers from the cabinet, he backed up into the light switches by the rear door and accidentally turned on the flood light.

The beer and crackers hit the floor.

Gus dashed across the kitchen to snap up the pistol. "Banks!"

His friend was in the kitchen in seconds. "What's up?"

Gus pointed out the window above the sink.

Shane was propped in a chair by the fire pit, staring blankly at the house. There was no doubt he was dead because his head and neck were at an impossible angle. They rushed outside with guns drawn. Banks watched Gus's back while he checked Shane for a pulse. There was no need. His flesh was ice cold.

"*We* did this," Gus said.

Banks didn't say a thing.

After checking the yard, they went inside and called Dawn James to let her know. As soon as Gus hung up, Emma called saying the young woman she was with was in a room and doing fine. Banks waited for the police while Gus picked her up and filled her in on what happened on the way back to his house. Tears snaked down Emma's cheeks.

They returned to a block filled with flashing lights. Gus's neighbors gathered around, asking what had happened and if he needed any help. He walked past them, unable to respond to them. Banks could barely meet his and Emma's eyes as they shuffled inside to give their report. The day that felt as if it would never end extended long into the night, leaving everyone in Springerville cored out and depleted.

# CHAPTER 39

When Gus and Emma awoke the next morning, both of them having slept like the dead once they hit the pillows, he said to her, "Honey, I think you should call your parents and let them know you need to stay with them for a little while." He'd slept with his shotgun leaning against his night table. Dawn James had said she would have a patrol car check on the house every half an hour, just to be extra cautious.

Emma's mother and father lived down in Sarasota in a two-bedroom house that didn't see as much company as they would have liked.

"I'm not leaving you," Emma said defiantly.

"I can't keep you safe here. And if I'm worrying about you all the time, I don't know how I'll be able to function."

She slipped on her robe, went around the bed, and sat next to him. "You're not stuffing me away in Florida. I can look after myself."

His head hung down and he stared at the rumpled sheets. Gus took her hand. "I can't risk losing you. If I lost you . . ."

Emma threw her arms around him and pulled him to her chest. "You're not going to lose me. I'm not going to find myself alone any time soon, and I'm not going to be unarmed."

Gus breathed in the comforting scent of her. "I don't think a pistol packing grammar school teacher gives the right, what's the word, optics."

"Don't forget. I'm not a teacher anymore. And I'm mad as hell."

He lifted his head and kissed her. "On that we agree. I'm feeling things I haven't felt since the war."

"That's a good thing. Because this is a war. So, get up and get used to me sticking around. We have work to do."

The night before, Gus had spoken at length with Dawn James and his suspicions about who was behind the day from hell. He also had to admit that he and Banks had leveled The Pennsylvania after finding a huge cache of drugs in Sniper's trailer. She agreed that Sniper had most likely gotten his pound of flesh and was on his way to Mexico by now. She had one of her men put out a BOLO for Sniper and his gang. During their stay, the police had managed to get their motorcycle makes and models, along with their license plates and pictures of their unsmiling faces.

"They'll ditch the plates, but not the bikes. A lot of them were custom jobs. I figure they'll keep to as many side roads as possible."

"But we don't know for sure they're on the lam," Gus said.

"I wish I could say we did."

Banks had wanted to find their tracks, if tracks were to be found, and pursue them. They all agreed no one was in any shape for a night of biker hunting. And James had warned them that any vigilante justice outside of Springerville would not be welcomed. Not to mention, she wanted it to stop here as well.

After the medical examiner had removed Shane's body in a black zippered bag and James and her team had left after being served jugs of coffee, Gus and Banks stood beside his Jeep talking about what they could do to find Sniper and his gang if they were sticking around. As much faith as they had in Dawn James and the entire Springerville police force, they were spread too thin and just as bone weary as the citizens they had sworn to protect. Besides, none of them were even remotely prepared for what the town had and was going through.

Today was the day to take action.

"You're sticking with me," Gus said to Emma after they'd showered, changed, and eaten.

"You don't have to tell me twice."

When he fired up his Jeep, the radio came on. The news talked about the hurricane touching down in South Carolina the next morning, only it had been reduced to a tropical storm. Rain and high winds were expected.

"Downgrading to a tropical storm is one good piece of news. Maybe our luck is turning," Gus said.

Downtown was deserted. Those who hadn't been wounded had fled overnight, gone back to wherever they'd come from, or maybe on to the next circus. They left behind their tents, garbage, and human waste. Gus parked right outside the embers of his luncheonette. Meeting in the Iron Works was out. He didn't want his friends enclosed in one place knowing Sniper could be lying in wait. Better out here in the open.

Naturally, Banks was the first to arrive with a thermos of coffee and spare disposable cups. "You get any sleep last night?"

"More like falling unconscious. But it feels like I never slept at all."

"We've been there before."

"I'd hoped to never return."

A patrol car cruised by and hit the lights briefly, Officer Iacovo behind the wheel. Gus watched him go down the block and turn the corner, glad he didn't decide to stop and chat.

Randy and Ashley came next, both with bags under their eyes. They had stayed with Randy's parents during the melee, wanting to protect them in case the violence came to their street. They must have been up all night waiting for the other shoe to drop.

"Wish I had a place for you to make some of your delicious pancakes," Gus said. "We could all use them today."

Ashley smiled wearily. "That makes two of us."

"Would be even nicer if Maddie Jackson was still around to supply the berries," Banks said.

"How many people we got?" Randy asked. He rubbed the back of his neck, and his eyes swiveled every which way, looking for trouble.

"There's Freddie Powell, and then Ron and Mike. That'll make sure everyone works in pairs."

"Ron and Mike?" Randy said.

"They were both military, believe it or not. Ron served in the army and Mike was in the air force. They want in, and they know what they're doing."

"Works for me. They have weapons?"

"They do."

The idea was to spread out and comb through the entire town, each team taking a direction on the compass. The criteria was that they had to have military experience and be armed, just in case. Emma was the only exception, but only in not having been in the military. Gus had been to the shooting range with her, and she was a deadeye. Even moving targets had a hard time avoiding her fire.

Dawn James had her team scouring the edges of town and beyond. Something told Gus Sniper was hiding close, maybe in plain sight. No one was to approach Sniper and his gang until everyone had been called and brought to their hiding spot.

Freddie, Ron, and Mike drove up in three separate cars. There was little small talk. Everything had been hashed out over the phone earlier. They knew what needed to be done.

"Freddie, you pair up with Banks."

"Got it." Freddie took his rifle out of his car and put it in Banks's Wrangler. With his free hand, he was running a finger along one of the wider scars on his head. It was a habit that got more pronounced when he was either deep in thought or tense. Right now, Gus was positive he was both.

"We need to keep in constant communication. Put your phones on vibrate so we don't give away anyone's cover if they're close to Sniper's men. I want check-ins every thirty minutes. If you find them, notify everyone and sit tight until we get there. We'll assess the situation then and decide what to do." The decision would involve calling the police or taking care of it themselves. Gus was inclined to get the police no matter what. Shane was already in a cold steel drawer. He didn't want any more death on his hands.

All eyes were on him. He took a moment to look at each of them, then said, "Anyone who wants to back out now can and there's no hard feelings or shame in it."

No one moved.

Gus nodded and patted his thigh. "Okay. This is a search party, not search and destroy. Your weapons are for defense. We all on the same page?"

Everyone muttered their assent.

A voice behind Gus said, "Are you looking for the people that did this?"

He barely recognized the uptight woman who owned the fancy soap shop. Her place had at first been spared, but then systematically torn apart as the crowd grew and lost control.

"We're just talking, is all," Gus said.

"I heard you say this is a search party," she said sheepishly. Gone was the haughty air she used to carry around. "What else could you be searching for?"

Of course, she would have to be the fly in the ointment. He was going to make up a lie when a man said, "We want in." It was the fellow who ran the cybercafe and several of his crew. They might have come down to clean up the damage, but now they wanted in on the action.

Gus held up his hands. "Look, this isn't what you think it is."

Suddenly, more people joined the circle around them. They started talking, and soon everyone was asking Gus what they could do, from tried-and-true townies to the locusts that had moved to Springerville over the past year. It was overwhelming to say the least. How could he run a secret search campaign if dozens of people were now wanting to get in on it.

"Look, I appreciate all of you wanting to pitch in. But this is dangerous work. Several people died yesterday, and there are many more in the hospital. I won't have that happen again. I ask that you please keep this to yourselves and let us do what we need to do."

A middle-aged man Gus had seen around stepped forward, and said, "Whatever you say, Gus. Maybe we haven't seen eye to eye with all of you," he looked around at the mix of people gathered around, "but I for one know when right is right. I'm not sorry for coming here last year. But I am sorry for what's happened the past few months. I think it's time we all worked together and stop letting our fears and prejudices tear us apart."

Gus couldn't have said it better himself. And this from a man he had called a locust. Maybe he needed to rethink his position on things after all. He held out his hand, and the man readily shook it.

"Okay, you all do what you have to, and please don't tell the police. When we need them, we'll bring them in."

"We'll start cleaning things up here," the man said. "And God help any biker that rides into town."

They left to a chorus of cheers and clapping, even on a such a dark day. It gave Gus hope.

"That was . . . interesting," Emma said.

Gus fired up the Jeep. "It was more than that. It was eye opening. He was right. Both sides had their heads up their rear ends. Neither gave the other much of a chance."

"Maybe some good can come out of this." She took her pistol out from underneath the seat and checked the chambers. "So, where to?"

"Stranger's house. It would be an obvious place to find Sniper, so most people would assume he'd be nowhere near it. That's what makes it a possible choice."

He pulled the Jeep over a quarter mile down the road from Stranger's house. Advising Emma to stay low, they made their way through the trees to his property. Gus had her wait behind a thick-trunked tree while he scoped out the area. There were no motorcycles in sight or hidden in the brush.

But there was something shocking.

Stranger's house had been vandalized to the point where it looked like it had been abandoned long ago. Splashes of red paint splattered the exterior. Windows had been smashed. Doors were knocked off their hinges. Pure white furniture had been tossed into the front and backyards and either partially burned or defaced.

Gus cautiously made his way to the front door, the only door still in place. With his gun held down along his thigh, he knocked twice, stepped back and to the side, and leveled it up.

Braden Stranger answered the door, though he was now a different man. His shirt was stained, his hair disheveled, his face drawn and pale. He had a full glass of amber liquid in his hand and his eyes were pools of icy water.

"Come here to gloat?" he said, his speech slurred.

"I've come to look for Sniper."

Waving his arm around the shambles that was his house, he said, "As you can see, his gang of miscreants were here, and made sure I knew it."

Gus tried to peer past Stranger to see if anyone was in the house. "Where are they now?"

"I don't know. Hopefully in hell."

Gus threw looks behind him, expecting an ambush. "Life must be hard without your guard dogs."

Stranger sneered. "What do you know? I didn't want them here. They were forced on me. And then they went ahead and destroyed everything. And you know what? I think that was the plan all along." He knocked back the rest of his drink and threw the glass onto the driveway where it shattered. "Talk about a patsy. I fell right into their trap. They used my ambition to blind me."

"Don't start feeling sorry for yourself now," Gus said. "You brought this on."

"You think I meant for this to happen? You're wrong . . . pardner. I was just put here to make people lose faith in the electoral process, and then show the world that small-town life was no place for a city person."

Gus nearly jumped when Emma popped up beside him. "What do you mean?"

Stranger squinted at her. "You're the teacher they threw out for teaching the book about that wizard kid. Even I thought that was ridiculous. My son loves those books. They won't make him a bad person." He wavered on his feet and looked down at his shirt. "No, I think my genetics have already set that in stone. You asked me what I mean. You might not know it here, but major cities have been bleeding residents for the past few years. If it keeps up, districts have to be redrawn, representatives in Congress will decrease. It's weakening our position."

"And what position is that?" Gus asked.

Braden waved him off. "It's not worth the breath. You know full well. You want to talk about terrorism? We have rich men, much wealthier than I'll ever be, planning for a new America. But the new America needs to keep power centralized. That can't happen if everyone is scattering . . . maybe finding a better way to live and think. Huh. I came here to bring the city to the sticks. Now I know, I was just a dirty bomb that accomplished nothing but chaos and fear. Screw them." He cupped his hands around his mouth, and shouted, "I'm done. You hear me? I'm done."

Gus grabbed him by his arms and shook him. "When were they last here?"

Stranger's eyes focused a bit. "When everything started blowing up. I heard them coming and I took off in my car. When I came back a couple of hours later, this is what I found." He pointed to what looked like excrement smeared on one of the few windows that hadn't been broken. "I think if I was here, I would have ended up just like the house . . . or worse."

"So they could still be anywhere," Emma said to Gus.

"Yep."

For the first time, Stranger looked down at the weapons in their hands. "You're not thinking of going after them, are you?"

"What's it to you?" Gus replied.

"You can't take them on. They're animals. Look at this place."

"They killed Shane Varrick yesterday. In my backyard." Gus's jaw ached from clenching. "Nobody does that and gets away with it."

"Come on, he's no use to us," Emma said.

Stranger raised his hands. "What can I do to help?"

"Help?" Gus said. "The last thing we want is help from the man who upended our town and lives."

"I'm not looking for redemption, if that's what you're thinking. You and I will never be buddies. We're from two different worlds."

Gus thought about how everyone, old and new, had gathered in the town earlier, and wanted to tell the sanctimonious schmuck how wrong he was.

"But we do have something in common. We were both screwed by the same people. And I'm not just talking about Sniper. If you can find him, do what you have to do. Then, maybe, we can work together to take down the real people behind this."

Now, Gus didn't know how he and a failed city slicker could hope to topple the one-percenter who had orchestrated this disaster. Stranger was angry and drunk. There was no sense taking anything he said as truth.

"If I give you my number, will you call me if Sniper comes back around?"

Stranger nodded. "Here's my phone."

Gus typed in his number and gave it back to him.

"I mean it," Stranger said. "I know it's hard to believe, but I want to be on your side. What happened here is unconscionable. But I promise you, this isn't the end. Hell, it's not even the beginning."

"Go inside and sober up. Then we'll talk."

"I'll go inside. I can't make any promises about getting sober."

Gus made a head motion for Emma to head back to the road.

He heard the *whup-whup-whup* of suppressed fire before he saw the damage.

# CHAPTER 40

Gus grabbed Emma and hit the ground hard. Emma shrieked. Glass tinkled around them, along with bits of shrapnel from the house. It ended as suddenly as it had begun.

"Are you all right?" Gus said, hearing retreating footsteps in the distance.

Emma was breathing heavily. She rolled onto her side with a grunt and clutched her thigh. Gus saw blood and his heart went into overdrive. "I think I've been shot."

He gently lifted her hand away to inspect the wound. There was a vertical tear in her jeans. He couldn't make out any damage through the blood.

"Don't move your leg," he said as he plucked his Swiss Army knife out of his pocket. It had been a high school graduation gift from his father and hadn't left his pocket since. He used the scissors to cut away the denim around the wound. Using the end of his shirt to mop up the blood, he nearly staggered with relief when he saw it was only a flesh wound. "You're going to be okay. It just nicked you."

"It sure stings like it's worse than that." She wiped a stray tear from her face with the back of her hand.

"Sometimes they do."

Gus had been grazed by enemy fire twice in the desert. It wasn't fun, but it beat the alternative. "Stranger has to have a first aid kit in the house."

That's when he saw Braden Stranger on the ground, eyes staring blankly into the sky, two seeping holes in his chest. He ran over to check his pulse, and was surprised to find one, even though it was faint.

"Can you call an ambulance?" he asked Emma.

"My God. Is he dead?"

"Not yet."

Emma sat up and fumbled with her phone while Gus dragged Stranger into the house, found a blanket, and draped it over him. He then ran up the stairs, found the bathroom and a brand-new first aid kit. After applying some peroxide to Emma's wound, he dressed it, all while handing her a towel and telling her to apply pressure to Stranger's chest.

"I need you to stay in here with him, and don't let up on the pressure."

"Where are you going?"

"Whoever shot at us can't be far."

"What if they come back?"

"EMTs and police will be here in a few minutes. You'll be fine. Shoot anyone that comes in not wearing a uniform. You got that?"

"Yes."

Stranger's face was losing color fast. Gus kissed Emma and ran his thumb down the side of her face. "I love you. You're the toughest teacher I've ever met."

Her smile was both pained and worried. "Be careful. Don't take them on alone."

He waved his phone. "I'm about to call in the troops."

Dashing out the door, Gus made a quick call to Banks,

Randy, and Mike, telling them what happened and where he was headed. He hadn't heard the roar of motorcycles, so whoever had shot Stranger was either still on the run, had a different vehicle stashed somewhere, or was waiting for him to come after them. All the more reason to proceed with caution. He couldn't let his emotions get the better of him.

Proceeding as quietly as he could through the brush while making as little noise as possible came easily. Aside from his military training, he'd been hunting most of his life. Every now and then, he paused to listen for any movements made by the shooter. He heard a branch breaking to his left and headed in that direction.

There was definitely someone there. A few hurried footsteps confirmed it. Gus estimated whoever it was had to be about forty or so yards ahead of him. He timed his movements, advancing when the shooter walked, hoping to hide his pursuit. Wary that someone could be hiding in the trees or behind a rock, Gus kept his finger on the trigger and his head and eyes in constant motion.

He was getting closer. The man . . . or woman for all he knew . . . ahead of him was getting more reckless. They must be close to their getaway vehicle.

A few labored minutes later, he caught sight of a man wearing a red bandana and leather jacket making his way over a narrow creek. It was tempting to take him down from his position, but he couldn't take a chance missing. He had to get closer.

When Gus's boot hit the water, he heard a familiar and unpleasant click.

"Gotcha."

A bearded man he'd seen around Stranger's house had a shotgun pointed at him.

"You should have stayed with your girl."

A gunshot cracked in the distance, right in the direction of Stranger's house.

"You son of a . . ."

"Bye-bye."

The next shot was closer. Gus expected to be leaking holes.

Instead, he tasted blood, and felt it running down his face. The bearded biker had dropped his shotgun. He had a surprised look on his face as he sank to his knees. The hole by his shoulder leaked crimson. When he fell, Ashley Early came into view. She looked over her shoulder.

"Randy got the other one."

Gus had never been so happy to see another human being in his entire life. Ashley held out a hand to help him up. She looked at her phone. "Your friend Banks caught someone sneaking into Braden Stranger's house. Emma's okay."

His first instinct was to hug her, but then he thought of what she'd been through and restrained himself. Randy came bounding over and looked down at the biker. "Is he dead?"

Ashley kicked him and he groaned. "If I wanted him dead, he would be. How about yours?"

"I got him in the calf and zip-tied him. He's not going anywhere."

Sirens seemed to be coming from every direction.

"I guess this proves they didn't head for higher ground," Ashley said.

"At least not all of them. They shot Stranger. I doubt he'll make it," Gus said. He wiped his face with his sleeve, spitting out the biker's blood. There was no telling what diseases the man had.

"I called the cops and told them where to find these

pieces of street grease," Randy said as he zip-tied the unconscious biker. "Do we stay and wait for them?"

Gus was on the fence. Emma had been wounded and Ashley and Randy could have been shot. But they were close. He could feel it.

"I'll tell Emma to head out with Banks. I'll tag along with you. Let's keep pressing."

The couple's faces lit up. Maybe this would be all the therapy they needed to move on with their lives. Gus only hoped they had many, many more years ahead of them after this. He followed them to their pickup, which was hidden off the road under a low hanging pussy willow tree. They waited for the ambulance and police car to pass. Then Gus called Emma and said to meet at his Jeep.

He was relieved to see her standing on her own. A white bandage was wrapped around her leg. Freddie Powell leaned against Banks's Wrangler with his rifle resting in the crook of his arms. Banks was breathing heavily.

"I owe Chris my life," she said when Gus took her in his arms.

"How many were there?" he asked Banks.

"Just the one. He had a rifle and was walking through the back. I got him in the ass. You should have heard him howl. He's all tied up like a present, waiting for the police."

"What about Stranger?"

Emma shook her head. "I tried."

"There wasn't much you could do. The bullet might have nicked his heart as well. Randy and Ashley got two of them, including one who was about to take me out. So, you and I both owe someone our lives."

"You can pay us back later," Ashley said. Her brow was creased as she looked at her phone. "Ron and Mike think they spotted some suspicious activity at the abandoned house on Whitlock."

Gus patted the hood of his Jeep. "Tell them to hunker down and we'll be right there."

Three vehicles burned rubber heading for the edge of town and, Gus hoped, the final standoff.

# CHAPTER 41

Don Runde called Gus before they could make it to Whitlock Avenue. Gus had left Don and Dennis out of their search party because neither had a military background and, to be honest, Gus worried about what Don might do.

"Hey, Don," Gus said, hitting the speakerphone and keeping an eye on the rearview mirror to make sure everyone was still behind him. He knew he was driving too fast because Emma had both hands on the dash.

"You'll never believe this."

"Believe what?"

"They're back."

"Who? The protestors?"

"Not as many as before, but they're filing in two by two, like Noah's little pets. I guess they all didn't fly north and west after all. I thought maybe we can all try to nip this in the bud before it gets out of control. Peacefully. I think we had enough violence last night." He was silent for a beat, and then said, "I heard about Shane. That's a damn shame. He was a good guy, even if he didn't have much common sense."

"Yeah. He deserved better than that. Look, I'm tied up at the moment, but I'll be there as soon as I can."

"You got it, chief. We'll hold the fort down best we can."

Gus didn't need this. "Why on God's green earth would people come right back to protest after what happened?"

Emma double checked her seatbelt. "I guess they all couldn't get away and they have nothing else better to do."

"That's a sorry excuse for pestering a town that's already hurting."

"That's the way cowards do it. Kick a man when he's down."

He made a hard right, just missing a parked car. "When we're done at Whitlock, I'll show them that this man's not down."

Then he got an idea. Randy and Ashley had just shot two men. Their nerves, no matter what they might have said to the contrary, were jangled. Putting them in another potentially dangerous situation was not in their best interest. He dialed Randy.

"Can you two head on over to Main?"

"Main?" Randy said. "What for?"

"Don just called me and said the protestors are back. Not all of them, but I guess enough to make him concerned."

"So what would you want us to do?"

"Just keep an eye on things. Protect whatever's left standing. I'll be there as soon as I can."

"So, you want us to babysit?" Ashley said.

"Just for a little bit."

"But you might really need us."

"I do. At Main Street. Please."

They both sighed, and then Gus saw Randy's car pull

away. "All right. But call us immediately if anything goes down."

"Roger that." Gus handed the phone to Emma. "If anyone else other than Banks and Ron calls, send it to voicemail."

She tucked the phone into her shirt and under her bra. "You did the right thing."

"I hope so." He drove on, wondering if he would regret not having their firepower on hand. He sure hoped not.

Randy turned onto Main three blocks away from the edge of the protestors. There weren't as many as before. But what were *any* of them doing there after so much had been destroyed and members of their ranks were dead or in the hospital?

"These people are out of their minds," Randy said. The signs were back up in the air and a man had a megaphone to his mouth, though with their windows closed, they couldn't hear what he was saying.

As he drove closer, the rain started to fall. It was a light drizzle, but the slate skies promised much more to come.

"You think the storm will send them scurrying?" Ashley said.

"Bombs, fires, and dead people didn't. So no, a little rain won't do a thing."

He stopped by where Gus's place once stood and they got out, keeping their guns tucked away inside. Randy worried about what would come next once the police had the men they shot in custody and they described who put them down and tied them up. Would they get congratulated for stopping stone-cold killers? Or would this end up like the New York justice system where the brave and the right were always in the wrong.

That would have to come later.

He spotted Don and Dennis and their friends outside the Iron Works, keeping an eye on the crowd. Randy wanted to jump in the middle of the interloping rabble-rousers and tell them how incredibly misguided they were . . . not just about Gus, but everything.

But, just as his father had said many, many times, you can't fix stupid.

"Wish we had a horse, some lassos, and a corral," Ashley said.

"That would be too easy."

They were both still riding an adrenaline high, so he thought it was best for them to hang back. If they got sucked into the madness, there was no telling what might happen.

After ten minutes had passed, and it looked like the mob had reached its capacity, Ashley spotted a group of people walking down the street toward the protestors. She pointed them out to Randy. "Reinforcements?" she asked.

He used his phone to get a closeup look and saw a sea of familiar faces. The leader of the pack appeared to be Sarah Birch. No one carried weapons as far as he could see, but the looks on their faces were daunting enough. They looked just the way Randy and Ashley felt—they'd had enough.

"Yes," Randy said, "for our side." He showed the zoomed-in picture he'd taken. There must have been a hundred residents, with others joining in from side streets. The great thing about small towns was how fast news traveled. He wondered who had started the idea to make a show of force to the protestors.

Don, Dennis, and their friends joined the group. The protestors carried on, oblivious, shouting at a city hall that was mostly empty. There weren't even spare police to man the locked doors.

The people of Springerville, even ones who were recent transplants that may or may not have joined the initial protests, surrounded the protestors. Every race, creed, and color that represented Springerville, both old and new, were united for the very first time.

The megaphone went silent and the misguided youths who had come to town to stir the pot stared at this new development with wide eyes.

Sarah Birch had a megaphone of her own. She brought it to her mouth, and said, "Since you don't seem to have the common sense God gave a salamander, we're here to make sure you leave our town and never come back!"

Randy felt another shot of adrenaline course through him. Ashley said, "This could get ugly fast."

A smile curled on Randy's lips. "I sure hope so."

"Me, too."

Their wishes came true.

The man with the megaphone misguidedly said, "Make us."

That was it.

The throng of Springerville strong descended on the protestors. Randy and Ashley saw cell phone after cell phone being ripped out of hands and destroyed. They pushed into the protestors, silent and menacing against their cries. It was almost eerie. The rabble-rousers this time around were outnumbered almost three to one.

No fists had been thrown because there were no true fighters in the group, but the message was clear. They were no longer welcome here.

"Hand over your phones and don't even think of recording or taking pictures," Sarah said. "Please don't give us stories about how much they cost. When you go back home, just ask your parents to get you a new one. Your cell phones are worth far less than the damage you've done to our home."

Don was especially gleeful as he collected cell phones.

"Should we help?" Randy asked Ashley.

"Most definitely."

The tension was thicker than a redwood as they weaved into the mob, taking phones and pocketing them. One man pulled his away just as Ashley was taking it. She grabbed him by the wrist and twisted until he cried out and handed it back. "Thank you," she said airily.

When they were done, Sarah said, "If you came by car, someone will walk you to it. If you came by train or bus, we've arranged rides to the station. We also have makeshift airport shuttles. You're going to make four lines and we'll do our best to get you home. Does anyone have a problem with that?"

To hear Sarah lay it all out like that, her tone informing all who heard her that there was no point in arguing with her, was as surreal as it was enervating.

Two men tried to push their way through the gathering. Don caught them each by the back of the neck with his meaty paws. Tears leaked from their eyes as he applied pressure.

"You can't get in line if you run away," Don said. "Now, are you a plane, train, or automobile?"

# CHAPTER 42

Whitlock was in the oldest and far from prettiest part of town. Gus remembered Wally telling him one of his jobs was to find a way to revitalize that neighborhood.

When Mike had mentioned the abandoned house, Gus knew exactly which one he meant, even though there were a few in that area. This was the one that had lain dormant since Gus was a teen. Over the years, it had gained a bit of a reputation as a place for kids to do naughty things, the centerpiece of a ghost story that had no merit, and a destination for urban explorers who wanted to step back in time into the old plantation house that had been built in the mid-1800s. Gus had it in mind to find the money to tear it down before someone got hurt.

He never thought it would end up the hiding place for biker thugs.

Well, maybe they could bring it all down around their heads. It would save demolition costs.

He saw Ron and Mike's vehicle a block away and pulled behind it. Banks slid behind him. The few standing houses were all ranches in need of repair. Front yards were littered with broken toys, rusted bicycles, shells of cars on cinderblocks, and household items that belong inside a home, not outside.

Ron and Mike were huddled behind a heap of appliances left in front of a house that, as far as Gus remembered, was home to a reclusive older woman who never came to town. Rain soaked them to their skins quickly.

Across the street was the infamous abandoned house. The four of them crouched beside Ron and Mike.

"What's the situation?" Gus asked quietly.

"So far, we've spotted three men in the house itself, and one outside who came out to smoke. They're all wearing leather or denim jackets and look about as friendly as pit bulls with a stick up their asses," Ron said. "I'll bet their motorcycles are parked in the back. There may be more. You know how big that house is. The others could be keeping low."

The Whitlock house had, as far as he recalled, five bedrooms, not to mention a study, living room, dining room, and game room. He'd gone in there as a kid and wanted to take the pool table home with him, but it was secured to the floor.

"You want us to make a wide circle and check out the back?" Banks whispered.

Gus said, "Yep. Emma, you stay here. I'll go with them so I can take a head count."

"Isn't this the part where you said we should call the police?" she reminded him.

"It is, though we did leave them a bit of a mess back at Stranger's." He felt a sudden rush of pity for Braden Stranger. He wasn't necessarily a good man, but maybe he was right and this was not what he'd signed on for. The real evil was somewhere else, and with Stranger dead, they may never know who he or they were.

First things first. They had to deal with Sniper before they could move on.

Motioning with his fingers, he, Banks, and Freddie

moved out, giving the house a wide berth so they could sneak around back. They had the advantage, because they knew every inch of the town like the backs of their hands. Banks pointed at the old game trail where white-tailed deer had been traversing for as long as they could remember. It was narrow and winding, but it would get them to a good spot to spy on the back of the Whitlock house.

No one said a word as they trod carefully along the trail. They came to a rise that had a boulder wide enough for five men to hide behind. It was covered with graffiti from generations of high schoolers who wrote their names and the year they were graduating.

Banks handed Gus a pair of binoculars. He focused them and saw a man smoking a cigar in back of the house. He sat on a tree stump and had a shotgun leaning against it.

"There's our man," Gus said, handing the binoculars to Banks.

Banks said, "I see six so far. Hold on."

Freddie ran his thumb along the barrel of his gun, cool as the other side of the pillow.

"Make that eight. Just spotted a couple of guys walking on the second floor."

"Wouldn't it be nice if that floor finally caved in?"

"It sure would. Save us a lot of trouble."

Motion behind them had them spinning around with their guns raised. Gus exhaled when he saw it was Dawn James with Officer Guy Hernandez.

"What are you doing here?" Gus said.

James peered over the rock. "Same thing as you."

"How did you know?"

"Old lady Washington called in some strange activity in her yard. We saw Emma and your buddies hiding out front. Then we spotted one of those biker assholes by the house. Thought we might find you here."

"We were about to call you," Gus said.

James shook her head. "Yes, most likely after the fact. I just came from Braden Stranger's place. He's dead, but I guess you know that. Thank you for the gifts. They were quick to tell us who had the jump on them."

"I promise it was all self-defense," Banks said.

"You're not under arrest," she assured him. "Now, what do we have here?"

Banks handed her the binoculars while Gus explained. "That guy smoking the cigar under the trees is Sniper."

"I remember him."

"Banks counted eight other men in the house. I don't think we'll be able to get them without a firefight."

James dropped the binoculars from her eyes. "I agree. We could call in the staties and some other precincts to get some help."

When she didn't expand on her thought, Gus said, "Or?"

"Or we take them out now. They made a mess of our town. It only seems right that we clean it up."

Gus smiled. "Remind me to give you a raise. I defer to you. What do you want us to do?"

"I'm not sure yet. Seems like they're waiting for something. Wanna bet it's the three guys you took down. When they don't come back soon, I think they'll make a move. Guy, call in for backup but tell them to keep it quiet. We don't want to spook them."

"Will do."

Guy walked away and spoke quietly into his walkie-talkie.

The rain started to come down harder. In a way, it was a good thing because the noise would give them cover.

Sniper flicked his cigar into the woods and strode back

into the house. Gus could see him talking to three other men in the kitchen. There was no furniture left inside, and his gang appeared to be getting antsy with no place to properly sit and wait. They were on their cell phones, eyes glued to their screens. Two men were clearly making calls, but not talking.

"I think they're getting the idea that the guys they stationed outside of Stranger's aren't coming back," Gus said.

"If they can wait five minutes, I'll have enough people to take them down."

The men upstairs came down to the main floor, and now all nine of them were in the kitchen. Seconds later, they walked out into the yard. One by one, they lifted their bikes out of the cover of leaves.

The motorcycles blazed to life. James hit Gus on the shoulder. "Let's go!"

They ran down the game trail, hoping to get ahead of the bikers before they hit the street.

It became quickly apparent they wouldn't make it.

They did see Ron pop up from behind the appliances and fire into the mix of hogs and criminals. Somehow, he missed. Sniper's men fired back. Ron spun sideways and hit the pavement. Gus and everyone with him opened fire, though they were at a bad angle. The motorcycles roared past them.

Emma and Mike were on their feet running toward Ron.

Gus sprinted for his Jeep. "How is he?" he called over.

Emma and Mike were on either side of Ron, who writhed on the ground. "He's hit in the arm," Emma said.

Most likely, he'd be okay, unless the bullet ricocheted internally and took out a major organ. Ron lifted himself up with a face twisted with pain and gave a thumbs-up.

"Stay with him!" Gus said.

Banks and Freddie hopped in his Jeep while James and Hernandez dove into the patrol car. They peeled out, hoping to stay close behind the bikers. Gus rolled his window down and rain sluiced into the Jeep. If he couldn't see the motorcycles through the darkening day and rain, at least he could hear them.

As they whizzed down Decatur, Gus spotted the bikers in the shortening distance. In the rain, the Jeep had a distinct advantage. Most of Sniper's men didn't wear helmets, which also meant they didn't have visors to block the rain from pelting their eyes.

Two patrol cars coming in the other direction hit their lights and sirens when they spotted the gang tearing down the road.

Nine red brake lights flashed as one. The gang turned left, taking a side road to avoid the incoming cars. James and Hernandez went into the oncoming lane and passed Gus, nearly going off the road as they headed after Sniper's gang.

Gus fought the wheel. The patrol cars were right on his heels.

As they rocketed down the two-lane road, Banks said, "You know where this road ends, right?"

Gus gritted his teeth and hung on to the wheel for dear life. "I do. Which is why we need to get them now."

There were very few houses along the road, though he knew there were several tucked away behind the trees.

The problem was, it ended at a turnabout, and that turnabout was right in front of the grammar school.

# CHAPTER 43

The melee with the protestors was short-lived. The young agitators wanted nothing to do with the angry townies who had had enough. Randy saw the burly woman who had opened a crystal and faith healing shop a few months ago shout down a waif of a woman and order her to get in line.

A stream of cars, trucks, and vans filled the street to take them where they needed to go.

When Joe Iacovo pulled up in his car, Randy came to his door.

"What's going on here?" Iacovo asked as he watched people file into the waiting vehicles.

Randy had gone to school with Joe all the way from kindergarten through high school. He said, "Just helping people get back home."

"Should I be concerned?"

"The opposite."

Joe got out and seemed to consider whether or not he should do something. He opted to lean against the open door and ask, "You hear what happened over at Braden Stranger's house?"

Randy and Ashley played dumb.

"Someone killed him. Looks like one of the bikers did it. We have three wounded in custody as we speak."

"Why would the bikers kill Stranger? I thought they were here because of him?" Ashley asked innocently.

"Beats me. I don't have a clue what's going on here anymore." He watched the ranks of the protestors thin out. "Like this. Not sure what's happening and who's behind it, but as long as it gets these people out of here— legally—I'm fine with it."

Randy pointed at Sarah who was directing people where to go. "Always trust your elders."

The radio squawked in Joe's car. Dispatch alerted all cars to a high-speed chase in progress by the elementary school.

Randy knew right away what that meant. "Ashley, get the car."

Joe jumped into his own. "I'll be back to check on this . . . situation."

Randy didn't respond. He was too busy running over to Don and Dennis. He told them what was happening. Don went to Sarah, and said, "We have to go. You got this?"

"Yes. What's happening now?"

Dennis gave her a quick rundown and headed after Don. Sarah looked to Randy. "They have to be stopped."

"I know. They will be."

"You don't understand. Even though they canceled school today, there are still after-school programs going on. I don't know how many children are there now, but more than zero is a terrible number."

Randy's blood froze. He sprinted for his car and urged Ashley to get to the school as fast as possible. He checked their guns as she drove, making sure they had spare ammo. He was afraid they were going to need it.

\* \* \*

Sniper and his gang were cornered. The roads were slicker than Vaseline thanks to the rain and there was nowhere for them to go. James's patrol car came to a sideways skidding stop, blocking their exit. She popped out and kept her door open, her gun trained on the bikers. Guy Hernandez did the same.

"Get off your bikes and get down on the ground!" she barked.

Sniper and his men didn't move a muscle. Gus stopped his Jeep so the two patrol cars could pass on either side.

He saw several cars in the parking lot and his stomach dropped.

"Call Emma for me," he said to Banks. Gus's own phone was currently in her bra.

When she answered, Banks put her on speaker. "Are you okay?" she asked.

"Wasn't school supposed to be closed today?" he asked.

She paused, then said, "Yes. I spoke to my friend Carol who's a second-grade teacher. They canceled school because of what happened yesterday."

"If it's canceled, should there be cars in the lot?"

Gus reached for his gun. Now six officers were shouting at Sniper's gang to put their hands up and get on the ground. The men stared them down, unafraid of the weapons trained on them.

Emma said, "I . . . I don't know. We have a couple of after-school programs for the children with special needs. They need consistency, so maybe they didn't cancel them. Why are you asking me this?"

"Because Sniper's men are in front of the school with no place else to go."

Emma gasped. "If they get in the school . . ."

"I know. Call you back."

He looked to Banks and Freddie. "You know the way to get around the lot?"

"Yes," they replied in unison.

"We'll take the drop-off that rings around the lot and find a way into the school. If Sniper and his men get in there, all bets are off."

Banks looked ahead at the standoff. "Then we better get moving because it doesn't look like they have much choice. They can't stare down the cops forever. They'll need cover."

Gus took a deep breath. "If this goes wrong, James will have every right to lock us up."

"That's why we'll make sure it doesn't," Banks said.

The second they left the Jeep, the storm intensified. Rain was coming down in thick sheets, soaking the ground that greedily suctioned their feet as they made their way around the lot. The wind angrily whipped their faces. Gus could faintly hear James yelling at the bikers.

They were halfway to the back of the school when the motorcycles revved like thunder. That was followed by shattering glass. Gus scrabbled up the muddy slope just in time to see Sniper's men drive straight through the front door and into the school. The engines echoed in the empty halls.

Gus, Banks, and Freddie ran across the lot, no longer needing to hide. Time was of the essence now. They had to get into the school and find the children and teachers before Sniper's gang.

The back door to the cafeteria opened and someone ran out. It looked like one of the janitors. Gus had a hard time seeing through the punishing rain. He sprinted to the door before it closed. Propping it open for Banks and Freddie, he closed it softly behind them.

Inside the school, the motorcycles sounded like the roaring of the four horsemen of the Apocalypse. And underneath that rumble that Gus could feel in his chest was the shrieking of children.

"You hear which way that's coming from?"

Banks shook his head.

They didn't have after-school programs when they attended, so they weren't sure where those sessions would take place. There were only two floors in total, with about twenty or so classrooms if Gus remembered correctly.

Tires screeched on the polished floors and the stench of exhaust made its way into the cafeteria. They had to find those kids now. Gus could only hope the children and teachers were on the second floor.

He waved Banks and Freddie on, taking a quick look around the corner and down the hallway. All was clear for the moment, though the racket from the bikers made it sound as if they were right in front of them.

Gus hustled past the bulletin boards displaying essays and artwork with Banks and Freddie right behind him. He stopped again when they came to a bend in the hallway. This time, when he craned his head to look around, he saw two bikers rumbling their way. The sound of screaming children appeared to be closer.

He flashed two fingers, and the trio stepped into the hall with their guns drawn.

The bikers brought their motorcycles to a squealing stop.

"End of the road," Gus said.

The men reached behind themselves and drew their own weapons.

They didn't get very far.

Gus blew out the man's kneecap on the left, while Banks and Freddie created a shower of sparks as their bullets hit the motorcycle, and then the rider, who flipped over with the top of his shoulder reduced to a pink mist. The heavy bike landed on his leg, trapping him. His howls of agony were more satisfying than Gus could have imagined.

Rushing over to grab their shotguns, Gus kept an eye out for their compadres.

"I'll freaking kill you," the one with the missing kneecap sneered.

"Save it for later," Gus said, before he brought the stock of the rifle to bear on his face. He went out instantly. Banks was about to do the same to the one pinned under his motorcycle, but he had the smarts to pass out first.

"Seven to go," Banks said.

The motorcycles sounded as if they were all around them. He thought he heard Dawn James shouting somewhere in the school as well.

The children yowled again, and Freddie pointed up the stairs. "I swear they're up there."

They hit the stairs running and crashed through the double doors to the second-floor corridor. There was no one to be seen, but they could hear the children much clearer now.

Unfortunately, they lived in a time where school shooter drills were common. The teachers had more than likely locked the doors and put something against them. Normally, they would shepherd the children to a closet or cubby room, or if none was available, usher them away from the door and under their desks, doing what they could to keep them quiet.

Children with special needs might not understand what

they were being told, simply responding to what sounded very scary to them.

Gus, Banks, and Freddie split up, trying door handles and looking inside. The first one Gus turned was open. The classroom was dark and empty. Freddie stepped inside the one across the hall. Banks did the same to another.

The crack of gunshots downstairs was deafening. The children's cries went up an octave.

Gus hurried to another classroom. This time, the door wouldn't budge. He looked through the window set in the center of the door and thought he saw movement. He knocked on the door.

"Is everyone all right in there?"

A child cried for her mother.

"It's Gus Fuller. I need you to stay inside."

A frazzled woman emerged from under a desk. Her mascara ran down her face. Gus had met her a few times with Emma. She was the fifth-grade teacher who lived three towns away. Maisie was her name.

"Just stay down," he said to her. "The police are here, too. Are there any more children or teachers in the school right now?"

"No."

"Okay. Don't open this door for anyone but me or the police."

She nodded and dipped back under the desk, pulling a wailing child close to her chest.

Gus said to Banks, "It's just this one room. We have to make sure no one gets near it."

There was another exchange of gunfire below. Gus could make out the distinct sounds of shotguns, rifles, and pistols blazing away. He wanted desperately to go downstairs to help James and her team, but his place was up here, protecting the children.

"We should wait in the surrounding rooms," he said. "The second one of those bikers pops up, we take them down. And unlike downstairs, we shoot to kill."

They slipped into three classrooms, keeping the doors open.

The gunfight on the first floor escalated. A man yowled in pain.

Gus felt the motorcycles riding up the stairs. The floor vibrated and the manic hum filled the hallway.

He stepped out of the room, ready to pull the trigger.

Freddie was in the classroom ahead of him, Banks across the hall.

The lead biker already had his gun out, wasting no time to let lead fly.

# CHAPTER 44

Freddie spun and crashed into the doorway when he was hit. He didn't make a sound. He just crumpled to the floor.

Banks and Gus returned fire, hitting the man dead center in his chest. He flipped off the back of his motorcycle, that continued to barrel at them. They had to sidestep back into the classrooms to avoid getting run over.

The biker behind the fallen man ran over him. His front wheel wobbled, and he lost control of the bike. It crashed into the wall. Gus took a shot and missed, reducing a piece of artwork pinned to a corkboard to confetti. Banks had scrabbled over to Freddie and pulled him into the room.

The biker whipped his shotgun from off the floor and fired at Gus. He was lucky enough to duck just in time as pellets zinged just over his head. Gus fired blindly as he dropped. The bullet ricocheted off the wall next to the fallen biker. The man frantically tried to reload. Gus took a knee, steadied himself, and shot him in the head. The blood splatter behind him painted the wall in garish crimson and gray matter.

Jesus. How was this happening in a modest school that

housed so many fond memories? It made Gus's blood boil.

"How's Freddie?" he called out.

"Bleeding bad," Banks replied.

Gus was about to see how bad when another bike exploded off the top step, riding the air until it came down just ten feet from where Gus stood. He shot at the biker, only managing to shred part of the motorcycle's seat.

Another bike came from the other end of the hall. Then another from the opposite side. There were too many for Gus to take on at once.

"Banks!"

The biker he'd fired at grinned when he saw Gus. He revved his bike and headed for the locked classroom, presumably to mow down the door and get out of Gus's line of fire.

"No!"

Gus pulled off several shots, one of them burying itself in the man's neck. He slipped off the motorcycle, but it still went through the door.

The children inside screamed loud enough to be heard over the motorcycles.

Gus heard a rifle's report, then felt something burn his side. The pain was instant and agonizing. He looked down at a ragged gash in his side. Blood poured out of the wound.

A wave of dizziness washed over him. He fell to his knees, looked up, and saw he was about to be shot in the chest.

The crack of two successive shots made Gus wince. When he fully opened his eyes, he saw the man slump over his motorcycle's handlebars before it fell onto its side.

Banks turned to Gus, saw he was bleeding, and shouted, "Are you . . ."

The biker at the other end of the hall opened fire, hitting Banks in the leg. The pistol fell out of his hand as he crashed onto his back.

Gus spun around and fired back. The motorcycle revved. Gus scooted into the room, keeping his arm out so he could suppress the biker's ability to advance.

Until he ran out of ammo.

Struggling to reload through the pain and blood loss, Gus despaired when he heard another biker roar onto the second floor. The children were beside themselves.

Gus craned to the side to see what was happening.

Sniper dismounted from his bike, looking at the carnage. Blood ran down his arm. When he heard the children wailing, his head snapped in their direction.

Gus slammed the magazine home and pulled the gun up.

He was too late.

Sniper was already in the classroom, shouting, "Get up and get over here! Now!"

Another motorcycle made it to the second floor. Gus could see Banks laid out on the floor. His chest and stomach were still moving. He had no idea what shape Freddie was in.

Where was Dawn James and her men? Had they all been killed?

Gus's ears rang. His vision wavered. He tried to think of a way to save the children, but his brain refused to cooperate.

He had to do something before he was no longer physically able to move.

With his palm down flat on the tiled floor, he felt a heavy reverberation. Could there be more bikers on the way? No, this felt different.

Then it *sounded* different.

It was the pounding of feet. Dozens and dozens of feet.

Dragging himself forward, he saw a throng of people—men and women—burst into the hallway from both ends. Randy and Ashley were in the lead on one side, Don and Dennis on the other. Before the bikers could react, they swarmed over them, toppling them off their bikes and pounding them with fists and feet. It was like watching a zombie movie, only in this case, the zombies were the good guys and very much alive.

The bikers screamed for help. They pled for mercy.

None was given.

Gus couldn't believe his eyes. The town had come, young and old, longtime residents and new, risking their lives, to save the day.

When Ashley saw Banks on the ground, she rushed over to check on him.

Gus pushed his back against the doorframe until he got to his feet.

Everyone stopped when they saw him. Don said, "Dude, just sit back down. An ambulance is on the way."

Gus took a sharp breath. "I can't. There's one more."

He staggered across the hall. He waved everyone off. Somehow, the children had stopped screaming and crying. When he stepped inside the classroom, Sniper had Maisie in one arm and an unconscious child in the other. A pistol was in each hand.

"Take one more step and they're dead," Sniper growled. He had the wild stare of a desperate man.

"Just put them down. It's over," Gus said, his breath raspy. "All of your men are dead. There's no way out."

"Not as long as I've got these." Sniper kicked at a boy who yowled in pain.

Randy popped into the doorway. Gus snapped at him. "Get back!"

Gus set his gun on the floor. "You want a hostage? Take me."

Sniper smirked. "I don't think you'll last long enough for me to make it down the street, Hoss. Besides, people care a lot more about kids than some dipshit fry cook."

"How far do you think you'll get anyway?"

"I just need to get out of this town. I got people who got my back. People who will be happy to destroy you and your pisshole of a town."

Gus sucked in a breath when the pain ratcheted. He wanted to grab on to something, anything, to hold himself up. He refused to show any more weakness than his bleeding wound to Sniper. "Well, you sure did try. But we're a tough nut to crack. We'll be just fine long after you're gone. Stranger's dead, and the men you left at his place are in jail. Unless the people who have your back can teleport you out of here, this is the end of the line."

"Keep talking smack. You might want to tell whoever else is out there to walk on out of the building, or I start shooting these little snot noses until they do." He cocked the hammer back on the gun near the unconscious child's head.

Maisie whimpered. Sniper tightened his arm around her neck.

Gus held out his hands. "You don't want to do that. They're just kids."

"Fine. I'll put a hole in teacher's head first. Then the kids."

Out of the corner of his eye, Gus spotted Dawn James on the ledge, just outside the window. In that instant, he knew there was no way she'd have a clear shot at Sniper. He had to keep the killer's attention on him.

"I wouldn't touch a hair on their heads if I were you," Gus said.

Sniper's forearm tensed, the muscles coiling like angry snakes. "What are you gonna do? Bleed all over me?"

"Why don't you come over here and find out?"

James was crouched, trying to lift the bottom pane of the window. Blood ran down the side of her face.

Sniper spit close to Gus's feet. "You got nothing. And I'm not stupid enough to drop these two just to hand your ass to you."

"Didn't your momma teach you that you should never judge a book by its cover? I've been worse, and I've beaten men ten times better than you."

"Keep talking. Maybe I should just put you out of your misery."

The pistol slowly turned from the child to Gus.

James had managed to crack the window open.

The window squeaked when she lifted it more.

Sniper whirled in her direction, dropping the child but sweeping Maisie off her feet as she struggled to breathe.

There was only one thing for Gus to do.

He charged at Sniper, letting out a war cry to get him to turn away from the window and James.

Sniper did just that.

And sent a hail of bullets his way.

It felt like getting charged by a bull's horns.

Gus was set on his heels, falling backward.

He heard another shot.

By the time he hit the floor, he was seeing black.

# CHAPTER 45

Wally Sturgis was dressed in his best suit. His somber expression seemed right for the occasion. A cool breeze whistled down Main Street. Their version of winter was upon them, and though there wouldn't be snow or ice, those who called Springerville home were not used to temperatures hovering around forty degrees.

Generations old and brand-new citizens of Springerville were out in force. Wisps of steam curled about their heads as they blew on hands to warm them and conversed with their neighbors. No one would utter the words *locusts* or *hick* anymore. What had happened was terrible, unconscionable, but it had also united the town and opened minds and hearts.

Framing for the demolished businesses were a sign of hope.

This particular moment was not about hope for the future. It was about honoring the past.

"You ready?" Wally said over his shoulder.

Gus winced when he stood, leaning heavily on his cane while Emma held his arm. He'd been sworn in as mayor from his hospital bed several weeks earlier. Today's event was his first order of business.

"Not really," Gus said.

Wally and Emma helped him to the podium. He stared out at a sea of faces that were old and new, but all familiar now. It was impossible to count the number of people who had come to visit him in the hospital. From old friends to the new residents, they all wanted to personally thank him for what he'd done. Gus was quick to remind them that he didn't do it alone, and there were other people in the same hospital who could use their support.

Ron was now in a rehab center, getting the strength back in his arm.

Banks made it out a week before Gus with a pronounced limp. He was back at work, fixing cars after hiring on Randy Early to help him out.

When Gus tapped the microphone, Banks, who was standing beside Emma, winked.

"I want to thank you all for coming. I know this isn't exactly ideal weather, and from the looks of it, quite a few of you need to rethink your winter coats." Several people laughed, especially those in light coats hugging themselves to keep warm. "We . . . we went through hell together. Yet here we are, standing as one, the past united with the present. It doesn't matter if Springerville is where your parents were born, or if it's the place that's recently captured your heart. This is our home, and I don't think anyone has fought harder to keep it that way than all of you."

Everyone clapped. When Gus turned to Emma, she was wiping away a tear.

Don, Dennis, Sarah, Randy, Ashley, and all of his closest friends were right up front by the grandstand in the center of the town. You couldn't see the lawn beneath their feet because just about everyone was there. Even

Aileen Wuhrer, dressed in her furs from head to toe, was applauding with a tremendous smile on her face.

"Now, I'm not one for speeches, though Wally here tells me I better get used to it." Wally smiled and nodded. "I think it's important to honor those who gave us this day. The ones who sacrificed their lives or had them taken from them unwillingly. By the summer, on this very spot, there will be a new monument, listing their names so we never forget them. Their blood is in the ground that supports us. That we call home. And they will always be a part of us."

There were sniffles along with cheers.

He noticed that Sarah had managed to sidle next to Banks, looping her arm within his. Banks, for once, didn't flinch or protest. Gus couldn't help but smile. It was about time.

The modest monument was currently in progress in Kentucky. It would have the names of heroes like Freddie Powell, Guy Hernandez, and the four other officers who were killed in the line of duty. It would also include Shane Varrick and Maddie Jackson, as well as the protestors who had died in the bombing and Braden Stranger. Wally tried to fight him on the last two, but Gus dug in his heels. They hadn't come to Springerville to die. They'd been sent by a shadow to foment distrust and anger. Even though things had gotten out of hand, Gus would bet his life that whoever had orchestrated it all was pleased in some sick way. What happened in Springerville had perpetuated the myth that all elections were to be distrusted, and small-town life wasn't the American dream anymore.

Gus would find a way to show the world that those were wrong assumptions. Very wrong.

For now, in place of the monument, under glass and within a beautiful wooden display case made by Banks, was the small bit of Gus's American flag that had survived a bomb and subsequent fire. No one could think of a more perfect representation of Springerville's undying spirit.

Dawn James stepped forward and helped Gus to his seat. He patted her hand, thanking her. She'd been put through the ringer trying to craft a narrative that wouldn't land good people in prison while Gus was in a medically induced coma. He'd meant that part about getting her a raise. That would be news for tomorrow.

Al had returned to rebuild his barbershop, even though he'd been thinking about retiring before everything had started. He stepped up to the podium and played "Taps" on his bugle. There wasn't a dry eye to be seen.

Sarah Birch read out the names of the deceased, followed by a prayer and moment of silence.

Gus had made sure to appoint several teenagers to record the event. It would be their job to edit the video and find ways to flood social media, because that was the way to get the word out in this new world. Gus wasn't ready to dive headfirst, though he was willing to learn.

When it was over, people filed by the spot where the monument would rest and left flowers.

Gus's body felt like it was being twisted into a pretzel. Fighting the pain, he walked on his own and left a white rose atop the pile.

Then he let Emma wrap her arm around his waist to support him.

"We're going to be okay," he said, looking around the town. His town. Their town.

"We are. We just have a lot of work to do."

"Work is something I can do."

As they headed for her car, they passed his luncheonette. The builders said it would be ready by late May. Gus couldn't wait to make biscuits in his new oven.

**Turn the page for a barn-burnin' preview!**

*National bestselling authors William W. Johnstone
and J.A. Johnstone know what it takes
to fight for the red, white, and blue.
And when the battleground is Texas,
the outcome is sure to be explosive . . .*

**FREEDOM IS NEVER FREE**

After the president agrees to hold civilian trials
for a gang of murderous, kill-crazy terrorists, some of
them are relocated to Hell's Gate Prison in West Texas.
Until a group of fanatical sleeper-cell shock troops
launch an all-out assault to "liberate"
their jailed comrades. There's just one problem:
they don't know that Army Ranger Lucas Kincaid
is working part-time at Hell's Gate.

With the town's high school team held hostage and in
danger of being executed one by one, Kincaid assembles
a ragtag band of survivors and aging hardcore cons into
a lethal fighting force to keep the unholy warriors from
their deadly mission. And Kincaid and his men are on
their own—everyone, from the president on down,
orders Kincaid to give in to the terrorists' demands.

But warrior Lucas Kincaid, outnumbered
and outgunned, won't back down.

One thing's for sure: when the enemy gets to Hell,
they'll know America sent them.

**NATIONAL BESTSELLING AUTHORS**
**William W. Johnstone**
**with J.A. Johnstone**

## STAND YOUR GROUND

**The line has been drawn.**

## Live Free. Read Hard.
**www.williamjohnstone.net**
**Visit us at www.kensingtonbooks.com**

**On sale now, wherever Pinnacle Books are sold.**

# CHAPTER 1

*Fuego, Texas*

The bright lights on the tall metal standards around the stadium lit up the night for hundreds of yards around. The cheers of the people in the stands filled the air. An autumn Friday night in Texas meant only one thing.

Fuego had gone to war.

And the enemy was the McElhaney Panthers.

The undefeated Panthers were ranked number six in the state in the 3-A classification and had come in here tonight expecting to crush the lowly Fuego Mules, who currently owned an unimpressive record of two wins and four losses.

Yet here it was, middle of the third quarter, and Fuego held a slender 14–10 lead on the visiting Panthers.

The people in the home grandstands were going nuts. They were on their feet with almost every play as they cheered for the local high school team. The band played the fight song at high volume.

Across the field in the smaller stands where visitors sat, Panther fans who had made the ninety-mile drive from McElhaney were fit to be tied. Their shouts were edged with disbelief as they implored their boys to hold the line.

Their dreams of an undefeated season were fading. The Mules had the ball and were driving for a score that would pad their lead.

At the big concession stand on the home side, operated by the Fuego Booster Club, Lucas Kincaid leaned forward and said over the racket, "I'll have two chili dogs and a Coke, please."

The booster club mom who was tired and harried from the press of hungry and thirsty customers blew a strand of blond hair out of her eyes and said, "Sure, hon. You want onions and jalapeños on those dogs?"

Kincaid shook his head and said, "No thanks. Just chili and cheese."

"You got it."

He saw her casting glances at him as she fixed the chili dogs. Probably wondering if he had a kid playing in the game or maybe in the band. He was fairly youthful in appearance but had touches of gray in his close-cropped dark hair, which made him old enough to have a child in high school. She didn't know him, though, and even in this day and age, everybody knew 'most everybody else in a small town like Fuego.

But not Kincaid. He didn't have any relatives around here, didn't have a kid who was a football player or a cheerleader or a trombonist or anything else.

That didn't stop him from attending the games. He wanted to fit in, because the more he fit in, the lower a profile he could keep. Everybody in Fuego went to the games, so he did, too. He didn't want to get a reputation as a reclusive loner. People remembered reclusive loners.

Kincaid didn't want to be remembered. He didn't want to be noticed.

That way if his enemies came looking for him, they'd be less likely to find him.

Make that when his enemies came looking for him, not if, he thought. It was only a matter of time.

The blond woman set the chili dogs in their paper boats and the canned Coke dripping from the ice chest on the counter in front of him and said, "That'll be five dollars."

"Thanks," Kincaid said as he laid a bill on the counter beside the food.

"Can you handle that okay?" she asked as he started to pick up the food.

Kincaid smiled and said, "Yeah, I think so." His hands were pretty big. He had no trouble holding the two hot dogs in one hand and the Coke in the other. He opened the can before he picked it up and took a long swallow of the cold, sweet liquid.

"Thanks," the woman said. Kincaid could tell that she wouldn't mind if he stayed and talked to her some more, even though more customers waited in line behind him. He had seen the appreciation in her eyes when she cast those hooded glances at him. He was a good-looking stranger, and she probably didn't have much excitement in her life.

Lucky woman, he thought as he turned away.

In his experience, he'd found that excitement was way overrated.


Andy Frazier's nerves were jumping around all over the place. He struggled to bring them under control as he leaned forward to address the other players in the huddle. He had to make them think he was calm so they would stay calm. He was their quarterback, after all. Their leader.

"Red fire right on two," he said, relaying the play that one of the offensive tackles had brought in from the sideline. "Break!"

The team broke and went up to the line. As they took their stances, Andy looked over at the sidelines. He saw Jill Hamilton leading cheers, her long, dark brown ponytail bouncing as she jumped around and waved blue-and-white pompoms.

She must have felt his eyes on her, because she paused and turned, and the connection between them over the green turf was electric. They'd been dating for six weeks and Andy knew she'd be riding him in the front seat of his pickup before the night was over, but it would be even better if they could beat those asshats from McElhaney first.

Andy bent over center and barked, "Hut, hut!" and Charlie Lollar snapped the ball to him. Andy turned, faked to Brent Sanger charging past him from the running back spot, and slid along the line with the ball on his right hip as he waited for Spence Parker to make his cut and come open on his pass route.

But then one of the linemen—Ernie Gibbs, big but slow and stupid—lost his block and suddenly a McElhaney linebacker was right in Andy's face. Gibby, you son of a bitch! Andy screamed mentally as he twisted away from the rush.

There was no pocket—the play was designed to look like a rush, so the linemen had fired out rather than dropping back—and as Andy curled back across the field he saw a sea of McElhaney red and silver coming at him. He dodged this way and that and looked downfield to see if anybody was open, or at least close enough to open that he could heave the ball ten yards over his head and get away with it. They were almost in field goal range for Pete Garcia, but an intentional grounding penalty, with its loss of both yardage and down, would push them back too far.

Then Andy caught a glimpse of a seam in all that red and

silver and cut into it without stopping to think. Hands grabbed at him, but he shook loose. Bodies banged into him, but he bounced off and kept his feet. He pulled the ball close to his body to keep it from getting swatted loose in all the traffic.

He was just trying to reach the first-down marker, but suddenly he came free and saw nothing but open field in front of him. The line of scrimmage had been the McElhaney 35, and he was past that now so there was no point anymore in looking for a receiver. Andy put his head down and ran as frenzied shouts went up from the stands on both sides of the field.

He passed the 30, the 25, and cut to his right as he sensed more than saw one of the McElhaney safeties coming in from his left. The diving tackle fell short, but the safety had forced Andy back toward the pursuit. He angled left at the 20 and saw the flag at the front corner of the end zone.

Now it was a race, and a hope that nobody behind him held him or threw an illegal block.

By the time Andy reached the 10, he didn't hear anything except his own pulse pounding in his ears. No, that wasn't his pulse, he realized, it was a couple of McElhaney players closing in on him from behind. He crossed the 5, left his feet at the 3-yard line just as they hit him. Momentum carried all three of them forward, and when Andy came crashing to the ground with nearly 400 pounds of McElhaney on top of him, the ball tucked under his arm was a good eight inches beyond the goal line.

Andy saw that, realized he had scored, and felt a moment of pure elation before he started screaming from the pain of his newly broken leg.

\* \* \*

Up in the stands, George Baldwin turned to his friend John Howard Stark and said, "That's a sign of true greatness, being able to make something out of nothing. You know good and well that was a busted play, John Howard, and it wound up being a touchdown."

"Yeah, but it looks like the kid paid a price for it," Stark drawled. "He's still down."

Baldwin, a burly, bear-like, middle-aged man with close-cropped grizzled hair, frowned worriedly toward the group of players, coaches, and trainers clustered around the fallen player.

"Damn it, I hope he's all right. That's Andy Frazier. His dad Bert works for me out at the prison."

"I hope he's all right, too," Stark said. He was taller than his old friend but weighed about the same. Stark had lost a little weight over the past couple of years, but to all appearances he was still a vital, healthy man despite being on the upward slope of sixty.

An apprehensive quiet settled over the stands during this break in the action. The crowd became even more hushed when a gurney was brought out from the ambulance that had pulled up on the cinder track surrounding the field. Everybody on both sides stood up and applauded when Andy Frazier was loaded onto the gurney and taken to the ambulance. His right leg was immobilized and probably broken, but he was awake and talking and holding the hand of a pretty brunette cheerleader.

The kid would be all right, Stark thought. Even with the way things were today, he had everything in the world to live for.

As the teams lined up to kick the extra point, Baldwin said, "You never have told me why you showed up out of the blue to pay me a visit, John Howard."

"Can't a guy stop by to see an old army buddy?" Stark asked with a smile.

"Sure, but you've never been what I'd call the sentimental type. Anything you ever did, you had a good reason for it." Baldwin frowned again. "I heard about your health problems. Hell, everybody heard about them. There was the trial, and all that crap with that drug gang—"

Stark winced and said, "I could do without all the notoriety. I'm just glad things have settled down and I can go places again without being recognized. I've been traveling around, seeing some of the old outfit I haven't seen in years."

"You're not going around and, well, saying good-bye, are you, John Howard?"

Stark laughed and shook his head.

"No, this isn't a farewell tour, George. Fact is, I'm in remission and feel better than I have in a year or more. But none of us are getting any younger."

"Boy, that's the truth," Baldwin said. He clapped as the Fuego kicker drilled the extra point and made the score 21–10. "I've got a hunch I'm about to get a lot older, too."

"The terrorists," Stark said.

"Yeah." Baldwin sighed. "All the places they could have put them, and instead of spreading them out they've sent all hundred and fifty of the bastards to Hell's Gate."

Stark knew exactly what his friend was talking about. The official name of the place was the Baldwin Correctional Facility—a privately run penitentiary with a contract with the United States government to house federal prisoners—but nearly everyone knew it as Hell's Gate because of a geographical feature just west of the prison.

A long line of cliffs ran north and south there, and the red sandstone of which they were formed made them as crimson as blood when the morning sun hit them. Then, in the afternoon, the setting sun lined up perfectly with a gap in the cliff, and anyone looking through that opening at the blazing orb would think that Hell itself lay just on the other side . . . hence the name "Hell's Gate."

The prison had been an economic boon to this isolated county in West Texas, which was larger than many northeastern states but had more jackrabbits and rattlesnakes than people, making it a good location for a maximum security facility. Hell's Gate was actually the largest employer in the county these days.

Because of the seemingly permanent economic downturn that had gripped the country for the past ten years, ever since the Democrats had learned how to buy national election victories by passing out benefits to low-information voters and how to steal the elections they couldn't buy, for a time it had seemed that Fuego was going to dry up and blow away.

Hell's Gate had changed all that, providing jobs for many of the town's citizens. Guards, administrators, service personnel, all benefited from the prison's being there. If the trade-off was having hundreds of violent offenders housed just a few miles west of town . . . well, so be it. Prices had to be paid.

But now, with the recent closure of Guantanamo and other off-the-books military prisons, finally fulfilling the promise of the president who had started the nation's precipitous slide into mediocrity, the population of Hell's Gate had swelled dramatically, and nobody wanted the newest prisoners: hard-core Islamic fundamentalists who had nothing in their hearts but hate for America and a burning desire to harm the country. Stark had run up against their kind before and knew how dangerous they were.

The Supreme Court had ruled that they had to be held in a civilian prison, though, and tried in civilian courts. It was a farce, an invitation to catastrophe, but age had picked off enough of the Justices so that the gate was wide open for anything the so-called progressives wanted to do, without any way to rein them in.

And that, John Howard Stark thought as he watched a football game on a Friday night in Texas, was the true gate to Hell for a once-great nation.

"Well . . . maybe it'll work out all right," he said to Baldwin, although he didn't believe that for a second.

"Maybe," Baldwin said, not sounding convinced, either. "Hey, you want to come out to the prison, have a look around?" He grinned. "I'll buy you lunch in the cafeteria. The food is actually pretty good."

Stark nodded and said, "I'll just take you up on that, George."

# CHAPTER 2

Despite losing their quarterback to an injury, Fuego hung on to eke out a 21–17 victory over the previously undefeated McElhaney Panthers. It took a great effort by Brent Sanger, who played defensive back as well as running back, to slap away a Hail Mary pass in the Fuego end zone as time ran out on the clock.

Jubilation filled the town as people in the stands used their phones to post the final score on social networks. Car horns began to honk, not only at the stadium but all along Main Street to the Dairy Queen and McDonald's at the other end of town. Soon there was such a cacophony it seemed more like the team had just won a state championship, instead of improving its record to one game under .500.

So yeah, maybe folks were overreacting to the win, Lucas Kincaid thought as he made his way through the parking lot toward his Jeep, but he was happy for them anyway. With the world the way it was, people needed a little something to celebrate every now and then.

A long line of red taillights stretched from the parking lot along the road in front of the high school to the state highway that ran past the school and the football stadium. Kincaid figured he would sit in his Jeep for a while and let the traffic thin out before he left. He hated inching along in traffic.

Loud voices from his left drew his attention as he walked across the asphalt with his hands in the pockets of his denim jacket. He looked in that direction and saw three men confronting a man and woman who had a couple of small children with them.

The three men were angry, and their comments were pretty profane. One of them said, "You people don't even realize what you've done. We were undefeated! You've ruined the whole season!"

The other two shouted obscene agreement.

So, disappointed McElhaney boosters, thought Kincaid. And from the sound of them, drunken ones at that.

The man and woman tried to lead their kids around the angry visitors. The trio cut them off.

"Whassamatter? You too good to talk to us? You think one lucky win makes you better than us?"

"Mister, my wife and I just want to take our kids home," the man said. He was in his thirties, a little heavyset, wore glasses. Kincaid thought he looked like a teacher.

As if three-against-one odds weren't bad enough already, the three men from McElhaney were all bigger and rougher-looking, the sort of men who worked outdoors in construction or oil and gas. Kincaid's eyes narrowed as he studied them. He had never liked drunks, especially mean drunks . . . like his old man.

One of the men shoved the guy in glasses and sent him stumbling back a step. The guy's wife made a sound that was angry and frightened at the same time. She maneuvered the kids, a boy and a girl, behind her.

Kincaid had slowed, but he hadn't stopped walking. He could just go on to his Jeep and forget about what was happening in this corner of the parking lot. He knew that was exactly what he should do.

No, he thought. He couldn't. Who was he trying to fool by pretending that he could?

"Stop that!" the guy in glasses said. "Leave us alone!"

"You gonna make us?"

"No," Kincaid said as he came up behind the three men. "I am."

They turned toward him, startled, and he hit the one in the middle in the belly hard enough to double him over. Then in a continuation of the same movement he slashed right and left and caught the two flankers on the sides of their necks with the hard edges of his hands.

The one on the left went down like a puppet with his strings cut, but the one on the right stayed on his feet. He was a little tougher than the other two, Kincaid supposed, and probably not as drunk, either, because he reacted fairly quickly. He bulled forward and caught Kincaid around the waist, slammed him back into the passenger door of a parked pickup.

If he could have just gone ahead and killed them, it would have been easier, but Kincaid knew he couldn't do that. Even getting in a fight was more notoriety than he ought to risk. Since he had to hold back, it threw him off a little, slowed him down, allowed the guy to ram him into the pickup. Kincaid's head bounced off the glass in the window.

Yeah, and maybe he was a little rusty, to boot, he thought. He had been lying low for a while. Skills deteriorated with disuse.

But muscle memory never went away completely.

Kincaid jerked his head out of the way as the man tried to punch him in the face. Another second and he would have the man on the ground, puking his guts out like the one Kincaid had hit in the belly.

Kincaid didn't get the chance. The guy in the glasses tackled the third man from the side. Both of them spilled onto the pavement. Glasses swung a punch into the man's face. The blow was slow and awkward and probably didn't have a lot of power behind it, but it landed squarely on the man's nose and broke it.

That ended the fight. The third man rolled onto his side, cupped his hands over his nose, and squealed in pain. Glasses climbed to his feet, where his wife grabbed his arm and asked, "Honey, are you all right?"

He pushed the glasses up on his nose and said, "Yeah, I think so. Thanks to—"

He stopped as he looked around for Kincaid.

It was too late. Kincaid was gone. He'd faded into the shadows because a crowd was gathering and somebody was bound to call the cops and Kincaid didn't need that.

As it was, nobody involved in the incident knew his name. Nobody would be able to describe him except in vague terms: medium height, medium build, dark hair, blue jeans and denim jacket. That description would fit dozens of guys who'd been at the game tonight.

"Stupid," Kincaid muttered to himself as he circled through the parking lot. Getting mixed up in a brawl in a high school parking lot wasn't keeping a low profile. Not low enough.

Not when a lot of dangerous people would have liked nothing better than to kill him.

\* \* \*

Andy Frazier floated on a cloud of painkillers. He didn't even feel his broken leg anymore. He was just coherent enough to realize he had a silly grin on his face as he looked up at Jill, who stood beside the hospital bed holding his hand.

"Did we win the game?" he asked her.

"We did," she told him. "Twenty-one to seventeen. Ashleigh texted me and let me know."

From the other side of the bed, Lois Frazier, Andy's mother, said, "He's asked you that four times already, Jill. I think there's something wrong with his brain. Did they check him for a concussion?"

"For God's sake, Lois, he's just doped up," Bert Frazier said. Andy's dad stood at the foot of the bed. "He doesn't know what he's saying."

He was tall and had the same shade of brown hair as Andy, but his was straight and thinning, instead of thick and rumpled. His face was broad and beefy, and his shoulders were heavy. He was a supervisor out at the prison, in charge of the correctional officers when he was on duty, which he wasn't tonight because he always arranged to have Friday nights off during football season.

Andy was glad his dad and mom were here. That made him feel better. So did having Jill hold his hand. But as he looked up at her, he felt a pang of disappointment.

"My leg's broke," he said.

She smiled and nodded and said, "Yes, I know."

"That means we can't—"

Her hand tightened on his and made him stop.

"I know," she said. "That means we can't hang out at the Dairy Queen with everybody else and celebrate the victory. But it wouldn't have been possible without you,

Andy, and everybody knows that. We'll just have to celebrate later, when you're feeling better."

"Okay," he said. That wasn't what he'd meant at all— he had been thinking about what they would have done out at the dry lake bed, just the two of them, alone—but if she wanted to act like that's what he was talking about, that was fine, because . . .

Oh, yeah, his folks were right here. So it was probably better not to say anything about the lake bed. Jill was smart that way, really smart. Probably gonna be valedictorian. Vale . . . dic . . . torian.

Andy started to giggle.

"Ah, he's stoned out of his mind," Bert said. "Come on, Lois. Let's go home and let him sleep it off."

"I'm not going anywhere," Andy's mom said. "I'm going to stay right here at the hospital. I can sleep in one of those chairs out in the waiting room."

Bert rolled his eyes. That just made Andy giggle more.

Then he stopped and asked Jill, "Did we win the game?"


There was only one motel in Fuego, down on the same end of town as the fast-food joints. It had been built in the fifties, with a one-story office building that also held the owner's living quarters in front of a two-story L-shaped cinderblock building with thirty rooms, fifteen on each floor. A swimming pool sat inside the L. Guest parking was on the outside of it. It was a fairly nice place, well kept up despite its age.

Stark had checked in earlier that day and told the clerk, who was also the owner, that he would probably be staying for a few days but didn't know exactly how long. That wasn't a problem, the man assured him. The motel did a steady business, since it was on an east–west U.S. highway, but it was seldom full.

When Stark got out of his pickup after the football game and started through the open breezeway leading to the stairs, he saw the motel's owner doing something to the ice machine that sat in the breezeway next to a soft drink machine. The man looked up and nodded to him.

"Hello, Mr. Stark."

"Mr. Patel," Stark said.

"Did you enjoy the game?" Patel grinned. "I could tell from the racket that we won."

"Yes, it was very exciting." Stark gestured at the ice machine. Patel had taken a panel off the side of it, exposing some of its works. "Problem with the machine?"

Patel shook his head and said, "Not really. Just doing a little fine-tuning on it." He chuckled. "You know, when things get older, they don't work as well. You always have to be messing with them."

"That's the truth," Stark said with a smile of his own. "Well, good night, Mr. Patel."

"Good night, Mr. Stark."

Stark didn't think any more about the encounter as he climbed the stairs to the second floor and went to his room.

What he had told his old friend George Baldwin about being in remission was true. The last time he'd seen his doctor, he had gotten an excellent report, which came as a surprise to both of them. A couple of years earlier, the doctor had told Stark he had maybe a year left.

So every extra day was a blessing, Stark told himself, but at the same time the days carried with them a curse. The longer he hung around this world, the longer it would be before he was reunited with his late wife, taken from him by violence several years earlier.

But Elaine would have wanted him to live as long as he could and enjoy every day of it, Stark knew. His friend Hallie Duncan, waiting for him back home, was the same way. She had encouraged him to go see his old friends, so that was what Stark was doing.

Despite what he'd told George, in a very real way this was a farewell tour, because Stark didn't know from one day to the next what was going to happen. It was all too possible that he would never see any of them again.

But then, every day on this earth was a farewell tour of sorts, because the past was gone and nothing else was promised to anybody but the present.

Tomorrow might not ever come . . . and the day after that was even more iffy.

As Patel was tightening the screws on the service panel after putting it back in place, a figure drifted out of the shadows to the side of the breezeway.

"That was him," the newcomer said in the foreign tongue that he and Patel shared. "The big American who has caused so much trouble for our friends in the cartel."

Patel nodded. His mouth was dry with fear—this man caused that reaction in him—so he had to swallow a couple of times before he could speak.

"Yes, that was John Howard Stark. I . . . I have no idea what he is doing here. He said he came to Fuego to visit an old friend, and it must be true. He could not have any idea what we plan to do."

"Well, it doesn't really matter," the other man said with

a shrug. "If he chooses to stay here, in a few more days he will be dead, too, along with thousands of these other decadent Americans."

Patel looked down at the ice machine and tried not to shudder.